D1531505

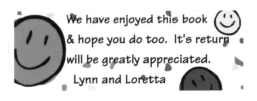

We have enjoyed this book & hope you do too. It's return will be greatly appreciated.

Lynn and Loretta

# HEROES

## OF GLORIETA PASS

# HEROES

## OF GLORIETA PASS

### A NOVEL

## BRAD E. HAINSWORTH
## & RICHARD VETTERLI

DESERET
BOOK

SALT LAKE CITY, UTAH

This is a work of fiction. Characters and events in this book are products of the author's imagination or are represented fictitiously.

**Library of Congress Cataloging-in-Publication Data**

Hainsworth, Brad E.
  Heroes of Glorieta Pass / Brad E. Hainsworth, Richard Vetterli.
    p. cm.
  ISBN 1-59038-474-1 (alk. paper)
    1. New Mexico—History—Civil War, 1861–1865—Fiction.   2. Glorieta Pass,
Battle of, N.M., 1862—Fiction.   3. Young, Brigham, 1801–1877—Fiction.
I. Vetterli, Richard.  II. Title.
  PS3558.A3323H47   2005
  813'.54—dc22                                 2005012289

Printed in the United States of America            72076
Publishers Printing, Salt Lake City, UT

10   9   8   7   6   5   4   3   2   1

# DEDICATION

★ ★ ★

 It was my coauthor, Richard Vetterli, who first conceived of a novel that would deal with two critical Civil War phenomena: the efforts of the Confederacy in attempting to split California from the Union and the critical battle of Glorieta, fought in the mountains of New Mexico during late March of 1862.

Though Richard passed away early in the novel's development, his spirit can be felt throughout the book. We had agreed that I was to write the middle portion of the novel, Richard the early chapters, and yet a third author, screenwriter and character actor, Leo Gordon, the concluding chapters. But it was not to be. Richard died having written only three chapters and sketches of two or three others, and Leo grew ill and also passed away before he could make any contribution.

It fell to me to bring our dream to reality. Only those who have set forth in writing anything so demanding as an historical novel can understand the obsession such an effort can become. So it was with me and, somehow, Richard's presence was nearly always there, prodding at my elbow from the moment I assumed the full burden of the novel until its publication contracts were signed. Something, perhaps it was he, would not let me rest. It was an unsparing, almost prepossessing task, and I am only now beginning to feel any sense of relief. Though, I must confess, the characters in the book are now following me around, demanding further life and final resolution in a sequel. Whether or not such haunting demands can ever come to fruition is of course dependent on the success of this effort.

For all the above reasons, and many more, this novel is happily dedicated to Richard Vetterli, Ph.D., Latter-day Saint, dedicated husband and father, professor, scholar, dreamer, and for me, brother under the skin. I miss his friendship and collaboration very much.

# PREFACE

★   ★   ★

*H*EROES OF GLORIETA PASS is a work of fiction, based on a little-known incident in the Civil War. Within these pages, fictional characters interact with real, historical figures. These fanciful actors perform in the historical drama in a manner the author imagines they would have had they actually lived in that time, place, and circumstance. Of course, as the plot of the story develops, license may be taken with various situations as they may actually have occurred, places changed or created, and incidents altered.

As in all historical fiction, dialogue is developed between actual personalities and fictional characters, and these are the products of the author's imagination, as are many places and scenes that, in fact, never truly existed or occurred. However, care has been taken not to treat historical figures unfairly and to portray them as the historical record suggests they might have been.

The fact that many of the individuals who actually lived and participated in the events dealt with in this novel have become legendary, their place in history so enormous, it is fairly impossible to portray them in any way but fictionally. Abraham Lincoln, Brigham Young, and Senator William Gwin and his brilliant wife, Mary, are the obvious examples in this story, not forgetting to mention Orrin Porter Rockwell, one of the more interesting men in Latter-day Saint and western American history.

Human motivations are difficult to determine at any time and under the most immediate circumstances, but they become even more incomprehensible when one tries to fathom them through the mists of receding time. The morality of personal political positions and the actions taken to further them, especially in times of war, are always colored by how those conflicts played themselves out. Where war is concerned, history, as they say, is always written by the victors.

In recent years, a number of alternative histories have been published, attempting to describe how different the world would be had certain conflicts gone the other way. For example, what would the world be like today had Nazi Germany and the Axis powers prevailed in World War Two? Or what if Nikita Khrushchev had succeeded in burying the West economically as he had boasted he would? Or, closer to our present interest, what if the South had won the Civil War? What would life be like living in America today, and where would a Confederated United States of America fit in the modern world?

One thing is certain, had these conflicts been won by those who in fact lost, the key players in those cataclysmic events would be judged far differently today.

Given these considerations, every effort has been made to portray actual historical personalities fairly. Those depicted in the following pages were each in their own ways great men—men of passion and achievement, each in his own way important to the development and progress of the United States; and the same must be said of the women who stood with them.

On behalf of my coauthor, Richard Vetterli, who is deceased, may I say that it was our hope that their depictions in these pages will again bring to life their illustrious heritages.

For Americans, there is no greater story to be told than their own.

Brad E. Hainsworth
Kanab, Utah Territory, 2005

# ACKNOWLEDGMENTS

★   ★   ★

ONLY A FELLOW AUTHOR OR someone who has spent time around the publishing industry can fully appreciate the time and effort that goes into publishing a book. It literally takes a small army many weeks to take a manuscript from the hands of a hopeful author and nurture it through the intricate and involved publishing process, and then see to its distribution through hundreds of retail outlets and finally into the hands of the reader.

There are those who must make the difficult decision whether to publish the work or for any number of reasons return it to a very disappointed would-be author. Then come the copy editors, graphic artists, typesetters, contract specialists, marketing professionals, and many others involved throughout the process. This list could go on and on. Suffice it to say, any author owes each of them his heartfelt thanks.

At Deseret Book, there are two very gifted individuals whom I am now happy to call friends. Cory Maxwell encouraged me at a time when my natural defeatist inclinations would have caused me to give up, and he did it at a very difficult time in his own life. His constant encouragement was that of a true friend. It fell to Richard Peterson, a superlative editor, to edit the manuscript and help me find better ways to say the right things. I was blessed with his support from the very beginning. Both of these men, I am grateful to say, I now count as friends. Among the three of us there are many shared values.

I express my gratitude also to designer Richard Erickson and typesetter Tonya Facemyer for their invaluable contributions.

And finally, there is one more who must be mentioned—my wife, Jackie. She read every word of the manuscript, pleased with most, but unafraid to suggest whatever changes she thought necessary. I'm happy to report that on the whole, she thinks it an admirable work. It must be said, in no uncertain terms, that no writer can succeed without the help of a fully supportive spouse. To say I am grateful for her is an egregious understatement—but it must be said.

★　★　★

Verily, thus saith the Lord concerning the wars that will shortly come to pass, beginning at the rebellion of South Carolina, which will eventually terminate in the death and misery of many souls; And the time will come that war will be poured out upon all nations, beginning at this place.

—DOCTRINE & COVENANTS 87:1–2

# PART ONE

★  ★  ★

# CHAPTER 1

★　★　★

CAPTAIN BEAUREGARD MAYFIELD turned in the saddle as his second-in-command, Lieutenant James Allen, reined in beside him, a cloud of thick, chalk-gray dust swirling high into the air. "When is it ever goin' to end?" Allen asked, removing his hat and wiping the dirt and perspiration from his forehead.

"Do yuh miss the South, Mister Allen?"

"More than you'll ever know, suh. Not just the South. I miss South Carolina more than words can say—Charleston, especially."

"Mmm," Mayfield nodded in agreement. "When we fired on Sumter, I never thought I'd wind up out here in the middle of such a barren wasteland, miles from anything remotely civilized."

"What was your hope, Captain?"

"Why, the cavalry, of course. I'd rather sit a horse than eat or sleep."

"Well . . . I reckon it could be said we're doin' that now, suh."

"Could it, indeed, Lieutenant Allen? Could it?" Mayfield said, turning his horse to look back at the long wagon train slowly making its way up the gentle slope toward them. "Just look at that motley horde behind us. Would you call that an army, Lieutenant? What would you call it? Rabble . . . ruck would not be strong enough. I tell you, Lieutenant, we are stuck out here in this hellish ocean of dust and dirt with the off-scouring of society—riffraff, trash, a swinish multitude at best—and we leave the real war behind us with every step we take. It's a shame, suh, that's what it is—an outright shame!"

The two Confederate officers looked back on a train of twenty over-burdened wagons, some pulled by mules, others by oxen, each wagon driven by a dirty, vulgar, tobacco-spitting teamster, each of them an employee of the freighting company of Russell, Majors, and Waddell, and accompanied by nearly a hundred so-called volunteers from Kansas and Missouri. Not one of them loyal, in any sense of the word, to the Confederacy. The entire group was ostensibly commanded by Mayfield, a cultured gentleman from Charleston, South Carolina, born and reared on a large plantation, where he had been brought up in the ways of the southern aristocracy—born to the horse and the gun.

Though a patriot, dedicated to the Confederate cause, Mayfield was less than pleased with his present command. It was humiliating, really. At the time he had committed himself to the secessionist cause—long before the attack on Fort Sumter—he never dreamed that he would end up west of the Mississippi, fighting the winds and dust of the Platte River trails, in command, supposedly, of what to him seemed the dregs of the human race.

Whenever he thought of the general orders that were to govern the wagon company, it brought a sardonic smile to his handsome face. All members of the train were to observe the Sabbath, due respect was to be shown to all persons encountered on the road, and profane language was prohibited. That in itself seemed an obscenity. Not a man in the lot had even the slightest familiarity with such values.

Mayfield's orders, which had originated with former United States Secretary of War—now a general in the Confederate army—John B. Floyd, had been unusual, indeed. He and Lieutenant Allen were to dress as civilians and "with due purpose and intent" proceed to a point some thirty miles east of Fort Kearney. There, they were to be met by agents of the freighting firm of Russell, Majors, and Waddell, who would provide them with weapons, supplies, and a sufficient number of men and wagons to ensure the success of their mission. They were then to proceed west with all possible speed to a newly established, but rapidly growing, riverfront town called Platte River Station. Thus heavily armed and provisioned, his command was to invest the town, declare martial law, and control passage over the Platte River Road. But of greatest importance, at whatever cost, the overland telegraph wires were not to reach Salt Lake City.

Floyd had warned them to stay clear of the major forts. Although there were but a few volunteer troops guarding them, the forts possessed their own abundance of provisions and were heavily armed. Each fort had cannon and likely could hold off a sustained attack for some time. The former Secretary of War assured Mayfield, however, that not one of the forts had the manpower to interfere with his control of Platte River Station.

In any event, the Union officers commanding those forts were charged with just two orders: protect and maintain the forts and keep the telegraph lines open—nothing more. As things now stood, they lacked the manpower to give the telegraph lines anything more than minimal protection. Only small Union details would occasionally venture out to survey and repair the lines. If avoided, they should not pose a problem.

The trip had been long and difficult. The bright, relentless autumn sun was overpowering, and the terrain overwhelming. It was not just direct sunlight that caused discomfort and short tempers, the reflection that rose from the scorched earth forced eyes to squint, and lips quickly cracked and bled. Traveling several hundred yards south of the Platte River, water was readily accessible to the wagon train, though often of poor quality. Yet, even frequent stops did not prevent white lather from appearing on the horses' necks and flanks, and brackish water frequently caused cramps and diarrhea among the men, making their tempers short and their language even more foul.

Between forts Kearney and Laramie, the wagon train had been plagued with high winds out of the west, blowing directly into their faces. Eyes, ears, and mouths of both men and beasts suffered from the blowing sand and dust, and many of the men suffered from severe eye irritation and even temporary blindness. But the worst was encountered east of Fort Laramie—flies, gnats, and mosquitoes, always a problem, turned the trek into a living nightmare. The weather had been hot, and the nights had not yet turned cold enough to rid the river of its swarming pestilence. Descending in black clouds just before sunset, their hateful, exasperating whine filling the air, the insects attacked man and beast with equal ferocity.

It was maddening—victims waving their arms, fanning their faces, brushing the tiny tormentors out of their eyes and ears, shaking their heads violently, all in a kind of primordial dance that seemed to border on insanity. At times, it was almost as if the entire company of men had lost total control of their bodies in some primitive, atavistic frenzy. After sunset, buffalo gnats joined the fray, covering anything that moved, engulfing men's beards, penetrating their ears and noses.

West of Fort Laramie, the trail at last began to rise toward the higher plains and eventually the Rocky Mountains. The sand dunes disappeared; the almost constant, harsh winds began to subside; the temperature and humidity moderated; and as the trail gained in altitude and the nights grew cooler, the flying pestilence became less vexatious. Though there was considerably more grass for the animals, it was brown and lacking in nourishment. Alkaline pots were frequently encountered, and the brackish water sickened the animals. A good dose of vinegar—force-fed—usually cleansed their systems and brought them around.

But new problems arose to plague the wagon train and further strain the patience of all. The Conestogas under Mayfield's command were built to carry no more than 2,000 pounds, but due to the nature of the mission, each wagon carried substantially more. Now, as they were approaching their destination, the men were paying for the excess weight in lost days due to frequent breakdowns—worn axles and hubs, splintering wheel spokes, and bent or loose iron rims separating from their wheels were frequent problems that ate up precious time. Repair of the huge, over-burdened wagons was not only difficult, but aggravating, and tempers flared almost without provocation.

Neither of the Confederate officers was a military neophyte. Mayfield, thirty-three years of age, proud, and by-the-book, was a West Point graduate who had dedicated nearly a decade of service in the United States Army before resigning his commission to join the Confederate cause. Lieutenant Allen, several years younger, slight, blond, and handsome, had been commissioned a first lieutenant by none other than General Albert Sydney Johnston during the Utah War. Neither man was without considerable experience in moving large numbers of men and materiels or in exercising command.

The surly lot that made up the Confederate "Platte River Command" was not only unruly, they were beginning to get out of control. Not a man among them had received any military training. In short, so far as Mayfield knew, he and Allen were the only men in the entire command to have worn a uniform and understood what that meant. As the days wore on, Lt. Allen had grown more and more uneasy about their venture. "This group," he had confided to Mayfield early on, "makes southern white trash look and act like aristocracy."

Somewhere, in one or two of the Conestogas, there had to be an almost endless supply of rotgut. Night after night the so-called "volunteers" bellowed and bullied around the campfires until early dawn. They slept in the saddle, more than a few periodically puking all over themselves or falling from their mounts. Of the six killings that had occurred since passing Fort Kearney, at least four of them were attributable to drunkenness, and the Confederate captain had long ago stopped counting the fights or interfering with them.

Realistically, however, there was little he could do about any of it. The first week spent with this ragtag command had taught him that much. It had also taught him that the true power of command rested with Wolfgang Striker—the one called "Wolf." Whenever Mayfield gave an order, Wolf seconded it, otherwise it was ignored. No one disobeyed Wolf. One teamster had, and Wolf had beaten him senseless and left him by the trail to die slowly, along with the embers of the morning campfires.

Wolf Striker was an anomaly among men. He was large in stature, standing well over six feet in height, and his tall frame was heavily muscled. In certain circumstances, he had the appearance of a large bear, but there was not an ounce of fat to be found on him. In surprising contrast to those over whom he exercised his seemingly innate authority, he was physically clean—clean shaven, cleanly clothed each day, and clean in speech.

But to Mayfield, at least, Striker's most interesting characteristic was his immaculate use of language. He was surprisingly articulate and spoke in a manner that indicated breeding and education. In short, there were times when he displayed the mannerisms of a highly cultured individual. In one or two brief conversations with Mayfield, he exhibited a familiarity with literature and history that was surprising, and his understanding of military strategy and tactics was equal to that of a West Point graduate, which Mayfield suspected he just might be.

Wolf Striker, however, was thoroughly ruthless and without scruple. At the slightest provocation, he might turn on a man with a degree of cruelty that, at times, stunned those around him. He would brook no disobedience, nor would he tolerate the slightest questioning of his demands. If crossed in any way, he was utterly unfeeling in his reaction and unapologetic for the consequences. To be around such a man was to be constantly prepared for the unexpected, and the unexpected could be sudden, brutal, and deadly.

Striker's almost constant companion, and in some ways his second-in-command, was a deranged, pathetically twisted creature known as Jubal Hathaway. Small in stature, but with the nature of a bully, Hathaway had been a wagon master for the same freighting firm—Russell, Majors, and Waddell—under Johnston's command during the Utah War. In one of the skirmishes, as Johnston's beleaguered army had struggled through the mountains toward Salt Lake City, the vicious little bully had been severely beaten—some thought, and many were willing to swear, by men in his own detail.

Hathaway's nose and cheekbones had been badly crushed, and a final kick to his face from some powerful leg and a stiff boot had made pulp of his left eye. As a result, the left side of his face was paralyzed, and the skin beneath the eye socket hung without support, exposing what remained of the dead eye, covered with yellowish ulcers that periodically drained down his cheek. Usually, he wore a black eye patch, but when he did not, even the most calloused among this ragtag assembly of misfits would turn away in revulsion.

But the damage went even deeper: the beating had so impaired his brain that his left side was constantly numb down to his waist, and his shriveled left arm hung uselessly at his side. Nonetheless, his right eye was sharp most of the time, and his good arm and hand moved with lightning speed, especially when he reached for the Colt .44 holstered on his right hip.

Jubal Hathaway worshiped Wolf Striker, but unlike Striker, Hathaway was devoid of any illumination whatsoever. The twisted little man existed solely on hate and was driven by lust for revenge. Most of all, he hated Mormons, seeing them as the sole cause of his baleful afflictions. Because of this, he had begged Wolf to let him come on this expedition. From the increasingly frequent bouts of dizziness that swept over him, the periodic blurred vision, and the almost unbearable headaches, Hathaway was certain he had little time left. All that was keeping him alive was hatred and lust for revenge.

It was a little past noon when Captain Mayfield, shading his eyes with his outstretched palm, caught his first sight of Platte River Station. The town squatted on the north bank of the Platte River, and a single dock with several canoes and a moored flatboat could be seen protruding out into the relatively shallow, slow-moving water. There were those willing to argue that the Platte was nothing more than wet, moving sand. A narrow bridge had been constructed across the river, but from where Mayfield sat, it looked none too sturdy.

Platte River Station was originally one of a planned series of way-stations along the Platte River trails. Over the years, where other efforts had been less successful, Platte River Station had grown steadily, especially during the Utah War. Now, more than three years later, it would be considered an established frontier town by any standard.

At the top of a gentle rise, Captain Mayfield threw his right arm in the air, bringing the long column to a dusty stop, and Wolf Striker galloped up and reined in beside him. "Well," Wolf said, in his usual patronizing manner, "what now, Captain?"

"You are askin' me, Mister Striker?" Mayfield said, his gentle southern drawl slightly more pronounced. "How solicitous of you."

As the two spoke, a wagon approached the bridge on the far side of the river, accompanied by two riders. Uncertain of what appeared to be some sort of invading force on the opposite bank, riders and wagon wheeled about and at full gallop headed back into the settlement.

"Look here, Captain," Striker responded, an uncharacteristic softness in his voice, "we both want this takeover to be as quiet as possible; however, it would appear that our presence has now been discovered. Moving with some dispatch at this delicate juncture might be wise, don't you think?"

"I like nothing about this expedition, suh, except its purpose. This rabble," Mayfield said, nodding his head in the direction of the wagon train behind them, "is almost beyond control. But I'll tell you what at this delicate juncture, as you put it, bothers me most, Wolf, and that is how your warped little friend, Jubal Hathaway, is going to respond. What bothers me even more is why you brought such a degenerate person with you in the first place, given the nature of what we are here to accomplish."

"Look, I do not want any reaction from Fort Laramie anymore than you do, Captain, if that is your concern. I have my reasons for bringing Hathaway along, and I'll do what's necessary to keep him under control. Now, what do you propose?"

Mayfield took a deep breath, looked away, then turning back to Striker said, "Alright, Wolf, let us agree to allow the town officers to remain in charge—for appearance's sake. It'll become obvious soon enough who's in control, and they will see that it is in their best interest to do as we tell them. We can accomplish what we must with as little unpleasantness as possible."

"Agreed. Now what?"

"Lieutenant Allen and I will go in with ten men. I'll explain all that is necessary—what we intend to do. If there is an agreement, I'll signal by waving to you. You lead the entire column to the west end of the town, pitch the tents, and line up the wagons. And from the looks of things, there will be plenty for your men to do. You'll quickly need to build more and larger corrals for the stock."

"Agreed, but Hathaway and I go along."

"Hathaway? Are you out of your mind, Wolf?"

Striker's face froze. "You'll do it my way, Mayfield," he snapped, his tone turning ugly. "Hathaway and I go along."

For the briefest moment, Striker paused, then continued, his manner almost overbearingly reasonable. "I don't want to leave him where I can't watch him, and he won't do anything stupid while he is with me. Back here, alone, now that we're here, who knows?"

# CHAPTER 2

★ ★ ★

WILL AND LUKE CARTWRIGHT sat in one of the two unoccupied cells behind the sheriff's office, concentrating on a game of checkers, when a rider rode up and dismounted out front. His boots made a hollow sound as he strode rapidly across the boardwalk and into the outer office.

"Who is it?" Will hollered, without turning around to peer through the jail room door. "We're busy—on official business in here."

"Yeah. If it ain't important, go away!" Luke hollered, with a chuckle. "King me."

"King yuh?"

"Yep," Luke, said as he banged his man across the board, jumping three of his brother's red men. "King me."

Will looked up as the man rushed into the cell room. "What is it, Chester?"

"Hell's fire, Will," the man said, his breath coming in excited gasps, "there's a bunch as big as a whole damned army a comin' over the rise across the river. In fact, that's exactly what it looks like—an army—an' it don't look to me like they're up to no good, neither."

"Slow down, Chester, and watch your language. What are you talking about?"

"Looks to me like maybe two or three hundred men, and I didn't stop t' count the wagons, but there's plenty of 'em. You best get out there in a hurry, Sheriff."

"Nuts," Will muttered, pushing his chair back, "and just when I was about to clean your plow."

"Clean my plow?" Luke said, following his brother into the outer office. "I don't see any kings among your men."

Strapping on their sidearms, the two brothers strode out into the street. Both were big men, but Will was the larger, and neither of them ever had been accused of being good-looking. Will wore two .44 Colts, just as did his mentor, Porter Rockwell. The younger brother, Luke, wore only one, ribbing his brother, when the occasion allowed, that one was all he needed.

As the two brothers left their office, the town was coming awake with the usual, comforting sounds of a small community. Somewhere a pump handle squeaked, and further down the street a door slammed. In the distance, a dog was barking, and two or three roosters repeatedly announced the coming of another day. At that early hour only a few people could be seen on the boardwalks of the main street. The chatter of birds could be heard in the trees and the fields surrounding the town, and across the street Jim Farnsworth, the owner of the town's mercantile, was sweeping the boardwalk in front of his store. It was a peaceful setting— the citizens of Platte River Station awakening to a new day, unaware that the Civil War in the east was tragically about to engulf them.

Climbing into their saddles, the two brothers trotted their horses toward the town's riverfront. They had barely reached the end of the main street when they came face to face with a half dozen strangers, two of them in Confederate uniforms.

Captain Beauregard Mayfield, drawing in his mount, was the first to speak. "Gentlemen, I hope you will excuse this unannounced intrusion," he began, the grace of his southern heritage more than apparent. "I am Captain Beauregard Mayfield, of the Confederate States of America. May I ask whom I have the privilege of addressing?"

Will Cartwright was a man quick to assess any situation, and his judgments were nearly always correct. He had no liking for what he saw. "I'm Will Cartwright, Sheriff of Platte River Station," he said, a cautious edge to his voice. "This is my deputy, Luke Cartwright."

"I see," Mayfield nodded, "does Platte River Station have a mayor?"

"You're looking at him," Will responded dryly.

"Am I to understand you are both sheriff and mayor?"

"*And* the judge. *And* the bishop."

A snicker arose from the riders behind Mayfield. "But right now, mostly, I'm the sheriff," Will continued, casting a hard glance at his detractors.

Mayfield cleared his throat. "I see. It would appear, then, that I am speaking to the town's officialdom."

"Whatever your reasons for being here, you are."

"I am obliged to inform you that we are under orders from the Confederacy to invest this place and hold it—for the time being, at least."

"You're what?" Will Cartwright said, looking suspiciously at the riders behind Mayfield, his right hand resting unobtrusively on the butt of his Colt. "What is the Confederate military doing here? I'm afraid I don't understand."

As Cartwright spoke, he locked eyes with the one-eyed Jubal Hathaway, and there was instant recognition between the two. A guttural whine, like that of a wounded animal, rose from Hathaway's throat, his teeth grinding, as his darkened, deranged mind began to lose whatever stability kept him under control.

Not fully recognizing the source of the odd sound, Mayfield tried to be reassuring. "We intend no harm to you or the people of this town. With few exceptions, you may all continue your regular tasks. I—"

Before those around him could react, Hathaway drew his Colt and shrieked in crazed frenzy, "I know you Mormon pigs!" His gun and Will Cartwright's pair fired in one shattering explosion, and pandemonium erupted. Hathaway was slammed backward over the rump of his horse by the impact of Will's two slugs, one in each shoulder, and Will dropped from his horse to one knee, blood oozing from a wound low in his abdomen.

Horses reared back on their haunches, others lurched sideways in reaction to the explosions around them, screaming in fear. Three riders were thrown from their mounts, including Captain Mayfield, who was momentarily knocked senseless. No longer in their saddles, the Cartwrights, on solid ground, had some advantage, while most of the others, fighting to control their frightened and skittish horses, attempted to level their guns at the two brothers. Taking slugs themselves, Will and Luke emptied their Colts into the swirling mass of confusion.

When the last shot was fired, all of the Confederate hostiles lay still, two with their dead mounts on top of them—none had survived the brief fight. Three riderless horses bolted and galloped down the town's main street, stirrups flapping at their sides, oblivious to the growing number of astounded citizens that dodged them as they flew by. A fourth followed closely, dragging a dead rider, his foot snagged in the stirrup.

Only Lieutenant Allen and Wolf Striker remained in the saddle during the melee. Allen, his pistol still in its holster, had not been touched as he fought to keep his horse under control. Striker, hit in the thigh by a wild shot, remained mounted, his horse relatively undisturbed by all the violence. Jubal Hathaway lay writhing on the ground, loud, effeminate cries of pain issuing from his saliva-streaked mouth.

The Cartwright brothers had each taken three slugs. Luke lay gasping on his back, a pink froth bubbling through the holes in his shirt as he struggled to breathe. Will, still kneeling in position, his now empty Colts held straight, slowly slumped forward, two red stains over his chest and stomach rhythmically soaking his shirt. The wound in his lower abdomen had already saturated his pants. Finally, falling onto his side, he lost consciousness.

Before the shooting had ended, fifty of Wolf's men had galloped into the town, while others had taken strategic positions around the community's perimeter. To the frightened townspeople, disappearing as quickly as possible into their shops and homes, the murderous, ragtag horde of invaders appeared to be everywhere.

Furious, Wolf dismounted, ripping the bandanna from his neck and tying it over the wound in his leg, all the while staring down at the bawling Hathaway curled at his feet. "You stupid, driveling idiot, this mess is your doing," he hollered, giving Hathaway a vicious kick in the ribs. Walking over to the Cartwright brothers, he said, "Look at them. Two or three more like them and they could have wiped out our entire command. The two of them are better men than a thousand like you or any of the rest of this mob."

Seeing the brothers were still alive, Striker hollered at no one in particular, "Alright, the skunk's out of the sack. Now we're going to show this town where the real power lies." Nodding at a corner building near the end of the block, where a sign hung over the boardwalk that read *Sadie's Bird Cage,* he gestured at two men who had just ridden up. "You boys get these two Mormons, or whatever they are, down the street, there, and hang them—hang them above the boardwalk, there, where everyone can see—right in front of Sadie's Bird Cage, the busiest place in town, more than likely. Then we go through this one-horse town and search every room, house, barn, doghouse, and outhouse. I want every gun, every knife, anything that could be used as a weapon. Nothing—I mean, nothing—had better be overlooked. Any resistance, shoot. I don't care who it is. You understand me? Now, get started!"

Wolf winced with the sudden and unexpected thrust of the muzzle of Captain Mayfield's gun in his back. "Now, you understand *me*, Mister Striker," Mayfield said, his voice hard, though he was still unsteady on his feet. "You're not hangin' anyone! Enough harm has been done to the citizens of this town. I told you not to bring that crippled ghoul down here with us. But now the harm's been done, let us all just calm down."

Typical of his upbringing, Mayfield's courage and southern chivalry outweighed any consideration of the impossible position in which he had placed himself. Still somewhat dazed, he did not sense the movement of several men behind him, and, as with most deadly, unexpected violence, what happened next was so sudden there was no time for reaction.

Still sitting his horse a few yards away, Lieutenant Allen

reached for his gun as he called out a warning to his commanding officer, but his weapon caught on the flap of its military holster. With Mayfield's attention momentarily distracted, Striker whirled, and in one fluid movement drove his elbow into Mayfield's face with stunning force, knocking him to the ground. With his other hand he drew his big Colt and coolly shot Allen, still struggling to free his weapon, from the saddle. The lieutenant was dead before his body hit the ground. In less than three or four seconds, it was over.

Looking down at Mayfield as the captain struggled to sit up, Wolf snarled, "You stupid, gallant fool! You're in no position to interfere with my orders. You'll never do it again." Reaching around, he snatched a revolver from one of the ruffians who had gathered next to him and pointed it at Mayfield's head. For a long moment the gun seemed to hang there, frozen in time and space, no one daring to breathe. Seeing nothing but spite and contempt in the southern soldier's bruised and bleeding face, Wolf lowered the gun and turned away. Something in the Confederate officer's manner had stopped him: courage, defiance, something that spoke to him, something not really understood but mutually shared only by true fighting men. "Take him away," he said to no one in particular. "There'll be a jail in the sheriff's office. I may need him later."

In spite of himself, Wolf Striker respected the southern officer. The man had fortitude, he told himself. He was a soldier, a fighting man through and through, and that demanded respect, even from one's enemies.

Five hundred miles or so to the west and two weeks later, Marshal Orrin Porter Rockwell sat in his dusty, cluttered office, located near the center of Salt Lake City, sorting through a stack of wanted posters he had neglected for too long. Lost in thought, he looked up only when a shadow fell across his desk.

"Sorry to bother you, Port."

"President Young," Rockwell said, rising from his chair. "What're you doing here, sir? All you ever have to do is send a messenger, and I'd come to your office, directly."

Waving off Rockwell's surprise, the big man slid a chair in front of the marshal's desk. "Sit down, Port. I need to do the same. I'm afraid this won't be a very pleasant visit."

A shadow crossed Rockwell's eyes. "Bad news, sounds like."

"Port, when was the last time you were at Platte River Station?"

Rockwell thought for a long moment. "Not since Will Cartwright was made sheriff, and his brother his deputy—must be on to two years, now." His eyes narrowed. "Is there a problem with those boys?"

"They're both dead, both of those fine boys."

Rockwell was stunned. "Dead?"

"I'm told they were both shot, then hanged."

What little could be seen of Rockwell's face was not pleasant. Beneath the full beard, his features froze, and his pale blue eyes, nearly hidden by bushy eyebrows, narrowed with the look of final judgment. A man of few words and not one to show emotion, even under the darkest of circumstances, Rockwell's entire body seemed to take on the solidity of a block of granite as he rose from his chair. "How?" he growled.

"Hear me out, Porter, please. Sit down and hear me out."

Slowly, Rockwell sank back into his chair. "Those boys fought under me through the Johnston invasion. The two of them were like sons to me, Brother Brigham," Rockwell said, his voice low with foreboding reaction.

"Yes, Porter, I know."

"How'd it happen?" Rockwell asked, more bluntly than he intended.

"The information I've received says that some months ago, near Fort Kearney, two Confederate officers were joined by a small army of mostly Missouri bushwhackers and a large wagon train, complete with muleskinners, bullwhackers, and such, loaded with weapons and provisions, all compliments of Russell, Majors, and Waddell, and under the orders of Confederate General John B. Floyd."

"Buchanan's Secretary of War?"

"That's the one. They immediately headed west, taking the lower Platte River Road, avoiding forts Kearney and Laramie, and as quickly as possible moving on to their destination, Platte River Station. When they arrived, they took over the town and fortified it. It was during the initial battle that Will and Luke were killed. From then until now, the Confederate force has controlled access to both sides of the river. From the station they've launched a reign of murder, robbery, and terror. The result is, they have effectively stopped overland transportation to California."

Rockwell again came to his feet. "Will and Luke?" he said through clenched teeth, his voice not much more than a deep rumble. "What about them?"

The Mormon leader shook his head and swallowed, his throat tight with a rare show of emotion. "Just as you would expect. They stood their ground. Against a hundred or more. Unfortunately for all, there was a shootout—at least ten invaders died before they were finally shot down. Then the leader of the mob had them dragged to the brothel in the middle of town and hung from the balcony. The next morning, their bodies were cut down and thrown into the Platte."

Dust mites floated in the light that struggled through the dirty windows of the cramped office, and neither man spoke, not wanting to trust their emotions.

Brigham Young was the first to break the silence. "Porter, I promise they'll be brought to justice. I've sent riders to find Major Smith. He and his men are probably at Bridger's Fort. Justice will be done. He'll—"

"Lott Smith? Brother Brigham, I've got to do this myself!" Porter said, more abruptly than he had intended, but somehow his voice would not soften. "Those Cartwright boys . . . well, they were my boys—like my own flesh, almost! I took them out there; they're my responsibility! Lott Smith can't do what has to be done."

"Porter, are you sure—"

"President Young, I want ten men, unattached; no more. Lott can supply more troopers if I need them when we get to Fort Bridger. I want repeating rifles and Colts for everyone, and more ammunition than we can possibly use. I assume Lott's men are armed with repeaters.

"Send a message to Phil Cooke at Camp Scott, if you would, sir. I want two wagons filled with powder, delivered to Salt Lake within a week."

"Just a minute, Porter," Young said, his voice betraying some alarm. "Are you sure he'll respond to that? And what do you need so much powder for? Those men need to be brought back for trial and sentencing."

Rockwell's grim smile contained a hint of sarcasm. "Yeah, Phil'll respond, alright. Tell him we're fighting on the same side again. He'll recognize this Confederate thrust west for exactly what it is—an attempt to block western overland commerce and to gain access to western resources for the Confederacy. As for those who did the killing, I'll see that justice is served.

"Oh . . . yeah . . . and I'll also need a letter from you giving me command over Lott Smith and his militia."

Brigham Young hesitated a moment, then responded with a chuckle. Reaching into the inside pocket of his coat, he pulled out a sealed letter and handed it to Rockwell. It was addressed to Major Lott Smith, Territorial Militia.

*How does the man do it?* Rockwell thought. *He knew. He knew all along I'd go, and under what conditions.* Rockwell shook his head, a look of admiration on his face. "I'll never understand you, Brother Brigham. Never."

Two weeks later, Rockwell and ten well-mounted, heavily armed troopers, trailing pack animals and two unmarked wagons loaded with hundred-pound kegs of fine grain black powder, each drawn by a six-up team of mules, wound their way through Emigration Canyon, headed for Echo Canyon and finally, Bridger's Fort on the Green River.

# CHAPTER 3

*  *  *

T HE HORIZON EAST OF PLATTE River Station began to lighten, sending confusing and ill-defined shadows crawling across the uneven contours of the high plains. As the sun melted the earth's rim and day broke, the clouds that drifted eastward above the devastated town and the surrounding broken country were bathed in an ominous, incandescent crimson that seemed to reflect the smoldering perdition below.

The destruction of Platte River Station was nearly total. Those few buildings that remained standing were little more than the shattered skeletal remains of what only hours before had been a small, sprouting river town, one pivotal to the plans of ambitious men in tumultuous times. And the fires that still raged threatened to leave nothing but an obscene, black stain as a memorial to those ambitions.

Two lone riders emerged from the dark shadows of the ragged hills to the southwest. Reaching the river's silted bank, across from

Platte River Station's main street, the two stopped to survey what was left of the town. Both men were struck with the totality of what had happened the night before.

Turning to his companion, Porter Rockwell said, "I was here, Ben, but even so, it's hard to believe what has happened."

"I can't believe my eyes," Ben Kimball responded.

Rockwell spurred his horse into the muddy, languid stream and said, "Come on. We need to find Smith and Ashworth pronto and make sure everything is under control. There's still a lot to be done, and you bringing more from Brigham Young doesn't help."

"Come on, Port," Kimball responded genially. "You know who the boss is. What needs to be done, needs to be done, and with little time wasted. The sooner we find Lott and get this place behind us, the better."

Ben Kimball, the one man Brigham Young trusted most when failure was not an option, a man never far from Young's side, had just made the ride from Fort Bridger with man-killing speed. The message he carried securely buttoned in an inside coat pocket would do much to change the history of the West and the course of the war now raging in the eastern United States.

A dismal pall of gray smoke hung over the scene of devastation as the two men made their way along what was once the town's main street. Here and there insistent fires fought for continuing life, casting odd shadows in the smoldering gloom of early morning, threatening to further add to the almost total wasteland.

Despite the violence and death of the night before, life was beginning to stir. People were emerging from whatever shelter they had been able to find, and many stood in stunned disbelief, their faces black with soot and gaunt from spent emotion, their orderly lives wrecked with the horror that had swept their town.

Subdued by the tragedy that surrounded them, the two riders

walked their horses toward what was left standing of the Platte River Saloon, where the Utahans had established their temporary headquarters. As Ben dismounted, Rockwell said, "You go on in, Ben, I see a fella I've got to talk to."

A short distance along the street several wagons were drawn up before their owners' smoldering businesses. What little could be salvaged was being loaded; any reason to remain in Platte River Station simply no longer existed.

Patrick Gilhooly Muldoon leaned against the single remaining support that held a dangerously sagging wood awning over the boardwalk, morosely watching the activity around the nearest wagon.

"Muldoon?"

"Ah . . . Rockwell," the short, stout Irishman said with a chortle. "Ain't this a sight?"

"Yeah, I'd say it's a sight, alright," Rockwell agreed, looking around. "Look, Muldoon, if I ever get my hands on Striker and that bunch, they'll pay."

"Pay, will they?" Muldoon said, taking a deep breath and glancing over his shoulder at the smoldering ruin of his once prosperous business, what had been the second largest saloon in town. "Well . . . it's gone now, sure enough. Those Confederates—that's what they called themselves, yuh know—did a real job on this place. Nothin' left t' speak of."

Not knowing what more to say, Rockwell removed his hat and scratched his head. "You seen Sadie?" he asked lamely.

"Sadie's alright. Like the rest of us, she's packin' whatever's left. Gonna leave."

"How about her girls? What are they?—"

"Three of 'em's dead. Killed in the explosions."

"Oh . . . there was no reason for this!" Rockwell said, as he hit the charred awning post with his fist.

"Careful, man . . . you'll have what's left of the place down on me head."

"What are you gonna do now, Pat?"

"Well . . . guess I'll head for California, with Sadie, maybe. Get started again. Won't be the first time. Likely not the last."

Rockwell reined his horse about and stopped in the middle of the street. Reaching into his pocket, he said, "Pat?" As the man looked up, Rockwell tossed a roll of currency to him. "Think of it as rent while the rest of us are here. Won't take *no,* Pad'ner."

Muldoon gazed at the wad of money in his hand for a moment and then pitched it back. "You ain't t' blame, man. You warned us. What's done is done. Simple as that. I'll make out. I always have, so don't you be worrin' yerself about me, none. Sadie, neither. She'll be okay, too. I don't—"

"Then give it to Sadie," Rockwell said, chucking the roll of bills back to the chubby saloon keeper. "Far as I'm concerned," he hollered over his shoulder as he spurred his horse back the way he had come, "the Irishman ain't been born that don't need help most of the time."

After tying up his horse, Rockwell entered the burned-out saloon, irritably kicked aside a broken chair, and walked over to the table where Dr. Charles Taggert was examining the ugly furrow an almost lethal bullet had dug across Clay Ashworth's forehead. "Looks to me like there ought to be a better place, Doc," Rockwell said, giving the wreckage of the saloon a disparaging glance. "What's left of this gin mill would come down with a sneeze in the right direction." The entire front of the obviously unstable building was gone, offering a panoramic view of the blackened, skeletal remains of the building across the street.

"Look, Doc," Clay Ashworth was saying, as he struggled to sit up. "All I've got is a headache. The rest of these men, and a lot of other people out there, need your help more than I do."

"You lie down," Dr. Taggert responded sharply, easing Ashworth back down on the unstable, once-ornate Farrow table, his long legs hanging awkwardly over its broken and tattered edge. "You've got more than just a flesh wound here, my friend. More than likely you got yourself a right proper concussion. Now hold still, and let me have a look-see."

"Better listen and stop complaining, Ashworth. I can't afford to loose you just yet," Rockwell said, his voice devoid of humor. "Besides, Brigham Young would have my hide if anything happened to you."

Bending over his unwilling patient, Charlie Taggert looked up at his old friend, Porter Rockwell. "And you. Uncomfortable with this place, are you? Well, just where in heaven's name do you suggest I go to treat these men? Those so-called Confederates did the job pretty near to perfection, didn't they, Kimball?" the doctor said, glancing in Ben Kimball's direction.

"Yes, sir," Kimball said, looking around with some admiration. "There's been a time or two when I thought I'd walked into hell itself, but this place beats all."

"By the way, what are you doing here, Ben?" Taggert queried, returning to his examination of Ashworth.

"Just the usual, Doc," Kimball said with a nod.

"You must be in hog heaven, Charlie," Porter Rockwell grumped. "In just one night, you got these eight victims here to work on, not to mention whatever else is lying around out there."

Turning toward the gaping front of the building, Rockwell glanced at Ben Kimball and said, "Get yourself something to eat and rest for a few minutes. You look all done in. I'm going to have another look around, and then we'll talk."

"Well, I could at least use something to eat," Kimball said, turning toward the front of the building. "I'll be right back. We've got business to take care of."

"Porter . . ." Clay Ashworth said, lifting his head from the table.

Rockwell glanced over his shoulder. "Yeah?"

"Before the doc dragged me in here, I was doing some poking around myself—"

"This man was walking around in a daze when I found him, Porter," Taggert huffed.

"Anyway, there's a man down in the jail you or Lott had better have a look at. I wasn't in any shape to get him out of the place."

"The jail?" Rockwell said, stopping to look back at Ashworth.

"Yeah. It's about the only building left standing in one piece— a small, rock building, next to what used to be the sheriff's office. The man says he's a Confederate officer and wants to speak to whoever's in charge. He looks to be dressed in what might have been a Confederate uniform. I couldn't find Lott, so you might want to talk to him. Might just be what he says he is."

"He say anything else?"

"Well . . . he knows something about Wolf Striker. Says Striker took off with all of the guns and ammo intended for the Confederacy, and he—"

At the mention of Wolf Striker's name, Porter Rockwell turned on his heel, jumped to the street, and was quickly lost in the smoke and stench of the previous night's carnage.

"Doctor Taggert," Clay said, leaning back on the table. "I've seen that look in Rockwell's eyes before. If he ever finds Striker

. . . well . . . I don't want to be in the neighborhood when he does."

"I know," Charlie Taggert said, pressing a piece of plaster tape over Ashworth's newly cleaned wound. "There are times when I think the man borders on the irrational, when his mind's made up on a thing. I think he's got the gift of Cassandra, if you get my meaning."

"I don't know, Doc. This time, it just might come true."

"Now, Clay, you best forget about all of this and head back to Salt Lake. You're going to need to take it easy for a while."

The small, stone building looked just as Ashworth had described it. The explosions had blown the solid, iron-strapped oak door from its hinges, leaving it lying at an awkward angle, forced inward, and jammed by its own massive weight between the shattered door frames. Except for a somewhat weakened and sagging roof, the building looked stable enough, with its walls and bars still intact. As far as Rockwell could tell, the place still made an efficient jail, a convenient fact he stored in the back of his mind.

"Over here," a softly accented voice rasped from the darkness of the corner cell. "Please . . . ah need some help here."

Pushing through the doorway, Rockwell found the man in the corner of a dank cell, struggling to get to his feet. The stench in the tiny space was overwhelming. The man, whomever he was, had been left to wallow in his own excrement, half-starved and, from the looks of it, nearly done in.

"If you'd be so kind, suh, ah need water."

"In more ways than one, mister," Rockwell said, yanking at the dirty cell door. With some effort, the heavy, rusted cell door, apparently jammed and left unlocked, grated open with a nerve-grinding, half-human screech. Grasping the man beneath his arms, Rockwell lifted him to his feet with surprisingly little effort and, half dragging him, got the Confederate officer out of the filth and into the outer room. Taking a closer look at the man, Rockwell said, "Let's get you out of here where Doc Taggert can get a look at you. Then you and I are gonna have ourselves a little talk."

# CHAPTER 4

★  ★  ★

Beau Mayfield, Captain of Cavalry, Confederate States of America, sat slumped on a wooden chair, sipping from a steaming bowl of broth, its fragrant, nourishing warmth slowly seeping throughout his weakened body. " . . . and that's God's own truth, Mistah Rockwell. My command was composed of mostly volunteers recruited in Missouri and Kansas, a hundred or so. An undisciplined lot that in the end were not loyal, excuse me, suh, *never* were loyal, to me, let alone to the Confederacy. They were, in fact, loyal to their own lusts and to that blackheart, Wolf Striker. A thoroughly miserable fellow, if ever there was one."

Sipping more of the tasty broth, the Confederate officer looked up, his face filled with a hatred Rockwell well understood. "My second-in-command, Lieutenant Allen, God rest his gentle soul, is dead. Gunned down when that miserable, twisted wretch, Jubal Hathaway, initiated all this violence. James Allen was as close a friend has ah have ever had, suh. In that regard, ah intend to set things right. On that you may rely. You must understand, suh, we were trying to control the situation."

As Mayfield was finishing his broth, Rockwell rose from his chair and began pacing back and forth. "Hathaway, that miserable little worm-eatin' cretin," he said, his voice revealing the depth of his hatred. "His time'll come, Mayfield, I'll guarantee you that. When I get my hands on 'im, he'll beller for heaven's mercy, because I will show him none."

"As it should be, suh. As it should be."

"So Striker lit out for the New Mexico Territory?" Rockwell continued, turning to look at Mayfield. "Did he take Hathaway with him?"

"Ah think he did, suh. If not, ah have no idea where Hathaway has gotten off to. You must pardon my vagueness, but ah think Striker left a day or two ago, if ah remember correctly."

"What did Striker take with him? How many men? How many wagons? What was in them?"

"Most of our wagons had broken down because of the weight of their contents, but ah think he left with three or four fully loaded wagons and perhaps fifteen or twenty men, aside from the skinners. I have no idea what happened to the rest of that scum."

"Porter, this man needs rest," Dr. Taggert broke in.

"In a minute, Doc," Rockwell snapped, waving Taggert to silence. "What was in those wagons, Captain Mayfield?"

"Guns—the latest Spencer Carbines and Colt Army pistols. Those weapons—the carbines, that is—are repeating—"

"I know what they are, and what they can do, Captain."

"Then you know, suh, his group is as well armed as any army presently in the field. Striker is capable of inflicting great damage, suh."

"Well, what the devil were you doing out here with that much firepower, guarded by that kind of rabble?" Rockwell spat.

"Ah am sure you are fully aware of our intentions, as I have explained. It was my duty to bring to a complete halt any travel or commerce between the Union and the western territories. We were to cut the telegraph wires, which you people have so jealously guarded between here and Fort Bridger, stop all migration, stop the stages, and above all, stop any supply wagons attempting to reach beyond this point."

Sitting back down at the table, Rockwell leaned forward on his elbows, his face only a few inches from Mayfield's. "Well, all you so-called Confederate gentlemen have managed to do is arm the Indian slave traders in New Mexico. You understand that much, don't yuh? That's where that stuff is going. Wolf Striker has no more interest in your chivalrous attempt to save your dying Southern civilization than I do. He's out to line his own pockets, and he'll do it with human blood and Indian slaves, thanks to you."

"Ah am well aware of that, suh. He threw it in my face the day he left. But let me make my position clear—"

"And one other thing," Rockwell said, cutting him off. "You and your Confederacy may be sure a good number of my boys are even now guarding the men stringing wires west from Fort Bridger. We expect to have the telegraph in Salt Lake City before the end of October," Rockwell said, thumping the table. "You can count on that, you Confederates."

"Ah do not doubt your intentions, suh. Nor do ah under-estimate your abilities. Ah want no misunderstanding with you, Mister Rockwell. When ah joined the Confederacy, ah joined to serve where ah was needed most. Aside from what's going on back east, it is important to deny the West to the Union and open it to

35

the Confederacy. That was my intention; it remains such still. And, I'll do what ah must to see that is done. And let me make one thing clear, suh," the Confederate officer continued, attempting to get to his feet. "Ah will do what ah must, align myself with the very Devil himself if necessary, to achieve that objective."

"Well, you sure enough did that when you hitched up with Wolf Striker," Porter Rockwell said, making no attempt to hide the disgust in his voice.

"Precisely, suh. And that is why you must take me with you when you go after him."

"Take you with us?" Rockwell said, incredulously.

"Make no mistake, Mister Rockwell. Ah want him as badly as do you, if for different reasons. Ah want justice, too, suh. But more importantly, ah must regain those arms he stole. Ah must regain them for the Confederacy, suh."

Rockwell's chair groaned dangerously as he leaned back and contemplated the man before him. "Well, it seems we have at least one thing in common."

"And what might that be, suh?"

"We need to stop—"

Both men turned at the sound of Lott Smith climbing from the dusty street into the ravaged saloon, followed by Clay Ashworth.

"Where have you been?" Rockwell spat, leaving little doubt of his evaluation of Smith.

Ignoring Rockwell's challenge and looking at Ben Kimball, Lott Smith said, "Kimball, what are you doing here?"

Pulling a soiled envelope from his pocket, Kimball said, "Something here from President Young you two boys need to read together. The envelope is addressed to Lott, but the message is for you, Port."

Pulling a chair beneath himself, Kimball said, "President Young told me to put that envelope in the hands of either one of the two of you—preferably, both of you. It's urgent. In fact, it's so urgent, I've just made one devil of a ride from Bridger. Think I broke some speed records doing it, too," he said, smiling at those in the room. "And while it may be comparatively warm here, the snow's becoming a threat between here and Salt Lake. I'm to wait for a response and head back directly, Port."

"Directly, huh?" Rockwell said, pulling the message from its envelope. "Must be urgent." Smiling at his old friend, he said, "If it's that urgent, you'd better go find a fresh horse, and we'll have a look-see at what all of this fuss is about."

"I've already done that. Soon as you come up with a response, I'm on my way back to Salt Lake," Kimball said, watching Rockwell's face intently as he read the letter.

The message was brief, to the point, and came as no real surprise to Porter Rockwell:

*Porter:*

*It is imperative that you and a sufficient number of battalion men of your choosing leave for New Mexico at once. Other considerations must wait.*

*Confederate forces are set to invade New Mexico Territory. Any move to the north could prove disastrous for Utah and the Union and negate our efforts at Platte River Station.*

*Leave at once and ascertain the nature of any threat. Take no action, but report directly to me.*

*The utmost secrecy of your purposes is imperative.*

*Lott Smith, Clay Ashworth, and the remainder are to return to SLC immediately. An important assignment awaits Ashworth's return.*

*Brigham Young*

Porter Rockwell looked up from the letter and, handing it to Lott Smith, stared off into the mid-distance, his eyes focusing on nothing but his own thoughts. *How does he do it?* Rockwell thought respectfully. *The man seems to know what I'm thinkin' as soon as the thought enters my head. He knew I'd be heading for New Mexico, anyway.*

Turning, Rockwell took the letter from Smith, and said, "Doc, you got a pencil?"

"Here," Taggert said, from across the room, throwing a worn stub into Rockwell's open hand.

At the bottom of Brigham Young's note, Rockwell scribbled one word and signed it:

*Done!*

*O.P. Rockwell*

Stuffing the message back in its envelope, Rockwell handed it to Kimball. "There. Now, get on your way. We're not going to be long here, either."

Lott Smith and Porter Rockwell watched Kimball carefully

place the letter inside his cavalry blouse, flip them all a careless salute and, with no further formalities, turn and leave the saloon.

Glancing at Rockwell, Lott said, "I'm heading for Salt Lake, and my orders include bringing Clay Ashworth with me. I don't know what's in store for you, Clay, but unless I miss my guess, I'll soon be on my way to the southern settlements and then on down into Navajo country, across the Colorado." He got to his feet. "The Indian slavery issue is heating up, sure as sin."

Rockwell chewed contemplatively on a thumbnail for a moment, and then looked up at Smith. "Well, you know where I'm going. 'Less I miss my guess, Wolf Striker's lookin' for those rebels. He'll be looking to sell what he's got to the first taker. When I put the poker to him, a lot of this Confederate misery will come to an end."

"You must take me with you, Mister Rockwell," Beau Mayfield said, getting to his feet.

"Take you with me?"

"Indeed, suh. Ah will follow on my own accord, in any event. We may as well work together, don't you think?"

Rockwell turned in his chair and stared out into the desolate street.

"Captain Mayfield, if you go with me, you will take my orders and make no attempt to assert your interests except as they fit with mine. Understand? I'm going to find Wolfgang Striker and bring him to justice—nothing more."

"If those are your conditions, then let us be gone, suh. You may rest assured, Mister Striker is at the top of my list, as well. And ah so give you my parole—as an officer of the Confederacy."

Looking at Lott Smith, Porter Rockwell rolled his eyes, and

said, "Oh, hell, lock him up, and he's to stay locked up until I'm long gone."

"But, suh . . ." Mayfield stammered.

★   ★   ★

When the last rays of the setting sun dimly reddened the still smoldering remains of Platte River Station with their fitting stain, only the town's still stunned and bewildered inhabitants remained to struggle with the task of reordering their shattered lives. To those who were not dazed beyond rational thought, one thing was painfully clear: Platte River Station would never rise again.

From the bluffs above the wide, black ribbon that was the river, the small army of Utahans could be seen splitting into two distinct groups as they slowly wound their way into the darkening distance, each responding to imperatives defined by forces beyond the control of any one man, but in the end led by the vision of only one—Brigham Young.

# CHAPTER 5

★   ★   ★

CLAYBORN RAYNOR ASHWORTH sat unsteadily on his big, dappled gray, his head filled with pain and his vision badly blurred. It would be days before he reached his giant ranch in the valley of Utah Lake, some fifty miles south of Great Salt Lake City, and he was not at all sure he was going to make it. Despite his weakened condition he resented the presence of the men Lott Smith had assigned to remain behind and nursemaid him until he got home. Lott and the others had hurried on ahead, and Clay knew these men were going to be desperately needed elsewhere.

"You okay, Clay?" It was Ben Kimball's voice that came to him out of the nagging darkness.

"Ben?"

"Yes."

"I thought . . . I thought you'd gone on ahead."

"Nope. By the time I got all my business finished . . . Say, you alright, Clay?" Kimball said, leaning closer, studying his friend's face. "You don't look so good, partner."

Before Kimball or any of the men around him could grab an arm, an unconscious Ashworth slid from his horse, landing hard on the rocky trail, the whine of a bullet ripping the air a split-second later just above his empty saddle, the crack of a rifle echoing off the rocky slopes of the shallow, wooded draw through which their trail wound.

The bullet lightly creased the rump of Kimball's horse, and its stinging bite sent the startled animal into a wild, whirling thunderstorm of back-humping, hoof-kicking, dirt-throwing hurdles that discharged a surprised Ben Kimball into the air and slammed him face down in the dirt and weeds some twenty feet from the prostrate Clay Ashworth.

Taken completely unawares, the small troop of Utah militiamen fought to control their frightened animals while desperately seeking some kind of cover to shield them from their unknown assailant.

The second shot caught Sergeant Jonathan Short in the back, just beneath his right shoulder blade as he fought to control his horse. The .56 caliber slug hit with the sound of a hand slapping putty, and ripped through the man's lungs, tearing away half of his heart, and blowing out the side of his chest in a pink spray as it exited his body. Short was dead before his body hit the ground amid the melee of flying hooves.

"Sergeant Short's hit!" someone yelled. "Where's it coming from?"

Groggily shaking his head and yanking his Colt Army .44 from its holster, Kimball hollered, "Roberts . . . act as horse-handler!" Waving his pistol at the man he yelled, "Get those animals behind that rocky outcropping yonder! The rest of you find cover!"

As Kimball struggled to drag Clay Ashworth to a place of safety, two more shots probed among the men and animals, spitting up dirt in the middle of the confusion, sending him and the others back into the dust in an effort to present as small a target as possible, and further spooking the already frantic horses. "Be quick about it, man!" he hollered at the horse-handler. "Don't lose those horses—we'll never find them in the dark!"

Some three miles to the southeast, at the sound of the distant shots reverberating among the hills to their rear, Orrin Porter Rockwell threw his right arm up, and bringing the column to a stop, concentrated on the faint but unmistakable clap of distant rifle fire.

Glancing at the Utah battalion officer riding at his left, Rockwell ordered, "Keep this column moving until it's too dark to go any farther." Then, reining about and setting spurs to horse flesh, over his shoulder he barked, "I'll find you."

In the rocks above the bloody scene of the ambush, Jubal Hathaway shuffled back from his place of concealment, dragging the heavy Spencer behind him in the dirt. In the rapidly fading light, a deranged frenzy seemed to burn in his single eye. Hatred was the only emotion Hathaway knew, and he was filled with it and the desire to kill—and kill again.

Three shots remained in the rifle's magazine, but the ferret-like cripple had two additional tubes of cartridges in a leather quiver that dangled from his belt, each tube containing seven copper rimfire cartridges—seventeen rounds in all. Enough to finish the job.

Afraid the muzzle blasts might have revealed his position, his mind filled with the single thought of killing as many of the hated

Utahans as he could. The twisted, malevolent little man sought additional cover in a jumble of boulders overgrown with sage and mountain juniper. It was a place of comparative safety and offered an even better field of fire into the killing ground below.

With the onset of autumn, darkness had come early in the high country, and the rapidly fading light had nearly put an end to his advantage. Yet Hathaway instinctively felt if he kept moving and shooting, the men below him might think there was more than one rifleman attacking them. Even so, deep inside, Jubal Hathaway knew he was going to die; it was just a matter of time. But in his twisted mind, the more of those he so intensely hated he could take into hell with him, the better. This was as good a place as any to finish his miserable life.

It was only the cool efficiency of the Utah militiamen that prevented the entire group from being wiped out in the deadly ambush. The horses had been quickly led into hiding and the wounded dragged to a place of safety away from the action. In the confusion following the initial attack, two more men had been hit, but their wounds were minor. Nothing remained on the trail, and each man from his place of hoped-for safety strained in the growing darkness to see how many were attacking them and who they were.

Seldom given to profanity, Clay Ashworth rubbed his aching temples and asked, "What the hell was that all about?"

"Don't know," Kimball answered, as he squinted around the trunk of a large pine tree. "It's so dark, I can't make anything out. I don't even know how many there were or if they're still out there."

"They're still out there," someone whispered from somewhere nearby.

"I can't see nothin', but I hear some shufflin' up there on that ledge, over on the other side of the trail," another further down the line said, squeezing off a shot. "Sounds like there might be two or three up there."

"Save your ammunition," Ashworth hissed. "Shooting now will get us little more than ringing ears. As dark as it is, you'll never hit anyone. Besides, shooting uphill almost ensures a miss, dark or no."

Jubal Hathaway lay in a black declivity between two large rocks, cursing the darkness and the cold mountain air. Aside from some random shots into the night, none of which did much more than make the men below uncomfortable, he had been unable to hit anyone or anything.

It was the cold sound of the voice behind him that turned Hathaway's blood to ice. "Roll over very slowly, Jubal. I want you to see everything that's going to happen, you sick, driveling, little halfwit." As he spoke, Orrin Porter Rockwell quickly ducked to one side.

At the sound of the hated voice, the demented little man twisted sharply, brought his Spencer up in one surprisingly swift movement and fired in the direction of the sound. "I'll kill yuh, Rockwell," Hathaway screeched. "Jest like them two Cartwrights I killed, I'm gonna kill yuh. I killed 'em good, too, Rockwell!"

Sliding around in an awkward attempt to locate Porter Rockwell, Hathaway brought the heavy rifle to his cheek with his good right arm and sighted down the barrel into the darkness, his shriveled, useless left arm wedged beneath him. "I can hear yuh breathin', Rockwell. Killin' you's gonna be real easy. In the guts, just like that big Cartwright fella," he said, cocking the rifle.

"How many shots you got left, Jubal?"

"Huh?" The involuntary response caught in Hathaway's throat, and his finger froze on the trigger. How many did he have?

45

He had reloaded his second tube, but he had no idea how many rounds he had fired since, only that he had shot several—maybe six or seven.

The pause was all the big Utahan needed. Lunging toward Jubal Hathaway, Rockwell kicked wildly in the dark, his foot catching the rifle at the base of the barrel, just in front of the receiver. From the force of the vicious kick, the weapon was driven up into Hathaway's face, the sharp end of the cocked hammer jabbing fiercely into his right eye, tearing flesh and tissue away as the empty rifle flew into the air and clattered down the rocky slope behind him.

To the men curled in their hiding places below, the macabre shriek that erupted from Hathaway's throat as his eye was torn from its socket was unearthly, something of another world—something out of hell itself—and it seemed to go on without end as the hideous sound echoed off the surrounding bluffs.

Now, for Jubal Hathaway, the darkness would be total.

With the first, cold light of false dawn, Ben Kimball and Clay Ashworth, along with several of the others, stood in a semi-circle around the crumpled, grotesque body of Jubal Hathaway as Orrin Porter Rockwell bent to examine him.

"Is he dead?" Ashworth asked.

"Unconscious," Rockwell said, pulling Hathaway's body free of the rocks and dumping him unceremoniously against the trunk of a fallen, long-dead tree. "Likely to be that way for some time. Bleeding like the stuck pig he is, too."

"Reckon we ought to find him some help," Kimball offered, his tone somewhere between a question and a statement.

Taking a deep breath and exhaling slowly, Rockwell looked methodically at what remained of Jubal Hathaway. "I'll take care of 'im. You boys collect your stuff and get going. It's a long piece to Ashworth's spread, and the weather's gonna turn real nasty any day now."

★   ★   ★

It was late in the day, long after Rockwell, Ashworth, Kimball, and the others had mounted and gone on separate ways— Ashworth and his group back to Utah and Rockwell to catch up with his New Mexico expedition—that Jubal Hathaway slowly regained consciousness. His weakened body was chilled to the bone, and the night was blacker than his tormented, pain-filled brain could ever remember: it had to be late, no moon, maybe even overcast. That would explain it; that would explain the darkness.

As the fog in his head cleared, the intensity of the pain drew his right hand to his face, and he knew he was blind: a bloody, empty socket all that remained of the light he had known. Filled with shock and disbelief as the memories of the previous night flooded his twisted mind, Hathaway struggled to move, but tight strands of rough, heavy rope bound his legs and feet firmly and strapped him securely to the tree stump, refusing him any but the smallest movement. It was Rockwell, he knew—it had to have been Rockwell.

Orrin Porter Rockwell had lingered, assuring the departing Utahans that he would see to Hathaway's needs. "I'll see he's taken care of," he had said, as the others had gone on. Then he turned to the savage who had precipitated the murder of the two men who had been almost like sons to Rockwell—the Cartwright brothers—turned to the one man whose irrational actions had assured the violent destruction of Platte River Station.

When Rockwell had finally mounted and headed back the

way he had come, only Jubal Hathaway's right hand had been left free.

Struggling to find the knots, the blind, tortured, little brute became conscious of the weight in his lap, something heavy that slid to the ground next to his leg. Groping in the dirt his hand came to rest on the butt of a large, cold revolver—a Colt Army .44. His fingers explored it carefully before he lifted the heavy gun in his shaking hand. Only one chamber was loaded, the other five tormentingly empty.

A gut-wrenching wail, like that of a wounded animal, filled the night, but it was cut short as a single, sharp thunderlike clap echoed off the surrounding bluffs.

Several miles to the south, Orrin Porter Rockwell hunched his big shoulders and spurred his horse to a faster pace.

New Mexico lay ahead.

# CHAPTER 6

★ ★ ★

Two weeks later, after Hathaway's aborted attack, Ashworth and his mothering troop of Utah militiamen reined their horses to a welcome halt in front of the large, sprawling ranch house and dismounted. Ashworth got off his horse more slowly than the others, his knees threatening to give way as he dropped to the ground. The big man leaned against the tall gray for support, trying to gather whatever strength remained in his aching muscles. It had been a long, physically and emotionally exhausting ride from the black stain that was once Platte River Station.

Clay had very much wanted to leave with Rockwell for New Mexico and the showdown with Striker but, Brigham Young's orders aside, Doc Taggert would have none of it, ordering him home. Taggert had been right, the recurring periods of dizziness had sapped him of his strength. More times than he could remember he had passed out and fallen from the saddle, each time

adding more aches and bruises to those he had already accumu-
lated. If it had not been for Ben Kimball and the others, he would
probably be lying dead somewhere along the trail.

Platte River Station. It had been a gruesome fight and a long,
dirty ride home, one Clay thought would never end. No one had
walked away from that fracas without something to remember the
place by. It had been a nasty business, what with the fire and
explosions. None of the Utahans had intended such cruel devastation. None of it had been their fault.

Yet, one fact remained: the single most important artery to the
West was now reopened and the integrity of the telegraph lines
assured. All of that had been swiftly and efficiently accomplished.
Even so, Striker, the one man responsible for all of the death and
devastation, had gotten away, and to that degree, their mission
had been a failure.

Of even greater importance, however, was the glaring fact that
all of the issues raised by the Southern rebellion placed the Utah
Territory in a pivotal position, a position critical to both the
Union and the Confederacy, in what was shaping up to be a long,
nasty war—a war among brothers. The assault on Platte River
Station, the unintended violence aside, had resulted in putting an
end to the Confederate's blockade, and that had been an absolute
necessity.

Tying the big gray to the hitching rail, Clay Ashworth climbed
the steps to the large, shady veranda and collapsed into one of the
many rocking chairs that littered the comfortable porch.

"Many thanks, gentlemen. More help is on the way. I can hear
her coming now."

He knew if the hollow sound of their boots on the rough-cut
pine did not bring her, the dust from their arrival would.

Despite the fact that the house was located high above the

valley of Utah Lake in a generous stand of mature pine trees, dust seemed to be a constant problem, especially to Emily, the old Mexican woman who took care of Clay and his home, much as his mother had done when he was a boy.

Clay had no idea how old she was, and he was too much of a gentleman to ask. But Emilea (Emily for short) Maria Consuela Salinas Montoya was the only woman in his life, and had been since the day he had rescued her from the Comanche slave traders who had murdered her husband and sons and taken her captive.

That had been another bloody fight that left more men lying in the dirt than were standing when he rode away, and the shock of it had robbed Emily Montoya of any memory of her past. She had quickly become mother, confidant, housekeeper, and friend. Over the intervening years, Clay Ashworth had come to love her as he had loved few others in his active life.

But this big, spacious house, and the fertile, sprawling ranch over which it presided, had been built upon his dream of a wife and children—somewhere in the future. But hard as he had worked, successful as he had become, that dream had not materialized. As the years slipped by and he had grown older, more and more conscious of each passing year, his feelings of emptiness had deepened, and he had become painfully aware of the incompleteness of his life.

Expecting to find Ashworth's ranch hands cluttering up her porch, the diminutive old woman hollered from inside, "How many times I gotta tol' you guys not to make so much dust, an' what you doin' here this time of day, anyway?" Emily Montoya spoke flawless Spanish, but her English never quite measured up. "You guys just not happy 'less you makin' me more work, that's all."

The screened door slammed as Emily hurried out onto the

porch and began heaping scorn on the men who were gathered around her entry area, a thing she truly enjoyed. To Emily Montoya, the men who worked for Clay Ashworth were her family, and it didn't matter how young or how old they were. If a man worked for Clay Ashworth, he was hers to scold to her heart's content. It was something she frequently did, to the delight of them all.

"What dust, Emily?" Clay said, rising unsteadily, hoping the pain and exhaustion would soon begin to seep from his body.

It was at that moment Emily realized this particular bunch of men were not her bunch. "What dust? What you mean, *what dust,* huh?" she said, looking around. Seeing Clay, her hands flew to her mouth and she rushed into his arms.

"Oh, Clay Ashworth, you tell me where you been and what you been doing all this time, huh? Don' you think I been worried sick 'bout you?"

Unsteadily, Clay wrapped his arms around her and smothered her in a huge bear hug. "Hello, Emily, I've missed you. Where's my big kiss?"

An embarrassed silence had fallen over the men on the porch, as Clay and Emily, overcome with the joy of seeing one another for the first time in many weeks, had forgotten their presence.

"Besides another big hug, what I need more than anything else in this world right now, and what my friends here need as well," Clay said, his eyes sweeping the group, "is a big mess of your tortillas and black beans. I think I'm starving to death."

The demand for tortillas and beans brought forth a chorus of agreement from the men that surrounded them.

"Clay Ashworth," she said, ignoring their encouragement and reaching up to cup his face in her hands, a look of motherly concern crossing her face, "what's happen' to your head? Jus' look at you. I knew when you left with that Rockwell fella, you was gonna get in trouble again."

Glaring at the other men, Emily Montoya grabbed Clay's hand and led him into the house. "You need more than jus' my tortillas. I gotta look at that forehead of yours. It sure don' look good to me, Clay Ashworth." Looking back before closing the door she said, "You jus' wait here. I'm gonna take care of you boys real good."

"I got a hunch she just might," someone in the crowd said, as the door slammed firmly shut.

"Yeah," another chimed in, "was that a threat or a promise?"

Clay Ashworth collapsed on his bed. "It isn't good, Emily. Something like this, something like what we've been through, is never good," he muttered, as she began carefully dabbing at the still seeping wound.

Despite Doc Taggert's best efforts, the wound had not healed properly, nor had the long trip home given Clay's head any chance to clear from the shock. Since the day that hot slug had dug its deep furrow across his forehead, he had not had time to rest; he had not had enough food to keep a sparrow alive, and he had not taken the time to keep the wound clean. And to top it off, the persistent headaches, dizziness, and blackouts meant Doc Taggert had been correct, he had suffered a concussion.

The touch of her affectionate hand felt good. It was the soothing feel of home, and Clay Ashworth was smart enough to realize Emily's loving care and home cooking was just what he needed. That, and a lot of rest. A lot of rest.

Clay struggled to regain full consciousness as three concerned faces slowly materialized through the haze. With increased intensity the headache had returned. "Oh, boy . . ." he said, reaching up to rub his throbbing head, "I feel like somebody stampeded a herd through my skull."

"Well," Dr. Peabody said, shaking a thermometer and stuffing it under Clay's tongue, ignoring his unwilling patient's weak protest, "Dr. Taggert was right, you've got a concussion. Not a bad one, most likely, but still, you'd better plan on staying down for a couple of weeks, even so."

"A couple of weeks?" Clay croaked around the awkward, brassy-tasting instrument in his mouth, as he struggled to sit up, quickly regretting it. "Oh . . . my head . . . that hurts!"

"Clay Ashworth," Emily said, stroking his forehead with her cool hand. "Don' you try to get up. You gotta do what you're tol', you hear?"

"You'd better mind Emily, Clay," the doctor said, withdrawing the thermometer without looking at it, shutting his old black bag, and turning toward the bedroom door. "I'll be back tomorrow. 'Til then, get some rest and lots of hot food."

"Well . . . now . . . just . . ." Further talk would have been useless as Emily followed the doctor out the door, their voices trailing off down the stairs. From what he could make out, Emily was receiving more instructions intended to add to his further discomfort and immobility. Still, Clay knew that in his present condition, resistance would only bring more fussing his direction from an already overly concerned Emily.

"I'm still here, Clay."

"Oh, Robby," Clay said, struggling to sit up now that Emily had disappeared. "Where've you been? I need some help here, friend."

"You think I look stupid, do yuh? You think I been thrown one too many times, maybe?" Robby said, as he dragged a straight-backed wooden chair from the corner, turned it around, and sat down, his chin resting on his folded arms. "I can tell yuh right now, I ain't gettin' into this dust-up fer nothin'. When Emily says you can get up, I'll help yuh, but not a minute before."

Owen Robshaw—nobody called him Owen—was as close to Clay Ashworth as any man alive. The two were like brothers, and had been from the time they first met three years earlier. Robshaw was foreman and top hand on the Ashworth ranch. In reality, he ran the place, giving Clay the freedom to disappear occasionally, sometimes for extended periods. Clay knew he could trust Robshaw and never have to answer unwelcome questions from him.

Though Clay Ashworth was not a Mormon, he had lived among them off and on for a number of years. No one seemed to know where he had come from, nor did anyone seem to know where he went during his not infrequent disappearances. But, when trouble brewed for Brigham Young or the Utah Territory, Clay Ashworth was not long in showing up.

He and Robby first became acquainted when Clay had joined the Mormon Militia early in its fight against Johnston's invading army. The militia had been bivouacked at Bridger's Fort, the Utahans' forward command post, one bitterly cold night in the late fall of 1857, when Ashworth had ridden in out of the dark sometime around midnight. Dismounting, he had asked one of the guards to point him to someone who could take him to General Daniel Wells.

After much discussion, it was Major Lott Smith who finally took him to the leader of the Utah Militia. The three had talked into the early hours of the morning, but when they emerged, Clay Ashworth had clearly established himself as one worthy of trust— as one of them. From that night on, he was a captain in the territorial militia.

"It was pretty tough back there, huh?" Robby asked.

"Yeah . . . it was tough," Clay said, attempting to punch a pillow in place behind his back. "You ever seen a town destroyed in a matter of minutes?"

"Can't really say as I have."

"Well, I'm not stretching the truth much when I tell you there's hardly a building left standing. Platte River Station was all but wiped off the map."

"You think it accomplished anything?"

"Oh, yeah," Clay sighed. "The leader of the gang responsible for all the destruction—fellow by the name of Striker—got away, but Rockwell'll run him to ground. What we did do was put an end to a likely Confederate blockade of the territory. That threat's gone now, at least for the time being.

"How're things around here, Robby? Seems like I've been gone forever."

"Everything's fine. Somehow we seem to just keep getting bigger and bigger. Could use some rain, but when wasn't that the case?"

"Yeah."

"Look, Clay, you better get some rest," Robby said, getting to his feet and placing his chair back in the corner. "You don't look so hot, and I don't want Emily chewin' on me fer botherin' yuh. I'll be back later or in the morning and fill yuh in on everything. Nothin' here that can't wait. Okay?"

Clay Ashworth slid back beneath the warm covers and closed his eyes. "Yeah. Later." He was asleep almost before the words were out of his mouth.

★   ★   ★

From the angle of the sunlight pouring through his bedroom window, Clay guessed it was late morning. The sounds of a hard-ridden horse being reined to a clattering stop in front of the house had awakened him from a fitful sleep, a sleep filled with odd, incomplete dreams: bloody, wild scenes of violence. Clay sat up as he heard the heavy sound of boots taking the front steps two at a time and hurrying across the porch, followed by an insistent knock at the front door.

"As bad as you look, you look better than the last time I saw you, Major Ashworth," Ben Kimball said, as he strode into the bedroom ahead of an obviously displeased Emily Montoya.

"Uh-oh, *Major*, is it? That doesn't sound so—"

"He still plenty sick, Mister Kimball," Emily said, making no attempt to hide the irritation she felt at Kimball's intrusion. "I been tellin' him he better stay in bed, jus' like the doctor said he should do. That's what."

"Oh, I don't know, Emily," Kimball said, scratching his chin. "From what I've seen of him in the past few weeks, he looks fit enough to me."

"Emily, my only true love, how's about you getting me and Major Kimball something warm to drink, while I find out why a man of his superior rank and advanced years has come all the way out here so soon after our last ride together."

"Sit down, Ben, and let's talk." Clay swung his legs over the side of the bed and sat up. "Oh . . . that feels good," he said, stretching his arms above his head, then scratching his ribs. "I'm getting saddle galls up my backside because Emily won't let me up. I honestly don't know what I'd do without that wonderful little woman, but I'll tell you, time comes when enough is enough."

"Well, how are you, anyway?" Kimball said, pulling a chair beneath himself. "You ready for some action, Major?"

"What's this *Major* business? How come now I'm a major?"

"Platte River Station, that's how come," Kimball chortled. "You ready for some more?"

"I been nailed in this fluffy coffin for two weeks now, and I'm starting to go nuts. As for any action, Major or not, this ranch needs some attention, I can tell you that."

"Well, that's what you've got Robby for, isn't it?" Kimball retorted, a smile crossing his handsome face. "You know darned well why I'm here. President Young would like to see you—as soon as possible."

# CHAPTER 7

★  ★  ★

THE RIDE FROM UTAH VALLEY TO Salt Lake City was not particularly long or rugged by frontier standards, but it could be tiring, especially when necessity urged a faster pace on man and animal. Even so, Clay Ashworth was pleasantly surprised at how good it felt after his brief convalescence to be on his horse again, and he was grateful for the opportunity to be up and moving.

A frontiersman to the bone, Clay Ashworth loved the squeak of good saddle leather and the jingle of bridle and spurs. Somehow it was the little things in life that always seemed to give the greatest joy. Nothing pleased him quite so much as the smell and feel of a good horse beneath him, and Clay Ashworth always rode the best.

By the time the two men tied their horses to the hitching rail inside the Young compound in the center of Great Salt Lake City, it was late evening, and both men and horses were tired from the pace they had been forced to keep.

"You feeling alright?" Kimball asked, as the two were led into Brigham Young's dimly lit office.

"Tired," Ashworth said, sinking into a chair in front of the massive table that served as Brigham Young's desk. "Nothing takes it out of you faster than a few days in bed. But to tell the truth, I feel great, even if it is late."

Both men got to their feet as Brigham Young entered the room.

Clay Ashworth had never been around the Mormon prophet without being awed by the sheer physical presence of the man. It was not that he was all that large in stature. Brigham Young was a big man, it is true, but size had nothing to do with it. It was the simple fact of personal dominance. Wherever he was, whatever his surroundings, Brigham Young was a presence. He dominated just by virtue of his being there.

The president motioned the two to sit, and his own chair squeaked as he leaned back. "How are you feeling, Clay?"

"I'm fine, sir."

"Mmm . . . well, we're grateful for what you've done. You are a real strength to this territory."

"He nearly got himself killed at Platte River Station, President Young," Kimball offered.

"Yes, I know. That scar is most becoming, Major. Though I'm sure such a badge of honor is not worth the risk behind getting it."

"Well, sir that's my feeling, as well."

"I'm concerned about what happened at Platte River Station," Brigham Young said, pushing away from his desk and turning to the window behind him. "Loss of life aside, I'm concerned because, regardless of our support for the Union, Utah Territory does not want to become involved in this ugly civil war that is bursting forth upon the nation back East."

Clay Ashworth cleared his throat, uncomfortable with a growing feeling of unease. "Well, sir, if you could see what's left of Platte River Station, you might think it's a little late."

"Precisely, Major Ashworth," Young said, turning to face the two men. "Exactly my point. I intend to send this telegram to Mr. Lincoln." He pushed a yellow piece of paper across his desk. "It flatly states our attitude with regard to Utah's position. Unfortunately, this does not reflect Governor Cumming's desires. The man, as I'm sure you know, is from Georgia and, as you may also know, he has left us to return to the South."

The message was as Brigham Young had just described it, straightforward: "Utah has not seceded but is firm for the Constitution and laws of our once happy Union."

"But Platte River Station—"

"Platte River Station had two purposes with regard to the war, Clay. First, the protection of the transcontinental telegraph, to assure it stays open until federal troops can guard the wires. I promised Mr. Lincoln we would happily see to that.

"Secondly, Clay, Platte River Station had to be neutralized in order to assure that the route of immigration would stay open, despite the war."

"I understand, sir."

"I can attest, President Young, that Platte River Station has definitely been neutralized—if you can call it that—thanks to Striker and his marauders. What these boys accomplished," Ben Kimball said, nodding toward Ashworth, "will guarantee that the goals you just stated have been achieved and will stay that way."

Brigham Young returned to his chair and leaned back, studying the men in front of him. "Yes. It's a terrible thing that there was so much loss of life. I would not have had that. I know it would not have happened but for the actions of those men who were occupying the town. Unfortunately, things all too frequently do not go as one might wish."

"No, sir. Under circumstances such as those, things have a way of getting out of hand very quickly," Ben Kimball offered.

"Indeed they do, Ben. But that brings me to my next point. What has gotten terribly out of hand—and the territory stands in real danger of being stained by it—is the slave trade carried on by a number of the Indian tribes out here in the Southwest, particularly throughout the New Mexico Territory south of us. The Comanches, the Utes, and the Navajos are openly trading in human flesh. Stronger tribes raid the weaker ones, carrying off women and children and selling them into slavery. They even raid one another. I tell you," Brigham Young said, slapping his desk, "it is a vile thing, utterly vile."

Kimball said, "But the people of this territory, certainly they can't be thought to be guilty of such things. How—?"

"I'll tell you how. These criminals—and that's all they are, murderous criminals—bring their captives into our communities and coerce our people into purchasing them."

"But surely they refuse."

"Of course they refuse. And when they do, the slave traders yank their victims' heads back by the hair and hold knives to their throats, screaming that if the Mormons do not buy these people, they will be killed on the spot. Their throats will be cut, then and there! And it has happened! Now I ask you, what's to be done?"

Clay Ashworth prided himself as something of a man of the world. He had, in fact, seen some harsh things in his years of hard living. It had been slavery that had driven him from his family and plantation lands in the South, because he could not abide seeing one man in subjugation to another, no matter what the color of his skin.

To see even the most primitive people so brutalized offended him no less. And, in the process, to see otherwise civilized and decent people blackmailed by the threat of the kind of violence President Young was describing was more than his temper could stand. "I'd have shot the dirty savage in his tracks, President Young, if you'll excuse my bluntness. That would have been my response."

"If only it could be so neatly done, Major Ashworth. However, it is never just one heathen with one knife to the throat of one victim. It is often one or two wagonloads of innocent, ignorant victims being swarmed by these savage tormentors, not one of whom would waste a second thinking about cutting a child's throat."

"Well . . . but, the Church . . . it's not involved," Clay offered. "How could you—?"

"But, of necessity, we are involved, Major Ashworth." Young rose and walked to the window. "Rather than seeing these Indians slaughtered, our people have purchased them. Of course they've let them go, but the point is, they've paid the extortionists to save innocent lives."

"But surely no one would blame them."

"Look, Clay," Ben Kimball said, sitting forward in his chair. "You know as well as anyone how we are viewed in the East. Shoot, the U. S. government sent an army out here over nothing more than rumors only four years ago. What do you think the eastern press would do with a story about slave trading in the Utah Territory?"

"That's exactly the point, Major Ashworth," Brigham Young said, turning to face the two men sitting before his desk. "We simply will not be dealt with fairly on an issue such as this. The eastern press is far from objective where the people of this territory and the Church are concerned. Our only course is to bring this nasty business to an end. That's why I asked Major Kimball here, to leave Platte River Station and return home. I'm sending him south, to deal with the problem. I want you to know that."

"Where the war back east is concerned, Clay, it's even worse," Ben said. "A bunch of secessionists held a convention and voted to attach New Mexico Territory to the Confederacy last March. That means the slavery issue is now out here—in the West. And Wolf Striker was headed for New Mexico when he left Platte River Station."

President Young leaned forward over his desk and said, "Clay, our primary concern is to end the slave trade, and end it quickly."

"But, President Young, why are you telling me all of this? You know I'm a committed friend."

"Yes, you are, Clay," Young said, resting his elbows on the back of his large swivel chair. "You've proved it many times." Young added, pausing thoughtfully. "And that, by the way, is something that has always interested me."

"What's that, President Young?"

"Why you are here in the Utah Territory," Young said, taking his seat and leaning forward on his desk. "Why you stayed here among the Saints. Tell me honestly, Clay, why didn't you go on to California? As I recall, that was your intent when you first arrived in these valleys, wasn't it?"

Clay studied the man seated across the desk. Brigham Young exuded energy and power. His every feature, his every movement, the way he carried himself spoke of innate authority and the willingness to exercise it.

As Clay well knew, at least two U. S. presidents had looked

upon the Mormon leader as a power to be accorded due regard and never to be taken for granted. Poor old vacillating Buchanan had even tried to neutralize Brigham Young and had only succeeded in making a fool of himself and a laughingstock of his administration. Manipulated by members of his own cabinet, the one-term president had only succeeded in weakening the military capacity of the Union through an unnecessary attempt to invade the Utah Territory and bring Brigham Young and his Mormons under some sort of subjugation. If anything, Brigham Young was stronger now than he ever was.

"And yet," Young continued, "you've not only stayed here, you've fought alongside us. And to boot, you own a ranch that seems to sprawl across half the territory—a wealthy man.

"Don't misunderstand me, Clay. You are a friend, and one we value, but you must admit it seems a little strange. There's a kind of mystery to it, don't you agree?"

An uneasy quiet had descended on the room with Young's unexpected interrogation, and the two men sat contemplating one another until Clay Ashworth started to chuckle, causing Young's eyebrows to arch in surprise.

"Well, President Young," Clay said, his face splitting into a broad grin, "if it's the truth you want, I was sent here to spy on you, to keep you and your people under continuing surveillance—by two administrations, no less. I honestly thought you knew. Why, if you'd have asked, I'd have told you as much. I guess I'm better at this stuff than I thought. I honestly thought you knew."

Glancing at Ben Kimball, Clay began to laugh at the look on Kimball's face—something like that of a cat caught with its paw on the canary. "I mean, I suspected Kimball here knew. And I for sure thought Rockwell was wise to me . . . a long time ago."

The room echoed as if a pistol had been fired as Brigham Young's hand slapped the desk, and the Mormon leader collapsed back into his big chair, the air exploding from his lungs in a wheezing laugh that turned his face a bright red from the exertion.

"Well, I'll be," Young finally gasped, trying to regain his composure, made all the more difficult by the contagious laughter his reaction had caused to come upon the other two. "Right in the middle of us," he said, gasping for air. "You know, that explains just a whole lot of things."

"Yes, sir," Clay said, the laughter gradually draining from his face. That Brigham Young might yet have the last word was just now occurring to him. "Like what, sir, for example?"

"Like this telegram, for example," Young said, tossing another yellow sheet of paper across the desk. "My, my, but things do have a way of catching up with a man, don't they? It's the law of the harvest, isn't it, Ben? You don't know it yet, Clay Ashworth, but you are going to become more closely involved in this American Civil War than you may think."

"I'm going to be more . . . ?"

"Oh, indeed. I wanted to have this discussion, Clay, before I gave you this telegram. It's for you, apparently from an old friend, as I understand it."

"Who would that be, sir?"

"Why, none other than one of the men for whom you've been such an effective spy—Abe Lincoln himself. And pursuant to that, there is a second telegram here," Young said, rearranging some of the papers on his neat desk and handing still another yellow sheet of paper to the surprised Clay Ashworth. "It came to me from Allan Pinkerton, with whom I understand you've had no small association in the past."

"Well, yes . . . some, sir," Ashworth responded, his eyes scanning the telegram from the president.

"Well, both Mister Lincoln and Mister Pinkerton have asked that I forward their messages to you—since we know your whereabouts, that is." The note of good-humored sarcasm in Young's voice was not lost on Clay. "Somehow they seem to have lost track of their surreptitious agent. And since both were addressed to me, I, of course, read them. It would appear that your country is in even greater need for your services than in the past."

"My services?" Ashworth asked, reaching out to take Pinkerton's lengthy telegram from Young's outstretched hand.

"There's more to this war than meets the eye, Major Ashworth—as we have unfortunately learned over the past four or five years. As always, it would seem there is no end to the complicity of scheming, conspiring men of inordinate ambition."

Ashworth's eyes began scanning the page in his hand.

President Young explained. "It would appear that men of power, both in the federal government and within the Confederacy, desire to capture the New Mexico Territory and Arizona for their mineral resources. They want our loyalty because we probably represent the single most militarily powerful group in the western territories, or potentially so. But perhaps more importantly, these conspirators intend to split California from the Union and make it an independent nation."

Clay looked up from the lengthy telegram in his hand. "Looks as if I have no choice, President Young."

"No, Major Ashworth, it looks as if you don't," Brigham Young said, stepping around his desk.

"It sure seems to have become one deep snake pit, Clay," Kimball said, as the two men got to their feet.

Brigham Young took Clay's hand and shook it as the three moved to the door.

"You know where we stand, Clay. You're one of us, a ranking member of the militia, and we trust you, spy or no. It is imperative that we end the slave trade, and we want the Union to win the war in the East."

"Much as I would like, there is no way I can avoid what Allan and the President have imposed on me, President Young. Not with the way things are developing now."

"No. Nor should you," Young said, as the three men stepped onto the front porch.

The night was cool and the smell of rain was in the air. The Mormon leader's face could not be clearly seen in the darkness, and he spoke almost as if to himself. "I can't help but wonder what would have happened if Douglas had been elected in 1860, and he had remained a true friend to the people of this territory. I don't think the Southern states would have had the excuse for their great movement of secession. It was Lincoln's election that persuaded them of that. If Douglas had followed the counsel he was given with regard to the great evil of slavery, this enormous tragedy of civil war might have been avoided."

Clay Ashworth turned to Brigham Young and took his hand for a final time. "President Young, what if . . . what if the South had freed the slaves and *then* fired on Fort Sumter? What then?"

"Interesting question. But all of the *what ifs* are nothing more than supposition, having no more substance than our breath in this night air. The fact is, our country is at war. The worst kind of war: civil war. Now, it would seem, it may be up to you to derail this California scheme Mister Lincoln and Mister Pinkerton have laid at your feet, and thus help restore the nation. And it would appear that the one man you must stop is Senator William McKendree Gwin."

As Clay and Ben Kimball mounted their horses, Clay asked, "How long has he really known, Ben?"

"Known what?"

"You know darn well *what*. Who and what I am."

"Oh, that," Ben said, offhandedly. "Since when you joined the militia—where we could keep an eye on you."

Clay could not see his friend's face in the darkness, but there was no mistaking the chuckle. "Well, I'll be. . . ."

"You sure will, Clay. Yes, sir, you sure will."

# CHAPTER 8

★  ★  ★

T HE EARLY MORNING SUN poured into the room, lighting
dust-spangled streamers that slanted in long luminous angles to
the floor as Clay Ashworth sat on the edge of his bed struggling
into his boots. He was still weak, and it was an effort that left him
a little winded. But as he pulled the last boot on and stood to
stomp his foot into place, he could not help smiling at the enjoyment he gained from this morning ritual of stomping into a pair
of big western boots. Somehow, they gave a man a feeling of
toughness and adequacy.

With the promise of a beautiful day, he couldn't help thinking also how much he loved this place, this ranch—*Rancho Los
Librados,* as it was known throughout the Utah Territory.

After a gratifying stretch that seemed to clear away any lingering aches and pains, Clay walked through the spacious bedroom's
big double doors and out onto the second-story deck. No matter
which direction he looked, the view was incomparable, and a deep

breath of the pine-scented air somehow cleaned a man's insides. Every acre in sight was his, thousands of them—from the lush grazing land stretching from the ranch house to the west, across Utah Lake and the valley to the barren peaks of the mineral-rich Oquirrh Mountains, and far into the pine-clad mountains behind him to the east. The ranch spread to the north as far as the eye could see, and south to where the valley spilled out of sight over a low line of purple hills, miles distant—all of it was his. Everywhere he looked, he either owned or controlled the land.

The spread was the largest in the territory, and it was the very center of his life. And though over the years he had come to view it somewhat casually, in the cool of the evening or the fresh light of early morning, when he stood on the expansive, second-story deck that encircled his home—a massive ranch house described by a few detractors as an arrogant display of wealth—it was impossible for him not to be humbled by the panoramic view.

But, in a sense, the sprawling ranch was not just his. Every cowhand who worked for him considered it his own as well, a part of his life, a place of happiness and industry. No one wanted to leave the place, and when a lucky cowboy found the right girl, he brought her back to *Rancho Los Librados* and built a cabin of his own where he could raise his own family.

The meadows and hills were alive with cattle, which were marketed periodically as far away as California and all throughout the Mountain West. There were hundreds of acres planted in hay, and the work of the ranch demanded the steady efforts of at least three dozen ranch hands—strong, reliable cowhands who returned to Ashworth a degree of loyalty that at times surprised him.

It was almost all he had ever wanted: this house, this ranch, this territory, the people he associated with on a regular basis. Still, something was missing. He longed for a wife, someone to love, someone to love him, someone with whom to share it all. But perhaps, he told himself, that would all come when his life, indeed the world, became less convulsive. He had been telling himself that for a long time.

Though at times he felt empty at the core, this sprawling ranch was truly his home, with all of its sights and sounds and smells. It was a place of freedom, a place of mutual esteem, shared values, and common vision. For Clay Ashworth, there was simply nowhere else on earth he could find peace, and he longed for the time when he could ride out from this heavenly spot and know for certain he was going to return.

It had been a long time since he left Georgia. Thinking back on it, there could not have been a happier place for a child grow up than Pine Haven, his family's large plantation. Its deep woods and fields, its barns and sheds, the slave quarters, all were perfect places for a child to play and grow, surrounded by a sense of love and safety.

But as he had matured, he had come to loathe nearly everything the plantation stood for: the medieval culture fostered by an artificial tradition of chivalry and over-elegant manners, the hypocritical environment thought to be based on some sort of virtue, but which was in fact based on the blood and sweat and misery of human slavery, causing the sanctimonious religiosity that permeated the South to ring hollow.

At first it had been difficult for him to understand why, as he grew older, the black children who had been his closest friends and playmates had become, in the eyes of his family and others, increasingly unsuitable as companions, or why one day some had simply disappeared while others remained. But as he matured into his teen years, he had come to understand the true nature of slavery, and he hated it.

With young manhood had come the necessity of spending more and more time with books and education. Yet, even as his days had become increasingly meaningful and fulfilling, his circumstances compelled him to watch as the Negro children, who had been his closest companions, were forced into the fields and burdened with increasingly exhausting labor.

Eventually, Clay had come to understand their plight. While his life was one of increasing leisure and privilege, the Darkies, as they were called, were consigned to a life of agonizing physical drudgery from well before sun-up until late in the evening—from "can't see to can't see." He came to see their narrow, dirty existence as a living hell, a horror for which he knew, in small part, he was responsible.

When his parents had died unexpectedly, Clay went on to manage Pine Haven with hard work and an even hand, frequently laboring in the fields alongside many of the slaves he owned, and the large plantation had become more profitable than ever before. Eventually, the persistent, nagging sense of guilt had become unbearable—the moral burden finally too much to endure.

Realizing what he had to do, Clay freed the nearly two hundred slaves his family had owned and sent them north, and then he sold the plantation. Without the slaves, Pine Haven had sold for far less than it otherwise would have, but the prewar sale still netted an almost unheard-of price.

Yet, as time went on, selling the plantation seemed an insufficient penance. He saw it his duty to do everything in his power to end the Southern rebellion and to stop men like Senator William McKendree Gwin, who doggedly clung to the evil that had divided Clay's family and driven him from Georgia. With his allegiance to slavery and the culture it had spawned, William Gwin was the symbol of human misery—a man who defended slavery, not entirely for the good of society, but to further his own purposes.

Clay Ashworth knew he must do his part, and do it well. And he had so ordered his life.

Taking one final stretch, Clay hurried downstairs and into the kitchen where Emily had filled a large pair of saddlebags with dried fruit, nuts, and a few pounds of beef and bison jerky—a supply of food that would see him through the next few weeks. There was also plenty of powder, caps, and shot for the big, ivory-handled Army Colt .44 he always wore strapped low on his right hip.

In addition, the floor was littered with large packs from their efforts the night before, packs filled with clothing, food staples, and additional ammunition for his prized, new 16-shot Henry rifle.

Watching Emily bustle around the kitchen, Clay knew just how much he was going to miss her. It was she who saw to his daily needs, working hard to manage the house and keep it comfortable. Most of all, he was going to miss the excitement that erupted as she kept his sometimes unruly cowhands in line when they intruded into her jealously guarded domain.

"Where's Robby?" he asked, as Emily finished tying off one of the packs.

"He jus' took some of this stuff out to put on your packhorse. He be right back, I think."

Hoisting a pack in each hand, Clay clomped through the spacious living room, across the large, elegantly woven Navajo rug that covered most of the polished wood flooring, and out onto the covered porch.

He was unprepared for the sight that awaited him there. The front yard was crowded, from the porch to the split-rail fence, with a large number of mounted ranch hands, and several more could be seen riding across the pasture toward the tall buck-gate at the front of the yard.

"I told these bums to get back to work, Clay," Robby said. "But . . . well, you know . . . there's times when none of 'em seems to hear so good."

"Word got around you was leavin' again, boss," Chet Langtree said, leaning over his saddle horn.

"That right, Chet?" Clay asked, tying one of the packs to the horse.

Stepping down out of his saddle, the big cowhand grabbed a bag, and said, "I'll tie that other'n, sir. Say . . . this packhorse of yours looks t' be gettin' pretty loaded. Maybe we ought t' get another'n. Looks like yer gonna be gone fer a time, huh?"

Chet Langtree was a big man, equal in size to Clay Ashworth and, among the ranch hands, he was the second in command— the *segundo* of *Rancho Los Librados*—under Owen Robshaw, always acting as ramrod in Robshaw's absence. An all-around cow-hand, he was a favorite among the others, good with everything from a gun to a rope. Langtree was nothing to look at physically—balding, heavy in the shoulders and narrow in the hips. By his own admission, he wasn't likely to stir a woman's blood.

With help from a couple of the hands, Clay finished securing the packs and, with an arm draped across the packhorse's rump, he surveyed the friendly crowd before him.

"Okay . . . what is it?"

An uneasy silence held until Rob said, "Chet there has been elected t' kind of speak for the rest, Clay."

"Speak for the rest, huh?"

"Uh-huh. Speak up, Chet."

"Well, sir," Chet said, clearing his throat, "to be truthful, there's times when you plain worry us," he stammered.

"Worry you? That'll be the day," Ashworth chuckled.

"Yessir, and it's today," was the surprisingly bold reply.

Ashworth's grin turned to a frown. "I guess this is serious. Out with it."

Langtree cleared his throat again. "Well, sir . . . you're just gone too often and stay away too long. Many's the time we don't know if you're comin' back at all—an' sometimes you come back kind of bloody."

"I guess that's true enough, but bloody or not, I've gotten back. Haven't I?" Clay turned and looked at his foreman. "Rob, you share these sentiments?"

"Maybe I'm not such a good one to answer, Clay. I know more than the rest of these men. Thing is, what would happen to us and our families if one day you *don't* come back? I think they've got a right t' know—more than most of 'em do."

Ashworth retreated to the porch and sat down on the top step. "Yeah," he said, thoughtfully. "You're right. My problem is how much I can tell y'all right now."

"Well, sir," Langtree said, trying to ease the unintended tension that had developed, "if it ain't none of our business, then we'll just take it as that an' let it go."

Ashworth sighed. "No, that's not the answer." Surveying the yard full of mostly mounted men, he continued. "Let me tell you what I can." Rubbing his chin and taking a deep breath, he looked around and said, "You all know what it means to owe somebody. We all run this place together—you owe me for your jobs, and I owe you for your hard work and loyalty.

"Well . . . I owe something else. It's a big debt, one that's always on my mind. I have to rid myself of that debt, and doing some of the things I've had to do is the only way I know how. Sometimes it means my life might be threatened. But I want you to know, it's for the cause of our country. That's really all I can tell you right now. When I leave, I'm not just running off to get away from here or for some reason that makes no sense."

"Is it the war back East?" Robby asked, hesitantly.

"In part . . . yes."

"But, Clay, that war's a long ways off," Robby said, removing his hat and scratching his head, "and the way folks out here have been treated in the past, it just seems like we'd be better off just minding our own business."

"Yes . . . at first glance, maybe. But when you get down to it, it's just not that simple. It's going to affect us whether we like it or not. Not too long ago, the Confederates whipped a Union army back at Bull Run in Virginia and sent those troopers racing back to Washington with their tails between their legs.

"We just had a nasty fight at Platte River Station. It's hard to believe, but the entire settlement was blown apart. The town, if you could call it that, simply doesn't exist anymore. It wasn't our fault, but it happened. We set out to secure the place, but thanks to a bunch of thugs that had been hired by some Confederate soldier, somehow things got out of hand, and they destroyed everything.

"Those Southern Confederates want to shut us off from the States and split California away as a part of the Confederacy or as a separate republic. That just can't be allowed to happen, that's all there is to it."

"Can they do that?" Robby asked.

"They *are* doing it. At least they sure as shootin' are making an effort at it. Just the end of July, Union troops abandoned Fort

Fillmore to Confederates down in New Mexico Territory. That's close enough to make me a little jumpy."

"What about us out here in Utah Territory?" one of the hands asked. "What are we gonna do?"

"Well . . . Brigham Young's determined that the Constitution be upheld—as the Founders saw it. That means he has no sympathy for the Confederate cause. That's one reason I've got to head for . . . well, you might as well know . . . California and try to derail some of the skullduggery being fomented. There are some powerful people out there, and back in Washington, who would like nothing better than to see this nation come apart. They want California for themselves.

"And, I'll tell you something else, there are European countries that would be over here in no time, exploiting this country's people and natural resources—gold, silver, you name it—not to mention slave trading, the kind that's already going on around here among some of the tribes.

"Where else can a man find the kind of freedom we've got here? Think about that for a minute. There are plenty of people willing to take it away; you can count on that."

For what seemed like several minutes, the only sound that could be heard was the soughing of a gentle breeze in the big Ponderosa pines that surrounded the massive ranch house and the occasional stomping and blowing of a horse, as the men digested what they had just been told.

Finally, turning to survey the unusually silent crowd behind him, Chet said, "Well, sir . . . some of us kind of felt somethin' was goin' on where you was concerned—we just didn't know what or how much. Anyway, we all took a vote, a kind of election— even the women spoke up—and I got chosen to go with yuh, t' kind of watch yer back trail, like."

"You what? Well . . . but—"

"Ain't no use balkin'," Robby insisted with a grin, "'cause we've all been talkin', and . . . well . . . that's how it's gonna be— you just said it yerself. We owe you."

Clay's throat tightened as he sensed the love and support these people were extending. It was not often he choked up, but he did now.

"Ain't no reason why you can't take a good man with you, Clay. Leastways, from what you've told me. Especially one who's as quick with a gun as ol' Chet here," Robby said, patting the muscular neck of Chet's big sorrel.

"We'd all sure feel better about it," one of the men said, accompanied by a chorus of agreement.

"Well, Chet, sort of looks like you're stuck," Clay allowed.

"Well, sir . . . not exactly. I guess you could say I sort of engineered the vote."

"Huh," Robby huffed, slapping Chet on his thigh. "The truth is, Clay, ol' Chet here wasn't about to have it any other way. At least not without some broken bones. One way or the other, as far as he was concerned, you were not leavin' here without him."

"Okay, Chet," Clay said, with a forced sense of resignation, "get your stuff, and let's get out of here. The sooner we get gone, the sooner we get back."

"Fact is, I got another packhorse around in back. Thanks t' Emily, he's all loaded and ready t' go."

"Emily?" Clay responded, rising to his feet. "I might have known it."

The door slammed behind him, and Clay turned, knowing full well that she had been listening to all of this. But what he saw stopped him dead in his tracks. The little woman he had come to love so much stood in the middle of the porch with her arms crossed and her feet apart, a stance that told him she was ready to do battle, and he knew it would be one he could not win.

Turning to re-enter the house, Clay paused, smiling down at her, and whispered gruffly, "You're sure getting good at keeping secrets, little mother, and one of these days you're going to stick that nose of yours in the wrong place."

Her response in most situations of this kind was to reach up and give his sunburned cheek a loving pat, but today all he got was a disdainful grunt.

"Oh . . . one other thing," he said, turning back to the crowd. "If the time ever comes when I don't come back, this ranch is yours—all of you. A deed to that effect is on file in the Territorial Governor's office, to go into effect upon my death. Now," he said, reaching for the door, "you all have things to do. I'll see you when I see you."

Blocking Clay's way, Emily placed her hand on his chest and looked up at the big man she adored, the man who had found her wandering in the New Mexico desert, her memory gone, who had saved her life, who had taken her into his home and created a new world for her, and whom she loved more than anyone else in her new, if incomplete, world, and said, "I tell you what's wrong with you, Clay Ashworth."

"Oh?" Clay responded. "And just what might that be?"

"I tell you what—you ain't married, that's what."

"Married?" Clay said, stepping back in surprise.

"You heard. You know what I'm sayin' to you. What you need is a good woman what keeps you home."

"Ah, but sweet señora, I have you," he said, patting her cheek affectionately.

Wanting none of his sweet talk, Emily pushed his hand away, and in a scolding tone of voice said, "Don' you give me none of your stuff, Clay Ashworth. You know what I mean. What you need is to go up to Salt Lake an' find yourself a wife. You need a good woman to keep your house, a beauty to warm your bed— somebody what's gonna keep your heart warm and your feet home, that's what," she said, her words coming in a flood, and tears beginning to spill from her large brown eyes. "Then maybe you gonna stay home."

Clay's neck turned a bright red as Emily swung about and stormed into the house, the screened door slamming with finality behind her. But even worse than not knowing how to deal with Emily when her Latin emotions began getting the best of her, he could hear snickers of agreement among the men behind him.

Somewhere out in the crowd, a cowboy turned to the man mounted next to him, and said, "That's sure enough what keeps me home."

"Yep," the other said, reining his horse about, "the ol' he-bull of these woods'll sure stay home then."

An "amen" came from somewhere in the crowd as snickers began turning to laughter at their boss's mounting embarrassment.

Grabbing Clay by the sleeve, Chet said, "Like yuh said, we better get gone. Ain't nothin' more t' be said here, that's fer sure. This here's one fight no man can win."

# CHAPTER 9

★ ★ ★

Senator William McKendree Gwin sat uncomfortably next to his attractive but increasingly short-tempered wife as the coach bounced jarringly along the rutted trail that crossed the high Nevada desert from Fort Hall to Carson City, the capital of the newly created Territory of Nevada. They had left Great Salt Lake City days earlier, and it would still be several long days before reaching Carson City. And then they would still have to travel over the rugged, precipitous Sierra Nevada Mountains to their home in San Francisco.

Pulled by a matched set of six big grays, it was an expensive coach, one befitting Gwin's station in life as a recently retired, two-term senator from his adopted state of California. The quality and comforts of the coach aside, the trail crossing this vast western wilderness remained so primitive that the occupants of the coach were constantly jostled about, sometimes with jolts so bruising, they were forced to hang onto the hand straps next to the windows to avoid being thrown to the floor or bounced into each other. And, as if the tortuous ride were not enough, the dust from the trail at times made breathing impossible, even with the hot and stuffy coach's leather shades drawn down and tightly fastened.

Travel across such barren, rugged country was physically exhausting, and by each day's end nerves became so frayed that tempers would quickly flare, often with no apparent reason.

The wheel of the coach struck a large rock in the trail, throwing everyone off his seat, drawing a fresh swirl of thick dust into the coach's interior, and sending Mary Gwin into a fit of temper.

"William! This is impossible! Have them stop this infernal coach before I'm beaten senseless or choke to death on this horrid alkali dust or both!" she shouted, her voice breaking with the jarring of the coach's wheels over the rocky, uneven trail. "I simply can't go on any further mile—not another yard."

William Gwin loved his wife deeply. She was a beautiful, educated woman of quality and refinement. Throughout her life, particularly as a young girl, she had been pampered and accustomed to the finer things in life—among them well-groomed or cobblestone streets. Furthermore, he was well aware of the fact that life with him had not been all that easy, though he knew she found great satisfaction in his achievements and in her role as the respected wife of a man of ever-growing importance. But he also knew there were times when she seemed called upon to endure more than most women would, or any woman should. This difficult but necessary trip was certainly to be numbered among those times, and the tone of her voice and her increasingly abrupt manner told him that, for today at least, his wife had had enough.

"Toby, don't just sit there, lean out and tell them to slow down and find a suitable place to camp for the night," the senator ordered, using his cane to thump on the ceiling of the carriage.

"Those two fools should know when it's time to stop. How many times do I have to explain it to them?"

"Yes . . . please do, Toby—for me," Mary Gwin implored. "I honestly think I'm more dead than alive."

Toby Bennington thrust his head and thin shoulders through the window of the carriage and hollered at the driver, not allowing his disgust with the trip and the continued obeisance his employer demanded of all his employees to show until his face could not be seen.

Thadius Penrod Bennington was a slight, bookish young man in his late twenties who, at his father's insistence, had been in Gwin's employ since graduating from Harvard at the age of twenty-two. Gwin, a long-time friend of Bennington's father, had known Thadius since he was a teenaged boy. Much to Thadius's disgust, the childhood nickname of Toby had stuck with him over the years, and the senator seemed to delight in using it just to humiliate or annoy him, especially when others were present—especially when Mary was present.

Bennington had to constantly stifle the urge to let the senator know just how little he thought of him. So far as Thadius P. Bennington was concerned, Senator William McKendree Gwin was a presumptuous, inordinately ambitious, pompous ass. Simply put, he thought the senator to be one of those individuals for whom history would have a difficult time accounting, one who, for whatever reason, had achieved a status in life far beyond his native abilities and talents.

As much as Toby hated his present circumstance in life, he appeared to be hanging on, perhaps gambling on the future. To everyone, it appeared he hoped a few years of such subservience might possibly bring him rewards beyond his fondest dreams—if the Confederacy prevailed, and if Gwin was successful in realizing his personal ambitions. That was the way it appeared. That was the way it had to appear.

As the senator's confidential secretary, there was, for the most part, little of Gwin's affairs with which Toby Bennington was not intimately familiar, or so it seemed. With Gwin, however, appearances could be and frequently were deceptive. Bennington needed to know more—nay, he needed to know much more, a great deal more. One day—and he could hardly contain a smile at the thought—he would have his say. One day he would see this pretentious popinjay brought low, and it was his intention to have a hand in, if not be the cause of, Gwin's downfall; the anticipation of that for the present made the wait worth the constant indignities he was called upon to endure in his current status.

What kept him going were the secret feelings he had for the beautiful woman seated across from him. Toby was hopelessly smitten with the senator's lady. Mary Gwin was the major distraction of his life and was constantly on his mind—an obsession of which he could not rid himself and which he had long since ceased to resist. To the dangerous exclusion of all other considerations, Thadius P. Bennington loved Mary Gwin with all of his heart.

Had anyone else suspected his feelings, they would have doubtless dismissed them as nothing more than mere infatuation with an older woman. But his passion ran much deeper than that; though he had confessed his love for her to no one, it was something he couldn't escape. And when he dreamed of the senator's fall, he dreamed of hers also: right into his waiting arms. And the more bitter he became toward the senator, the more intense his feelings for Mary Gwin grew.

With the thumping of the Senator's cane and the instructions sharply hollered from below, the two men on the driver's seat at the top of the coach looked at each other with the pained expressions of men tired of taking orders.

"I just hope we get t' 'Frisco 'fore I decide t' kill one of them two pork eaters," the driver muttered to the guard at his left as he hauled back on the reins, bringing the clattering coach to a dusty stop.

Toby opened the door and leaned out of the coach as the driver stepped down to the rutted trail. "We need to camp here. Find a suitable place."

"Mr. Bennington, you tell the senator that there ain't no suitable place. Not fer at least another ten miles. Out here there's just sage—nothin' else, no water or feed for the horses, no trees, not nothin'."

Thrusting his head through the window, Senator Gwin glared at the driver. "Well . . . why haven't you made better time? Find a place, and now! Look at those hills over there, they are covered with trees, man."

"Senator, why them's just sparse cedar and the like. They don't make cover of no kind."

"Mrs. Gwin does not have ten miles left in her," he said sharply. Waving his hand at the driver in dismissal, he commanded, "Do it now, man. And be quick about it."

The frustrated driver dragged his dirty, stained hat from is head and scratched his sweaty scalp vigorously. Turning to climb back up to his seat, he said half to himself, "His wife ain't got no ten miles left in 'er, he says. So jest what am I supposed t' do, anyway?"

"Will," the guard said, gesturing off to their left as the driver settled in his seat, "appears like there's a draw over yonder."

"Yeah," Will said, his voice filled with disgust. "Maybe we can make some sort of dry camp over there." Slapping the heavy reins along the backs of the exhausted grays and releasing the coach's brake with his foot, he muttered to the guard, "I ain't so worried about them folks down below, Lem, as I am these here horses. What we need, and need bad, is water and some good graze."

As the coach lurched forward, Lem looked at the driver and said, "Yuh know, Will, I don't think either of them two has ever used my name. What about you?"

Struggling with the heavy reins, Will hauled the lead horses around and eased the six-up and coach down into a wide, brush-filled draw that appeared deep enough to offer some protection from the chill of the desert night wind. He responded, "Well, sir, I can't recollect as they have, but the lady . . . now, she's some, alright. But them two roosters . . . well . . . I suppose you're right, neither one of 'em knows I've got a name. 'Bout sick of it, too."

The farther Clay Ashworth and Chet Langtree rode into the high Nevada desert, the more sign they saw, and though they had not actually sighted any Indians, the sign was getting more frequent, heavier, and worrisome. Where possible, they had kept to the low ground—and where cedars and juniper crept out into the sage, they attempted to stay well within the sparse tree line. Under such circumstance, the only safe assumption was that anyone or anything that moved was an enemy and to be cautiously regarded as such. The two frontiersmen knew you had to see them before they saw you, or you were in for possible trouble—often big trouble.

Reining their horses to a welcome stop in the middle of the rutted wagon track that constituted the main trail from Salt Lake City to Northern California, the two men sat studying the tracks they had been following.

Mopping his face with the big bandanna that hung loosely from his neck, Clay looked at his partner, and said, "Chet, something bothers me about all of this. If this wagon or coach is the one Senator Gwin and his wife are in, they're by themselves, no outriders, there's just the coach. They're trying to cross this wilderness by themselves. How do you read it?"

Shifting in his saddle to ease the pressure on his hip, Chet scratched his stubbled chin and said, "Well, sir, appears these are their tracks alright. I mean, we ain't seen any others. And when a feller contemplates the numbers of unshod horses that keep crossing their trail, ain't but one conclusion that feller can come to. These here folks's surely done the wrong thing, and if they ain't in trouble now, they're likely gonna be, an' soon, too. Ain't that about how you see it, boss?"

"I don't see any other way to look at it," Clay said, stepping down from his horse to study the tracks more closely. "How long do you figure it's been since they passed here?"

Chet took a deep breath and let it out slowly. "Late yesterday; this mornin', maybe. Them tracks're still sharp and clear, and there ain't been no wind to speak of. I figger they ain't all that far ahead of us. An' neither are them Injuns, either, from the looks of it."

"Uh-huh," Clay said, running his finger back and forth across the tracks in the sand. "Something's going to happen, if it hasn't already."

Not more than a mile farther on, the trail curved sharply to the right and disappeared around the point of a range of low hills that were generously covered with juniper, piñon, and cedar, and the late afternoon air was lightly scented with their fragrance.

Rising from his study of the tracks, Clay took in the surrounding terrain. "It's getting late," he said, "not a whole lot we can do now, and I'm tired. Let's make camp. That looks like a good place over there where that gulch comes out of those hills. Good cover."

"Yessir, I'm for that. If we stop now, we can make a small fire for cookin' and have it out afore dark. Better t' be safe than sorry on a night such as this."

Remounting, Clay reined his horse around and the two spurred their mounts into an easy lope toward the relative safety of the not too distant gulch.

The fires burned low and the night was cold, and so was Mary Gwin. Abruptly rejecting her husband's advances in the dark coach, she said, "I'm sick of this. I mean, I'm sick of it, William. I have been jostled and bounced around in this awful coach for over three months now. I've nearly been beaten to death on these horrible trails. I can't remember the last time I soaked in a hot tub, or even had a bath of any kind. I don't know when I have been so miserable and unhappy."

"Mary . . . dearest . . . don't be like this. Another day at the most, and we'll be in Carson City. You can soak in a hot bath for as long as you like, and then it won't be long before we are home in San Francisco. It's almost over, and I—"

"Don't do that," she said irritably, pushing his hand away. "I'm tired, I don't feel good, and I don't like it."

"Mary?"

"Besides, Toby is right under us. He can probably hear us right now, and . . . those horrid men out there . . . they always seem to be awake."

"Well, that's what makes them so useful—they're our guards."

"I really don't understand why we couldn't have taken a boat.

There are other ways you could have accomplished the same things, and we'd have been home long ago."

Frustration gave way to anger, and the senator snapped, "You *do* know, Mary. You know very well. You know, because I have explained it to you a hundred times or more. And when we started out on this trip, you were in full agreement. In fact a good deal of what we set out to accomplish was your idea—as well as mine.

"There are people, very important people, I have had to speak with. Influential, powerful people—especially in Kansas and Missouri—not to mention Utah."

"Yes . . . please don't mention Utah."

Ignoring her incessant petulance, the senator continued. "The hostilities along the Kansas–Missouri border, and the activities of those in sympathy with our plans will aid us immensely in our efforts out here in California."

"True or not, I had no idea, *William,* just how difficult and primitive this trip would become—or how long." Mary Gwin had an irritating way of pronouncing her husband's name with unmistakable disapproval when she was angry.

"You could have done it without me, if you had given any thought to my needs and comfort. All of my beautiful clothes are ruined," she sniffled, on the edge of real tears. "My hair is a rat's nest I'll never be able to untangle, and I just know I must smell awful. You do."

"Well, be that as it may, my dear, your hair will be fine and your clothes can be easily replaced in a few short weeks, perhaps even in Carson City in a day or so. The important thing is that our conversations with Governor Jackson and Lieutenant Governor Reynolds will bear sweet fruit for us and very bitter fruit for Union sympathizers all throughout that region. On that you may make book, so to speak," Gwin said, his anger from his wife's refusals beginning to abate.

William Gwin was aware of the causes of his wife's anger, that her obstinacy and argumentative mood were a result of her exhaustion. And he knew, as everyone who knew her was well aware, she had a political mind that was the envy of many powerful men whose talents and knowledge would never measure up to those of Mary Gwin. And both he and Mary knew that out of such disagreements frequently came an uncanny clarity of thought and like-mindedness between the two of them.

"But that awful place has been in a state of war for over five years now," Mary Gwin said, warming to the issues that held such promise for their future. "I mean, there is no order to be found there. The people are positively wallowing in anarchy."

"So you have pointed out before, my dear," the senator said, yawning and turning on his side, away from his wife. "Slave stealing, looting, arson, all of these things we must take full advantage of and encourage. It's not called bloody Kansas for nothing."

"Yes . . . Kansas is a mess," Mary Gwin said, thoughtfully, "but what of Missouri? Somehow it just doesn't seem so—"

"Missouri is a radical hotbed of the kind of violent pro-slavery people we need to keep the Union in turmoil and encourage the Southern rebellion—bring the Union house of cards down, in fact. That is precisely why this trip was so important," Gwin stressed. "Even so, there are too many in Missouri who at least tacitly support the Union, maybe even a majority of them, God forbid. That's why we must do all we can to constantly encourage the hotheads and keep all the others off balance."

"After your talks with Jackson and Reynolds, do you really think they can be counted on to keep the pot boiling, William?"

"I think so. If armed and motivated, the secessionist element can exert an influence far beyond their numbers. I got Jackson to promise me he will do all he can to see that those Southern sympathizers get the weapons they need. He assured me that he and his friends are going to start collecting guns and ammunition from strategic spots around the state and see they get into the right hands."

"Can he do that? I mean, how on earth will they do that?"

"I carried important information for the governor, informing him that the federal arsenal in St. Louis holds at least sixty thousand old muskets and over a million rounds of small arms ammunition, along with a lot of arms manufacturing and repair machinery. He's now convinced he must get his hands on that materiel as quickly as possible and use it to arm those in support of the Confederacy."

"Really? Why . . . I had no idea, William."

"The fact is, Mary, I was sworn to secrecy. But that, my dear, is why the sacrifices you and I are making are of such importance, and you need to know it. Now that the war has begun in earnest, everything must be done to take full advantage. No hardship is too great if it enables us to be successful in establishing a new California Republic."

Mary Gwin turned and lay her arm over her husband's side. "Well . . . still . . . I couldn't get away from that terrible place fast enough," she said, letting her hand wander across his body. How well Gwin knew that nothing warmed his lady quite like the thought of power, of becoming the first lady of what would soon become the new Republic of California, *their* Republic of California.

Her touch renewing his ardor, Gwin turned to his wife. "I know how hard it has been for you, Mary," he whispered in her ear. "But it's almost over, my dearest, and when you get discouraged, turn to me, and remember it will soon be *our* California."

Taking her husband's wandering hand in hers, she said, "Let's hope so, but you have one big problem that remains unsolved."

"You're telling me?" the frustrated senator said, taking a deep breath and rolling onto his back.

"That's not what I mean, William."

"Mmm, of course. Then, just what do you consider my *big problem* to be?" he asked, staring at the ceiling of the coach, irritation creeping back into his voice.

Reaching over and running a finger lightly along her husband's jaw, Mary said, "Not *what,* dearest one, but *whom.*"

"Alright, *whom* might that be?" he asked, his irritation increasing.

"Now, don't be cross, dear. You know very well *whom,*" she said, with some emphasis. "That nasty Brigham Young just might be the biggest stumbling block in our way. That so-called prophet has visions only for his own ambitions."

For a moment, Gwin said nothing, his mind re-exploring his recent conversations with the real power in the Utah Territory, federal appointees notwithstanding. "Mmm . . . that's one for the history books, all right. Still, I find it hard to dislike the man," he said, with a sigh. "You've got to hand it to him, Mary, he's the nearest thing to a true monarch you'll likely ever find on this continent. I rather admire the man, if you must know the truth."

"I don't have to *hand* him anything, and why in the world would anyone, least of all you, admire him? What on earth for? In the end, he could be the cause of the Confederacy's downfall, William—and ours. If we don't get California, if the Confederacy fails, it could be his fault as much as Lincoln's, when you think about it."

"Of course, you're right. Think about the absurdity of it, Mary. Here is a man whose territory was invaded, not four years ago, by a massive Union army, sent by the president of the United States himself, and still Young is emphatic about his support of the Union.

"That's really where and when this war started, you know—that foolish Utah expedition. Were I Brigham Young, I would personally take up arms and shoot the first Union blue belly I laid eyes on. But not Brigham Young. Oh, no, not the great, all-seeing Mormon *prophet,*" he said, with sarcasm. "Oh, no, not the great American Moses. He runs to genuflect before that bearded mongrel, Lincoln. Don't those two make a pair?"

They lay for a time in the darkness, then Gwin continued. "The really frightening thing is, Mary, when you stop to realize it, the Utah Territory literally dominates the western half of this entire continent. On top of that, Mormon colonies are spreading out all across the West. From the Salt Lake Valley in every direction—the New Mexico Territory, Arizona, you name it—and every one of them look to Brigham Young for leadership. His word is law to them. Now, that is *real* power, Mary."

"California, too," Mary offered.

"Yes, two colonies in Stanislaus County alone, and a third down south in San Bernardino, not to mention a considerable population in San Francisco. I mean, if Brigham Young decides to stop us, given the territory he controls . . . well. . . ."

"He's just another Cassandra, another kind of croaker—just more dangerous, that's all," Mary said, sharply. "The only difference is, he's just not in the South with the others that are betraying the Confederacy."

"Do you realize, Mary, if he took it into his head to really get into this war, that man could field an army at least equal to that of the Confederacy? Heaven help us if he does."

"I detest the man. He frightens me, the old lecher."

"Mmm. Nonetheless, I can't help but admire the man," Gwin said, thoughtfully. "Still, you'd think a man who has become known as some sort of colonizer would have some understanding of the kind of civilization this new Confederacy will be. I tried to explain that very point to him. We are building something that will equal the likes of Greece and Rome."

"And he couldn't see it?" she said, her voice subdued by unbelief.

"No. I explained that just the simple act of separating ourselves from the North has started the process—bloody as it has now apparently become—that will lead to glory."

# CHAPTER 10

* * *

ORNING CAME COLD AND EARLY on the high desert. Will
Gibby and Lem Suggs sat across their fire from each other, sipping
hot coffee and watching Toby struggle near the coach with the stub-
born embers of last night's fire. As usual the two had established
their own camp a few yards from where the Gwins and Toby had
settled for the night—the Gwins in the coach and Toby beneath it.

Toby Bennington was quickly losing patience with his seeming inability to rekindle the fire. Throughout the trip, the senator
had insisted that the driver and guard make a separate camp, but
to be close, in case of need. Toby did not like the two men, sensing their disapproval of him, but making them establish their own
camp served no purpose. It just made more work for him and
placed him in the role of a servant—right where the senator
wanted him, Toby bitterly suspected.

"Reckon I ought t' go help that poor greenhorn?" Will said,
with a deprecating chuckle, nudging his companion.

"Somebody should. Life'll be a misery fer us all if'n that senator gets up cold, and there ain't no fire nor coffee for him and his missus. Looks t' me like *Mr. Bennington*," Lem said, with some disgust, as he stood and stretched, "is into something what's bigger than he is, tryin' to get that fire started. Well, maybe I—argghh!"

The air in Lem's lungs exploded through his nose and mouth with such force that the resulting belchlike, snorting sound caused a startled Toby Bennington to look up from his struggle in rekindling his fire.

The man was standing next to the fire he had shared with Will, a look of shock and disbelief on his ashen face, his right hand tightly grasping the arrow that had impaled him. The ugly shaft had struck him with such force it had split his sternum and pierced his heart, the metal point protruding from a neat tear in the back of his shirt.

Before Lem's dead body folded to the earth, the cold morning air was shattered with the high-pitched shrieks of a Ute war party charging along both sides of the draw, the air around the small camp quickly filling with dust and exploding with the crack of rifle fire and flying arrows. The attack was so sudden and unexpected that both Toby and Will momentarily froze before the magnitude of what was happening struck either of them.

Drawing his revolver and diving for cover behind the fallen log he and Lem had used for a bench near their fire, Will hollered, "Get under the coach, Mister Bennington! Don't let them red devils get you, too."

Scrambling under the coach and staying out of the line of fire, Toby hollered, "I don't have my gun! What'll we do?"

"Stupid greenhorn," Will muttered to himself, as he fired off a shot. "Just stay put," he shot back. "Maybe all they want is the horses."

"No! Don't let them get the horses," the senator shouted, his contorted face appearing in the window of the coach. "We can't be stranded out here afoot, you fool. We'd be almost totally helpless. Protect those horses at all cost!"

An arrow thudded into the window brace of the coach with a vibrating twang and chips flew with the impact of several bullets, sending Gwin out of sight, tumbling to the floor of the coach, next to his wife.

"Uh-huh," Will mumbled to himself, as he twisted to give better covering fire in the direction of the six big horses. "I don't see the great man doin' nothin' too brave t' save them horses at all costs hisself."

"Senator? Drop my gun belt down," Toby yelled. "We need to hold these savages off somehow."

"Come and get the blasted thing yourself," came the muffled reply. "I'm paying you to take the risks."

Toby heard a faint, but unmistakably angry reply, and a moment later his gun belt landed with a dusty thump near the rear wheel of the coach, not far from his hand. It had been Mary. *If the senator had her gumption,* he thought, *if only*—

With bullets spitting dust around his feet and the din of battle shattering the air around him, Will slid under the coach with a crablike scramble. "Looks like this is where we gotta make our stand," he said, looking at Toby. "We should be able to cover them horses from here. Start shootin', son."

"Kindly do not refer to me as your *son,*" Toby responded irritably, as the Colt jumped in his hand and a grotesquely-painted Indian tumbled from his horse.

"Say . . . that's not bad shootin', son."

"Don't call me *son,* I told you . . . and make every shot count," he growled, rapidly snapping off shots until his gun emptied.

Quickly reloading and nodding at the floor of the coach above them, his tone almost dismissive, he said, "I don't know how much help we'll get from up there.

"Mary! I mean . . . Missus Gwin . . . you stay down on the floor!" he hollered, as arrows thumped into the side of the coach.

A rifle barked above them and another attacker slid from his horse and tumbled awkwardly among the sage.

"Maybe he heard yuh, huh?"

"Huh," Toby grunted. "More than likely it was Missus Gwin. She's a pretty good shot with a rifle. Not bad with a pistol, either."

"How many do you make out? How much trouble are we in?" Senator Gwin hollered from the coach.

"With them redskins, we're in a heap of trouble, that's what," Will yelled back, squeezing off two more shots. "Them looks t' be Utes—maybe a dozen of 'em—and they're painted for war. Could be more, too. Hard to tell in this ruckus."

"Damnation," Toby said, again stopping to reload his Colt. "I keep missing them."

"Shootin' uphill is the worst kind—you'll keep shootin' above 'em if yuh ain't careful. Aim lower, that's the trick."

Toby aimed carefully and another painted warrior slid from his horse.

"That's the spirit," Will hollered above the noise of the attack. "Keep it up, and aim for one of them feathered red devils. If yuh hit a chief, maybe they'll break off their attack."

"Why would they do that?" Toby hollered, over the sound of his big Colt.

Will took careful aim at a feathered attacker and squeezed off a shot that jolted the Indian from his galloping pony. "Because maybe they'll think their medicine's gone bad and break off—at least long enough to settle on a new leader."

"And if that doesn't work?" Toby asked, taking aim with his revolver, carefully squeezing the trigger. The heavy gun jumped in response.

"Gibby, what are we going to do?" Gwin hollered over the noise from their guns.

"Make every shot count, and save your last two bullets. One fer yerself and one fer yer missus," Will shouted. "You, too, son," he said, glancing at Toby.

"For ourselves?" Toby said, incredulously.

"And the missus," Will said, jerking his thumb toward the floor of the coach—in case he can't do it. You don't want them savages t' get their hands on yuh, least of all on her."

Toby's face drained of color. "You mean we aren't going to get out of this?"

"Well now, son," Will said, taking careful aim at one of their painted attackers, "just you take a look-see out there. Odds surely ain't lookin' too good, are they, boy?"

Will's rifle punched into his shoulder with a deafening slam, and another Indian jerked violently from his horse, tumbling into the dust, his naked arms flailing loosely around him as if he were no more than a dirty rag doll.

Toby's ears rang loudly from the resounding blasts of Will's big Henry next to his head. It seemed as if he had suddenly gone deaf, as if he could hear nothing over the maddening sound in his ears—only Will's words: *Odds surely ain't lookin' too good, are they, boy?—are they, boy?—are they, boy?*

The brightness of the early morning sun touched the tops of the cedar and pinon that surrounded their camp as Clay Ashworth and Chet Langtree were starting to move about, rolling up their bedrolls, getting ready to move out. Intent on an early start, the two worked quickly and in silence.

A light breeze out of the northwest filled the trees with its soft, mysterious sound, and the cool desert air became heavy with the scent of cedar and piñon. Somewhere out in the sage, the beautiful song of some desert bird reached the camp, causing both men to stop for a moment and listen.

It was one of those indescribably beautiful mornings, the kind that brings deep feelings of gratitude for life. Such moments make a person want to just sit down and breathe deeply of the clean, crisp, fragrant air, relax, and take it all in.

Though he would never confess to it, inside, Chet Langtree was a poet. He never had to admit it. Those who had spent any time at all with him knew he had the soul of an artist, a dreamer, a true romantic. They also knew better than to mention it—to him or anyone else. Mornings such as this made something well up from deep inside him, something he longed to put into words, but somehow they just wouldn't come, not in any really satisfying way.

Chet had just tightened the cinch of his saddle and was about to lean against his horse and commment on the beauty of it all when he suddenly stiffened, staring across the animal's neck toward the ridgeline above them.

"You hear that, boss?"

"Gunshots, and not too far off, either," Clay said, swinging into the saddle.

"That trouble we was talkin' about yesterday? Looks like it's found somebody."

"Yeah, and guess who."

★　★　★

Without warning, the pattern of the attack broke as three heavily feathered Indians, each with a large-bore rifle, reined their mounts brutally about and charged the coach, their frenzied screams distorting their grotesquely-painted faces as all three raised up and fired almost as one, the deafening blast from their muzzles momentarily drowning out all other sound. The huge lead slugs slammmed into the coach, causing it to lurch violently on its leather suspension, splintering its doors and side, tearing into its interior, and filling the air with Mary Gwin's screams of terror.

"Mary! They've killed Mary!" Toby heard himself screaming, as he lunged from beneath the coach and stormed toward the on-coming braves, his Colt relentlessly jumping in his hand, spitting a deadly fire. "Those filthy savages have killed Mary!"

"Get back here, you fool! They'll kill yuh fer sure!" Will hollered, frantically scrambling from beneath the coach in an effort to give Toby some covering fire. As Will brought his rifle up to his cheek, drawing careful aim, a bullet slammmed into the stock, driving the splintered butt cruelly into the side of his head, knocking him into the front wheel of the bullet-riddled coach. Attempting to hang on to the yellow, iron-rimmmed wheel, Will groaned, twisted, and slowly slid onto the dirt, unconscious.

One of the attacking savages pitched violently from his balk-ing horse as a slug from Toby's gun tore into his chest. The other two, flinging their now empty rifles to the ground, pulled their tomahawks, and with renewed screams leapt from their horses and rushed at Toby.

Realizing he had emptied his Colt, Toby Bennington hurled the pistol at the nearest attacker, the heavy gun slammming squarely across the Ute's nose, causing him to drop his ugly weapon as his hands reflexively flew to his bloody face. Filled with unreasoning rage, Toby plowed into the second big warrior, and the two tumbled to the ground, twisting and turning, clawing and gouging, each struggling for advantage in a grotesque, dust-filled dance of death.

Recovering his war ax, his faced covered with blood, the second brave screamed and danced above them. Filled with renewed blood lust, seeking an opening for his brutal weapon, the frenzied man suddenly left the ground, blown into the air in a cloud of pink spray, the boom of a big-bore rifle coming from the splintered door of the coach.

It was Mary Gwin. "Toby! Somebody help Toby!"

Under skilled hands, the horses carefully picked their way further back up the rock-strewn gully to a point where, over the years, the deep cutbank had sloughed away, creating a steep, but stable, slide leading to the sparsely timbered slope and ridgeline above.

Pulling their rifles from their saddle scabbards, Clay and Chet slipped to the ground and, staying hidden in the brush, made their way to the ridgeline. Lying on their bellies, careful not to skyline themselves, the two peered down on the battle taking place in a shallow draw two hundred yards or so down the steep slope from where they lay.

"The way things look, boss, them folks've about had it."

"Uh-huh," Clay said, drawing careful aim. "Especially that fella who's about t' get his head split by that big buck," he said, squeezing the trigger.

"He surely could've." Chet said, the blast from Clay's big rifle echoing off the surrounding hills.

"Looks like two left in the coach, probably Senator Gwin and his wife, and two dead, or at least down."

"Yeah," Clay said, the air resounding from the blast of his rifle, "but from the looks of things, they've put up a real fight."

"Yessir . . . and they're about to lose them horses."

"This ought t' put a stop t' that."

Both rifles roared almost as one, and two Indians jerked violently, tumbling awkwardly in the dust, the hoofs of the big, frightened grays pounding the earth around their lifeless bodies. With every shot Clay and Chet quickly rolled to different positions, hopefully making it appear to those below as if there were more than just the two of them.

# CHAPTER 11

★ ★ ★

T HERE MUST BE SIX OR SEVEN up there," Toby said, scrambling through the shattered side of the coach.

"Hurry, Toby," Mary said, pulling on what was left of his shirt. "Get in here where it's safer."

"Maybe more," Gwin responded, his voice filled with renewed hope. "One of them sure saved your scalp, Toby boy. Just look, those red devils aren't sure which way to shoot."

"Whoever they are up there, I'm surely glad they showed up. I thought you were dead, Mary. You, too," he said, glancing at Gwin.

Struggling to his knees, Gwin said, "Look! There are two riders coming off that ridge."

Struggling to reload his reclaimed Colt, Toby shouted, "We've got to give them as much help as possible."

"Them red devils ain't through yet," Will offered, his dazed-sounding voice coming from beneath them.

"Will, is that you?" Mary cried.

"Yes ma'am, it surely is."

"Oh," she said, collapsing against the far side of the coach, her body beginning to shake with sobs. "I thought Toby and you were both dead."

"Well, speakin' fer m'self, ma'am," Will offered, his voice muffled by the floor of the coach, "it'd take more than some Injun's bullet t' put this ol' he-coon outta commmission fer long."

At some point in all of the confusion, Will had regained consciousness and, his head pounding, he had crawled back under the coach. "Start pourin' lead into 'em," he cried, his gun barking beneath them, "much as y' can, folks. I think we're gonna make it, now."

"Will you look at that!" Toby shouted with excitement, as the two strangers slid their powerful mounts down the steep slope in a cloud of scattering rocks and dust, bursting into a dead run toward the coach.

Both riders charged headlong into what was left of the confused and disorganized band of Indians, causing them to scatter, almost as if they had been blasted apart by some shattering explosion.

Both men held a rifle in one hand and a large horse-pistol in the other, and with every shot damage was done. One stood in the stirrups as his horse darted among the scattering braves, his big guns barking death, each shot knocking another warrior into the dust.

"Hot diggity! One of them fellas has been hit," Will hollered, scrambling out from under the coach, flame spitting from his Colt with every step. "We gotta help 'em, Toby. Get out here, son, and sling lead! By the eternal, we've won! Jest look," he whooped, putting one more slug into the back of a retreating Ute.

"They're leaving!" Mary Gwin cried from the coach. "Look! They're leaving!"

"Stay down, ma'am," Will said, leaning against the coach, his head still throbbing. "Best you stay down 'til we're sure it's over an' check t' make sure all them redskins is dead."

Clattering to the edge of the wash, Clay and Chet reined in their heaving mounts enough to allow the animals to step over the cutbank and slide to the dry streambed at the bottom. Before his big horse had completely stopped, Clay dismounted and looking at Will said, "Everybody here all right?"

Thrusting his hand toward Clay, Will exclaimed, "We sure are, thanks to the two of you. Another few minutes and we'd have been out of luck. Just like poor ol' Lem over there. That there was Lemuel Suggs, my partner. I'm Wilbur Gibby—jest call me Will. Over yonder is. . . ."

"I am Senator William Gwin." Taking Clay's outstretched hand, he continued, "I'm confident we would have eventually prevailed here. I am, however—that is to say—we are grateful for your help."

"William?" Mary Gwin stepped between her husband and Will and offered her hand to Clay.

"Oh . . . I'm terribly sorry. Yes . . . well . . . may I present my wife, Mrs. William Gwin."

Dabbing at her tear-stained face with a corner of her skirt, Mary took Clay's hand and gave it a gentle, feminine squeeze. "Please, call me Mary. I can't tell you how grateful we are. You saved our lives."

Glancing at the senator, Clay said, "Looked to us like you were really giving it back to that bunch."

"Appears as you was really whippin' them Injuns," Chet

offered, leaning over his saddle horn, the sarcasm in his voice betraying his true feelings.

Clay glanced up at Chet. "Well, now it's time for me to apologize. Name's Clay Ashworth. This is my partner, Chet Langtree."

"Oh, dear. Your friend has been hurt," Mary said, stepping toward Chet's horse.

Stepping down, Chet ignored the others and took Mary Gwin's hand. "I'm most honored, ma'am, and it really ain't nothin'. Just a scratch from a poorly shot arrow is all."

Having been thoroughly ignored, and annoyed with Mary Gwin's concern for the big cowboy, Toby cleared his throat and stepped between Gwin and their two rescuers.

"I'm sorry," Gwin said, "what with all of the confusion. This is my aide, Toby Bennington. We all call him Toby."

"Yeah . . . you may as well, too," Toby said, with a glance of disapproval toward Gwin. "Everyone else does." There was, perhaps, nothing Toby Bennington hated more than being referred to as the Senator's *aide,* especially by Gwin. "I don't know which of the two of you knocked that Indian off of me, but I owe you an enormous debt of gratitude."

"I really don't know what we'd have done without Mister Bennington," Mary said, turning to slip her arm through Toby's, sensing his embarrassment and anger. "I thought there for a moment we had lost him. He's the one who makes things work for us, really."

"Thank you, Mary . . . uh . . . Missus Gwin."

"An' he was a reg'lar catamount when that coach got shot up, I'm tellin' you. A dern good shot is what he is," Will enthused, giving Bennington an approving thump on the back. "I'm purely proud he was with us, an' that's a fact."

Feeling a certain loss of control, Gwin took his wife's arm and pulled her away from Bennington. "Gentlemen. How safe are we? Do you think those savages will return soon?"

"Prob'ly best we move on, I'd say," Chet offered. "If that coach is still workin', that is. What about you, Clay?"

"I'd say so," Clay responded, trying to get an unobtrusive look at the wound in the unwilling Chet Langtree's side.

Not wanting to cause his friend any undue embarrassment, Clay turned to Gwin, and said, "Undoubtedly one of those you shot was their chief, Senator. They've withdrawn thinking their medicine has gone bad."

"Oh, I hardly think it was—"

"Soon as them redskins choose another leader," Chet interjected, "we can count on 'em comin' back. Utes ain't the ones t' leave a fight without some scalps, an' they shore don't like bein' mauled the way you all was givin' it to 'em. Clay's right. Best we move right shortly."

With the stage loaded, the horses hitched, and Suggs adequately buried, Toby joined Will on the driver's seat as Gwin helped his wife into the coach. Turning to Clay Ashworth, the senator said, "When do you think we can reach Carson City, Mister Ashworth?"

"Get away from here as far as possible today, and if you break camp early in the morning, you should have no trouble reaching Carson some time in the afternoon—by dinnertime at least, I'd say."

Climbing through the gaping side of the coach and leaning toward what was left of the window, Gwin said, "And what of the two of you? Won't you ride along with us? At least long enough to ensure that we have escaped another attack?"

"Oh, yes. Please do," Mary said, leaning forward with a pleading look on her dirty, but lovely, face. *"Please do."*

Clay glanced at Chet, a slight smile crossing his face. "Well, I guess we could do that. We were sort of drifting toward Carson City, anyhow. How about it, Chet?"

Chet leaned down and looked into the coach. With a smile for Mary Gwin, and ignoring her somewhat annoyed husband, he said, "Surely fine with me, ma'am."

"Times like these, there ain't never enough help," Will said from the driver's box. "Sure hope you fellers'll join up with us."

★   ★   ★

Later that day, Will Gibby slapped the heavy reins along the backs of the big horses, and the coach lurched forward at a faster pace.

Spurring his big gelding alongside the driver's box, Clay hollered, "Over in that grove . . . good place to camp."

Along toward dusk, Chet Langtree shot a deer, and with the wild onions and berries Will had shown a tired but willing Mary Gwin how to gather, the evening meal seemed a feast for kings. With everyone's stomachs comfortably full, conversation around the fire came easily—and, despite their aches and pains, lasted well into the night.

With Mary and Toby eagerly rehearsing with Clay the narrow escape they experienced early that morning, and the distance they had been able to put between them and the bloody draw they had camped in the night before, William Gwin turned to Chet Langtree.

"Tell me—Chet, is it?"

"Yessir."

"Tell me, Chet, how's your side?"

"Aches some, but that's kind of t' be expected. I've had a scratch or two before."

"Mmm. Wait here."

Returning from the coach with a small black valise, Gwin drew Chet aside from the others and sat down next to him. "Among other things, Chet, I'm a physician. I have to admit I haven't practiced much in the last few years, but I'm going to insist on a look-see, my friend," he said, pulling Chet's shirt free from his belted trousers before the startled cowboy knew what was happening.

"Yes. Just as I thought. Hold still, Chet, this needs cleaning, and I mean right now." Following a few deft pokes and prods, Gwin said, "This may hurt some, but that scratch, as you put it, is starting to look uncomfortably septic, and don't tell me it doesn't hurt. I can see that it obviously must."

Pulling a worrisome-looking bottle from his bag and dipping a piece of white cloth into it, Gwin began cleaning the wound and, in an off-handed manner said, "Tell me, Chet, what do you two fellows think about this so-called war between the states?"

Wincing from the vigorous cleansing his wound was receiving, Chet said, "Well, sir, I try real hard not to think about it at all, Senator."

"Yes . . . I'd have guessed as much," Gwin said, studying the wound carefully. "Tell me, Mister Langtree—"

"Senator, why don't you just keep callin' me Chet? Seems like out here," Chet said, glancing around the rough camp, "in these circumstances, anyhow, talk'd come easier."

"Yes, thank you. Then, tell me . . . Chet," Gwin said, applying a clean patch and plaster to Chet's side, "is that a southern accent I hear in your voice now and then?"

"Yessir, I guess it must be at that. Yuh see, I was born in Georgia, but Paw moved Maw and all us kids out t' Texas when I was hardly of any age at all. By rights, I'm a Texican, an' right proud t' be such, too."

Gwin straightened from his work. "That should take care of that wound for now, but it needs to be watched carefully for the next day or two, Chet."

"Yessir, and many thanks."

Gwin studied the man's face for a moment. "Well, I'm sure there is great sympathy for the South throughout Texas," he offered, prodding to test Chet's thinking and possible loyalties, much as he had the ugly wound he had just treated.

"Yessir. Fact of the matter is, Texas has already seceded—last winter, in fact. A lot of Texicans are gonna be in that war, Senator. You can bet yer last Yankee dollar on that, sir."

"I take it, then, your sympathies are with the South."

"You surely can. Y' see, down in Texas, we all feel that folks oughta do what they think is best. Ain't nobody got any right t' force 'em one way or the other, let alone t' start shootin'. That's how Texas and the others got t' be in the Union in the first place. They ought t' be able t' do the same the other direction."

"And does your friend, Clay, feel the same—about the secession of the southern states, I mean?"

Chet turned and glanced at Clay. "Well, sir, t' be downright honest, I ain't exactly sure where he came from—before I hooked up with him, that is. But, Clay, he ain't what I'd call a southerner—not by a long shot. But nobody could rightly call him a Yankee, neither. What I mean is, I ain't heard 'im say much on the subject, but he feels the same way I do about folks takin' care of their ownselves an' such."

Chet scratched his chin and thought for a moment. "I guess he feels like I do, folks oughta do what they think is right and be left alone."

"But, as you say, he's not a southerner," Gwin said, a slight smile crossing his face. "You can tuck your shirt in now, by the way, but try to keep your belt off of that wound."

"Many thanks, an' no sir, he ain't," Chet said, carelessly tucking his shirt into his trousers. "Like I say, don't really know too much about his past, where he came from an' such. Nobody does, I reckon. Out here it don't matter much, but I guess a feller'd have t' call him a westerner, if there is such a thing."

"Oh, I think there definitely is, Chet. That is really how I think about myself and the people who support and follow me. We have those same values—values very similar to those of you southerners."

"Well, sir . . . those're my feelin's on it, anyway," Chet said, stretching and looking over at the others.

Not wanting to lose Chet just yet, feeling the need to probe just a little further without raising unnecessary suspicions, Gwin said, "I mean, how would you fellows feel if the federal government told the Nevada Territory that it would conform to eastern trade and mercantile policies, and that you'd have to change the entire fabric of your economy and society or they would invade your territory with federal troops?"

"I guess we ain't mentioned it, but we've spent most of our time in Utah."

Attempting to hide his complete surprise, Gwin said, "You mean you two are Mormons?"

"No sir, we ain't Mormons. But we've spent a lotta time up in Utah, and a few years back, that territory was invaded by them so-called federal troops you're talkin' about. Wasn't a pretty sight, neither."

"Well, then, you—"

"Mind if I get in on this conversation?"

"No," Gwin said, turning at the unexpected interruption. "Certainly not, Mister Ashworth. Please join us."

"I'm Clay to my friends."

"Well, since I hope I can be counted in that group, Clay, please do join us."

"I couldn't help but overhear some of your conversation," Clay confessed, pulling a short log up near the fire. "It might interest you to know, Senator, I fought in that war."

"War?"

"The Utah War, as we think of it out here."

"Indeed?"

"I guess I'll never get over the arrogance of Buchanan and his henchmen sending an army out here to put down a nonexistent, so-called Mormon rebellion."

Gwin leaned toward the fire and shoved another small log into the hungry flames.

"We probably ought to let that fire die, Senator," Clay said, trying to sound helpful. "It's getting late."

"Yes. . . . You're undoubtedly right. Uh . . . a 'nonexistent rebellion,' you say?"

"Well, I'm not a Mormon, understand, but those I know are fine people, and they certainly were not involved in any kind of rebellion against the United States. All they've ever wanted is to just be left to worship their God as they believe to be right and to govern themselves, if you know what I mean."

"Yes. . . . Yes, I think I do."

Clay continued. "That invasion was as rotten a thing as I have ever witnessed." Clay thought a moment, studying the man before him. "And I don't mind telling you, Senator," he said, his eyes intently searching Gwin's, "I would do it again in a minute— without a moment's thought."

"Oh? Really?"

"Reckon that's about how we both feel about it, Senator," Chet said, getting up and stretching.

Clay looked up at his friend. "Thanks for fixing this old hoss. He'd rather die than admit something hurts."

"I'm glad to have done it, Clay. And he just might have—died, that is—without having that wound cleaned. It was starting to look ugly."

"It isn't as if either of us didn't know better," Clay said, winking in Chet's direction. "Frequently Indians on the warpath dip the points of their arrows in their own excrement. Makes for a nasty wound. That's why in an attack a war party will often use arrows along with whatever guns they might have."

"Yessir . . . that's true enough," Chet said, attempting to further tuck his shirt in without putting too much pressure on an already painful wound.

"I had no idea," Gwin said, his face covered with a look of disgust. "No wonder that wound was becoming badly infected. We need to watch it very closely, Chet, that being the case. Septicemia will remain a threat until it heals."

Nodding his understanding, Chet said, "Much obliged. Well, see y'all in the mornin'." Turning directly to Mary Gwin, he smiled and said, "Pleasant dreams, ma'am."

Toby Penrod Bennington lay in his blankets listening to the muted, languid talk between husband and wife in the coach above him, growing more and more resentful with the intimate noises that came through the floor all too clearly. Between the hardness of the lumpy ground beneath him, the chill of the night seeping through his inadequate blankets, and his resentment over the woman now sharing Gwin's bed, Bennington's obstinate antipathy toward the senator was seething into a barely concealable hostility that at times threatened to boil over into an uncompromising hatred, and tonight it seemed about to overwhelm him.

In an attempt to clear his mind, Bennington turned his thoughts to the conversation he had overheard between Gwin and the two men from Utah. "There are times," he grumbled to himself, "when that man's hypocrisy knows no bounds. But it will be stopped."

Toby rolled over and ground his hip into the dirt in an effort to find some comfort, however inadequate. *That lying hypocrite knows more about that so-called Utah expedition than those two fools could ever guess,* he thought.

Finding little comfort, Toby rolled on his back and laced his fingers behind his aching head. *Utah expedition! What a despicable joke! War is what it was, alright, and war is what it is. Right now—war is what it is, alright.*

*I wonder,* he mused, his eyes growing heavy from the need for sleep, and his mind beginning to drift, *what those two big Utahans would think if they knew they had actually fought in what amounts to the first actions in this civil war—right out here in their Utah Territory, way out here in the West, and that their newfound friend, the Honorable Senator Doctor Gwin, has been mixed up in a conspiracy to split the Union apart for years, including that so-called Utah war.*

*I wonder,* he thought, his heavy eyelids closing. *What if I were to tell them. I wonder . . .*

# CHAPTER 12

★ ★ ★

CLAY ASHWORTH CUT INTO THE thick piece of roast beef that had been placed on an elegant, gold-embossed china plate by a black, liveried servant whose use of the English language would have equaled that of the highest-born British nobleman, had one been present at Senator and Mrs. William Gwin's sumptuous winter dining table. The elegantly prepared, steaming slice of roast, blackened around the outside and a juicy, delicate pink on the inside, nestled among boiled new potatoes and crisp, sautéed carrots, was exactly to his liking.

For several reasons, the evening had been less than comfortable for him. To begin with, the Gwin's guest list included most of San Francisco's elite, at least those who were entirely sympathetic with the senator's secessionist ambitions for California—Democrats mostly. Consequently, the pre-dinner conversation had entirely to do with the progress of the war back East and was enthusiastically pro-South. Having established himself in the senator's confidence, Clay's unease grew from an acute awareness that the slightest slip of the tongue could undo all of his efforts since the day he and Chet Langtree had ridden into the Indian attack on the senator's coach weeks earlier.

What had come as a complete surprise, however, was the presence of the French Consul—an intense, humorless, foppish man who fancied himself a favorite of the ladies—Count Pierre Ladouc de Moppausaunte. The count left no doubt of his support, and that of his government, for the Confederacy, and displayed an obvious disdain for things American, particularly anything western.

From the moment they had been introduced, Clay disliked the man. His handshake was so weak, the big rancher felt as if he were grasping one end of a dead snake. Even worse, the palm of the man's hand was sweaty enough to make Clay feel like wiping his own down the front of his pants. The Frenchman was a man for whom one could quickly cultivate a determined abhorrence.

No sooner had Mary Gwin introduced Ashworth and de Moppausaunte to each other than she hurriedly turned to greet more guests arriving for her elegant dinner party—described the day before by San Francisco's newspapers as the city's gala affair of the coming winter season. Clay noted the Frenchman's effeminate face and wondered if Count de Moppausaunte had ever been faced with the manly necessity of shaving.

As Clay was trying to think of something to say to the consul, the Frenchman rudely pushed past him toward the front entrance where some newly arrived guests were removing their coats. With rapidly mounting disgust for the man, Clay turned his attention to the large, beautifully appointed living room, but as he did so, a flash of color in the crowded entryway caught his eye over de Moppausaunte's retreating shoulder.

A young woman had stepped from behind two men and, along with a somewhat older woman, had immediately become the object of Mary Gwin's excited attention. As the three happy women embraced, the older of the two men, graying and dignified in his demeanor, turned to help the young woman with her coat and parasol, handing her things to the now heavily burdened butler. As he did so, he deftly maneuvered the gentleman with him in the direction of the approaching French Consul, cutting off de Moppausaunte's hurried and apparently unwelcome advance—a subtle maneuver accomplished with such skill that nothing appeared to be out of place.

"Thank you, Father," the younger woman said, with a smile so captivating Clay Ashworth found it difficult not to gape. The unpretentious melody in her lightly accented words matched her startling beauty, but her low-toned, throaty, and completely feminine voice for a moment did not. It was somewhat lower, maybe half an octave or so, than might have been expected of a woman of her age—a kind of lilting contralto, Clay thought—and it carried with it an undeniably disquieting, though completely innocent, sensuality.

She stood shoulder high to her father, a large man near in height to Clay Ashworth. Her black hair, with the slightest suggestion of a natural curl, hung just below her bare shoulders, which Clay could see beneath a delicately woven, steel-gray shawl. All his eyes took in appeared to be soft and shapely, an unblemished, creamy white, temptingly revealed in the folds of her low-cut, red evening gown. Her large, dark eyes flashed as she quickly assessed the crowded room, and as they rested for the briefest, appraising moment on Clay Ashworth, the tip of her tongue lightly moistened her full, exquisitely shaped lips.

Without doubt, she was one of the most captivating women

Clay had ever laid eyes on. That she was a woman accustomed to the attention of men was more than apparent; that she enjoyed, even expected, such attention was equally obvious. With her glance, Clay caught himself and turned away, not wanting to be the least conspicuous in his admiration. He did so, however, with a vow that he would know much more of this exquisite woman before the evening was ended.

It was Mary Gwin, the always alert political operative and quintessential hostess, who provided the unexpected opportunity. "Clay," she said, smiling at de Moppausaunte as she maneuvered her distinguished guests around him, hurrying them toward Ashworth. "You've already met Count de Moppausaunte. Now I want you to meet our special guest for this evening, the governor of the state of Sonora in Mexico, our good neighbor to the south, Gobernador Luis de Garcia Salinas and his lovely wife and my good friend, señora Salinas. And this exquisite young woman is his beautiful daughter, señorita Maria Emilea Consuela Salinas. Oh, also, this gentleman is his aide and confidant, señor José Rodriguez Zamora."

Looking fondly at Clay, she continued, "This wonderful gentleman is one of Senator Gwin's most trusted associates and a friend to whom we are greatly indebted—Mr. Clay Ashworth."

Clay took the governor's offered hand. "I'm pleased to meet you and your lovely family, jefe," he said, briefly glancing at both women. "I have been anxious to meet you, sir. Senator Gwin has spoken of you a great deal in the few weeks I have been in California."

Salinas's handshake was firm, and the governor studied Clay's face intently. "It is my pleasure, I assure you, señor Ashworth. It is my hope before the evening is concluded, we will have the chance to talk. I, too, have heard much of you."

"It would be my pleasure, sir."

Returning Zamora's measured, almost hostile, stare, Clay nodded, and said, "señor Zamora?"

"Mr. Ashworth?" Zamora coolly responded, as he quickly moved to Consuela Salinas's side.

Two things struck Clay Ashworth about the man, Zamora. The first was his possessive attitude toward Consuela Salinas—an attitude that Clay found surprisingly annoying. The second was the nearly total lack of accent in the man's voice. Though obviously Mexican, or Hispanic, Zamora spoke and handled himself like a European: polite enough, but reserved in his evaluation and not too concerned about Ashworth's impression. That Zamora would make a dangerous enemy was more than apparent. He was undoubtedly a man to be reckoned with, to be approached with caution. And that he harbored an immediate dislike for Clay was unmistakable.

Sensing the tension between the two men, Mary Gwin gestured and said, "Well . . . yes . . . shall we mingle with the other guests, then?"

At dinner, Consuela Salinas sat across the long, sumptuously-laden table at the far end from Ashworth, at Mary Gwin's right hand, and the two had talked animatedly through the meal. Though Clay could catch only a word now and then through the lively chatter that flooded the table, it was obvious the two women were very close.

"Pardon me, señora," Zamora said, leaning forward to speak around the woman at Clay's right. "Tell me, Mister Ashworth, are you comfortable with all of this talk of secession and of California's independence?" His tone was one of appropriately mild interest—deceptively so. And he spoke just loudly enough to be heard by those at Clay's end of the table, including Gwin at the head of the table and Governor Salinas at the senator's left. "I understand you are from neither the South nor from California, but from one of the western territories."

Catching the intended challenge in Zamora's tone, Clay reached for his wine glass and took a slow, deliberate sip, enjoying the blushing liquid's unique California bouquet. Smiling at señora Salinas at his left, he turned and leaned forward just enough to make eye contact with Zamora. "As I was just saying to señora Salinas, I am from the Utah Territory, to be exact, Mister Zamora." Leaning back and looking across the table at the governor, he continued. "And I think that is where you will find my loyalties lie."

"Well spoken, Mister Ashworth," Governor Salinas said, raising his glass toward Clay in polite salute.

"You are a Mormon, then?"

The throaty, feminine voice from the other end of the table took Clay somewhat by surprise. Though he had watched her throughout the dinner, studying her carefully out of the corner of his eye, he had no idea that Consuela Salinas had been paying him the slightest attention.

"No, Miss Salinas, I am not," Clay responded, surprised at her unexpected intrusion, but delighted at the opportunity to expand his slight acquaintance with her. Keeping his smile cool, he continued, "Believe it or not, one can live in Utah without being a Mormon; the territory covers a great deal of country."

"How very interesting," she said with a beguilingly friendly smile, a smile much like that of a beautiful predator about to pounce. "Word has it, however, that Brigham Young controls the rising and the setting of the sun."

"Oh . . . well," Clay responded, clearing his throat, his eyes alight with opportunity, "when it comes to the exercise of such cosmic powers, señorita, you must not forget the moon and the stars, as well. After all, there are a good many who have no doubt the man is a prophet of God. From someone of such an exalted status," he said, lifting his glass in her direction, "it would only be reasonable, for those who don't know him, to expect such omnipotence."

"Mmm . . . then you are familiar with this Brigham Young fellow?" the governor asked, cutting off any further response from his daughter and casting a mildly disapproving glance in her direction.

"Actually, Governor, I know him quite well."

"Then, tell us, Mr. Ashworth," Consuela said, ignoring her father's glance, "how can you be loyal to your Utah Territory without first being a Mormon or loyal to Brigham Young—your so-called Prophet of God?"

With Consuela Salinas's mildly abrupt challenge, the dinner table fell silent, each guest turning to watch the exchange that was developing between the big Utahan and the obviously intelligent daughter of the gobernador of Sonora, Mexico.

"You must forgive my daughter, Mister Ashworth," the Governor said, his tone mild in its reproof. "I am afraid her enthusiasm for politics at times exceeds my own."

"Believe me, jefe, I take no offense at Miss Salinas's interest. Quite the opposite, I assure you."

"How gallant, Mister Ashworth," Consuela said, her smile not fully camouflaging the edge in her voice. "But you have not answered the question. He controls the territory, does he not?"

Clay Ashworth had always prided himself in his ability to assess people, but looking into the beautiful face of Consuela Salinas, across a table crowded with some of the most powerful people in the California separatist movement, he knew he had taken too much for granted where she was concerned—perhaps dangerously so. Having allowed himself to become distracted by her undeniably appealing physical characteristics, he now found himself surprised at her obviously superior intelligence, her forward attitude, and her aggressive and dangerous challenge to his loyalties.

"I'm sorry, Mister Ashworth," she said, arching one delicate eyebrow, "have I embarrassed you?"

"Not at all, señorita Salinas. The truth is, I—"

"Word has come to us in Mexico that this Brigham Young fellow stands with *your* Union," Zamora cut in, sensing an opportunity to attack this big gringo for whom he had taken so sudden a dislike. The man was not to be trusted.

Ashworth leaned back while a servant removed his plate and placed a dessert dish before him. Ignoring Zamora's challenge and smiling at Consuela, he said, "I assure you, Miss Salinas, I am not a Mormon. And while I have great respect for Brigham Young, I do not attribute cosmic powers to the man."

"How very interesting," she retorted. "But he does have rather cosmic political powers, does he not? And señora Gwin tells me that you seem to have some definite opinions about the war and the secession of *your* southern states."

"He does, and it is not *my* Union, nor are they *my* southern states, Miss Salinas," Clay said, finding her challenge a little too presumptuous and allowing a slight edge to creep into his voice. "Frankly, being out here, I find the war to be of little immediate concern—to me, at least. I, of course, can't speak for Brigham Young."

"The truth is, gobernador," Senator Gwin cut in, "Clay is a rancher, and he owns one of the largest spreads in the Utah Territory, where he runs very large herds of cattle, I understand."

"Ugh, boots." Conseula groaned, pulling a face at her friend, Mary Gwin. Though the comment was directed at her hostess, she had intended that it be heard by all at the table, especially Clay Ashworth.

Totally at a loss to understand the meaning of Consuela's last remark, Clay turned toward Governor Salinas. "That's right. As Senator and Mrs. Gwin are well aware, I am a rancher in the Utah Territory, and a happy one. And though Brigham Young is a man of, what some might think to be, inordinate power," he said, with a glance at Consuela, "I certainly don't mind telling you, Governor, why I regard him so highly: he never bothers me— except, perhaps, to occasionally ask my opinion on some matter or other. I have lived and ranched in the territory for a good many years now, and I have yet to be bothered by him or his people. The honest truth is, my interests coincide with Brigham Young's only in wanting to be left alone, to live my life as I see fit. No one understands that desire better than he."

"It would be wonderful if we all had such luxury, Mister Ashworth," Consuela Salinas said, the tone of her voice deceptively innocent. "But isn't that truly the point of your southern rebellion?"

"Our daughter means no offense, señor Ashworth," señora Salinas said with an apologetic smile. "And we should allow you to enjoy your dessert."

"Indeed," the gobernador agreed cheerfully. "But one must recognize that there is great confusion abroad because of the American war in the East. It leaves this part of the world in a good deal of turmoil. That is so, is it not, Count de Moppausaunte?"

"It does, indeed," the Count quickly responded, lifting his napkin and dabbing daintily at his lips. "As you all know—with the possible exception of Mr. Ashworth, of course—what is needed in order to bring stability to this unfortunate hemisphere is the best of European influence."

For a brief moment, Clay had allowed himself to relax, thinking the gobernador's question had diverted everyone's attention to the French dandy sitting at Mary Gwin's left at the foot of the table. It had come as a welcome relief, but with de Moppausaunte's obviously disdainful slur, all eyes again turned to the Utah rancher.

Yet neither the Count's demeaning remark nor the renewed attention was nearly as annoying as the expectant smile that now animated Consuela Salinas's lovely face. But what irritated him most was the fact that she had felt free to attack him in such a forward manner to begin with. This woman—this girl, really—had forced him to keep on his toes almost from the moment she had entered the house. What was even more annoying was the fact that she was obviously enjoying his aggravation.

Why had she chosen to focus on him? Why did she care one way or the other how he felt about anything? The Gwins obviously saw him as a friend and confidant and, yet, he had been challenged right from the first. Before she had walked into the Gwin mansion, he had had no idea Maria Emilea Consuela Salinas even existed, nor she him, he supposed. What kind of game was the woman playing, anyway? And what for?

Zamora's voice broke into Clay's thoughts. "I am surprised that you have no response to the Count de Moppausaunte's comment, Mr. Ashworth."

"Response to what, señor Zamora?" Clay said, staring into the Mexican's smirk. "Do his comments about French or European influence in this hemisphere—despite his appalling ignorance of the Monroe Doctrine—require some response from me? Or are you referring to his comment on my supposed lack of understanding? Or perhaps you refer to my disinterest in what he thinks, one way or the other—on this or any other matter."

The bluntness of Clay's response caused a gasp from one of the women on the other side of the table, and de Moppausaunte's face seemed to drain of color.

Zamora, obviously a man unused to such an abrupt response from someone he considered to be an inferior gringo, twisted in his seat, his smirk turning to something dark. "Then perhaps, señor, you will respond if I—"

"Oh, gentlemen," Mary Gwin broke in, "I declare, there are times when dinner conversation just doesn't go quite like it should. Isn't that right, dear?" she said, flashing a quick look of exasperation at her husband.

"Well . . . Mary, dear . . . I frankly would like to hear Clay's opinion on the matter," Gwin said, clearing his throat. "Another time, maybe." He rose from his chair.

"But, perhaps, gentlemen, we should continue our conversation in the library over brandy and cigars, and the women can retire to the drawing room and enjoy what is left of the evening."

"That would be lovely," Mary responded, the relief in her voice a little too obvious. "Shall we, then?" she said, as de Moppausaunte rushed to help her with her chair.

Troubled with how the evening was going, Clay hung back in leaving the table. He was not anxious to rush into the library and hoped that by the time all of the men were settled, each with a snifter of brandy and a cigar to enjoy, feelings would have cooled and the topic of conversation might shift in a less provocative direction. Unfortunately, it was not to be so.

As the group noisily crossed the large hallway, the women turning toward the drawing room and the men entering the large, book-lined library, Clay felt pressure on his elbow and Zamora's breath on his neck. "Your eyes offend me, señor," the Mexican said, his voice low and threatening.

"My eyes offend you?" he asked, twisting his arm from the man's grasp, his mounting irritation with Zamora's presumptions more than obvious. The hall had emptied and the two men stood alone, almost toe to toe. "What are you talking about, Zamora?"

"I am talking about señorita Salinas."

"Señorita Salinas? What about her?"

"Keep your vulgar eyes off of her, and do not approach her for any reason, señor."

"Wait a minute, Zamora. You are—"

A knife glinted in the dim light of the hallway as Zamora slowly raised it toward Clay's chin, their bodies blocking the view of anyone who might have been watching. "You have been warned. Try not to make it too easy for me, señor. Your blood on my hands would feel good."

Shoving the blade aside, Clay stepped closer to Zamora, knocking the man slightly off balance. "Now you listen to me, Mister," he said, his deep voice close to a snarl. "You put that knife back where you found it, or this expensive carpet you're standing on is going to have somebody's blood all over it, and it's as likely to be yours as it is mine. And it just might be easier for me than for you. You understand me?"

Before a surprised Zamora could recover from Clay's unexpectedly aggressive response, the two were interrupted by an explosion of raucous laughter from the library, and Senator Gwin stepped into the wide doorway, a brandy snifter in each hand, gesturing the two men into the comfortable room. "Come on in here you two. I need some support."

"Yes!" Governor Salinas, hollered from his place by the

crackling fire across the room, his face alight with laughter. "You really must hear this story, Mr. Ashworth."

As Gwin handed the two men their drinks and turned to join the others, Clay elbowed Zamora slightly, causing the man's brandy to slop over the edge of the small snifter and splatter across his hand and onto his highly polished boots. Zamora swore softly, stepping backward and lifting his glass in an effort to steady the liquid and prevent further spillage.

"And another thing, Zamora," Clay said, threateningly, almost too low to be heard, but close enough to the man's ear. "I'll look at her when I please and how I please, and I'll talk with her *any* time *I* choose. And, if I were you, I wouldn't presume to speak to me of this again. Understand?" Turning, Clay strode into the library.

As Clay entered the comfortable library, Senator Gwin was filling the last of his guests' brandy snifters, their laughter beginning to ebb. "Well, gentlemen," he said, setting the decanter on the desk, "so much for my token imprisonment. Our good Senator Broderick has gone to his final reward, and that is reimbursement enough for me for whatever time I spent in a Union jail. In the end, it was well worth it.

"Though some division remains in this state over the question of slavery, it is safe to say California is solidly Democratic. Try as they might, the Unionists will not prevent California from achieving her true independence, even if we are forced to divide the state in half. But never fear, I'm certain that such a course will prove to be unnecessary. Why?" he asked rhetorically. "Because most of the men in positions of power and influence in this state are men of southern birth—many of them right here in this room this evening."

"Here, here!" several responded.

Clay was surprised at the number of men in the library. The

dinner had clearly been for a few select friends of the Gwins. The rest had arrived for the after-dinner political conversations, and the entertainment that would come later.

"Clearly," Gwin continued expansively, "southern interests and beliefs guide our affairs."

"If anyone needs proof of that," an older, distinguished-looking man said from the opposite side of the library, "think what it means for the Unionists left in our state that Lincoln only garnered a measly eight hundred vote plurality. There would certainly appear to be little support for the Union out here."

"My friends," Gwin said, lifting his drink, "I give you California. Soon to be an independent state of the Pacific."

"I think you are most assuredly correct, Senator Gwin."

All eyes turned to the doorway, where an elegantly dressed gentleman was handing his wrap to one of the servants.

"Milton! How good to see you," Gwin said, extending his hand as others joined in the greeting. "Gentlemen, I'm sure you all know my colleague, Senator Milton Latham. Am I to understand you have come all the way from Washington, D. C. just to correct me, Senator?" Gwin said, jokingly.

"It's good I arrived when I did, William. Someone must keep my honored colleague in line," Latham said, with a friendly, truly contagious laugh.

"How so, sir?" Gwin said, laughing with the others.

In a more serious tone, Latham replied, "As you and others here well know, I have long advocated splitting California in half. That was my position as governor, and I'm still convinced that might be the best solution for gaining some stability out here, regardless of what happens back east.

"As I'm sure you are all well aware, things are going well

enough for the South. Our southern boys, despite the Union blockade, seem to be keeping the Union's troops on the run."

A murmur of approval swept through the room.

"Please excuse my intrusion, Senator Latham," Governor Salinas said, his tone somewhat apologetic. "I am a foreigner here, but the people of Mexico have always felt a sense of unity with your interests here in California."

The irony of Salinas's statement caused a smattering of friendly laughter and applause to erupt in the crowded library.

"Our interests remain much alike," the governor continued, a smile lighting his handsome face. "Therefore, in Mexico we are most interested in the progress of your Civil War. The likelihood of European intervention is very real, is it not?"

Latham responded. "It's hard to tell, Governor. The boarding of the British packet, *Trent,* and the recent seizure of our commissioners, James Mason and John Slidell, by Union forces have shown just how far the tyrannical Union government is prepared to go in strangling our efforts to secure our independence. It was nothing less than an act of war against Britain, but it remains to be seen just what the long-term effect might be."

"But the war—how goes the war?" another interjected.

"As I said, it goes well enough. With our victory at Ball's Bluff in October, we have gained more momentum, and old Stonewall Jackson remains the scourge of northern Virginia. Poor Lincoln, his biggest mistake seems to have been his appointment of that rooster McClellan to head his military efforts. I'm told there is real tension between the two. McClellan is a great planner, but so far not much of a doer—thank goodness. On the negative side, I'm sorry to say, gentlemen, the Union blockade is likely to turn into a real stranglehold.

"One can only say for sure, it's going to be a long and bloody conflict. That's why I can't help but feel that if California were bifurcated, the southern half pro-slavery, and the north not so, then regardless of the outcome of the war back east, we would enjoy some stability out here."

"But, Senator," Gwin offered, "why divide our spoils? As you yourself have said, this state has resources not duplicated by any other. We are more than qualified for independence. Why weaken our position by yielding any territory to those who now support the Union?"

"Yes, Senator Latham," another guest said. "Senator Gwin may well be correct. Both the North and the South have shown themselves to be incapable of living in any kind of harmony. Wouldn't such a division place two Californias in exactly the same position, one to another?"

As the debate heated, Clay unobtrusively slipped from the room, not wanting to be drawn into any controversy that might lead to inquiries into his background and loyalties—at least no more so than had already occurred. His having become the center of attention at the dinner table was just the kind of thing he sought to avoid.

California was a hotbed of dissidence in which everyone was suspect and where loyalties were a matter of momentary expediency. No one was to be trusted, and the Gwin home was a cauldron of intrigue, as the evening's events had shown. Given his purpose in California, it was imperative that Clay avoid any controversy, and that was best accomplished by keeping to himself as much as possible. Under such circumstances the wisest course was to be trusted by a powerful few and remain a stranger to all others.

"Are you leaving us so soon, señor Ashworth?" It was she, and her voice stopped him, almost reflexively, somewhere between flight and fight.

*Damnation,* Ashworth thought. He had just reached the entryway, thinking he would be successful in slipping out of the house without being seen. Though he very much wanted to see Consuela Salinas again, this was neither the time nor the circumstance.

"I'm afraid so, señorita Salinas, I—"

"I was hoping," she cut in abruptly, her eyes flicking in warning to the hallway behind him, "that we might have the opportunity to speak once more, señor Ashworth. Much remains to be said, I think."

Clay studied the beautiful face, the warning in her eyes, then glanced over his shoulder. Zamora was standing outside the library door watching them.

"Nothing would give me greater pleasure," he said, reaching down to take her hand, his voice loud enough to be heard by Zamora. "I will speak to your father."

Lightly squeezing his hand, she glanced toward the library. Zamora was no longer to be seen. "You must be careful, Clay Ashworth," she said, her eyes searching his. "Things here are not always what they seem."

Before he could respond, she quickly turned and entered the parlor where the other women were gathered.

# CHAPTER 13

★ ★ ★

MORNING ALWAYS CAME EARLY for Clay Ashworth. This one seemed unusually so, since he had found it difficult falling asleep when he had finally retired for the night. Before drifting off, he had lain in the darkness staring at the ceiling, thinking of Consuela Salinas, as he had every night since that magic evening he first saw her.

What kind of woman was she? There was certainly much more to her than her stunning beauty. She was not just smart; her bright and challenging conversation at the Gwin dinner table left no doubt that she was possessed of a marked intelligence. But what had she been up to in challenging him the way she had? Why her interest in him and where he came from and where his loyalties lay? Her antipathy toward Brigham Young was not hard to understand, given her almost ungovernable attitude as a woman. She had been more than adamant in her challenges.

Why? And why him? And then, why had she gone out of her way to stop him in the hallway and warn him of Zamora's presence?

Whatever else she might be, the woman was intriguing: beautiful, intelligent, well-informed, and sufficiently self-possessed to challenge any man—all of whom she obviously considered herself the equal. That she was, Clay Ashworth had no doubt, and it was a quality he greatly admired. What would it take to win such a woman? With Consuela Salinas at his side, a man could own the world. But then, it would probably take at least that, not only to win her, but to keep her.

He and Chet Langtree arose just as the fog densely covering San Francisco Bay had begun to take on the delicate hues that suggested the impending sunrise already tinting the peaks of the Diablo range to the east. Their stomachs growling, the two quickly bathed, shaved, dressed, and hurried down to the luxurious dining room of the newly opened Saint Francis Hotel, where they had been staying as Senator Gwin's guests.

Of the nearly sixty hotels in the booming city, Gwin had put them up at the best. Located on the corner of Grant Avenue and Clay, the St. Francis was rapidly becoming the most luxurious and cosmopolitan hotel of the 1860s—in San Francisco or anywhere else.

In the elegant dining room, the conversation of the two had been uncommonly laconic, each concentrating on a sumptuous breakfast of eggs, bacon, sausage, hash-browned potatoes, toast, and a colorful variety of fruit.

Pushing his plate away, Clay sipped his coffee and watched Chet over the rim of the expensive China cup. Though he had always liked Langtree and respected him as a thoroughly competent ranch hand, one he inherently knew he could trust, he had not come to fully appreciate how intelligent and dedicated the man was, and how much he genuinely liked him, until they had ridden and fought together on this trip.

Sensing Clay's stare, Chet looked up, and asked, "Somethin' wrong, boss?"

"Oh . . . sorry," Clay said, replacing the cup on its dainty saucer. "I didn't mean to stare. I was just thinking that I really did not want anyone with me on this trip, but you'll never know how valuable you've been, Chet, and how glad I am that you're here."

"Wouldn't have settled fer less, an' neither would the rest of the boys back home."

"I know," Clay said, leading forward on his elbows, "and . . . well . . . I'm grateful."

Somewhat embarrassed at Clay's forthrightness, Chet lifted the heavy silver coffee pot the waiter had left for them. "Some more coffee?"

Clay nodded and pushed his cup forward. "Chet, I've got to meet a contact in a few minutes down in the livery stable. I need to start getting word back about what's going on out here. I'm supposed to meet—"

"Ah, Clay, there you are."

"Oh, nuts," Clay whispered, with a smile and wave, as Gwin and another gentleman threaded their way across the crowded room toward them. Leaning toward Chet, in a confidential tone, Clay said, "Listen, Chet, if I get stuck here, you've got to get down to the livery for me. Go the stall where our horses are and you'll be contacted."

"Yessir, but what'll—"

"Just tell him what you know, and—"

"Clay, I haven't seen you since the dinner party last weekend," Gwin said, taking a seat and motioning the man with him into the empty chair next to Clay. "Chet? Good morning to you, sir.

"Gentlemen, I'd like you to meet Congressman John Burch."

As Clay and Chet dropped their napkins and started to rise, Burch thrust out his hand and said, "Please, gentlemen, not on my account. It's good to meet you both."

"These are the two I was telling you about, John," Gwin continued. "They are men we need and can take into our confidence." Nodding toward Burch, Gwin continued, "John, here, arrived late last night on the packet from Panama. He has spent the last two years in Washington as a member of Congress, but given all that has happened in the past few months, has decided that the future looks better to him out here in California."

"Seems true of a lot of folks lately," Chet said, pushing his empty coffee cup away.

While not unfriendly, Burch's attitude was reserved and his glance appraising. "Senator Gwin has told me a good deal about the two of you."

"Well," Gwin responded, "I can honestly say, had it not been for them, in all likelihood Mary and I would not be here today, John."

Clay watched Burch closely. The man seemed too reserved in his demeanor, perhaps more so with strangers, but that he appeared unwilling to take others at face value, especially when given such an obvious endorsement, made Clay uneasy. "We had a few exciting hours together, certainly," Clay responded, smiling at Gwin.

Turning to Chet, Gwin continued, "And how was the food here this morning?"

"Senator Gwin," Chet said, with an exaggerated sigh, "I can truthfully say I ain't had a breakfast like this since I left Texas, and that's true of just about every meal we've had since we got here."

"Amen to that," Clay added, glancing sideways at Chet with a barely perceptible lift of his chin.

"It's a pleasure meetin' you, Congressman," Chet said, struggling to slide his chair away from the table, "but if you all will excuse me, I've got some things that need doin'." Then nodding at Clay, "I'll see you later, boss."

Rising with Chet, Gwin said, "If you are through, too, Clay, we can all walk out together. Events in the East are beginning to move rapidly—accelerating, in fact. With the Confederacy's rather conspicuous victories these past months, I'm one who feels the war may be over sooner than any of us anticipated, and much remains to be done here in California. There is someone I want you to meet. He's here at the St. Francis, as well—right upstairs."

The broad hallway of the top floor of the St. Francis ended with two heavy, ornately-carved wood doors, above which were engraved the words, *Presidential Suite.* The stateliness of the place left no question as to the importance of whoever was staying on the other side of those double doors, which in almost immediate response to Gwin's urgent knock, swung open, and an officer wearing the uniform of a Union major, recognizing Gwin, stepped aside.

"Well, Gwin, it's about time," a deeply masculine voice said from the bedroom at the left. Entering the large sitting room, the speaker wore the uniform of a full Confederate general. "I've been waiting all morning, man."

Clay was immediately taken with the presence of the Confederate officer. Standing well over six feet, broad in the shoulders, dark and handsome, with an elegant handlebar mustache and a broad forehead that bespoke superior intelligence, the man had a military bearing that caused him to dominate the entire room. The oak-leafed emblem of rank on his collar and the piping on his sleeves were not necessary in determining that here was a leader of men.

"My apologies, General Johnston," Gwin responded, his voice even and certain, attempting to match Johnston's level of dominance. "What with the press of events, I have had much to do, and I was not informed of your completely unexpected arrival until less than an hour ago."

"Well, be that as it may, I've just—who's this?" Johnston said, looking over Gwin's shoulder at Clay and Congressman Burch. "I know Burch, here," he said, dismissively shaking the Congressman's hand, then turning to Clay. "But I don't know this gentleman."

"Excuse me, General, I—"

Stepping around Gwin and seizing Johnston's hand, Clay said, "I'm delighted to meet you, General Johnston. I'm Clay Ashworth."

Johnston frowned, his eyes penetrating. "Ashworth? Ashworth. Do I know you, Mister Ashworth?"

"I doubt that you do, sir. Though I must confess, there have been times when I've wished I'd had the opportunity."

"Oh, really? What would have—"

Attempting to regain some control of the situation, Gwin broke in, "Clay is from up in the Utah Territory—a place you're not unfamiliar with, General."

"Indeed," he said, a frown darkening his handsome face. "One of Brigham Young's boys, then." It was a statement, not a question.

"No, sir. I happen to own a ranch south of Great Salt Lake City. Down in what is known as Utah Valley."

"Oh, yes. Now I place you. Your ranch . . . what is it called?"

"We call it *Rancho Los Librados,* General."

"Yes, now I recall. But weren't you—"

"There were few who welcomed what appeared to be a full-scale military invasion, General. Being *one of Brigham Young's boys*," Clay responded with a hint of irritation, "was not a prerequisite."

Responding to Johnston's apparent mistrust, Gwin said, "Clay Ashworth can be trusted, General Johnston. He and his friend saved Mary and myself from sure destruction at the hands of a marauding band of Utes, and I have come to trust him implicitly. He's just the kind of man I—that is to say, we—need here in an independent California."

"Independent California, indeed," Johnston said with irritation, turning from Clay. "We're going to be damned lucky if we're not all hanged in the end, and your independent California's back in the hands of the Mexicans."

Shocked at Johnston's blunt retort, Gwin stammered, "Why, General . . . I'm afraid I don't understand. Things are going so well in the East, one Confederate victory after another. I'm afraid I don't understand."

"Confederate victories be damned, man!" Johnston huffed, turning toward the window, his gaze sweeping the bay. Clasping his hands behind his back, he began pacing the length of the room. "I've just returned from Los Angeles, and I'll tell you, sir, there's the devil to pay for what is happening. It's all too soon!"

"All too soon?" Gwin said, his face coloring with anger and frustration.

"Yes. All too soon. I'm telling you, the attack on Fort Sumter was idiotically premature. It was premature by at least a year."

"You can't be serious, General."

"Serious? I couldn't be more serious," Johnston said, turning to face Gwin. "I'm telling you, Senator, the moment Beauregard ordered Sumter fired upon, the war was lost, let alone our efforts out here in California. If they had just waited. Think, man. The fort was going to be abandoned by April fifteenth. All they had to do was prevent or forestall any Union re-supply effort, not fire on the fort itself—not start a war!"

"Not so, sir. What of—"

"Nothing was accomplished but what others have predicted. We've wantonly swatted at a hornet's nest, and legions that were quiet are going to swarm across us—across the South—and sting us to death. It's just that simple, gentlemen."

"But, General Johnston," Gwin pressed, quickly losing patience with such defeatist talk, "what of Manassas, Bull Run, . . . and Ball's Bluff . . . good grief, General, with the surrender of the federals at Fort Fillmore, we control the New Mexico and Arizona territories . . . and after Wilson's Creek, we control Missouri—everything west of the Mississippi, sir." The words came in an increasing torrent of emotion, serving only to further irritate Johnston.

"Oh, stop and think, man," Johnston snapped, with an irritated, dismissive wave, his blunt attitude that of one well-accustomed to being obeyed. With a sigh that obviously sought patience, he continued, "Senator, when the North gets over the shock of actual hostilities and gets organized, blood is going to be spilled as seldom seen in history; and that, sir, you may write down for your posterity. There is going to be hell to pay before this thing is over.

"All that idiot Beauregard succeeded in doing was to play right into Lincoln's hands—placing the man on the moral high ground."

"The moral high ground, General? Why that's—"

"Don't you see?" Johnston cut in. "Abe Lincoln could not have prepared a better scenario if he had devised it himself."

"But—"

"Now Lincoln the unknown has suddenly become Lincoln the powerful, given the chance to take the offensive without appearing to be on the attack!" Johnston said, his voice cracking. "It's so perfectly simple, you see," he continued, in a somewhat more calm voice. "The South has attacked the North, and the North is morally outraged."

The room had fallen silent, each man reflecting on Johnston's argument. What he said was painfully true, and each in his heart knew it.

Taking a deep breath, Johnston continued, his voice again becoming more strident with each word. "Lincoln can now recruit troops and be successful. He can now use crushing force to put down the South's so-called rebellion."

Pausing to look around the room, he continued, "We lost California by a handful of votes, and we've lost Utah. Utah was my fault, and I freely admit it. But Lincoln *had* to fight the South," Johnston emphasized, slamming his fist into the palm of his hand, "to put an end to any further talk of rebellion and subdue any movement toward secession once and for all. He now has the moral authority to do just that—to take advantage of our weaknesses and our mistakes—and Beauregard handed it to him on a silver platter."

As Gwin sank into a chair, struggling to control his temper, Congressman Burch said, "General, with all due respect, sir, we have the momentum." Waving a pudgy finger in the air, he said with repeated emphasis, "We have the momentum, sir!"

Johnston stopped in mid-stride and turned toward Burch. "Oh, really, Congressman?"

"Indeed we do, sir."

"Momentum? Against what, Congressman? Our beloved agrarian South—almost devoid of industry, with the exception of cotton ginning, of course—our beloved, chivalrous, pre-industrial South against an industrialized North? Against an enemy that can produce the weaponry, heavy and small, and the ammunition—all of the machinery of war, sir—in amounts that will soon overwhelm us like hornets out of their nest? And what will we use in our muskets, sir, cotton bolls?"

Gwin sighed heavily in an effort to control his rising anger, then spat, "The one fact upon which we can all agree is that the war has begun—it is a reality. Recriminations at this point are useless."

"I'm telling you, Gwin, it's all useless," Johnston said. "Until the South fired on Sumter, Lincoln was paralyzed. He would have had to watch us take Utah, New Mexico—even Mexico itself for that matter—and sit with his hands tied. He would have remained paralyzed.

"Now, it doesn't matter what you could do with Sonora, it will remain a part of Mexico—you couldn't defend it if you had it. And, Senator Gwin, what will you do if Mexico marches its troops into California? With the war in the East, who will stop them?"

"Are you suggesting surrender, General Johnston?" Gwin retorted, his emotion rising at the mention of Sonora. "Are you suggesting, sir, that we give up, that it was all just an unfortunate mistake?"

Johnston fell into a chair opposite Gwin. "Don't be absurd, Gwin. You can see how I'm dressed."

Taking a deep breath, Johnston continued, "I have no idea, gentlemen, how you are going to solidify the position of California as an independent state in the Southern Confederacy. I have resigned, as have nearly all those officers who are from the South. And large numbers of our enlisted men have not even bothered to resign. They have simply gone, left in droves, deserted the Army to return east to protect their homes and families. Perhaps *deserted* is not a fair word. They'll fight, and they'll die—for what, I'm not sure."

"There are those here who will fight for California, General," Gwin said evenly.

"Gwin . . . do you have any idea how many men we have lost? How many enlisted men have gone, and those left here with no officer corps to speak of? Do you, sir?"

"Why have so many left, particularly among the enlisted ranks, General?"

"These are simple men, gentlemen," Johnston said, glancing around the room. "Unlike their officers, most are barely literate. They have no knowledge of politics, let alone military strategy. All they know is that their families are in danger. In the face of that, they have no care of what we have been attempting to do here in California—they are frightened for their families. It's as simple as that."

"But . . . but this desertion," Gwin stammered. "It must be stopped, it must—"

"Gentlemen," Johnston cut in, his voice calm, "I have just come from Los Angeles, where I have seen firsthand what is happening. I have witnessed military order and organization fall completely apart as men struggled with their loyalties—and with their friendships as well. In reality it is no different with the enlisted men than it is with their southern officers.

"I spent a great deal of time with Captain Winfield Scott Hancock. I rather doubt any of you know him. Hancock is the quartermaster for this department of the army, a graduate of West

Point, a veteran of the Mexican war, and a Union loyalist, along with a large number of other officers who have served together for years.

"In fact, we had dinner at Win's house," Johnston continued, his mind drifting from the room, "a lovely meal prepared by his wife, Almira, one of the most beautiful women I have ever laid eyes upon. It was, perhaps, the saddest experience I have ever had. All of us, everyone there, recognized that one day we would face each other over some killing ground, not as fellow officers committed to the same noble cause, but as enemies, sworn to kill one another.

"I think it struck Lew Armisted the hardest. He and Win are the closest of friends. They were classmates at West Point, you know," he said, pausing reflectively, a hint of sadness in his voice, "and they fought together in Mexico—I knew them both there." Johnston caught himself and sat up, strength returning to his voice. "Lew's a Virginian, and he has left already, not even bothering to resign, I think."

Gwin drew a deep breath and turned on Johnston. "General, if I didn't know you better, I would swear that you are on the edge of panic."

"Panic? Panic? What are you talking about, Gwin?"

"General Johnston, you have all but declared the war lost, and it has hardly begun. How can that be? Things are not going all that badly in the East. And out here in the West, the so-called buffalo hunters have marched out of Texas and taken the New Mexico Territory. That strikes me as admirable progress, General. All right, what if, for the sake of argument, shooting started a year too early. So what?"

"So what?" Johnston shot back, jumping to his feet, his temper rising. "I just described for you what is happening."

"Even so, things are not going badly back East, or out here in the West for that matter. As a matter of fact they are going quite well. Oh, perhaps there have been some minor setbacks out here, but this state is crawling with southern sympathizers. All they're lacking is leadership, and I fully intend to give them that leadership. We will," Gwin said with emphasis, "make California and Northern Mexico separate and independent, an empire of the West in and of itself. That, sir, you may bank on."

"Gwin," Johnston shot back, his patience growing thinner by the word, "the more I listen to you the more convinced I become that your so-called loyalties to the Confederacy are nothing more than a sham."

Gwin jumped to his feet. "A sham, sir? A sham?"

"Indeed."

"By the eternal, sir," Gwin shot back, his face red with anger, "if an apology is not forthcoming, that statement demands satisfaction."

Alarmed at the growing level of hostility between the two men, Congressman Burch moved toward them in an effort to forestall any physical confrontation. "Gentlemen, gentlemen, please . . . let's remember we're all on the same side here."

"Are we really, Burch?" Johnston said, his voice low and threatening. The general's arm rose slowly from his side and, with an accusing finger pointing like a dueling pistol directly at Gwin's face, he growled, "This man is interested in nothing more nor less than an independent republic, one he can rule himself; and it doesn't matter a whit to him who wins this ill-advised war, the South or the North. If the Honorable Senator Gwin, here," he continued more calmly, turning his back on Gwin and stepping toward the window, "has his way, California will be a part of neither, and I have no intention of apologizing for that statement. Unless, Senator, it is untrue."

"Well, you are right about this much, General," Gwin said, refusing to yield to Johnston's accusations. "I am most assuredly interested in what's best for California."

"Yes, I thought as much," Johnston said without turning.

Letting the general's insulting behavior pass, Gwin looked at Burch and said, "Tell us, Congressman, how far is it from Washington, D. C. out here to San Francisco?"

"Well, what's that got to do with anything?" Johnston blurted, turning from the window with renewed impatience, only to be cut off as Gwin raised his hand for silence and looked at Burch.

"Oh . . . what?" Burch responded. "Say, three thousand miles or so."

"Thereabouts. Three thousand miles, more or less, of nothing but wilderness. I can vouch for that, because my wife and I just crossed it in a stagecoach—the worst trip either of us has ever experienced. West of the Mississippi there is little more than wilderness clear out to the Mormon settlements in the Utah Territory—nothing but wilderness and wild savages. The only realistic way to get out here to California is by steamer to Panama, a dangerous trek through diseased-filled jungles, and another boat trip up the west coast. It takes weeks, sometimes months."

"Well, what's your point, man?" Johnston snapped, sinking into an empty chair.

"My point, General, is that if there is going to be some kind of union, a loose confederacy of some sort is the only arrangement that can work, and, frankly, I have my doubts about that. And to listen to you, there won't be any Confederacy, anyway. How, General, do you expect California to be governed from Washington? How could even a confederacy really work across such a wide, untamed, and very nearly impassable continent? Certainly a federal union such as the North envisions won't."

"I thought as much," Johnston huffed. "You are no more for the Confederacy than you are for the Union, are you?"

"Practically speaking, I really don't see how either can govern here in California. And that is because each state is diverse—diverse people, diverse culture, diverse economic needs, and each state should be left to govern itself accordingly. That's true of the southern states and that's true of California. From a cultural standpoint, California has nothing in common with the states—north or south."

In the silence that filled the room, only the clatter of the traffic in the street below could be heard. Johnston stood and withdrew a paper from his pocket, handing it to Gwin. "Well, let there be no doubt where I stand, sir. As you can plainly see, gentlemen," he said, turning to the others in the room, "and I hope was never in doubt, my allegiance is with the Confederacy.

"As a consequence, I have sent a letter to Hancock as Chief Quartermaster of the District of Southern California, informing him of my actions, and I have so advised the war department. There you have a copy of it. And now that my replacement has arrived, I am leaving immediately for Los Angeles and then on to New Mexico to see if I can be of help there, then on to Richmond."

Gwin looked up from the letter in his hand. "Who has replaced you?"

Ignoring the question, Johnston turned back to the window, and said, "As you know, Senator, I was appointed last January by Secretary Floyd—who knew of my rather pronounced southern sympathies—to become commander of the newly merged military department here in California. It was his hope, as it was mine—and I thought yours, sir—that I could neutralize California and hold it somewhat aloof from whatever hostilities arose—stay neutral until it became feasible to attach the state to the Confederacy. Events have now made that impossible."

Turning to face Gwin, Johnston continued. "My replacement is your worst nightmare, Senator."

"Really," Gwin said, in as casual a manner as possible. "And who might that be?"

"General Edwin V. Sumner, a tough, highly competent cavalry officer, and a Union loyalist to the core."

"It sounds as if you know him."

"Know him? I've known him for years. We were at the Point together, and I fought with him in Mexico. And I'll tell you something else, Senator, there are few men for whom I have more respect."

"A Union loyalist, General?" Gwin asked, incredulously.

"Yes, a Union loyalist," Johnston retorted. "He's a soldier, and they don't come any finer, and that is exactly what is so awful about this war."

"What's so awful, General?" Gwin asked, his eyebrows arched with moral superiority. "The man's the enemy."

"Exactly so, Gwin. This is a war among brothers, among friends, and like most family feuds, it's going to get very nasty."

"Well," Gwin said with dismissal, "had I any choice, his name would have not appeared on any list of worthies. Given all you've said, how tough can one man be? Oh, I know his reputation," Gwin continued, waving his hand in the air, "but it is he that is stepping into a hornet's nest, not I. There is little sympathy in this state for what he stands for, I can assure you."

"You're dead wrong, Gwin," Johnston said. "As I said, he will become your worst nightmare. I'm telling you, all of our efforts at organization, all of our efforts to get this state in the position I thought we were all agreed upon, are all but lost—all the planning, all our labors out the window. One more year and things would have been in order. Now, all of that has been rendered a nullity."

Clearing his throat, one of Johnston's officers interjected, "Bill Grasley and Dan Bryant were shot and killed not too long ago, General."

"Grasley and Bryant, dead? Killed?" Gwin said, turning to the man in disbelief.

"Thank you, Captain," Johnston responded. "Yes, dead. They were shot while on their way to what was supposed to have been a clandestine southern sympathizers' meeting; and to make matters worse, the meeting was broken up and several more men wounded—a few seriously. Things are not so pat, are they, my friend?"

"And Joséph Trumble, sir?"

"Oh, yes. In case you haven't heard, Senator, Trumble was lynched by a Sacramento mob not in sympathy with our cause. And as far as I can tell, no authority has taken a step to bring the culprits to hand."

"Yes, Trumble was a terrible loss. He was the key man in that area. His loss was truly a disaster."

"Exactly. Under these conditions, for me to stay in California would be suicidal. My men and I are leaving right now, before Sumner can find me and place me under arrest, and I suggest you do the same, Gwin, before you find yourself rotting in some federal prison—or worse, dangling from the end of a rope."

"And just where do you propose to go, General?" Gwin asked.

"I told you, Senator," Johnston snapped, his dislike for Gwin more than obvious, "I'm leaving to fight for the South. I for one, sir, have loyalties that extend beyond my own selfish ambitions."

Ignoring Johnston's insult, Gwin responded smugly, "Well, sir, it sounds to me as if you really don't believe all is lost, General—despite all of your so-called setbacks."

Johnston studied Gwin's face, looking for some clue that the man understood the gravity of their situation. Taking a deep breath, Johnston said, "Senator, there's one chance, and it's probably the Confederacy's only chance, and that's where we're headed now. I'm taking what men I can—a hundred, a hundred and fifty, I doubt I can find more—to join the Texas regulars in New Mexico. If we can hold New Mexico, perhaps we can pull some of the fat out of the fire.

"As for you, here in California," Johnston said, glancing at the others, his meaning obvious, "I think you're all dead. You're just not smart enough to fall down."

Before Gwin could respond, Johnston spun on his heel, and with his men following, left the room, slamming the big double doors behind them for emphasis.

# CHAPTER 14

★  ★  ★

Leaving the St. Francis, Chet hurried to the bottom of the hill and crossed the damp, cobbled street. The city was still locked in an early-morning, deathlike shroud of fog as he made his way to the livery stable where he and Clay had boarded their horses.

The growing light of morning had barely penetrated the darkness, and the earthy, pungent smell of the horses occupying a generous number of stalls permeated the spacious barn. Hurrying along the wide center aisle separating the two rows of stalls, Chet found his horse's stall and stepped inside it where he gave the animal a gentle pat and began currying it with a stiff brush. He worked intently but slowly, listening for any sound in the building that might not fit, might be out of place, a signal of danger. There were noises, but they were those of horses in other stalls restlessly waiting to be fed.

"Where's Ashworth?"

Though not unexpected, the sound of the gravelly voice from the adjoining stall caused Chet to jump and instinctively reach for his gun. "Jehoshaphat, man, can't you give a body some warnin'?" Chet said, beginning to turn toward the voice behind him. "Clay couldn't come."

"Don't turn around," the voice said harshly. "Ashworth knew I was to meet him here. Where is he? He's supposed to be my contact. It was important that he meet me, and he knew it. Where is he?"

Chet took a deep breath and leaned against his horse, looking over its back, away from the unnatural-sounding voice and into the growing light at the front of the barn. "Gwin showed up with some other feller—a congressman, or was one—and wanted him to meet somebody else upstairs in the hotel. Clay told me t' meet yuh here."

"Any idea who?"

"Fella's name was Burch."

"I know Burch," the man said, impatiently. "Watch him, but he's not a heavyweight in all of this. I'm asking, who has Ashworth gone to meet?"

"Never said—leastways, not while I was there."

"You tell Ashworth next time we're to meet, he's to be here and not send someone in his stead."

The man's bluntness was annoying, but there was something else that troubled Chet. The voice had a familiar ring to it. It was obvious the man was speaking unnaturally, disguising his voice. Still, it was bothersome—familiar . . . something. Chet was positive he had spoken with this fella before, but where? When?

"Mister, you just hold on a minute," Chet said, his patience growing short. "This here's how it's gonna be whether you like it or not. Clay ain't here, not because he don't want t' be, but because it looked like he'd better go along with Gwin. Now, do yuh want to do business or not? If so, just speak up, or else let's stop wastin' each other's time."

"Ashworth's to get word back that Gwin's setting things up to split California away as an independent republic."

"Clay's already figgered that much out for hisself," Chet said, shortly. "Gwin's really taken him into his confidence."

"Not as far as you two might think. Remember, I know Gwin. And I know him much better than the two of you. He's not to be trusted."

"Just who the devil are you, anyway?" Chet said, half turning.

"I told you not to turn around. You don't need to know who I am," the man said abruptly. "You just tell Ashworth I said not to take anything for granted and not to underestimate Gwin. The man's shrewd. Don't trust him any farther than you would a rattlesnake. He'll use you and Ashworth just like he uses everybody else, then he'll get rid of you—one way or the other."

"I'll tell him," Chet said, swallowing a growing sense of anger at the man's presumption. "But, mister, you better understand something yourself: Clay Ashworth's no fool."

Ignoring Chet's petulant response, the man cleared his throat, forcing his voice lower, and said, "Two points need to be made with Ashworth's superiors: First, Gwin talks as if he's fully in support of the Confederacy, but the truth is, he supports it only as it suits his purposes. There's no mistaking the fact he has done all he can to encourage the war between the states, and he wants the South to win at all costs, but the end of it won't be a Confederacy that includes California. What he wants is an independent Republic of the Pacific that will include both California and Sonora, Mexico.

"Second, as a part of this, while he was in Kansas and

Missouri, Gwin met with Governor Jackson and Lieutenant Governor Reynolds. Washington needs to know that Jackson is doing all he can to get Union arms and ammunition into the hands of the secessionists, and they'll do all they can to keep that area in constant turmoil. By now most of the arms and ammunition in Kansas are probably already in the hands of the rebels, and those materials will be used to close off the West to the Union and guarantee its resources to the Confederacy."

"How sure are you of that?" Chet asked.

"Positive. Make certain Ashworth gets that word back as quickly as possible. But they need to understand the end of it won't be a Confederacy that includes California. I'm telling you, Gwen's interested in the Confederacy only as it suits his purposes."

"Is that it?"

"No. There's one more thing."

"And what might that be?"

"The U. S. Army out here is in a state of complete confusion, if not outright disintegration, and that plays right into Gwin's hands. It's a snarled-up mess, desertions right and left—mostly southern boys, but officers and enlisted men alike. A lot of northerners are looking to leave, too. The war back East has made a real mess out of the army, and Gwin knows it and will take full advantage of it. He's already making plans to do just that.

"Tell Ashworth to get word of all of this back where it needs to go as fast as possible. He'll know what I mean."

"I'll tell him. Now, since you know so much about what's goin' on out here, let me ask you a question or two."

"Make it quick."

"Well, there's a real bad hombre with Salinas, feller by the name of Zamora. I don't know—"

"José Rodriguez Zamora," the man said, resignation in his voice.

"That's his name, alright. Clay's already had a run-in with him. Seems this Zamora feller thinks Clay's got eyes for that young Salinas gal. He's already threatened him with a knife."

"Tell Ashworth not to underestimate Zamora. No one seems to know much about him—I certainly don't. My hunch is he may, in fact, be the real moving force in this Mexican arrangement. But what we need to know is whose side he's on—Salinas's or Gwin's. Or is he in it for himself? He's too cozy with certain French officials—that we know for certain. Right now, Ashworth's probably in a better position to find out more than anyone else. I can't get too near Zamora. But tell Ashworth to trust the man like a coiled rattlesnake. Find out what's going on and who's pulling the strings."

"I think Clay has that much figured out for hisself. Zamora's probably in thick with the French."

"Tell him, if he must, to find a way to accompany Salinas and his party back to Mexico." The voice was again deeper and more raspy. "Any kind of a Mexican alliance with the California separatists has got to be stopped—and as soon as possible."

"They've pulled out for Mexico by now. Leastways that was their plan."

"I know that. Tell Ashworth to find an excuse to get down there. He's got to prevent any alliance from developing or solidifying between Gwin and Salinas. Furthermore, he's got to watch Zamora, and if necessary, somehow eliminate him."

"Eliminate him?"

"You heard what I said. *Eliminate him,* neutralize him—whatever. Just get him out of the picture."

"Anything else?"

"I'll be in touch."

"I'll tell him. He's gonna want to know when we can expect to hear from you."

Half turning, Chet asked again, but the only sounds were those of the restless horses and the heavy front doors of the big barn grinding inward as a stable hand opened the place for the day's business.

★　★　★

"That miserable, rotten traitor," Gwin exploded, as the double doors slammed behind Johnston and his entourage. His jaw clenched and his hands clasped behind his back, Gwin growled, "The man's given up. He's a fool."

"I may be wrong," Clay said, watching Gwin closely, "but I have had some experience with Johnston—much more than I would have liked—and if I'm convinced of one thing, it is that our General Johnston there is no fool."

"Ah," Gwin said, waving his hand in angry dismissal, "the man's a pessimistic fool." Turning to face Clay and Burch, he said, "If I've ever seen a man on the edge of panic, gentlemen, it's General Johnston."

"Well, Senator," Clay said, with a deep sigh, "the man's wrong about one thing—dead wrong."

"Only one?" Gwin said, the look on his face hard to decipher.

"At least one, Senator. It's never too late—not for us here, not for the South, nor for anything else. The only thing that can defeat a man like Johnston, or us, is inaction. It may have defeated him—I can't say—but there's no excuse for it to overcome us."

"That's the kind of talk I like to hear, Clay," Gwin said, turning toward Burch. "And what do you think, Congressman?"

When the door had slammed behind Johnston and his men,

Burch had slumped morosely in a large chair and sat staring at the floor. Looking up at Gwin, he said, "It can't be denied that much of what he said is true, Senator."

"What?" Gwin said, a dark look crossing his face.

"What's the point, William? Johnston's no fool," Burch said, his voice rising. "Why, he's considered by many to be one of the brightest lights in the military. He may be right. Things are starting to cave in out here, what with all that has happened recently—the wholesale desertions, Trumble lynched, Grasley and Bryant dead, and who knows what else."

"I can't believe what I'm hearing," Gwin said, taking a seat across the coffee table from Burch. "Look, John, things are not going that badly in the East. Why, they're going quite well, as a matter of fact. You know as well as I do, the Confederacy has won some impressive early battles.

"Now is not the time to let Johnston's pessimism get to you— to any of us. Maybe there have been some setbacks out here, but this state is alive with southern sympathizers, and I intend to provide them the leadership they are looking for."

"But what about this new general?" Burch asked, anxiously. "What's his name?"

"Sumner, Edwin V. Sumner," Gwin said, his impatience with Burch growing. "Why? What about him?"

"General Johnston called him your worst nightmare."

"How big a threat can this Sumner be, anyway?" Clay chimed in. "This whole thing has just gotten started—on both coasts. Now is not the time to panic, Congressman. What we need right now is some real leadership—regardless of Sumner or anyone else."

Gwin turned, studying Clay's determined face, seeing him in

somewhat of a new light. "Yes, Clay, that's right. I really had no idea you were all that committed."

"Neither did I, frankly," Clay said, leaning back in the soft chair. "At least, not until this morning. Oh, don't misunderstand. I've always felt that people ought to be free to go their own way, to associate with whom they please, and especially to be governed as they choose. But, somehow, listening to Johnston, things suddenly began to solidify within me."

"Oh, really?" Gwin said, a lingering doubt just below the surface of his voice.

Clay got up and turned toward the window. "It just struck me, Senator. Your argument about the distance between Washington, D.C. and San Francisco is so obvious, one wonders why others can't see it."

"That's all true enough," Burch said, with impatience. "What's your point?"

"My point, Congressman, is that a confederacy is the only form of government that can possibly work over such a wide expanse, just as the Senator has pointed out. How can it not be seen? How *do* they expect to govern California from Washington—or any other state for that matter? Well, the answer is obvious, they can't. That's the Senator's meaning," Clay said, nodding toward Gwin. "Each state is different—different people, different culture, different economic needs, and each state should be left to govern itself accordingly—and that idea, sir, is worth fighting for, and not at all unconstitutional."

Gwin sucked in a deep breath and began pacing the room. "Exactly, and a bloody fight it's going to be."

"That goes without saying, Senator, and it has just begun," Clay said.

"That, gentlemen, is why I'm not ready to roll over and play dead just because Johnston has decided all is lost and there's a new general in town. The first shots have only just been fired."

Gwin spun about and continued, his face flushed with renewed excitement. "Look, Clay, I can't leave now to go to Mexico. I need to stay here and start consolidating support. You and Chet go."

"Me and Chet? But—"

"Clay, there are few men I would trust more than you. You've got the whole picture. If California is ever to be fully independent, we need Sonora, and to get that, I need Salinas's complete cooperation."

"Well, you've got that, haven't you?" Clay said, getting to his feet. "I got the impression you two were in tight together."

"I think we are, but who knows about Mexicans? The French are down there doing what they can to expand their influence. I think I can trust Salinas, but I'll tell you frankly, I don't trust Zamora. I really don't know where his loyalties lie. I wouldn't be surprised if he weren't in cahoots with the French. One thing is obvious, though, the man has too much influence over the governor."

"But if we—"

"Clay," Gwin said, rounding the coffee table and placing a hand on Clay's shoulder, "that's why I need you in Mexico. Get down there and find out who and what that miserable Zamora fellow is. Then, if it's called for, neutralize him. But most of all, make sure Salinas is solidly in our corner."

"Alright, we'll go—leave before first light tomorrow. But we'll need supplies, lots of them—enough to last for at least a couple of months. That includes a generous supply of ammunition, a couple of extra horses—good riding stock—and a couple of strong pack mules with plenty of bottom."

"No problem. Now, let's get out of here. By the time we turn in tonight, you'll have everything you need and more. We can do this, Clay. I'm convinced of it."

★ ★ ★

Before first light the next morning, Clay leaned over the back of the pack mule he and Chet had just finished loading. "And that's all he had to say?"

"Yessir, that's about it. Watch out for Zamora, and get word back to the right people. Everything else, you already know."

"I'll take care to do both—as quickly as possible."

"Who was that feller, anyway?"

"Well," Clay said, cinching a rope tight. "He's a Pinkerton agent who has been secretly keeping Gwin under surveillance for some time, now. That's all I know, and I don't want to know any more than that."

"Suits me, I reckon."

"Chet, I need you to get back home and get telegrams off to both Lincoln and Pinkerton. Make a full report to both. Here's some notes. Also, report to Brigham Young on just what's been happening here. One way or the other, all of this will have an impact on him and his people. He needs to be fully informed, and the sooner the better."

"You want me to tell 'im everything?"

"Everything. We have nothing to hide from him."

"Whatever you think's best. I'll tell yuh right out, though, I don't like the idea of your goin' into Apache country alone, or facin' Zamora by yourself, either."

"You've been a big help, Chet. I could not have gotten this far without you. But what I need to do now, I can best accomplish alone. You need to get back up to Utah and report. On top of

164

that, now winter's here, Robby can use your help. He and the ranch need you, and I need you up there, as well."

★   ★   ★

With two pack mules and a spare horse, Clay had made good time from San Francisco to the growing pueblo of Los Angeles. There, after a day's rest for himself and his animals, he had replenished his supplies and headed south to the small but beautiful coastal town of San Diego where he turned east on the jackass mail route into Arizona.

He followed the newly established stagecoach trail, which offered the easiest and fastest access through the mountains and across the Apache-infested desert to Apache Wells—a small, lawless border town that offered scarcely more safety than the open, hostile desert surrounding it.

The town resembled a pile of sun-bleached bones baking in the desert sun. And though in the heat of the day its single dusty street was devoid of life, a stranger quickly got the uncomfortable feeling he was being watched. The place consisted of a ramshackle feed store and stable located directly across the narrow, dusty street from a public eating place and a sagging, false-fronted, two-story clapboard building with a sign above the grungy, covered boardwalk that read (for those who could read):

*H-O-T-E-L.*

*Maria's Cantina,* located on the north side of the hotel, consisted of a worn plank floor supporting a rough frame of warped two-by-fours covered with sun-rotted canvas. A large woodburning cookstove squatted at the rear, and the place was crowded with old, wooden trestle tables that would hold at least six customers on each side, if they were friendly.

The hotel, a dingy, two-story, wooden building that had never known a coat of paint, consisted of a small lobby on the ground floor, with sleeping rooms on the second, each room containing six beds. The sleeping arrangement depended on how much pocket change the proprietor—Maria, of *Maria's Cantina*—felt she could extort from a tired cowboy or exhausted outlaw on the run.

No one had ever cheated Maria.

"Well, you don't look like no outlaw. Leastways not to me. What're you doin' in a place like this?" It was obvious from the look on her heavy face that she expected an answer.

The woman on the other side of the counter was formidable-looking. She stood as tall as Clay, well over six feet, and outweighed him by at least fifty pounds, if not more. The hair piled on top of her head might once have been black, but it was now generously streaked with grey.

That she was a woman who knew her way around and one who would brook no foolishness was obvious. That she could be a valuable ally, if not a friend, was equally obvious. Clay cleared his throat, and said, "Oh, I've been over the mountain a time or two, I suppose."

"Uh-huh," she said, obviously not satisfied with the answer.

"I'll tell you one thing, though. I've spent more nights sleeping on the ground lately than I can keep count of."

"I suppose you want a room, then?"

"With a bath, if you've got one," Clay responded, in an effort to appeal to her lighter side.

"Well, as you can see, we've got a convention in town," she said, her hand sweeping the empty room. "You can have any room upstairs you want. That'll be two bits—in advance. If you can find a tub somewhere, the bath'll be free. There's one hangin' on the side of the outhouse out back, as I recollect."

"And feeling the need for a bath, where do I find the water?"

"If you didn't bring none with yuh, that's your problem. Of course, if you're the enterprisin' sort, you might find a pump down near the stable."

"I'll just do that," Clay said, grabbing his saddle bags off the floor and turning toward the stairs.

"I suppose you're hungry?"

"All the time, but right now I could eat my horse."

"There'll be some beans and beef on the table in the cantina next door in about an hour—your animals'll be safe enough in the stable."

Freshly bathed and shaved, Clay sat down at the trestle table farthest from the stove, where Maria had set a plate covered with thick cuts of beef and a huge pot of dark, sticky, brown-sugar beans. A plentiful stack of tortillas shared the middle of the table with a small jar of butter and a bowl of chunky salsa, which he soon found to be the best he had eaten since he last tasted Emily's. It was a meal he had not expected.

"Maria, this is some of the best food I've eaten in a long time."

"Well, as you can see," she said, looking around the empty tent, "my cookin' attracts a crowd."

Returning with a large pot of coffee, the large woman seated herself at the end of the table. "Now," she said, filling his coffee mug once more, and one for herself, "what're you doin' down in this godforsaken place, anyhow? I'm purely amazed you've still got your hair."

"Why's that?" Clay asked, swallowing a mouthful of sweet, brown-sugar beans.

"Surely you been seein' sign . . . wherever you've come from. The Apaches is been makin' life miserable in these parts now for some time. Cochise has been on the warpath most of this year.

Butterfield Stage stations've been burned. Hell, there ain't been a Butterfield stage in the southern part of the territory since last March."

"There's plenty of sign, alright," Clay said, setting his mug down, "but I'll bet I've come through three or four of the heaviest rainstorms I've seen in a long while, just in the last week or so—washed a lot of it out. And the lightning—I don't know when I've seen bigger storms."

"Uh-huh. Worst year I've seen in a long time, and that's what's got them Apache riled up."

"The lightning?"

"That lightning is big medicine to the Apache. Makes 'em feel invincible. Their shamans are tellin' them now's the time to drive the White Eyes out of the territory—wipe 'em out altogether. And they've about done it, too. I don't know how many ranches have been burned out this past summer. Miners and ranchers killed time and again. Why, I'll bet there ain't more than two hundred people left up in Tucson, tough as that place ordinarily is. Patagonia ain't got but a few left neither, and Cochise has vowed he's gonna wipe both them places out. Ain't but a few whites left in the whole territory."

"What about the army? Aren't they doing anything to quiet things down?" Clay asked, reaching for another tortilla.

"The army," Maria huffed. "Them blue bellies is more the problem than the solution. Anyhow, they abandoned Fort Breckenridge, up on the San Pedro, last summer. May be some at Bascom, but not many, I expect."

"And what about you, Maria? How have you survived all this?"

"Me? Shoot, Cochise ain't gonna let nothin' happen to me. I'm one-fourth Apache—and a cousin of his'n to boot. Ain't

nothin' stronger in this world to an Apache than his family ties
. . . even if I am part white.

"But you . . . you're somethin' else. They'll kill you on sight,
not a question asked. Course, first they'll have some fun with
yuh—just to see what yer made of. Them Apache'll see your
dyin'll take a long time—and real painful, too. If you're smart,
you'll light a shuck outta here before first light."

Clay sighed and pushed his plate away. "They'll have to catch
me first, and I'm not easily caught when I don't want to be."

"I don't doubt that's true. Have some more coffee, and set a
spell. Maybe I can help yuh."

"Help me?"

"You're followin' 'em, ain't yuh?"

"Following them?"

"Yeah, that bunch from Sonora, the gobernador and his family, they're the only ones to come through here in months. And
then you show up. Don't take much guessin'."

"No, I suppose it doesn't. And, yes, I'm trying to catch up
with them."

"You and a bunch of Cochise's braves."

Clay set his mug down, spilling coffee on the table. "What?"

"That Salinas bunch left here over a couple of days ago, and
Cochise and a large band of Chiricahua came through here the
next day, hot on their trail."

Clay's stomach turned over and he almost choked on his
coffee. "How big was the Salinas party? Did he have any guards?"

"Old Salinas?" she chuckled. "I never knew that ol' hoss thief
t' take a chance of any kind. He didn't just have some guards; he
had almost an army. If Cochise catches 'em, and he will, there's
gonna be one gosh-awful fight."

"But if there are so many—"

"If there's one thing an Apache hates more'n a white man, it's a Mexican—and that's probably more true of Cochise than any other. Cochise ain't gonna see an army, he's gonna see Mexicans, and that's gonna light his fuse."

# PART TWO

★ ★ ★

# CHAPTER 15

\* \* \*

Tᴀᴇ ᴄᴏᴀᴄʜ ʙᴏᴜɴᴄᴇᴅ ʜᴀʀᴅ, causing Consuela's mother to grumble in her sleep, and Consuela reached for Zamora's hand, taking it in her lap. The ride had been long and hot and dusty, plagued with the fear of Apaches, but the thought of each mile bringing her nearer to the sprawling Salinas *hacienda* caused her heart to grow lighter. The massive Mexican ranch was home.

Educated in the eastern United States and Europe, and widely traveled, what throbbed at the core of Maria Emilea Consuela Salinas's being had always remained on her father's ranch, with her books and music, her horses, and her freedom. These were the things she cherished, and the ranch was not only her home but the center of her world.

The Salinas ranch had always been a highly cultured world, one of literature and art, of music and gaiety, of politics and power. Throughout Consuela's life, it had been a world presided over by her father, the jefe of their ranch and the gobernador of

Sonora, a highly educated man whose opinion was sought and respected throughout Mexico, and in her eyes, a man of enormous gentility.

As far back as Consuela could remember, her father's table had hosted leaders of government, education, religion, industry, and the arts, stimulating people from every walk of life, not just in Mexico, but from the United States and Europe as well. During the years of Mexican tumult, especially, the powerful, and those who sought power, had ceaselessly vied for the gobernador's support, and failing that, his opinion.

Though such attention could be dangerous for a man in his position, the violent waves of revolution had yet to penetrate the sanctity of the Salinas *casa*—her father would not allow it, and his word was law within its walls. Even in the most tumultuous of times, conversations in the Salinas home centered on books and culture, politics and history.

Events that were currently convulsing Mexico, and the influence of European countries throughout the hemisphere were not ignored, but it was understood by all that such discussions were to be conducted only in the most calm and civilized manner. From Consuela's youngest years, her father had taken care to see that she was a part of it all. She had never been merely an observer but always a participant, and she had been made to feel that her opinion was of importance.

Though raised a Catholic, Catholicism had not dominated their home, as it had throughout Mexico. Her father, a supporter of the liberal movement, had kept the Salinas residence perpetually open to the free discussion of ideas, to the examination of new and emerging theories of science, economics, and human behavior. In Consuela's world, nothing lay beyond intellectual exploration.

How her father had accomplished it, she would never know. In the midst of bloody civil war, he had kept his household and extensive holdings insulated from the social upheavals that continually tore at the fabric of their country, threatening to destroy it. The Catholic Church had been dethroned, along with the conservatives, and it appeared that Mexico was now emerging from its long tradition of theocracy.

The war appeared to be over, Juarez had been reelected for another four years, but the violence continued, and the times were no less dangerous. Scenes reminiscent of the French Revolution were repeated almost daily throughout Mexico—church treasuries robbed, their archives plundered, and their libraries burned. Recently, even bishops had been stoned to death. Nuns, though they had spent their entire lives cloistered, had been forced from their convents, turned out into the world with nowhere to go.

Though her father was not anti-Catholic, and was appalled at the violent reaction against the Church, it was his firm belief that church and state in Mexico must be forever separated. It was his conviction that throughout history, when the Church mingled in civil affairs, the people inevitably suffered. A religious base to any culture was an absolute essential, giving rise to those values that made true community possible, but it was not for the Church to govern beyond those matters that would always remain sacred and holy.

Despite the spiritual and emotional difficulties of the time, at the center of Consuela's existence was an undeniable spirituality that permeated everything, a reverence for all that surrounded her family as well as for things holy. For her the Salinas ranch had been a warm, safe, comfortable, and exciting place, in many ways a precursor of the Mexico that might be possible under Benito Juarez. But, still, the doubts remained, and now her father was exploring an alliance with an independent California, perhaps even union.

"How much farther, José? The closer we get, the more difficult for me the wait becomes."

"One more night under the stars, beautiful one," Zamora said, smiling as he lightly squeezed her hand. "You should be in your own bed tomorrow night."

"Oh, a hot bath, clean linen. It's too good to be true."

"It has been a long and tiring trip for you, has it not, my little one?"

Consuela turned her face away. As fond as she was of Zamora, perhaps even in love with him, his condescending attitude at times was more than she could tolerate. "I'm sure it has been tiring for all of us, José," she said, moving his hand from her lap, her manner abrupt. "And please do not refer to me as your *little one.*"

Consuela knew her resentment of his demeaning little endearments annoyed Zamora. She was aware of the fact that she frequently said and did things that annoyed him—at times, perhaps, even to provoke him. He saw many of her reactions as a reflection of her attitude of superiority, an obvious assumption on her part that she was the equal of any man. Well, she was, whether he appreciated her outspoken manner or not.

Still, he hovered over her with an exasperating, overly possessive attitude. She knew Zamora's future plans, whatever they were, included her. That he wanted to marry her was more than obvious, and she was unsure how she felt about such a union. That she enjoyed a freedom known to few women of her time she knew irritated and at times angered him, and were he to become her husband, she knew her world, however safe, would shrink to the dimensions he thought appropriate.

Consuela studied his handsome face out of the corner of her

eye. Zamora's attitudes and reactions were not unlike those of other Latin men—most men, for that matter—and perhaps it was time for her to assume a more traditional role, though she hated the thought. She never doubted that he would one day be a man of great power. With him she could go far. Without him, her choices were, perhaps, limited.

There was also, of course, the gringo, Clay Ashworth, the *norteamericano* from the Utah Territory of Brigham Young. At the Gwin's dinner party, she had found him absolutely fascinating, in many ways the only real man there, aside from her father. Right from the first, there had been a disquieting air of mystery about him, a kind of political obscurity that only added to his innate charm.

And she knew, as only a woman can know, that despite his somewhat unyielding attitude, he had been taken with her. Thinking back on that wonderful evening, it seemed as if those qualities Zamora found most objectionable in her, this Clay Ashworth fellow had seemed almost to enjoy—almost.

Thinking about the big gringo brought a smile to her face. Clay Ashworth was handsome, though not too handsome, very intelligent, and he had more than held his own when she and the others at the table were doing their best to back him into a corner. The more she thought about him, she could not imagine the circumstances under which such a man could be defeated. One thing was certain: she very much wanted to see him again. Yet the likelihood of ever doing so was almost nonexistent.

The thought of not seeing him again was most depressing and with an enormous sigh, she turned toward the window. Suddenly, her world seemed less full, less promising. "I will be so glad when we are finally there," she said, unable to hide the resignation in her voice.

Zamora studied her lovely face. He knew he had to have this woman regardless of her frequently infuriating behavior. She was truly the most beautiful woman he had ever seen, and that made her eccentricities easier to bear. Besides, she was essential to his plans. Once they were married, once her father was out of the way, she would be shown her place and kept there, subject to his will alone. "Tomorrow, Consuela, the trip will be behind us all," he said curtly.

"Yes, and none too soon," she said, ignoring the edge in his voice. "There is much to be done, what with our guest from California. The gobernador wants señor Bennington to be comfortable while he is with us. He has left it to me, and I think we must have a reception for him soon—something truly elegant, something befitting what he represents. Next week, I think."

Zamora did not respond, his thoughts turning to Bennington riding alone in an older coach toward the rear of the column, the man who had been sent by the schemer Gwin to solidify Salinas's treacherous alliance with California. At the thought of Bennington eating their dust, Zamora's lips twisted into a cruel half smile—it was as it should be. The *norteamericano* represented the frustration of all Zamora's plans. He was a threat to the future of Mexico, and Zamora disliked him intensely.

Bennington had complained of his place in the column, and the gobernador had argued with Zamora, but as the military commander of the expedition, Zamora's decision in the matter was allowed to stand. The *americano* remained at the rear of the column, followed only by a wagon carrying supplies and luggage and a small rear guard.

Dust billowed through the open coach window as a rider drew close alongside, his uniform stained with perspiration and dirt. "General Zamora!"

Zamora leaned forward. "What is it, Captain?"

"Much dust behind us . . . most of the morning. The Apaches we have been warned of. They grow closer."

"Cochise?"

"*Si*. It would be him, jefe."

At the name, a chill passed through Zamora. There was none as dreaded as this one great Apache leader. "How close, Captain?"

"An hour, perhaps less . . . it is hard to tell."

"Yes. They are not burdened with coaches and wagons."

"And *women?*" Consuela asserted, her voice raised in an effort to be heard over the noise of the coach, her eyebrow arched in female challenge.

Looking down at her, Zamora smiled condescendingly, his face darkened by the merest suggestion of inherent cruelty. *One day*, he thought, turning toward Consuela, *she will be made to learn proper respect.* "Yes, my dear," he said gravely, "*and women.* I would not want you or your mother or any other woman to fall into the hands of the Apache. You must remember, women have limited uses for them—especially Mexican women. Especially *beautiful* Mexican women."

Abruptly, the smile slid from his face as Zamora turned back to the window. "Where is gobernador Salinas?"

"He rides with my officers at the front of the column. It is he who sent me to seek your counsel."

"You should have said so, Captain."

"*Excusame, mi general,*" the officer said, stiffening in his saddle.

"Order the column to move more swiftly. We must reach Diablo Springs quickly. It is defensible, and we can face them there. But first, order some of the troops to fall back to the rear. If we are attacked, they must deploy as a rear defense and hold the savages away from the main column. They must hold the Apache off at all costs until the main column is safely away. Have I made myself clear, Captain?"

"*Si,* jefe," the captain said, saluting Zamora.

"Then go! *Rápidamente, hombre!*"

★ ★ ★

Bennington's coach lurched forward as the driver flipped the heavy reins along the horses' backs, snapping the lone passenger's head back against the hard, worn, leather seat.

With a mumbled curse, he pulled himself forward and leaned out of the window, dust and dirt flying into his face. "Hey, up there!" he hollered, squinting up at the driver. "What's going on? Why are we going so fast?"

The man looked down at Toby and said something in Spanish, but the clatter of the coach and team drowned out his voice as he whipped the overburdened horses to a full gallop in an effort to keep up with the column.

Filled with frustration, Toby slumped back into the seat, the jolting coach making it almost impossible for him to settle comfortably. He was angry—angry with Zamora for the treatment he had received since leaving San Francisco, angry with Salinas for allowing it to happen, and angry with that fool Gwin for forcing him to accompany the Salinases to Mexico. He could accomplish much more by remaining in California, where he could have stayed close to the Gwins, and perhaps done more to force an even deeper wedge between Mary and that pompous-ass husband of hers.

A smile crossed his face at the thought of Mary Gwin. He had made more progress in that department than he had thought possible, though the letter she had slipped into his hand at dinner the night before he departed seemed to shut the door on any further developments there—for the time being, anyway.

*Maybe this is best,* he thought, trying to put a more positive slant on his present situation. *There is much I can accomplish in Mexico. I would have had to force my hand by insisting on staying in California. This way, maybe I can be even more effective, concentrate on Salinas, derail his plans down here rather than San Francisco. That fool Gwin's fall from power is all but certain—only a matter of time. Funny how things work out.*

He had managed to get a message off to his superiors before leaving, but there had been no time for a reply, and with the Union army falling apart in California, no means of communication remained secure. At this point, their approval of his decision to follow Gwin's orders made little difference. He would make it work.

Toby Bennington was so immersed in thought, he did not hear the scream of the soldier riding behind his coach as the man fell from his horse, his body impaled by three Apache arrows.

# CHAPTER 16

★　★　★

THE EARLY-MORNING SUN WARMED Clay Ashworth's back as he lay on his stomach in the sparse grass, peering down into a wide draw. Below him what looked to have been a coach and three wagons smoldered, still in the shade of the deep cutbank. They were the Salinas wagons, or at least some of them, of that he was certain. They had been overturned, ransacked, and set ablaze. What had not been taken or destroyed had been left thoughtlessly strewn about. It was obvious that a hasty defensive circle had been attempted with the wagons, perhaps even as the column was being overrun by its Apache pursuers, but the defenders had been quickly overpowered.

It was an ugly scene, but one typical of an Apache attack. The bodies of Mexican troops dotted the area, their bodies terribly mutilated. To Clay, it looked almost as if no organized defense had been possible. Rather, the attack had been so overwhelming, each individual had been forced to defend himself against overpowering numbers right where he stood.

It was not atypical of the clash of two diverse civilizations—a conflict becoming increasingly violent across the breadth of virtually the entire North American continent west of the Mississippi River. One civilization, composed of hunters and gatherers, to whom any notion of property ownership was for the most part, alien, pitted against an encroaching civilization in the midst of a social and industrial expansion that was to a large extent dependent on the ownership and control of property. Neither culture seemingly capable of understanding the imperatives driving the other. Yet to both, access to the land was essential.

All across the content, Native American tribes were being pressed from every side by the encroaching White Eyes. It was as true of the Apache tribes in Arizona and New Mexico as it was of any other. The white man, seemingly without thought, considered the West and its resources to be rightfully his. Gold, silver, minerals of all kinds abounded in the mountains of the Southwest, and the voracious white man descended on ancient tribal lands like hoards of locusts.

In reaction, the Apache fought and killed for what had always been taken for granted. In defense, the white man killed to be rid of the red man's threat, even killing Apache infants, declaring that "nits grow up to become lice."

To the south were the Mexicans, long the enemy of the Apache. Throughout centuries of contact, Spaniards and Mexicans had used other Indian tribes, Yaquis and others, traditional enemies of the Apache, to drive the Apache north of the border, or to raid Apache camps for women and children to be used as slaves or to be sold into slavery far to the south.

Of both Cochise had finally had enough. Early in 1861, war

between the Chiricahua Apaches and Americans living through-out the southwest had broken out in one bloody fight after another. One of the most violent encounters took place at Apache Pass, where Cochise and five members of his family had been cap-tured by U.S. soldiers. Cochise had subsequently escaped, but his brother and two of his nephews had been hung. The Apache chief was so filled with rage that no white man or Mexican remained safe.

One of the wagons lay tipped at an odd angle, its side resting against a large rock. Strapped to one of the wheels, the body of a man hung upside down. It was obvious that a fire had been built beneath his head. Whoever it was must have suffered horribly, but from where Clay lay it was impossible to tell if the man might still be alive.

Nothing moved.

Several buzzards, the only sign of life, circled in the air above the carnage, not yet convinced it was safe to land and begin their macabre feast.

Clay studied the gruesome body hanging on the wheel. *Maybe,* he thought, *whoever it is isn't dead yet. Those birds would have landed by now.*

Retrieving his horse, Clay made his way down the steep slope to the ravaged wagons. Dismounting, he kicked the charred, still-smoldering wood and ashes from beneath the wheel and knelt to examine the man that hung there. The stench of burned human flesh more than he could endure, Clay retched and bile heaved up, stinging his throat. It was Toby Bennington. He had been scalped and then tortured, his head and shoulders charred black.

Unmercifully and inexplicably, the man was still alive, and there was nothing that could be done for him. Even to attempt to cover him would have accomplished nothing but more pain. In his near-death delirium, Bennington's glassy eyes seemed riveted on some object across the camp.

Following Toby's stare, Clay saw a piece of red cloth hanging from the thorny branch of a mesquite bush at the edge of the draw. He would never forget that color. It was a fragment of the dress Consuela Salinas had worn at Mary Gwin's dinner party—the party where he had first laid eyes upon the most beautiful woman he had ever seen.

"Oh, dear God, no," he said, struggling to his feet and retrieving the piece of shredded cloth. "Not that. Not her."

Bennington groaned, but did not move. "Gone . . . rear guard gone . . . all gone . . . left with rear guard. Dead . . . couldn't stop them . . . Zamora . . . all gone . . . dead."

"Dead? Who's dead, Toby?" Clay begged, turning back to Toby and desperation flooding over him. "Where's Consuela? Where're her father and the rest?"

The man was clearly near death and out of his head with pain. "Apaches . . . too many . . . too fast. All gone."

Desperate for information, Clay reached for his canteen, "Here . . . let me get you some water. You've got to—"

"No! No water . . . don't touch. South . . . Apaches . . . all gone south. Let me—"

"Toby? Toby, what do you mean, south? Who's gone south? Did the rest get away? Where's Zamora, Toby? Are they still alive? Toby? Toby?"

In the gravel bottom of the wash, using a short-handled shovel he had found under one of the wagons, Clay dug a shallow common grave for Toby Bennington and those with whom he had died, a hole in the rocky earth he hoped was deep enough to keep wild animals and desert scavengers away from their mutilated bodies. As he threw the last shovelful of dirt on the grave, Clay felt some relief knowing Toby was at last free from the horrible agony he must have endured.

Yet two things troubled him. First of all, Toby had been scalped, and Apaches were not known for scalping. In fact, as far as Clay knew, up to now they had done very little of it, and while the Mexican troops' bodies had been mutilated, they had not been scalped.

Secondly, Toby had been horribly tortured. For some reason, the Apaches must have seen him as some kind of warrior to have tested his bravery in so brutal a fashion. Torture to an Apache had a kind of sacramental meaning to it, a way of testing manhood, measuring the worthiness of an enemy, or as a right of revenge.

Because Apache warriors always retrieved their dead, it was impossible to tell how many might have been killed. Yet judging from the carnage around the wagons, it had been a raging, hand-to-hand battle. The Apache loses must have been great, at least equal to those of the wagon train, and undoubtedly Toby Bennington had acquitted himself well. That fact alone would explain his treatment at the hands of the Apache.

Returning to the wagons, Clay began sifting through what remained of their contents. All of the boxes and trunks had been hacked open and looted, and what little remained was badly burned. It was the typical scene of an Apache raid: complete devastation, nothing left untouched, people's lives strewn about, desecrated, destroyed. It looked to be a form of malevolence far beyond anything comprehensible to a white man. Clay knew it was not, of course. Brutality, as he knew full well, was a vice common to all races, certainly to white men.

Kicking through the spilled contents of the last wagon, the

wagon to which Toby had been strapped and burned alive, Clay discovered an unopened briefcase buried beneath several trunks that had tumbled from the wagon as it had been overturned. What was left of their contents lay in such a way as to conceal anything buried underneath. Near the handle, embossed in gold, were the initials T.P.B. It had belonged to Toby, and it was locked—double locked. From the design of the case, it was intended to be a secure container. Clay had seen such luggage before. In fact, he had a similar one of his own, issued by the Pinkerton Agency to agents in the field.

Sitting down in the skimpy shade of the wagon, he looked up and guessed the hour to be near noon. *So, Toby was my contact,* he thought. *He had me fooled. Who'd have guessed that kid was a Pinkerton agent? Somebody did. That may explain the special attention he received here.* Clay looked around. *Strange there aren't more bodies. The Salinases had to have gotten away, or there'd have been more bodies. Apaches hate Mexicans more than anything else on earth. But only Bennington had gotten the special treatment—and scalped, of all things. They might have kept Consuela as a slave or to trade, but the others—I wonder. . . .*

Jamming his knife blade under one of the locks, Clay pried it open and went to work on the second, which proved to be more difficult, but finally yielded. After shuffling through some telegrams and other correspondence, he found a personalized envelope he recognized as one of Mary Gwin's.

Setting the dainty envelope aside, Clay quickly read through the remaining correspondence. There was nothing he did not already know, with the exception of instructions for Bennington to act as his contact for getting critical information out of California. Aside from that, the man's mission had been to do everything possible to undermine Senator Gwin's efforts to split California from the Union.

The devastating scene, burying the dead, and now, the revealing correspondence, all served to fill Clay's mind with self-reproach. *I should have met with him,* he thought. *I had no business sending Chet. Maybe this somehow could have been avoided. If I had just known.*

Judging from some of the documents in the case, Bennington had been a Pinkerton agent for some time while acting as an aide to Gwin. It had been the perfect setup. With Bennington in place, Gwin had had few secrets, at least where information accessible to his top aide was concerned. The question was, how much information had Bennington managed to get out of California, and had he been discovered? If so, by whom? And how much did Gwin know? Had Clay's own mission been compromised?

Picking up the envelope on which Mary Gwin had written Toby's name in her elegant, feminine hand, Clay hesitated. It almost seemed too personal for him to intrude. Thinking of Toby's infatuation with Mary brought a smile to Clay's face. One would have had to be blind not to see it—everyone but her husband. *Or had he?* Clay thought, glancing at the pile of rocks that marked the common grave. *Or had he? They say the husband is always the last to know, but Toby had made little effort to hide his infatuation with Mary. If it had been a ruse to drive a wedge between the senator and his wife, it just might have worked—too well.*

The letter's tone was soft and feminine, obviously written by a woman who cared for the man to whom she was writing, afraid of hurting him, but attempting to turn away his not entirely unwelcome attention—for the good of all concerned, for the good of California and their future.

She blushingly confessed to a time when she had even thought of a much closer, though discrete, relationship, but events were simply moving them all beyond personal considerations. And now that he was leaving for Mexico on such an important mission, there must be nothing between them that could be misconstrued or open to criticism. He would always remain her special friend, but he must be the perfect aide, and she beyond reproach, as she knew he would want her to be.

Clay gathered the documents together and stuffed them into one of his saddlebags. *The perfect aide,* he thought, with a reflective smile. *There was nothing Toby Bennington hated more than hearing himself called Gwin's aide. Who could blame him?*

"Poor kid," he said to himself, as he mounted his horse and began circling the camp, studying the sign in an effort to better understand what had happened and where the rest of the Salinas party had gone. "Toby Bennington deserved better, far more. I wish I had known . . ."

Studying the sign, it was obvious what had happened. The troops at the rear of the column had fallen behind to set up a defensive position that would allow the governor and those with him to escape. Unfortunately, Toby's coach had been at the rear of the column, and he had gotten caught up in the defensive maneuver and the desperate fight that followed. Perhaps by accident, perhaps not. The rest had gotten away, apparently at a full run: coaches, wagons, and all.

"Must have been one wild stampede," Clay said to his horse. "Must have worked, too, because I don't seen any Apache sign headed in their direction. And that, old boy, means Consuela got away." Patting the animal's neck and lightly touching spur, his heart much lighter, he urged, "Now, let's you and I go and find her."

# CHAPTER 17

★ ★ ★

CONSUELA STOOD ON THE VERANDA of the large, rambling, stucco ranch house, watching a full moon rise beyond the timbered bluffs to the east. The huge Salinas ranch sprawled across the foothills of the Sierra Madre and extended well back into the mountains. It was the perfect *hacienda*, sustaining herds of cattle that numbered in the thousands; and farther back in the mountains were no less than fifteen Salinas mines that annually produced tons of high-grade ore, containing gold, silver, copper, and other minerals. She had never been allowed to visit them—too dangerous, her father had repeatedly insisted—but she daily enjoyed the undeniable wealth they produced.

The evening was cool, and she pulled her shawl tightly about her shoulders. Something about the moon, the chill of the night, or the music coming from the party inside caused an ache deep within her. It was a troubling sensation she had never really experienced before and could not explain, a painful hollowness, an emptiness she longed to somehow have filled.

The whole evening had not seemed right. She had not wanted to give the party, so many having just died. It had been intended as a reception for the *norteamericano* killed in the Apache attack. Still, her father had thought it best to proceed, to provide an opportunity for entertaining those on whose support and loyalty he relied in his precarious alliance with Gwin.

She could not help but feel sorry for her father. Mexico was in upheaval and had been for years. While he had been a moderate member of the country's constitutional convention five years earlier, it was difficult to tell where Mexico's future lay, and he was walking a narrow, dangerous line.

The bloody civil war—the War of Reform between liberals and conservatives—that had racked Mexico for the past few years had only just come to an end with the defeat of the conservatives. And now, the country's first Indian president, Benito Juarez, had suspended payment of Mexico's foreign debt for two years. It was a bold move, and a dangerous one. And, as one might have expected, word had arrived that France, England, and Spain had signed an agreement intended to compel Mexico to pay up.

No one now could deny that European hegemony and French imperialism undoubtedly would become a reality in Mexico, a reality her father hated and could not afford to ignore. Neither he, nor those closest to him, wanted French subjugation for Mexico, and a new civil war seemed likely. The realities were fraught with danger for the unwise.

If, on the other hand, Senator Gwin were to be successful in bringing about California's independence from the United States, an alliance with Sonora would keep the unwanted French to the south and her father in a position of power in what possibly could become a new nation.

A heavy step behind her brought Consuela from her thoughts. "Oh, José, it's you."

"Out here by yourself, little one? The laughter and the dancing is inside. Come," he said, grasping her elbow, "you should return to your guests."

Twisting her arm from his presumptuous grip, she cried, "You're hurting me, José. I'll return when I choose, and I am not yet ready."

"But your guests, they ask for you."

"I'm sure I am greatly missed," she snapped. Her words were heavy with sarcasm, and she immediately regretted them.

Zamora fought to control an angry reaction. "Really, Consuela, I—"

Turning to him, she said, "I'm sorry, José. I did not mean to be so shrewish, but they are Father's guests, and Mother is there. I'm sure they are quite happy."

"But you are out here, little one, and that makes me unhappy." His hand again found her elbow. "I will stay with you and together we will take advantage of the moonlight, eh?" he said, with a suggestive chuckle that only served to further aggravate her.

Turning back toward the hills and the moon, she said, "Please, José. So much has happened I would like to be alone for a while. I'll join you and the rest in a moment."

"Very well, if that is how you wish it, Consuela," Zamora said, turning abruptly and entering the brightly lit house.

He was angry, and Consuela knew it. But, somehow, it did not matter. She truly did not want to go back into the house, nor did she desire Zamora's company. Since their arrival at the ranch, she had been possessed with a sense of restlessness, and for some reason it was particularly acute on this night. Out here, on the veranda, in the dark, there seemed to be an expectancy about the night that reached the emptiness she felt within. Zamora's presence served only to stifle her feelings, and that annoyed her.

With Zamora's ill-tempered departure, a breeze had picked up out of the north, and the evening turned colder. Yet, it felt good on her body: cooling, calming, comforting—oddly intimate. Stepping from the porch, the wind in her face, Consuela slowly walked down the drive toward the large, ornate iron gate in the wall that surrounded the house and its gardens, separating it from the pastures and orchards that lay on every side. The brightness of the moon intensified the shadows of the trees, and the silvered air was heavy with the sweetness of honeysuckle that grew in abundance along the wall.

A movement in the dark shadows of the trees, down where the road turned sharply to the west and away from the mountains, caught her eye, and Consuela froze where she stood. She had been repeatedly warned of going beyond the wall at night. Marauding Apaches or *banditos* were always a threat, and she was now dangerously far from the protective wall and its big iron gate. Stepping into the shadows, she watched the distant patch of darkness closely, but nothing moved. Then, just as she was about to turn and hurry back to the house, she saw it again. Something stirred, but it somehow did not seem threatening.

It was a horse, and it was standing under a large, old apple tree occasionally switching its tail, as if at annoying flies. Yet at this time of night, flies were not a problem. Watching the barely visible animal closely, Consuela slowly moved toward it, almost unaware she was doing so until it became apparent that something or someone was on its back. Approaching cautiously, she saw that it was a man, and he was slumped over the saddle horn.

Melting into the darkness of the trees, she stood very still, watching, remaining as motionless as possible. What if it were some sort of ruse? What if he were just waiting for her to come near so he could grab her by surprise? What if he had an accomplice? Someone waiting in the darkness? What if there were more than one?

Fear began to prickle her skin. What a stupid thing it was for her to be out alone this far from the house. She was helpless. No one would hear her screams over the noise of the party and the wind in the trees. She was too far away.

Zamora stood at the punch bowl and watched an old Mexican servant pour an expensive brandy into the watery beverage that was already there. Angry with Consuela, he thought, *There is no excuse for such a waste of expensive liquor. These fools deserve much less.* Looking around the crowded room, his eyes stopping to study a face here and there, he found some comfort in the thought that in the not too distant future they might all be in prison—or dead.

He was getting anxious for things to happen, for the needed changes to take place. Without the French, with Spain's—his Spain's—powerful influence, Mexico had no future, and these fools were too stupid to understand that. *Too many of them, especially that fool Salinas,* he thought, watching the governor engaged in animated conversation across the room, *are walking a narrow ridge with Mexico on one side and California on the other. They are straddling something that will quickly become razor-sharp and cut them in half, and none too soon.* The thought that the day soon would come when he would take the daughter and destroy the father brought a malevolent smile to his lips.

Zamora had just turned back to the table and was reaching for the punch ladle when Consuela rushed into the room, disrupting the small crowd around her father. Following a few hushed words, the governor followed his daughter from the room, trailed by those who had been close enough to hear, and the room quickly began to drain out onto the veranda.

Casually filling his cup, Zamora turned and leaned against the table, watching the room empty. Then, with a sudden sense of unease, he dropped the cup, spilling its contents across the white linen, and pushed away from the table, forcing himself to walk unhurriedly to the door. In the darkened courtyard, the governor and two men were lifting an unconscious man from the saddle.

"*Madre mia* . . . it is señor Ashworth," señora Salinas said, quickly crossing herself. "Here . . . bring him into the house. There is a bed in the south wing. We must get him there and care for him—quickly."

Consuela was holding the horse's reins, and the look on her pale face caused Zamora to flush with anger. "*Allí está el toque!*" he hissed. "So, this is the heart of the matter." Pushing through the crowd, he took the governor by his arm. "*Qué pasa,* gobernador?"

"Ah . . . Zamora, I am glad you are here. It is señor Ashworth, and it would appear he has been shot. Help us get him into the house."

"Allow me." Never taking his eyes from Consuela's, Zamora slipped Ashworth's arm over his shoulders. Lifting the unconscious man to his feet, and with the help of some of the others, he pushed past her and into the house.

"He is heavy, this one," one of the men grunted.

Somehow, Zamora had known this would happen. From the night of the Gwin dinner party in San Francisco, weeks ago, he had suspected that there was something between Consuela and Ashworth. Nay, inside, he had known it to be so. But how? How could this happen? How could she, she who is so level-headed, be taken with this Utah gringo?

Struggling down the hall, they wrestled the unconscious Ashworth into a bedroom and dropped him onto the bed.

"Oh . . . do be careful," Consuela said, brushing past Zamora. Propping a pillow under Clay's head, she began fussing with the bedcovers, seemingly unaware of the others in the room.

Stepping away from the bed, Zamora watched Consuela, something beginning to seethe deep within him. "He is not hurt badly," he spat. "It would appear to be nothing more than a shoulder wound."

She did not answer, but began loosening Clay's clothes, unbuttoning his shirt and pulling it away from his neck and the slowly draining wound in his shoulder.

"Consuela," her mother said, taking her by the arm. "This is not for you to do. Leave the room, and he will be taken care of properly."

*He will, indeed,* Zamora thought staring at the gringo who had invaded his life, and who, by his very presence, threatened to undo all of his plans. Consuela aside, this man was a menace to everything he had worked so hard to achieve—to the future of Mexico, to his future. With no effort to hide the grimace that distorted his face, he thought, *I will see he is taken care of, as the señora says—properly.*

# CHAPTER 18

★  ★  ★

"FROM HERE, AS FAR AS YOU can see," Consuela said, her hand sweeping the horizon around the rock outcropping where they sat enjoying the cool of the shade, "it is my father's ranch— our ranch, the Salinas ranch."

"Goodness me. All of it?" Clay asked, his manner teasing. "Even the mines back in the mountains?"

"All of it. And, yes, even the mines, and far beyond," she said, watching him closely, not trusting his mood. She had learned during his all too brief convalescence what a tease he could become.

It was Clay's first venture from the Salinas ranch house since he had been shot in a running encounter with a small band of Apaches two weeks earlier. The wound had not been all that serious, and he had healed quickly, but Consuela and her sometimes imperious mother had forced him to remain in bed until they were satisfied the wound would not open with movement. The possibility of infection was always present.

Anxious to be on the move and to discover as much as possible about Salinas and his interests, Clay had badgered Consuela into giving him a horseback tour of the ranch holdings, at least those not too distant from the main compound. It had been a short, but tiring ride, and they had dismounted to sit for a time in the shade of a grove of trees.

"How did you know there were mines in the mountains?" she asked, her face intent, and the suspicion in her voice more than apparent.

Clay was not quick in answering, attempting to give his response some thought without being too obvious, since he had no idea where he had heard it—perhaps from Gwin or someone else. But he knew the mines existed, and he knew they were worked by slaves—Apache slaves. It was something he intended to investigate as soon as his strength returned, at least to the point where he could ride alone.

Clearing his throat, he said, "Maybe we ought to get back. I'm a little weaker than I thought. Getting on and off of that horse has put some strain on this shoulder," he said, gently kneading the heavily bandaged wound.

"Don't do that," she commanded, taking his hand in hers and pulling it into her lap. "You might start it bleeding, and that would put you right back in bed."

Clay studied her face. There was so much to be seen there. Beauty, certainly. It was a kind of beauty that often served to put men off, made them wary, gave rise to a fear of possible rejection—a degree of beauty that made them vulnerable and that somehow threatened their masculinity.

But not for him. Hers was a face at which he knew he could never tire of looking, nor to him was it the least bit intimidating, perhaps because there was so much more than beauty to be found there. She radiated a depth of intelligence, a quickness of personality and wit that gave animation to her every mood, her every expression. It endowed her with a quality, a charm, so captivating it could not readily be put into words.

Looking at her, Clay Ashworth knew there was one thing of which he was certain: he wanted this woman. Never before had he felt this way about another human being. Just being with her filled him with an inexplicable joy and stirred him physically. He wanted her to be his, totally and completely, for deep inside he knew only she could fill the void that had made his world so incomplete. Yet, at this moment, nothing seemed more impossible.

"You did not answer my question, señor Ashworth. How did you know my father had mines in the mountains?"

Her question brought him from his thoughts, and he suddenly became aware of where his hand was resting. The intimacy of it made him color with embarrassment. For all her intelligence and beauty, she at times seemed possessed by an innocence of upbringing that made her a little too bold.

"We need to get back," he said, ignoring her question as he rose unsteadily to mount his horse.

"Oh . . . what is this?" she said, taking his elbow as she came to his aid. "You can't even stand up straight. I knew you were moving too soon—and riding a horse, too," she scolded.

"No . . . I'm fine . . . really. It's nothing. Here, Consuela . . . I can get mounted . . . really. I'm just fine . . . really."

"Yes," Consuela giggled, "let's get you back on your horse."

Gubernador Salinas looked up as Zamora entered his study. "I would appreciate it, Zamora, if you would do me the courtesy of knocking before you enter my study," he said, lifting what appeared to be a letter from the papers on his desk and slipping it into a folder.

Ignoring Salinas's annoying rebuke, Zamora complained, "I am concerned with Consuela's behavior, gobernador. She spends too much time with the gringo, Ashworth."

"Really? And how is that?" Salinas's response was cool and distant.

"She has been with him almost daily during the past days, and now they ride together in the hills."

"And what is that to you, señor Zamora?" the governor asked, setting his pen aside and leaning back in his chair. "She has aided her mother in nursing señor Ashworth back to health. Nothing more."

Zamora studied the governor's face. The man had never displayed such an abrupt attitude with him before. "That is true, gobernador, but now that the gringo is back on his feet, is it proper for her to ride with him unchaperoned?"

"I must say, Zamora, I am somewhat surprised at your concern. Señor Ashworth is a man in whom I have the utmost confidence, and she acts merely as a guide and riding companion for him, nothing more. Furthermore, I have asked her to show him much of the ranch. There is nothing improper about it, I assure you.

"Now, if you will excuse me," he said, reaching for his pen and dipping in its inkwell, "I have much work to do."

Struggling to suppress his anger, Zamora shot back, "I had thought there was some understanding between your daughter and myself, gobernador. An understanding that had your approval."

"And what understanding is that, señor?"

"Betrothal," Zamora said, his voice growing low, his face coloring.

"Betrothal?" the governor said, leaning back in his chair and tossing his pen on the desk. "There has been no formal betrothal, señor."

Taken back by the gobernador's abrupt response, Zamora struggled to regain his composure. It would not serve his purposes to alienate the governor of Sonora—not when his plans were so close to fruition. "I beg to differ, el gubernador!" he said, half bowing. "I know there has been nothing formal, but things seem to have been understood between us, and now this stranger, this gringo has—"

"Perhaps you have assumed too much, Zamora," the governor said, abruptly rising from his desk, tucking the folder firmly under his arm. "Perhaps we have all assumed too much—too much about many things."

"Gobernador?"

"I shall speak with my daughter. However, I suggest that you remember your place where she is concerned, señor. She is a woman capable of very sound judgment and would do nothing inappropriate."

Zamora struggled to control his anger. He just had been insulted beyond acceptability. Had any other man spoken to him in such a manner, he would have called him to account. As much as he detested this inflated little man, so filled with self-importance, Zamora knew he could not afford to lose Salinas's confidence, nor his access to Consuela. It was obvious that his abrupt approach had invoked an unintended and potentially harmful chill between them.

"Gobernador, I assure you, I—"

"Let me remind you, señor, you are here to aid me in my efforts to secure the future of Sonora, perhaps even Mexico," the governor said, stepping toward the door at the rear of the room leading to the back of the house. "Not to pursue my daughter."

Turning the ornate knob, he gave Zamora a level stare. "Perhaps there has been some misperception on your part, señor, one that can only lead to further embarrassment for yourself, if not for Consuela. It is my wish that you refrain from speaking with her until I have done so. We will talk further of this matter in the morning. Until then, good day, Zamora."

As the door closed behind Salinas, Zamora cursed under his breath and turned from the desk, his face ashen. *I could kill that miserable little hijo de perro,* he thought, turning toward the door and stepping into the outer hallway. Stopping in mid-stride, he looked back at the door. Troubled by Salinas's churlish attitude, he stepped back into the study and went directly to the desk. Something had caused Salinas's surprisingly curt, almost hostile, reaction, and Zamora knew it could not have been his irritation with Consuela. The two men had spoken of his relationship with her many times in the past. And despite Salinas's denial, there *had been* an understanding—nothing formal, but an understanding nonetheless.

Quickly sorting through the few papers Salinas had left on the desk, he uncovered an envelope that had been tucked out of sight. The address was written in Spanish, and it had come from a law office in Madrid, one not familiar to him.

"Madrid," he whispered to himself, turning the empty envelope over in his hand. "He has had no business with anyone in Madrid—unless. . . ."

Replacing the envelope where he had found it, Zamora turned and left the study. Hurrying to the barn, he ordered a stable hand to saddle his horse, and he rode from the yard, taking the road to the dusty little settlement of Bavispe, some twenty miles southeast of the ranch headquarters.

Arriving there, Zamora tied his lathered horse to a rusted

metal railing in front of the old Spanish mission that dominated the village square, and he entered the church. Quickly striding down the empty nave to the second of two confessionals set against the church's outer adobe wall, he slipped into the dark booth, drew its curtain, and rang the silver bell that would summon one of the priests.

It was relatively cool in the quiet building, and the darkness of the booth was relaxing after his long, hot ride. Zamora's eyelids grew heavy and he dozed.

"What do you wish, my son?"

It was the voice, not the words, that brought him fully awake. "Forgive me, Father, for I have sinned."

"I thought it was you, Zamora, but I had to be certain. We are alone, but be quick. What do you have for me?"

"A letter has come from Madrid."

"From?"

"A law firm," Zamora said, carefully repeating the string of names. "It is one of which I have no knowledge."

"And?"

"Salinas has no business with anyone in Madrid that I know of. It can only mean one thing. Someone is informing him of French intentions."

"But you are only guessing."

"Of course I am guessing," Zamora snapped. "But can we afford to wait until we have proof? If it is what I suspect, it will quickly solidify Salinas's plans to join with Senator Gwin in creating an Independent Republic of the Pacific. They must strike while the United States is torn by civil war and before any kind of French rule can be established here. That means they cannot afford to wait. They must act, and act quickly."

"So quickly? How can they? Plans to put Maximilian on the

throne of Mexico are well underway. A few weeks, months at the most, and it will be accomplished."

"There is an agent of Gwin's here at the Salinas ranch, a *gringo* named Clay Ashworth. I am certain he is here to see that such an alliance takes place. Luckily, he was wounded by Apaches in coming here, but he heals quickly."

"He must be removed. But you must do it in a manner that does not suggest any political motivation on your part. Do you understand?"

"Certainly. That will not be a problem."

"One more thing, Zamora."

"*Sí?*"

"Gubernador Salinas's brother is here."

"Where?" Zamora asked, his palms becoming sweaty despite the coolness of the building.

"Here. Back in Mexico."

"But he is not at the ranch."

"No matter. He soon will be."

"That confirms my suspicions. He has been in Europe. Salinas knows, or he will know with his brother's return, even if the envelope is meaningless. The letter may even have come from him."

Somewhere in the building a heavy door swung on loudly complaining hinges, and the voice in the confessional quietly said, "The Governor of Sonora must be removed as well, Zamora. An alliance with California is unacceptable under any conditions. Eliminate them both as quickly as possible."

Before Zamora could respond, the air stirred, and he knew the booth on the other side of the veiled, ornately carved wooden screen was empty.

# CHAPTER 19

★  ★  ★

"Oh, José, come in and see who's here," Consuela said, leaving the others to take him by the arm and lead him into the formal dining room. "I have been looking for you all afternoon and wondered where you were."

The room was dimly lit, pleasantly so, with a cozy fire crackling in the large fireplace at the far end where the others stood enjoying their drinks. The rustle of Consuela's full, ankle-length skirt and the soft smell of her perfume somehow added to an uncomfortable sense of intrusion that seemed to fill the room as he entered. Though the long dining room table was set for six, obviously to include himself and Ashworth, never had he felt so apart.

Zamora's busy eyes flicked throughout the room, glancing from one individual to another, trying to appear as casual as circumstances would permit. Studying their unrevealing faces, he had the uncomfortable feeling they knew—they had to know. At least the gobernador and his meddlesome brother knew. He could see it in their look, in their attitude, this very moment. And señora Salinas had yet to acknowledge his presence. Even the gringo, with his sideways glance, knew.

Somehow Zamora was certain. Ashworth must be the first—tonight. The *norteamericano* spy would not live the night through. A way would be found to eliminate him, and do it quickly. And do it without losing Consuela.

As for Consuela, he would have her tonight. She had been his—it was understood to be so—and her presence always solidified his sense of control. Without her, he would lose it all: the ranch, political power in the new Mexico, the Mexico of the future—everything he had worked so hard to achieve. He would not allow it; it could not be.

Though things suddenly felt different, they were simply more immediate, nothing more. All that remained was to bring events into line with his plans, but it must be done quickly—and finally.

"Yes, do come in, Zamora," Governor Salinas said. "You are expected."

"Thank you, gobernador. I do not wish to appear rude, but I must excuse myself."

"No dinner, Zamora? Well . . . surely you can stay long enough to enjoy some wine and renew your acquaintance with Lazaro here," the governor said, nodding toward the stocky man standing next to Clay Ashworth and handing Zamora a delicately carved flute filled with a deeply crimson liquid. "It is our vintage, you know."

The subtle aroma of fruit and alcohol made Zamora's mouth water, suddenly making him realize he was hungrier than he had thought.

"Please stay, José," Consuela said, "the evening will not be complete without you. It has been months since we last saw Uncle Lazaro, and he has much to tell us of Europe."

"Yes . . . do, Zamora," Lazaro Salinas said, leaving his place by the fire and shaking Zamora's unenthusiastic hand. "There is much of which we must speak."

"Indeed?" Zamora said, quickly withdrawing his hand, sensing some ominous undertone in Lazaro Salinas's voice. The man's look, while not unfriendly, was distinctly guarded. "Then we must do so very soon, señor."

"Without doubt," the gobernador added.

"Come. We should be seated—so the food may be served," señora Salinas said, with a wave of her hand across the elaborate table. "And, yes, please stay, señor Zamora. If it would please Consuela."

Zamora smiled and shrugged his shoulders. "Perhaps I will stay. The wine is excellent, and with you here, Lazaro, the evening promises to be an interesting one. It has been a long time."

The muscles in Zamora's jaw worked rhythmically. Every nerve in his body told him he must act now. But first, he had to determine just how much Salinas and his brother actually knew, or if they were merely guessing, putting things together, but not really knowing. Still, one way or the other, he had to act, and act quickly.

For Consuela the dinner was an unexpectedly uncomfortable affair, pleasant in some respects, but the atmosphere had been too stilted for the evening to have been truly enjoyable. Inexplicably, there seemed to be some distance growing between Zamora and her father, and that was troubling to her.

She had feelings for this man, despite his, at times, domineering attitude toward her. She had often wondered what life would be like as his wife, a thought she had entertained for no

209

other man, at least not until Clay Ashworth had entered her circumspectly patrician world.

After dinner, Consuela permitted Zamora to escort her out onto the veranda.

"Isn't the night beautiful, José?" she said, slipping her hand into his. "The moon makes it so bright, and the chill in the air makes me feel so alive."

Zamora suddenly turned her to him and grasped her shoulders.

"José, you're hurting—"

"You are alive, little one. You are life itself," he said, passionately crushing his mouth to hers as she disappeared within his embrace, his entire body seeming to envelop her.

Suddenly filled with panic, Consuela felt as if she were being consumed, as if he would devour her.

Her lips hurt terribly from the hardness of his mouth, and she struggled to push herself free.

Tearing her mouth from his, she cried, "José, stop it! You're hurting me! Let me go!"

"No! No, little one," he growled, struggling to keep her within his painful clutch, "you are mine." His breath was strong from the wine, and his mouth again sought hers. "No one loves you as I do. No one."

"No, José! I am not yours. Not yet . . . maybe never, José. Let . . . let me go!" she said. With a final shove she broke free and stood staring at the man whom she now barely recognized.

Never before had she seen him like this. His actions had always been so correct, so gentlemanly, almost courtly. Nothing in their past relationship had prepared her for the urgency of his embrace, for the frightening totality of his demands.

As he seized her arms, again pulling her within his grasp, a hand slammed down on Zamora's shoulder, pulling him violently back, the force of its grip causing him to wince as he let her go, twisting away from her. Before she was completely free of his hold, Clay Ashworth's massive fist connected squarely with Zamora's jaw, snapping his head to one side and knocking him off his feet onto the tiled floor, badly stunned, but not unconscious.

"You'll never know how good that felt," Clay said, rubbing his throbbing fist.

Dropping to Zamora's side, Consuela looked up at Clay and said, "Clay Ashworth! Look what you have done."

"Well, he was molesting you, and I thought—"

"Never mind what you thought," Consuela said, lifting Zamora's head into her lap, gently rubbing his temples. "He has done nothing to you, and he would do nothing to hurt me."

"Can you be so sure, Consuela?"

"What do you mean by that?" she snapped.

"His almost total sense of possession is what I mean, Miss Salinas," Clay said, feeling a flush of embarrassment and anger toward her. Looking down at her, he continued. "The man acts as though he possesses you—you, the ranch, your father, every-thing."

"Please, señor, don't be ridiculous," she snapped.

"*Ridiculous?*" Clay said, blanching at her obstinacy.

"*Sí.* Ridiculous."

"Then perhaps you can explain to me his true loyalties."

"*True loyalties?* His true loyalties are to my father and to me."

"And not to France or Spain, not to himself?"

Consuela caught her breath. "What do you mean *to France or Spain?*"

"Oh, come now, Miss Salinas. You're a woman of the world," Clay said, his tone slightly tinted with ridicule. "Surely you can see what's happening. His attempt to rather roughly subdue you here, just now, had nothing to do with his desire to control this ranch and secure his place in a French-dominated Mexico? Surely it had nothing to do with attempting to scuttle your father's plans with Senator Gwin because they would interfere with his own chicanery?"

As Zamora slowly rolled onto his elbow, shaking his head, Consuela rose to her feet. Saying nothing, she looked squarely at Clay, her face hard with resentment and frustration. Then turning, she stormed past Clay toward the entrance to the house, trailing an angry torrent of Spanish behind her.

Turning to watch her retreat, utterly astonished by Conseula's unexpected defense of Zamora—her seemingly blind refusal to recognize the man for what he was—Clay was not aware that Zamora had struggled to his feet behind him.

"You see, señor Ashworth, she truly is mine. I have won, and I will soon control it all: her, this place, and northern Mexico."

Clay turned to look at the sneering man. "You seem to have forgotten one important factor, Zamora."

"And what might that be?"

"Her father."

"Her father," Zamora scoffed. "He is a weakling, less than nothing, and will soon be exactly that—nothing.

"I should let you go back to your Senator Gwin and tell him of your failure. But no, señor Ashworth," he snarled, rubbing his jaw, "you are going to answer to me. You have your choice of weapons, but not of time and place. We will meet just before sunup, in the small meadow outside the compound wall. There will be no quarter asked and none given. Do I make myself understood?"

Clay studied the man's darkened, hate-smeared face. "It would seem I have—"

"It would, indeed, señor. Your choice of weapons?"

"A duel, then? You're challenging me to a duel?"

"I am, señor. A duel. Now, enough talk—your choice of weapons?"

"Ah . . . well . . . if there is no other way, señor Zamora, I have my cavalry sword. I suppose that—"

A smile cracked Zamora's hollow face. José Rodriguez Zamora was known throughout both Mexico and Spain as an accomplished swordsman. To enter into swordplay with him was to court death at his convenience.

"That will do nicely," he cut in, his gratification all too apparent. "Do not be late, señor."

"Yes. Until then," Clay said, half to himself, as he turned and walked back into the still brightly lit ranch house, a smile playing at his lips.

As a cadet at West Point, eventually graduating fourth in his class—a time and accomplishment in his life few were aware of— Clay had worked hard developing his expertise as a swordsman, a skill he then deemed essential for any military officer. While still a student, he had trained with the blade constantly, almost to the detriment of his scholastic studies. But his determination had resulted in a proficiency that had won him a wide reputation and numerous awards.

Despite the fact he had not used a sword in some time, and his deftness with a blade had undoubtedly suffered, he now found himself looking forward to his next encounter with the mysterious José Rodriguez Zamora—an encounter he hoped would end at least some of the duplicity he had been sent to forestall.

# CHAPTER 20

* * *

Clay Ashworth stepped from his room into the hallway outside his bedroom, strapping his sword to his side.

"You won't need that this morning, señor Ashworth," Consuela said, eyeing his cavalry sword. "I have our horses just outside, saddled and ready. We have a long day ahead of us."

"*A long day?*" he asked. "I thought after last night, we—"

"It is *because* of last night, señor Ashworth," she said, her tone cold and efficient. "With my father's encouragement, I am going to show you as much of the ranch as possible. You will see just how powerful my father's influence is, and how baseless your mistrust of señor Zamora."

"But I have never doubted your father's influence or his power, and as for Zamora, I—"

"Nonetheless," she said, turning toward the door, "we must leave now if we are to be back for the evening meal, and Father has important guests coming he will want you to meet. We must hurry."

"But . . . I . . ."

"Leave your sword and come," she ordered, disappearing through the door, her abruptness leaving no room for dispute.

Following her directions, Clay returned the sword to his room and hurried to follow her out of the hacienda.

The mountains east of the ranch almost seemed to claw at the black sky, tearing open a ragged gray wound above them. The air was cold and bracing, and it felt good to be in the saddle, riding next to this woman. It annoyed him though to realize just how important and impossible a place she had come to assume in his life, how her words and behavior affected his reactions. What she thought and how she acted were starting to interfere with what he had come here to do. In a situation as dangerous as this, such feelings could quickly become a weakness—a fatal weakness.

As for his meeting with Zamora, it would happen; but for now, it would have to wait. This was his chance to get into the back country.

"And just where are we headed, may I ask?" he said, as they mounted their horses in front of the house.

"I want to show you one of the mines. You needn't worry, it is the nearest one. I have been there before."

"And the others?"

"They are farther back into the mountains, and I am unsure of their location. We will go to the nearest for now."

"I will go to the nearest with you, if you will come to one of the others with me."

Consuela studied his face in the dim light of dawn. "Why? Why is it of such importance for you to see another?"

"I don't think it's of as much importance to me as it might be for you—when you see what goes on there."

"What are you talking about?" she snapped, reining her dancing horse to a stop. "What goes on there?"

"You honestly don't know?" Clay said, turning in his saddle to face her.

"I don't know what you are talking about," she insisted, the hostility of the previous evening again entering her voice. "If I knew, do you think I would ask?"

"It would be easier if I showed you."

"Show me what?" she demanded, her resentment mounting.

Clay felt himself losing patience. His voice harder, he said, "Very well, Consuela, I'll tell you, but only if you promise to come with me, help me find one of the other mines."

"Oh, all right," she said, slapping her leg with her quirt in frustration.

"Your father and Zamora are engaged in slave trading and in slavery. Those mines are profitable because they are worked by Apache slaves who are kept on the edge of starvation and worked until they drop."

"What?" Consuela's face paled, and her voice quavered with shock and resentment. "How dare you!" she said, swinging her quirt at Clay. "My father would never deal in slaves! Never!"

Ducking her angry swing, Clay grabbed her skittish horse's bridle. "Will you come with me," he said, jerking her horse around to avoid her quirt, "or are you going to hide from the truth?"

"It's not true," she blurted, tears beginning to well in her eyes. "You haven't seen them. You've never been to our mines. It's not true."

"No, I haven't, and you've only been to the nearest. One of the reasons I'm here is to verify what seems to be widely known north of the border and is seen as a major cause of the trouble everyone's having with the Apaches. Now . . . will you come with me, or are you going to hide from this, too?"

"What are you talking about, *this too?*"

"Zamora. You and Zamora."

"My relationship with señor Zamora is none of your business. For your information, I intend to marry him."

"Marry him? You'd marry him, knowing what he is?"

"He is a gentleman," she insisted, her pretty nose in the air. "He would never behave as you have."

"As I have? Lady, you haven't seen anything yet," Clay declared, slapping her horse on its rump, causing the animal to bolt forward, nearly unseating her. "Now, señorita Salinas," he shouted over the drumming of the horses's hooves, as he spurred his mount alongside hers. "Find me those mines, if you have the courage to face the ugly truth."

After watching the confrontation between Consuela and Clay Ashworth from the early-morning darkness at the side of the house, Zamora slunk back further into the blackness and considered their heated exchange, the thoughts streaming through his brain in a storm of confusion.

The situation was rapidly getting out of hand. If Consuela had not interfered, Ashworth would be dying or dead this very moment. But now . . . now things had to be brought to a head, and quickly. He had no idea that Ashworth knew of the slaves, or even had any interest in such an issue. He was here to solidify the relationship between Salinas and Gwin—or was he? *Who the devil is this man, anyway?* Zamora thought, rubbing his forehead. *What is it he really wants? What kind of game is he playing?*

For Zamora, the only certainty now was that he had to act fast to eliminate Salinas and his brother—they were both on to him—and then to kill Ashworth. Consuela would then be his—hadn't he just overheard her say that she intended to marry him anyway? She had told the gringo straight to his face. Though he knew she had spoken in anger, she had committed herself nonetheless. That much had been good news. With that accomplished, the ranch would be in his hands, and northern Mexico would be under his control when the French took control of Mexico City. Then, and only then, could he begin turning Mexico toward Spain.

By the time Consuela and Ashworth had ridden off, a plan had taken form in Zamora's mind, and turning, he entered the hacienda home through a back passageway. The hour was still early, and the house dark, the only sounds those tiny, secret noises of a household at rest.

Making his way silently down the dark hallway, stepping carefully to avoid any sound on the red-tiled floor, Zamora stopped at the door to Clay Ashworth's room. Slowly depressing the handle, he pushed the heavy door inward and stepped into the dark room. Lying on the bed was the weapon he sought: Clay Ashworth's cavalry sword, carelessly discarded as he had left with Consuela.

Quietly slipping the long, gracefully curved blade from its decorative metal scabbard, Zamora turned and made his way to the gobernador's bedroom. Luckily, the old woman slept in an adjoining room. Slowly pushing the door inward, he stepped to the bed.

Salinas lay on his side, his back to Zamora, his breathing deep and regular. In the sanctuary of his own bed, his gray hair disheveled by sleep, the gobernador looked surprisingly older, even frail. Without hesitation, Zamora lifted the sword high above his head and struck with terrible force.

The awful sound of the old man dying seemed intense, and for a moment Zamora feared it would be heard, then all fell silent. Zamora stood considering what he had done. He had killed men before, but never like this. Without wiping the bloodstains from the blade, he turned and made his way back to Clay Ashworth's bedroom where he replaced the sword in its scabbard and quickly left the house.

# CHAPTER 21

★  ★  ★

IT HAD TAKEN CLAY AND CONSUELA most of the morning
to reach the nearest mine. For nearly the entire distance, they had
ridden in silence, each resentful of the words that had been
spoken earlier.

"You see," Consuela said, dismounting in front of the shack
near the entrance to the busy mine. "There are no slaves here."

"No. You are absolutely correct, señorita Salinas," Clay
declared in mock agreement, swinging his right leg over the saddle
horn and sliding easily to the ground. "This mine of yours would
appear to be a model of admirably honest efficiency. Just as one
might expect."

Consuela arched a delicate eyebrow. "As one might expect?"

"Certainly. This is where all of your father's guests are brought,
isn't it? At least those who are interested, anyway?"

"Of course," she declared, haughtily tossing her head. "The

other mines are much more difficult to reach, further up in the mountains."

"Uh-huh."

"Oh! There are times when I very much want to like you, Clay Ashworth. But, you are the most difficult and arrogant man I have ever known."

Clay leaned against his saddle and grinned at her. "No exceptions? Not even one?"

Stomping her foot, Consuela turned away, fighting to suppress the annoying urge that threatened to lift the corners of her lovely mouth into a smile. The man bothered her no end. How could he so consistently anger her, yet fill her with this inexplicable longing, a desire for him that frightened her with its intensity?

She had never known a man like Clay Ashworth. He was more man than any she had known before—and that included Zamora. Perhaps that is what made him seem so difficult. When she was with him, she felt safe, as though no possible harm could come to her.

As much as it hurt to admit it, this big Utahan was more open, more direct, more honest in his mannerisms and actions than anyone she had ever known, including her father. At one moment he could be so completely charming she was willing to do anything for him, and in the next, drive her to distraction. The truth was, she trusted him.

*No,* she thought, *the truth is, I love him—desperately.*

Assuming her most businesslike manner, she turned toward Clay and with as much chill as she could force into her voice, asked, "Do you wish to see this mine, señor Ashworth, or not?"

Clay took a deep breath, savoring the scent of pine and the chill of the mountain air. Watching her a moment, he said, "No, ma'am. Not this one. I want to see one of the others. I really don't care which, just one of the others. The choice is yours."

"You are still convinced my father deals in slaves, then?"

"I haven't seen anything to change my mind yet. Have you?"

"I know my father," she said, climbing into the saddle.

Watching her, Clay could not help but smile. Consuela had a way of lifting her chin and looking down her nose when she was delivering what she considered to be the final word on a subject. He could not decide what it was that so delighted him whenever she did it. It was not a gesture of snobbery or snootiness. On the contrary, to him it was one of her most endearing mannerisms, another one of those little traits she possessed that so totally captivated him.

Reining her horse about, she looked squarely at Clay. "You needn't be so smug about it," she said, reacting with annoyance to his smile. "He would not do such a thing, nor would José."

It was mid-afternoon when the two rode into the littered assembly yard of the next mine. It had not been hard to find. They had simply followed a deeply rutted wagon road farther back into the Sierra Madre.

Dismounting near a badly weathered shack they walked to the entrance of the shaft. Narrow-gauge tracks emerged from the dark hole and split, one branch running past the shack and out onto a dangerously dilapidated loading bunker, beneath which stood a huge wagon half-filled with newly mined ore. The other ran to the edge of the spreading discard dump.

The place was a clutter of old, rusted mine cars, badly corroded track, frayed cable, broken winches, and other worn out, cast-off mining machinery. It looked more like a junkyard than a producing mine. Had it not been for the freshly excavated rock and dirt heaved over the edge of the dump and down the steep mountainside, the mine would have almost appeared deserted.

At the mouth of the mineshaft, someone had crudely carved the words *Estar a la Muerte* deeply in the overhead support beam.

Clay nodded toward the ill-boding message above the dark, gaping portal. "Looks like an efficient operation," he said, sardonically.

"I don't understand," Consuela said, looking around. "There should be an overseer . . . and mine workers."

Clay stepped to the mouth of the mine. "Oh, they're about. Come and listen."

"How far back in are they?" Consuela asked, peering intently into the grimy blackness of the shaft.

The dull, rusted tracks slanted downward, quickly disappearing into the darkness, and muffled, disquieting sounds could be heard deep inside the mountain.

"Should we go in?" she asked, taking a hesitant step past the entrance. "Do you think it is safe?"

Clay leaned against the tar-coated bracing at the mouth of the shaft. "Not a good idea. Without a light it would be easy to get hurt. In fact, from the looks of the place, it would be easy to get hurt with a light."

Almost imperceptibly at first, a low, grinding rumble began filling the shaft, slowly growing in intensity, oddly punctuated with sharp, snapping or cracking sounds.

"I think I see a light back in there," Consuela observed. "Someone's coming, I think."

"Best stay out of the way," Clay said, casually. "They are probably bringing a carload of ore up."

Somehow reluctant to move from the mouth of the mine, Consuela slowly turned and carefully made her way to the log bracing that extended outward from the tunnel's outer support beam and angled away from the tracks. Stacked on their sides, pyramid fashion, the longest on the bottom, the big logs kept the loose dirt of the mountainside from sloughing onto the tracks where they emerged from the tunnel.

Daintily sweeping some dirt off the lowest log with her hand, she sat down across the tracks from Clay, watching his reactions out of the corner of her eye.

"Careful you don't get a sliver," he chided.

From where she sat, Consuela could not see more than a few feet into the tunnel; but increasingly uncertain of what they were going to discover in this dismal place, she had begun to feel somewhat irresolute and vulnerable. Even for a mine, the place was unbelievably filthy.

It suddenly dawned on her that what was missing was any sense of pride, the pride so obviously taken in other Salinas operations. There was no dignity here. In fact, a spirit of hostility and shame seemed to permeate the entire area, and somehow she sensed it growing stronger as the noise coming from the shaft grew louder.

Clay slowly rose to his feet, the look on his face betraying an intensity of anger and hostility she had never seen, nor would she have thought it possible. His jaw was clenched, and his hand moved involuntarily to the big Colt at his side. It was a look of pure hatred.

"Clay, what is—"

Four Apache men slowly emerged from the mouth of the tunnel. Except for the ragged breach clouts that sagged from their scrawny loins and the rough leather harnesses that bit cruelly into their bloody shoulders, the sweating, emaciated men were naked, their heavily chained feet leaving a trail of blood on the sharp rocks that littered the track bed. Bowed with the weight of their struggle in pulling the heavily loaded ore car from the mine, they were completely unaware of anyone watching them.

Suddenly, a single, sinuous, black snake shot out of the mine from behind them, leaving a bloody welt as it sliced across the back of one of the men nearest the heavy ore car. No sound escaped his throat, but the searing pain caused him to lose his balance, and he fell across the tracks, the iron wheels scraping at his nearly fleshless legs.

Bringing his big Colt level with his shoulder, Clay snarled. "You two drop your guns and come out of that tunnel. Do it now, and do it very carefully."

From inside the mouth of the tunnel, Consuela heard, "What the—?"

"You heard me. Any more conversation, and I'm going to blow one of you away."

Guns clattered on the track, and two men stepped into view. They were white men, not Mexicans, and Consuela did not recognize either of them.

"Who are you, mister?" one of the men asked.

"Never mind who I am. You recognize either of these two vipers?" Clay asked, glancing toward Consuela.

Stunned at what she saw and at the unexpected swiftness of Clay's reaction, Consuela could only shake her head.

"Who's she?" one asked, looking her over carefully. "Ain't never seen the likes of her around here b'fore."

"No, and it's unlikely you ever will again. Now, whichever one of you has the keys to those leg irons, unlock them, and be fast about it."

"Ain't got 'em," the bigger of the two said, a little too confidently.

Looking at the other, Clay said, "Too bad, because if he doesn't unlock those irons, and do it fast, I'm going to blow out one of your knees. You'd better convince your partner he has those keys."

"Look here, mister, you ain't got no right t' do this. These here slaves belong t' Governor Salinas. All you're likely to do is wind up in there chained up with 'em. Now—"

The blast from Clay's gun reverberated down the tunnel as the slug slammed into the support beam above the two men, falling dirt dusting them liberally. "Next one draws blood," Clay said, leveling the gun at the men.

Consuela started at the sound of the shot, but it had been the mention of her father that made her catch her breath and sink back down on the log. "It's not true," she said, half to her self. Looking up, her eyes misting with tears, she saw Clay glance her way, the look on his face a mask of contempt for what they had found, what he had known to be true. "It can't be true," she cried.

"Oh, it's true alright, Consuela. It's—"

Suddenly the black snake shot out again, wrapping itself around Clay's neck with an ugly crack, cutting off his air, and yanking him cruelly from his feet. The big gun flew from his hand as he clawed at the whip and landed between the tracks a few feet in front of Consuela.

"Yeah, I got the keys, mister," the big man snarled, giving the whip a vicious tug. "An' since yer s' concerned fer these here miser'ble redskins, you can jest help 'em move this ore out to the loading rack. Then we'll see what else we got t' keep yuh busy."

"I'm gonna take care of missy, here," the smaller of the two said, leering at Consuela, as he moved from behind the ore car.

Like the crack of that ugly whip, something snapped inside Consuela. The horror of what she was witnessing, the realization of betrayal, of her life having been lived at the unspeakable cost of such human suffering, flooded her mind. And the realization was as abrupt and shocking as if someone had thrown ice water over her naked, fevered body.

A scream born of bitter anguish tore from her throat as she threw herself from the log onto the tracks. Clutching Clay's big Colt, Consuela rolled onto her back, the big gun a natural extension of her arm. Her first shot tore into the chest of Clay's assailant, the second shattered the skull of the man desperately reaching to grab her ankle.

Within less than an hour, working together, Clay and Consuela had subdued the remaining two slave masters and freed the captive Indians—most of whom were Apache—liberating them to find their way back to their respective tribal bands. Many of them were so weak as to be near death, but feeling the chains drop from their ankles, and finally understanding that they were at long last free to flee, to take flight into the sunlight and fresh air, they disappeared like shadows melting before an early-morning sun, renewed strength somehow flooding through their pain-wracked, emaciated bodies.

As the chains fell, so too did the sense of guilt that had flooded Consuela, nearly consuming her. With each chain, she felt increased expiation, and with the last, what only could be called absolution. Finally, as they trudged from the now-empty mine, she turned to Clay and stepped near to him, causing him to take her in his embrace, not quite understanding what her actions meant.

"Clay," she whispered, tears welling in her eyes. "I . . . I can't. . . ."

Gently grasping her shoulders he held her back and looked

into her eyes. "It's not necessary, Consuela. You had no way of knowing."

How she loved this man. How she wanted to tell him. How she wished he would take her back into his embrace and crush her to him. How she wanted to feel his lips on hers. At this moment she would happily give herself to him without hesitation—right now, right here in the dirt. But he did not understand. She could see it in his face, and she had no way of telling him. Not now.

# CHAPTER 22

★ ★ ★

It was dark when Clay and Consuela rode into the ranch compound. The house was brightly lit, and at least a dozen horses were tied at the hitching rail. Something was not right—very wrong, in fact. Clay had felt it the moment they rode into the yard.

As Clay dismounted and stepped around his horse to assist Consuela from her mount, the front door suddenly banged open, slamming into the door casing. A flood of men poured out of the house to surround Clay and throw him to the ground. The sudden noise and confusion caused the horses to panic and set them to dancing and straining against their reins.

Fighting to stay with him, Consuela was torn from Clay's side as the men surrounded him, kicking at him and pummeling him with their fists.

Pushing Consuela toward the porch, one of the men yelled back to the house, "Bring the rope out here."

Bolting up onto the porch, Consuela turned and screamed, "Stop this! Stop this at once!"

The tone in her voice left no doubt as to her authority in this place, and except for the scuffling of the men dragging Clay to his feet, the yard fell silent.

"What is the meaning of this?" she demanded.

Zamora stepped from the house. Speaking her name softly, he said, "Please . . . come inside. There are things you must know."

Consuela gestured at the mob surrounding Clay. "But what is the meaning of this?"

Taking her elbow and gently pressing her toward the door, his tone reassuring, he said, "They will not harm him—not now." Turning, he commanded, "Bring the gringo inside."

"But . . ."

"Come inside, my little one, and sit down. I will explain."

As the two disappeared into the house, the crowd again closed around Clay, several of the men continuing to batter him with their fists, shoving him from one into another. Twice he was knocked to the ground and kicked as he struggled to regain his footing.

Suddenly wrenching one hand free, Clay lunged upward, driving his left fist into the belly of his nearest assailant, doubling the man over. His right landed squarely in the face of another, bone crunching with its impact.

Enraged, the mob closed, hands grabbing, feet kicking; and in the dim light spilling from one of the windows, Clay glimpsed a rope being thrown over a tree limb at the corner of the house.

In one last effort to somehow save himself, the big Utahan cocked an arm ready to swing, but Consuela's anguished scream pierced the gathering darkness, causing the struggle to collapse into silence, her cry of denial and disbelief filling the night.

The mob shoved Clay through the door and into the house ahead of them. Consuela sat hunched over on the large leather couch in the great room, her face in her hands, her body shaking with sobs. Zamora stood behind her, a comforting hand resting on her shoulder. In his other was Clay's sword.

Clay looked at Zamora. "What is going on? What are you doing with my saber? I—"

"As you well know, señor Ashworth," Zamora said, the sneer on his face revealing his utter contempt for Clay. "gobernador Salinas is dead—by your sword. Foully murdered by you, sir."

"Dead? By me? But I—"

"What you don't know, señor, is that señora Salinas has collapsed and now lies at death's door as well. Her physician does not expect her to last through the night."

Consuela looked up at Clay, her tear-stained face distorted by shock, incomprehension, and anguish.

She seemed to choke as she spoke his name. "Clay?"

"Consuela, believe me. I know nothing of this," he pleaded. "Surely you believe me. Surely you know I could never have done anything to harm your father—or any of your family."

Clay watched the face he had come to love so desperately, hating Zamora's hand on her, looking for any sign that would indicate she did not think him guilty of such an act.

Tears still streaming down her cheeks, Consuela dragged the back of her hand across her wet face.

"Please, Consuela, I. . . ."

"Just this morning you accused him of slavery," she said, her voice heavy, her words filled with reproach. "You were not willing to rest until you had proved it to me."

"But . . . Consuela, that's. . . ."

Zamora cut him off. "Take this gringo outside," he ordered,

rudely gesturing to the men surrounding Clay. "I am going to bring him to justice in the way he seems to understand best—with the blade—his own blade."

"José, no. It is not the way we deal with this," Consuela said.

"Quiet, my little one," he cooed. Lifting her elbow, he continued. "Come. You are in shock. You must rest. This matter is not for your eyes, and you must trouble yourself no further. Your father will be avenged this night, little one."

Pulling her arm free, Consuela turned to Zamora. "Where is my Uncle Lazaro?" she demanded weakly. "I need him—he will help me know what I should do."

"He is not here," Zamora said abruptly. "It is not necessary. I am here, and I will see that this matter is quickly resolved. Now go," he demanded, gesturing to one of the servants. "See she is taken to her room and made to rest."

"José," she complained, attempting to pull herself free. "I do not . . . wish to. . . ."

Zamora caught Consuela as she collapsed. "She is in a state of shock," he said, lifting her into the arms of one of the house servants. "Do as I say. See she is taken to her room and cared for," he said, his tone leaving no room for argument. Turning to the men behind Clay, he said, "Take him outside and wait for me. We will put an end to this—now."

★　★　★

Clay's gracefully curved cavalry sword glinted in the dimming moonlight as it came up quickly to parry Zamora's unexpected thrust. *So, this is how it is to be,* he thought. *No trial, no formality, just accusation and a brutal fight to the death.*

Stepping back, Zamora struck swiftly, his blade slashing downward toward Clay's chest, but with Clay's upward thrust to block the well-aimed blow, the blades slid to their hilts, and the two stood locked toe-to-toe, eye-to-eye.

The small cluster of men closed around them, each anxious not to miss a word or stroke of the exchange, each wanting to see the end of the hated gringo, Clay Ashworth.

For most of the men present, he had killed their friend; for the others, a much-loved *patrón*. All loved and respected the señora, now near death, and the señorita. Now, all of them were eager to see the horrible crime avenged, and none doubted Zamora would prevail. The gringo's end would come quickly.

"This will be quick, señor Ashworth," Zamora said, his eyes lifting from the blades. "You will suffer for only a short moment, then you will die. But suffer you must."

"Maybe you speak too soon, Zamora," Clay said, refusing to break eye contact. "Over-confidence can kill."

Shoving Zamora away, Clay thrust, and their blades crossed, each surprised at the other's skill, each knowing that nothing could be taken for granted.

The two fought in silence, their blows reverberating as they circled, tested, came together, and parted in the cold night air. The moonlight flashed repeatedly from each blade, mesmerizing the crowd that opened and closed with the rhythm of this graceful dance of death.

Disengaging, the two stepped away, their sabers waving gracefully between them, each studying the other for advantage.

"You are surprisingly good, señor Ashworth," Zamora purred. "But you will not be good enough. Too much is at stake."

"Too much?" Clay said, lifting the deadly point of his saber toward Zamora's face. "Your concentration must be weak, Zamora. The blade requires focus. It's too late for scheming. You can lie to everyone but the sword. Here, only the truth will tell."

Zamora's eyes grew large, and the man seemed to expand like a balloon about to burst. "Damn you, Clay Ashworth!" Zamora screamed, grasping his sword with both hands and springing toward Clay, hacking as if the saber were an ax. "Damn you to hell!"

Clay ducked quickly to the left, and Zamora's wild swing slashed past him. In that instant, lifting his right foot, Clay caught Zamora's ankle, and kicking upward, sent him tumbling into the dirt, his sword flying into the air and landing at Clay's feet.

Kicking the sword aside, Clay watched the man struggle to his knees, hands searching for his saber. Knowing Zamora's humiliation would be overwhelming and his reaction violent, Clay braced himself to deliver the killing stroke.

"That will do, señor Ashworth." It was Lazaro Salinas. "We know it was not you who killed the gobernador, and we know who did. Get up off your knees, Zamora, and stand like a man. It is you who must pay the penalty for this brutal crime. Tonight you must answer for two.

"It was you, Zamora. It was you who killed my brother—and now my sister-in-law, as well. It is you who must answer, *asesino.*"

At the sound of Salinas's voice, Zamora froze, his head slowly turning to face his accuser, his brain unbelieving.

Surprised at Salinas's appearance, Clay lowered his blade and turned as the crowd reacted with stunned silence to the unexpected news. Not only was the gobernador dead, but so was his wife.

As those nearest the steps parted, Clay could see Consuela standing next to her uncle on the steps of the veranda. Gone from her stricken, tear-stained face was the accusatory look that had burned into his brain; gone was any sign of doubt. His only thought now was to take her in his arms, to help her understand how deeply he loved her, and how much he hated what had happened—the death of her father, and now the loss of her mother. All he wanted in life was to make it up to her, to restore stability and love in her life.

Uncomprehendingly, Clay watched her hand fly to her mouth and heard her scream as a thin line of icy pain slashed across his cheek and shoulder.

Springing back for a second and final blow, Zamora lifted his sword and yelled, "No! You die, gringo! Now you—"

As Clay turned to counter the coming blow, Zamora's chest blossomed with a spray of red, his words choking in his throat, as the report from Lazaro Salinas's pistol rang out across courtyard.

The sword fell from Zamora's hand, and filled with shock, his eyes searched Clay's face, as if looking for some answer, as if looking for an explanation of what was happening. Why had things gone so wrong? How had he lost? Why?

The following week had gone quickly and, for Consuela, it had been a terribly upsetting time. She was relieved to learn of Clay's innocence in the death of her father. Zamora's guilt had been confirmed by one of the house servants who had been up early and seen Zamora emerge from Governor Salinas's bedroom, bloody sword in hand. In the face of Clay's impending lynching, the frightened little woman had found the courage to inform Consuela's uncle, absolving Clay of the crime.

Lucky to have been only superficially wounded by Zamora's desperate, final attack, Clay had watched with admiration as Consuela dealt with each problem in its proper order. Her parents were now gone, buried on a hill not far from the house; a badly wounded Zamora was recuperating in prison awaiting a date with the hangman, her feelings for him crushed beneath her contempt; and the future of the ranch seemed now to be in the capable hands of her uncle, a man for whom she felt nothing but love, and in whom she had the utmost confidence.

As for Mexico, only time would tell.

With Zamora's arrest, all of his plans had come unraveled. Lazaro Salinas had returned from Spain with proof of Zamora's duplicity, and it would have been only a matter of time before his schemes were revealed—and Zamora had known it. He had been plotting with the Spanish and French to bring about French supremacy over Mexico, and he had been scheming to gain control of the ranch and all of its holdings when the French would enter Mexico City sometime within the next year. It was now obvious to everyone that Zamora's intention had been to become governor of all of northern Mexico. And unknown to Consuela, she had been the key to it all. With her as his wife, everything he had worked for would have fallen into place.

For Clay, there now remained nothing for him to do in Mexico. Gwin's plans for an alliance between Sonora and California had died with Governor Salinas. The would-be California president was now on his own. If the Confederacy could not open a southern route into the New Mexico territory and on into California, it was unlikely that California could ever become an independent republic. Without access to the mineral wealth of the West, the future of the Confederacy would remain very much in doubt.

Clay knew the war between the states would continue, and he knew, as only a soldier could know, it was likely to be long and bloody. But for now, he had done what he had been sent to do. Not only had he seriously undermined Gwin's plans, a factor that would impact the course of the war, he had also had an impact on the slave trade between Arizona, New Mexico, and northern Mexico. He had not put an end to it by any means, but he had disrupted the trade in Apache slaves that was a major cause of Cochise's rampages back and forth across the border. Whether what he had done would have an impact on the slave trading around the Mormon colonies, he did not know, but perhaps it was a beginning.

It was time to return to Utah and to the ranch that was the center of his world.

# CHAPTER 23

★  ★  ★

M Y PLACE IS HERE, IN Mexico," Consuela said, not knowing whether to look at Clay or her uncle. "I am needed here.
Besides," she said, lifting her cup, "this is the only life I have ever
known."

"Consuela," Lazaro said, affectionately touching his niece's
hand, "this place will run itself. What real need is there for you
here? You have your own life to live. Go and live it. There is no
future here, not the kind you surely desire.

"Besides," he continued, self-consciously withdrawing his
hand, "how much have you really been here in the past? For long
periods each year, you were away becoming truly educated; you
have traveled; you have grown to womanhood. This has been a
place to which you always returned, and it shall always remain so,
but the time has come for you to make a life of your own."

Clay pushed his chair back from the table and looked at

Consuela, his face solemn. "I think it would be best if I left early in the morning. I need to get back, and it's a long way."

In the previous few days, Clay and Consuela had broached the subject of the future many times, attempting to deal with the doubts and fears that threatened to separate them. Each time, the issues dividing them had been left unresolved.

This place was her home, the only home she had ever known. She had traveled widely and spent long periods of study in the eastern United States and Europe, but it was at the Salinas Ranch and northern Mexico where her heart had always remained. It was the kind of emotional affinity she could never put into words.

Yet she recognized that Clay was needed back in Utah, back at his *Rancho Los Librados*. He was a rancher, and though she had been raised on a ranch, she had grown to adulthood convinced that she could never marry a man who wore boots and worked with cattle and horses and all the smelly mess that went with them—a cowboy, a *vaquero*. Horses were to be ridden for enjoyment, brought to her gentled and saddled—their preparation, care, and keeping left to others.

Here in this place of intellect, culture, and gracious living, she had been shielded from the on-going, earthy realities of ranch life that daily surrounded her just outside the *hacienda* walls, and the big boots every vaquero and cowboy wore had come to symbolize all of the dirt and grime that unwanted men dragged into her clean, orderly surroundings. In fact, those boots had almost become a fetish in her thinking.

In her mind, the contrast couldn't be more clear: her father's ranch was a place of comfort, refinement, and safety—a place to leave from and a refuge to which she could always return. What it took to create and maintain such wealth and comfort never entered into her thinking.

"There is always a home for you here, Clay," Lazaro said, wondering if this was a subject he should avoid. Clearing his throat, he continued, "If you will pardon me, I must attend to some matters before I retire."

"Don't leave just yet, Uncle Lazaro."

Turning to Clay, she said, "He is right, Clay. We could live here. Uncle Lazaro can run the ranch and you and I can travel, see the world, and have a marvelous life together."

"As wonderful as that sounds—and I thank you both—I really must return to Utah. I have obligations, too. Obligations that I can't avoid."

"Would that be enough for the man you would want, Consuela?" Lazaro asked. "Could you love a man who had no more purpose in life than pursuing leisure?"

Clay watched Consuela carefully. How could he live without her? He loved even her independence, the way the light danced in her eyes when she spoke, how quick she was to smile at those around her, even when someone asked her an annoying question. It would be so easy to give up everything he had worked so hard to achieve, to turn his back on everything for this woman.

He loved her more than he could put into words. But deep inside, he knew it would not work. He had tried to explain his feelings to her, that he would not just be turning his back on the growing nation that was so much a part of him, on the rugged Utah Territory, on the ranch he had worked so hard to build, and on those who depended on him—he would be denying himself, his own identity.

"Besides," Consuela said, staring into her cup, ignoring her uncle's question. "I am not a rancher or a rancher's wife. I am sure I would hate it—boots and everything else. I would have to wear those awful boots, and do the kinds of things that make women old before their time."

"My dear," Lazaro Salinas said, with a chuckle, "where do you think you have been living?" His hand swept the room. "Is not this a *rancho?* Have you not been living on a ranch all your young life? I have not noticed that you have aged too drastically because of it."

"That's different, Uncle Lazaro. The ranch is run by others. Father was a *patrón,* a *jefe.* His was not the difficult life of a rancher. He was a gentleman, a *político,* a statesman."

Turning to Clay, her eyes pleading, she said, "Stay here—with me. We could be so happy here. We can travel and do things together. The ranch would almost run itself under Uncle Lazaro's direction."

Lazaro chuckled as Clay said, "I'm afraid you really don't know that much about ranching, do you? It's a hands-on way of making a living, a demanding life, but the best life anyone could ask for. Here your Uncle Lazaro is going to have his hands full, and up in Utah, I will, too. In fact, I have been away far too long.

"I want you by my side, Consuela. And you're right, we could have a wonderful life together, you and I. You need never worry about hard work. The kind you seem concerned about will be done by others. On our ranch, you will be my queen, my *reina de los prados, ulmaria.* And such a queen is never compelled to wear boots."

"Mmm," she hummed, studying his face, as she so often did when attempting to fathom his thoughts. Finally she said, "Come, let us walk in the moonlight before it's too late."

Though not warm, the night air held only a slight chill, and the moonlight caused contrasting shadows to litter the meadow that sloped gently away from the back wall of the compound where Clay and Consuela lay lost in the deep, sweet-smelling grass. Not far away horses could be heard grazing, the sound of their cropping and chewing somehow reassuring. And in the distance, the soft lowing of cattle settling for the night added to a feeling of peace and rightness.

Consuela leaned over Clay, her face close to his. "How can I convince you, Clay Ashworth?"

"Convince me of what?"

"Of how much I love you, and how much I need you."

Clay gently pulled her to him. "There's no need for convincing," he said, as their lips met.

It was a long embrace, one in which each felt for the first time the thrill of their bodies touching so thoroughly, so intimately, so intensely. Though they had kissed before, neither had experienced the touch of the other so completely. Neither had felt the joy of so totally converging in the warmth of the other. To both it seemed as if individuality were at last being lost as they melded momentarily within each other's arms.

After a time, Consuela pushed herself up and looked down upon the man she had come to love so desperately. Breathing heavily and rising to her knees, she whispered, "I love you, Clay Ashworth. I need you, and I want you."

For Clay, seeing her kneeling above him, opening herself so completely, the light of the moon touching her hair and body with silver, her eyes filled with passion, it was the most thrilling moment of his life.

From the instant he had first laid eyes on her that night at the Gwin's dinner party, when she had challenged him at almost every word, he had adored her, wanted her to be his. From that moment on, his feelings had only grown more intense. She was the most perfect woman he had ever known—perfect in body, perfect in mind, perfect for him. If he could not have her, he knew he would never truly want another.

Gazing up at the perfection of the woman so completely opening herself to him, he was struck nearly dumb by her exquisite form. Never in all of his dreams had he expected such beauty, such generosity. His voice was deep with desire and wonder as he struggled for expression. "Oh . . . Consuela." No other words would come; none were necessary.

Clay pulled her to the ground and buried her beneath him, his mouth crushing hers. There, in the moonlight, in this perfect place, it was as if they thought as one, as if there were no reaction, only oneness, a perfect cohesion. Through it all, from California to this moment, she was at long last about to become his—totally, completely.

The thought that what was happening was not right, was in fact horribly wrong, suddenly flooded Clay's heated brain with the force of an icy deluge.

Pushing himself away, he whispered, "No."

For a moment, Consuela did not understand, and then her mind slowly began to fill with doubt. "What did you say?"

"Consuela, I . . . I can't. This is wrong."

"*Wrong?* Don't you love me?" Her voice suddenly filled with embarrassment and then anguish. "How can it be *wrong?*"

"It is because I love you that I can't allow this to happen." It was the wrong thing to say, and he knew it the moment he said it.

Quickly, Consuela rose to her feet. "*You* can't *allow* this to happen?" she hissed, her humiliation turning to anger. "Have *I* nothing to say?"

"Please, Consuela, let me explain."

"You had better make it fast, señor Ashworth," she said, tears beginning to flood her eyes, "because right now I don't think I ever want to see you again."

"Consuela, where I come from, this sort of thing . . . this, well . . . this . . . you know—what we were doing . . . about to do," he stammered. "Well . . . I live among a people who consider it to be sacred, to be saved just for those who are married—for man and wife. It is *sacred*, and I thought—well, I couldn't dishonor you."

"*Dishonor* me? Dishonor *me*, Clay Ashworth?" Consuela spat and brought her slim arm back into a roundhouse swing, her slap landing squarely and loudly on Clay's bewildered face. "Only *I* could do that, and I thought I was too much in love with you for the question of *honor* even to arise."

"But don't you see, Consuela," Clay pleaded, attempting to get to his feet. "I love you too much to have you for just one moment. I want you forever—the right way."

Storming toward the hacienda, the words streaming over her shoulder as embarrassment returned and anger gave way to tears, she blurted, "Dishonor me? Have I had nothing to say? Who do you think you are? You . . . you . . . you gringo, you."

Cochise watched the lone rider pass beneath the rocky promontory on which he sat his horse. On each side of the great Apache chief sat two of the former slaves Clay had freed. The two gestured as they spoke, explaining their extraordinary rescue at the hands of the white man and his woman.

Approaching from behind him, as yet unnoticed by the man below, was a coach accompanied by several outriders, obviously pressing to overtake him.

Cochise nodded as the men continued to gesture toward Clay and then toward the coach. Then, lifting his hand in the air silencing the two, Cochise reined his horse about and rode into the tree line where a large band of mounted warriors awaited them.

This white man and those with him would travel in safety through Apache territory, no matter how long or what the distance.

Hearing the rumble behind him, Clay turned in the saddle to see the large coach and six-up team top the rise behind him, the outriders careful to stay near but out of the dust. Urging his horse off the deeply rutted road, Clay waited for all of the dusty commotion to pass him by.

As the coach approached, the driver heaved back on the heavy reins, bringing the six big horses to a noisy, stomping halt, the coach door a few short paces beyond Clay's stirrups. Aside from its size, and the fact that heavy leather curtains had been drawn across each window, there was nothing remarkable about the coach, no identifiable markings, and none of the riders now surrounding Clay at a respectful distance appeared familiar to him.

Looking up at the driver, Clay was about to ask what this was all about when the coach door slowly opened, swinging away from him, and a slender, shapely, very feminine leg appeared. The skirt had been drawn high enough to prevent its being dirtied or torn and to perhaps reveal more than modesty might dictate. But the most remarkable thing about that beautiful leg was the elegantly tooled boot, the top of which rose only a few inches above her delicate ankle—a boot he had never seen before, but one that uniquely depicted the fullness of his future. Truly, it was the most beautiful thing he ever could have hoped to see: the end of his solitude, a new beginning, the promise of fulfillment.

At last he would be whole.

# PART THREE

★  ★  ★

# CHAPTER 24

★ ★ ★

HIGH IN THE SAN JUAN MOUNTAINS of the New Mexico Territory, somewhere southwest of Taos Pueblo, a cold wind kept a dark stand of ponderosa pines and leafless aspen in constant motion, making the sound of anyone approaching the meager camp impossible to detect. For the lone figure who sat morosely staring into a small fire, the possible approach of an enemy seemed of little concern.

To begin with, the hour was late, and the trees harboring the camp were entirely surrounded by a wide, snow-covered meadow. In addition, the deep, fresh snow which had fallen in the high country during the past two days reflected the light of an almost full moon, making the meadow nearly as bright as day. Any unseen approach would have been next to impossible, had anyone in the camp been keeping watch. But the greatest protection for any intruder was the apparently total lack of concern on the part of the camp's solitary occupant.

Despite the bitter cold and the late hour, Wolf Striker sat hunched near a crackling fire, now and then throwing a small log or branch into the wind-fanned flames, sending a bright shower of sparks spiraling into the cold night air, further announcing his presence to any and all who might be watching. In an area frequented by Apaches, Kiowas, and sometimes Utes and Comanches, it was just plain unhealthy for a man to sit close to his campfire, outlining himself for any enemy to see. And staring into the flames all but guaranteed his helplessness if attacked. Regardless of the brightness of his moon-lit surroundings, his night vision would be next to nonexistent. It almost appeared as if the man were inviting attack, intent on committing suicide.

At least that is how it looked to Orrin Porter Rockwell, a very cautious and skeptical tracker, as he lay in the snow some thirty yards from Striker's camp. It was a worrisome thing to find a man like Striker throwing all caution to the wind. The man was an experienced fighter, a killer, one wise and skilled in the arts of death. He did nothing by accident; Striker always knew what he was doing. That's how he had stayed alive when others around him had not. The man had to be setting a trap, using himself as bait. Either that, or he just no longer cared, and that made no sense at all. Yes, indeed. What a cold, short-tempered Porter Rockwell was looking at was a worrisome thing.

Rockwell had been on Wolf Striker's trail since the day that he and his fellow Utahans had left the burned-out town of Platte River Station, splitting up, each group to pursue separate—yet not unrelated—missions. Every time Rockwell thought he had caught up with the man who murdered two of his closest friends, Striker had managed to disappear, slipping from Rockwell's grasp just as he was about to close the noose. It was uncanny how the man could leave so little or no sign, obliterate any trace of his passage, or lay a false trail. Whether as a result of obvious skill or just dumb luck, Striker had always managed to stay just beyond Rockwell's vengeful grasp.

This time it was going to be different. After weeks of failure and frustration, Striker was well within reach, right where Rockwell wanted him, tantalizingly close, and Rockwell's patience was well-nigh spent. Lying in the blowing snow, stiff from the penetrating cold, it was all he could do to keep from rising up, screaming his lungs out, and charging the camp, regardless of what lay behind Striker's apparent carelessness.

Trap or not, Rockwell hungered for the feel of Striker's neck in his hands, to feel the man struggling beneath him, fighting for the precious air he would never again breathe. A knife from behind or a shot in the back would never do. Vengeance had to be up close, face-to-face, where he could look into Striker's eyes as the man died, where Rockwell's was the last face Striker would ever see. Wolf Striker had to die knowing that he had been brought to justice for the brutal murders of Will and Luke Cartwright, and that he was dying at the hands of Orrin Porter Rockwell, his judge and executioner.

As Rockwell studied the camp and the man slumped before the fire, all of his senses told him something was wrong. After weeks of tracking, trailing, and close calls, finding Wolf Striker sitting by a fire showing himself to the whole hostile world made no sense, not the kind of sense an experienced lawman and tracker like Rockwell expected. It just did not stack up, and if Orrin Porter Rockwell was anything, he was a cautious man. As easy as it looked—and it looked too easy—he was not about to walk into any trap set by Wolfgang Striker. Not now. Not this close. Not after all that had happened.

It had been late summer when Platte River Station was

destroyed, one of the ugliest scenes Rockwell had ever witnessed; and he had seen some of the worst. The whole town had been reduced to smoldering ruins in no more than a few minutes. Rockwell had always prided himself in having a certain toughness, looking in the face of human suffering and feeling nothing but an insatiable drive to turn it around, make it right, get even. He was a Mormon; he knew suffering; he knew what it was like to be burned out of house and home, to see women, even young girls, driven out into the snow and raped, to see men and boys shot down in cold blood, all for their religious beliefs.

No one knew better than Rockwell that the law was not always there when its protection was needed most. Even worse, there were times when the law was used as a weapon of oppression, when Lady Justice was not only blind but turned her back or used her sword in betrayal. Neither the law nor Lady Justice had been there when an oppressed people, his people, had been marked by Lilburn W. Boggs, the governor of Missouri, for extermination. There were times when someone just had to stand up and set things straight, and the governor's signing of his *extermination order* against the Mormons was such a time. From the moment the shot had been fired into the back of Boggs's head, every accusing finger had pointed at Porter Rockwell.

The ex-governor and U.S. Senate candidate had been sitting in his study one evening, reading the newspaper, when someone had shot through the window, the balls striking Boggs in the back of his head and neck. Oddly enough, the serious wounds did not prove fatal, a fact Rockwell had always considered a sorry shame. It was not surprising he had been accused of the attempted assassination, but the local authorities could find nothing to link him directly to the shooting, and it drove them crazy. The only thing he had ever said to his accusers was that he had never done anything of which he was ashamed, nor had he done anything criminal. On one occasion, however, he did confess that if he had shot Boggs, the *sonofabitch* would have been dead. All that had happened twenty years ago, and there was still a Missouri warrant outstanding for Rockwell's arrest.

What had happened at Platte River Station, however, was something else. None of it was his fault nor the fault of the Utah Militiamen who had been sent there to prevent the Confederate investment of the town. They had gone there ready to do what was necessary to free Platte River Station from the Confederate control and guarantee the protection of the telegraph lines and the river trails, not to harm the innocent. It had been their plan—his plan, really—to infiltrate the town under cover of darkness, find the Confederate headquarters, armory, and supply area, capture or destroy them, and reestablish civil government—nothing more.

The whole thing literally blew up late one night when Jubal Hathaway had discovered—actually stumbled over—two of Lott Smith's men who had been laying fuse between hidden barrels of black powder they had stashed around the Confederate supply encampment at the far end of the town's main street. The two had heard Hathaway cursing to himself as he shuffled toward them through the deep grass behind the tent containing all of the stored Confederate munitions and explosives. The grotesque, deranged, little man had been on his way to his tent, returning from Sadie's Bird Cage, angry and frustrated because he had been refused by every "fallen angel" in the place. Even the most calloused of Sadie's girls could not stand the thought of his revolting touch.

Unknown to Rockwell or Lott Smith, before their arrival, Striker had ordered every building in Platte River Station mined with explosives as a means of keeping the town's residents in line.

Any attempt to organize and confront Striker and his men would have resulted in the town's immediate destruction.

As Hathaway grew nearer, the two men had flattened themselves in the grass, certain of not being seen in the dark. In his blind anger, however, Hathaway had tripped over one of the men's legs and landed on his face in the grass. In the brief struggle that followed, the little man had managed to free his pistol and take a couple of shots at the two intruders as they scrambled for cover. As things would have it, the shots missed their intended targets and hit a box of explosives inside the munitions tent. The whole shebang went up, one explosion after another igniting the charges that mined the settlement, and the entire town suddenly burst into a wild conflagration. No one, not even Striker, had been prepared for what had happened.

Now the man who was responsible was nearly within Rockwell's grasp. Wolfgang Striker had a lot to answer for, and Porter Rockwell rose up from his hiding place in the snow determined to bring that man face-to-face with his guilt—and his punishment.

Another telegram—two, in fact—had just arrived by courier from Salt Lake City. Clay did not want to open them, and he had sat for nearly an hour staring at the yellow envelopes, knowing their contents could only mean trouble. This new telegraph system was proving to be a real nuisance. It had been two telegrams that sent him into California and Mexico, and there was no doubt in his mind that these two were likely to be just as disruptive, if not more so. On the other hand, he would never have met Consuela but for those two telegrams, and he would not have missed that opportunity no matter what it entailed.

Maria Emilea Consuela Salinas Ashworth was the center of his life, everything he had ever hoped for in a wife. Because of her, the last few weeks had been the happiest he could remember. She was the most beautiful woman he had ever laid eyes on, and she had given herself to him without reservation. Though it had been only months since she had confronted him in her captivatingly abrupt way at the Gwin banquet table—challenging his allegiances, attempting to fathom his character, and generally putting him off balance in front of everyone present—he could not imagine life without her. In fact, it seemed now as if she had always been with him, and in many ways she had. She was his lifelong dream: beautiful, smart, knowledgeable, the intellectual equal of any man, independent, and yet completely his.

They had driven up to his ranch house, now their home, scarcely a month before, and he could not begin to say where those few precious weeks had gone. The moment Consuela saw the ranch, she knew it was her home, and with Emily's help, she had set about making it Clay's paradise on earth. Fortunately, the two most important women in his life had liked each other immediately, and each in her heart had made room for the other.

That had been his only worry as he and Consuela made the difficult trip from Mexico to the ranch. How would Emily react to another woman taking control of the house? How would Consuela feel about another woman in the house, especially one who had lived there managing the house as her own? Would they get along? He would never part with Emily, and he could not imagine life without Consuela. It just had to work, and it had. The two women loved each other from the start—almost as if they were family. Since their arrival, Consuela had commented on more than one occasion how much Emily reminded her of her own father: her mannerisms, the line of her jaw and the set of her mouth, and other not quite identifiable characteristics.

He knew living with Consuela was going to be a challenge. She was a woman with a mind of her own—a very bright mind—and with it came opinions, very strong opinions. Furthermore, she had not been happy with the thought of being a "ranch wife," as she had repeatedly put it, and having to live with "boots," her one phobia in life. But all of that had changed the moment her dainty foot touched the front porch of *Rancho Los Librados*. All of her apprehensions fled, and she knew this beautiful place was hers. It was now, without question, her home.

"You can't read them if you don't open them, my darling."

"Oh . . . sweetheart, I didn't hear you come in. I've missed you."

"Robby rode with me a ways back into the hills—I'm still stunned by all of this. I wanted to visit the line shack up above the falls—the one you pointed out on our ride last week."

"Oh, yes. Well, I could have—"

"I knew you were busy. Besides, I'm planning a surprise, and I don't want you to know what it is until it's time."

"A surprise?"

"Never mind. For now, anyway. Now open those envelopes. My curiosity is killing me."

"Mmm. You and the cat."

"The cat?"

Clay picked up the knife he used as a letter opener, stared at the two bodeful missives, and sighed deeply. "Never mind, sweetheart. I already know who they're from. And I have a sick feeling I know what's in them."

"You know who they are from?"

"Uh-huh," Clay replied morosely, "and what they contain."

"Goodness, how could you . . . ?"

"One's from the president."

"The president? President who?—whom? What president? Not that Brigham Young person!"

"Sweetheart, you are going to love President Young when you meet him. Just wait and see if I'm not right."

"Huh. Well . . . we shall see, my sweet, just who's right about that man."

"This president," Clay said, cutting the envelope's flap, "is Mister Lincoln, and this other telegram is from Allan Pinkerton. That's who they're from, just as sure as the sun will set tonight. Neither one of them could be good news."

Consuela sat down on a large, overstuffed, leather sofa that dominated one wall of the comfortable, book-lined study. "Should I begin crying now or later?"

"Let's start with this one," he said, opening the thinnest envelope. "Then we'll see when and whether we should both get unhappy.

"Well . . . here goes," he said, scanning the short message, then reading it aloud.

> California mission unqualified success—in more ways than one, I understand. Congratulations on both. Services needed even more urgently in New Mexico Territory.
> You are hereby commissioned major in United States Army, unattached. Your acceptance understood.
> Details follow from Pinkerton.
> A. Lincoln

"I knew it," he said, reaching for the other envelope and extracting a much longer message. "I just knew it."

"New Mexico Territory," Consuela said, a sigh escaping her pretty lips. "For how long? I'm going with you."

"Uh-uh. Way too dangerous." He read for a moment, then said, "It would appear the war in the East has found its way to the West. It seems that a Confederate force of 2,500 men, under the command of Brigadier General Henry H. Sibley, has crossed the Rio Grande River, rebuffed a superior federal force and, to make a long story short, has occupied Santa Fe."

"Is that serious? What does it mean for us?"

"Oh, it's serious, alright. It means that if they are successful in controlling the New Mexico Territory, they will have opened access to the west coast and control of the mineral wealth of the southwest. They will have negated all of our efforts at Platte River Station and everything Chet and I were able to do in California and Mexico."

"Not everything, dearest husband," Consuela said, a giggle underlying her meaning.

Clay looked at his wife and smiled. "No, not everything. I'll tell you what's kind of funny, though."

"What's that?"

"I can't help but wonder if the boys in Richmond have heard of Cochise. Still, they can use their supposed control of the mineral resources throughout the southwest as a means of financing the war. A million dollars in credit could bring them ten million in arms and supplies from Europe—even European intervention. It would be a disaster for the United States, a disaster that can't be allowed to happen."

A depressingly lucid silence flooded the room as both Clay and Consuela lost themselves in thought, each fathoming the meaning of their future. Both were frightened, neither wanting to articulate the doubts and fears that were filling their hearts, as if putting their apprehensions into words would hasten the inevitable.

Clay was the first to speak, trying to avoid what both knew had to be said. "It says here I'm supposed to form a detachment of cavalry and proceed immediately, by forced march, to Fort Union where I'm to aid in driving the Confederates out of Santa Fe, if necessary. Further orders will await me and my men there. Other Confederate forces are headed toward New Mexico, and a major battle could be in the offing. According to this, I'm to be at Fort Union within thirty days. Thirty days? They can't be serious."

"That's just what I think," Consuela said, slapping the arm of the sofa, doing her best to mimic her husband. "*They can't be serious!*" It was her way of helping to ease his tensions, and she had quickly learned that in his eyes, she could do no wrong. To her surprise and joy, everything she did delighted him, whether she intended to or not.

"Those people in the East have no concept of what it's like out here," Clay huffed.

"No, they surely don't, do they?"

"How big, how rugged the West is, how almost impossible it is to go any distance at all without taking weeks to do so. I mean, think of it!"

"Yes . . . *think of it,*" she said, striking the sofa again.

Almost as if he had not heard her, Clay said, "Well, my sweet, you are going to have your opportunity to meet Brigham Young. We'll leave first thing in the morning. Nuts, anyway!"

"Yes," she said, slapping the sofa once more, "that's exactly what I think. *Nuts, anyway!*"

Clay stopped and looked at his wife and, as their eyes met, they both broke into laughter. Each knew it was either that or tears.

# CHAPTER 25

★  ★  ★

T HERE IS NO MORE DEADLY SOUND than the two chillingly distinct clicks made by a Colt .44 army revolver as it is being cocked, nor is there any mistaking its meaning. Striker never moved. He sat almost as if he were asleep—or dead—his big shoulders slumped forward, his head hanging over his chest. But he was not asleep, and the lethal sound came almost as a relief. There would be no more struggle, not tonight, no more bitterness. He had run his course, such as it was, an evil thing with no point to it but the atrocities that had resulted from it, no meaning but corruption. The time had come to end it.

Striker knew the gun was no more than three feet from the back of his head, and he knew who held it. "Go ahead, pull the trigger, Rockwell," he said, the exhaustion and resignation in his voice unmistakable. "You'd be doing me a favor. Damn you, Rockwell . . . pull the trigger."

"If I pulled this trigger, the damnation would be yours, Striker. You ready for that?"

"You here to preach religion, Mormon?"

"Couldn't do yuh no harm," Rockwell said, as he moved around the one man he hated most in all of creation, never taking the gun from its intended target. "No sir, wouldn't do yuh no harm at all."

"It's taken you long enough to get here, preacher," Striker said weakly, his sunken eyes, luminescent beneath dark, bushy brows following Rockwell. "Past few days, I've left a trail a blind man could have followed."

Rockwell studied the man before him, the firelight making the hollows in Striker's gaunt face dark and indistinct, making him appear almost as if he were dead already. This was not the Wolfgang Striker that Rockwell had known and pursued, the man whom he had longed to bring to justice. This was not the cold, brutal blood-letter who so calmly destroyed a town, not caring who was killed, the despot who left people crying out in agony from the flames as he headed south, the lucrative slave trade of the southwest beckoning to him like a lewd woman. The man who now sat slumped in the snow and the cold was a broken, defeated hulk, full of self-loathing, a thing ready to die just to be rid of itself.

"Well, I'll be," Rockwell said, half to himself. "If I hadn't seen this with my own eyes, I wouldn't have believed it. I don't need t' kill you, Striker. You're worse than dead, and I ain't about to put you out of your misery. That'd be an act of mercy you don't deserve."

"Maybe if I were to reach for my gun. . . ."

"Naw. To start with, it ain't where yuh can reach it," Rockwell said, glancing at Striker's big Colt, tucked safely in its holster and draped across Striker's saddle, both covered with a light dusting of snow. "But, to tell the truth, I don't think yuh care enough to try. You look like a coyote caught in a trap, gnawing hisself apart, watching hisself bleed to death just to be rid of the trap. Life's become a trap for you, ain't it, Striker?"

"A philosopher?" Striker said, his words beginning to slur. "You're a man of surprising depth, Rockwell. Either that, or you see before you a kindred soul. One who reminds you of yourself, perhaps? Is that why you don't shoot and get it over with? Would it be too much like putting a bullet in your own head?"

Striker was about gone, that much was obvious. There was still some stubbornness left in the man slumped on the other side of the fire, he could still use words as weapons when nothing else was at hand, but he had little strength left to hurl even them. "Still some life in yuh, ain't there, Striker? Smart talk like that don't come from a corpse."

"Shoot, Rockwell," Striker gasped, his voice breaking from the effort. "Shoot. Please . . . shoot, I. . . ." His strength gone, Striker slowly rolled onto his side, a stain blackening the snow beneath his body. Almost as an afterthought, a large pistol slipped from beneath Striker's coat into the bloody snow near his hand.

"Huh," Rockwell grunted. "Now, what do I make of that? Still the same old Wolf under all that misery. Maybe I should've shot 'im. Still. . . ."

Consuela watched Brigham Young from across his desk as he studied the two telegrams that had been sent to her husband, and she was fascinated by the man. He was not what she had anticipated. Nor was this place, Great Salt Lake City, nor this home and office where they sat, what she had presupposed. Thinking about it, Consuela really didn't know exactly what she had expected, but this certainly was not it. Everything she had seen from the moment she and Clay had ridden into town late the day before bespoke culture, industry, orderly growth, a people that knew where they belonged and who cared for everything around them. Clear, cold water ran in the irrigation ditches along the tree-lined streets, yards and gardens were well cared for, and the farms surrounding the city were obviously abundantly productive.

Furthermore, there were stores lining the wide downtown streets offering goods of all kinds, some even displaying the latest fashions in their windows. In some respects, the big cities of the East could have offered little more, and in many respects, they provided much less. In short, she had encountered a remarkable civilization in the middle of the western wilderness, and she had been taken completely by surprise.

None of that, however, as astonishing as it was, had prepared her for Brigham Young—the man everyone referred to either as President Young or Brother Brigham. The Mormon leader's physical presence was almost overwhelming, his massive head resting on a body that seemed to radiate the strength of the granite mountains that surrounded the city. This was a man who, by his mere presence alone, dominated everything around him. Yet from the moment he entered his office and greeted them, he exhibited a charm that quickly defused the animosity she, for some reason, had been predisposed to feel toward him. Doubts remained, but in spite of herself, she knew she was going to like this Brigham Young fellow—like him very much, in fact.

Why? She wasn't sure. Perhaps because he showed such respect and affection toward her husband; perhaps because he had made her the center of all that had occurred since their arrival; perhaps because he exhibited the kind of leadership that made her feel, no matter what happened, everything was going to work out in the end. He made her feel comfortable, at home, at peace, safe. He somehow gave her assurance.

"Well, Clay," Young said, looking up from Allan Pinkerton's telegram. "I knew this was coming. Furthermore, there has never been any doubt in my mind that you were the man to head such an expedition from Utah. I'll see that you have the men you need by tomorrow morning—good, experienced cavalrymen. Many of them will be men who were at Platte River Station with you."

"I couldn't ask for better, President Young. I'll need a culled-down company of from, say, forty to sixty riders."

"Supplies?"

"That's difficult, given the time frame and the terrain. We've got to move fast, and the middle of winter in the mountains doesn't offer the best of conditions."

"Yes, well, the truth is, Clay, you will not get to Santa Fe in the time you've been given. However, a Union force is being assembled in Denver, along with several other units from some of the surrounding mining camps. They are under orders to move south into New Mexico, hold Fort Union, retake Santa Fe, and either destroy whatever Confederate forces are found there, or drive them back into Texas. Joining up with the Colorado force would be the more efficient means of accomplishing your goal, I think. Besides, getting to Denver from here is not nearly so problematical as getting to Santa Fe. The stage route, such as it is, out through the basin will give you the best chance of getting there before it's too late. You can stop at the small settlements along the way for provisions and forage.

"I see two advantages to that alternative, Clay. First, you won't be burdened with your own supply wagons. They would slow you down far too much. Second, in joining up with the Colorado forces, not only will it enable you to use their supplies, it will multiply your strength in numbers until you get there. Also, I'll send with you some letters of introduction for the bishops along the way, asking them to help you with provisions, and one for Governor Gilpin. He'll see that you get hooked up with an appropriate unit or units, if they haven't left before you get there. After that, you should have little difficulty."

"We'll get there in time, sir. Without supply wagons, we should average forty miles per day or better, at least where the terrain permits. That should get us there in about three weeks, if we don't get bogged down in snow."

"Fortunately, this has so far been a mild winter in the mountains," Brigham Young said, returning the telegrams to their envelopes and handing them to Clay. "Let's hope it stays that way until you get there."

"Those Colorado troops are not going to 'see the elephant' without us, that much I can promise."

Young pushed back from his desk, a quiet signal that the meeting was nearing its end. "That's an admirable attitude, Clay," he said, walking around the desk, "but you've done an enormous service for your country already. It would not break my heart if you and your men missed the fighting altogether. Don't you agree, Mrs. Ashworth?"

"I certainly do," Consuela said, taking Young's offered hand and casting a worried look at her husband. "He can *see the elephant* right here with me anytime he feels the need."

Both Young and Clay burst into laughter at Consuela's quick retort. "I'm certain Clay has discovered the truth of that already," Young said, grinning at the two of them, as they walked out into the hallway. "How long have you two been married now?"

"Long enough, President Young," Clay said, taking his wife's hand. "Only a few weeks, and I quickly learned not to do anything to provoke warfare at our house. I wouldn't stand a chance."

"Mmm. Surrendering to a far superior force before the shooting starts can be the smartest defense."

"Yes, sir. Much more fun, too. And let me tell you, she is the superior force."

The night following their visit with Brigham Young had been a sleepless one for both Clay and Consuela but, neither knowing how long their separation would be, they had made the most of it. Now, in the early hours of the morning, both lay staring at the ceiling of their rented room in the Salt Lake House.

"You awake, sweetheart?" Clay asked.

"Uh-huh. I can't sleep. Not now. The time's too short." Rolling on her side, Consuela threw her arm across Clay's chest, propping her head on her hand. "I just had a wonderful thought. Why don't I come with you? You'll need a cook. I can cook for you and your men. Just think—"

Clay leaned over and kissed her, breaking her cascade of words in mid-sentence. "Not on your life, my sweet. We are going into a war, and that's no place for a woman—especially such a woman."

"What do you mean, *no place for a woman?* Women have been caught up in wars as long as men have." Rolling on her back, she huffed, "'No place for a woman,' indeed."

"What about *Rancho Los Librados?*" Clay asked, hoping a strategic change of direction would help his case. "With the master gone, our ranch needs its mistress. Robby and Emily can't run the place alone."

"Tell me about her. Emily, I mean," she said.

"There's not much to tell," Clay said, slipping his arm around Consuela and pulling her nearer. "She's been like a mother to me for a number of years. I don't know what I'd have done without her."

"But how did you two meet? I mean, how did you come to live together?"

"Believe it or not, I found her wandering in the desert near Fort Defiance. She was in a state of shock, badly sunburned, and dehydrated. Another few hours and she would have been dead. The doctor at Fort Defiance probably saved her life, but her memory was gone."

"You mean she doesn't know anything about her past?"

"Nothing. All we could determine from what little she said was that Indians had attacked their wagons and her family had been killed. Apparently she was either not found when they sacked the wagons or she was left for dead. I took some troops out for a couple of days, but we couldn't find where the attack had taken place. She evidently had wandered quite a ways, maybe even for several days.

"Anyway, she had nowhere to go, so I brought her to the ranch where she has lived happily ever after. Neat story, huh?"

Consuela rolled on her side, facing her husband. "Very nice story, but it's just like you to do something like that. Maybe that's why I love you so much."

"I hope so. For whatever the reason."

"It's funny, though."

"What is?"

"My father had a sister who disappeared years ago," Consuela said, pensively, "and there is much about Emily that reminds me of my father and of Uncle Lazaro."

"Didn't you know her? Your aunt, I mean?"

"The last time I saw her I was very young. She and her family were coming to be with us when they all disappeared. You don't think. . . ."

"Oh . . . you never know, but I don't think I would make too much of it. When you get back to the ranch, sit down with Emily and talk about it. Anyway, one way or the other, she now has you, as well as me, and you have her. That's why you need to go back to the ranch and take care of things there."

"I was named after her. Did I ever tell you that?"

"After your aunt?"

"The Consuela part, anyway. My mother and father sometimes used to call me Connie after her. My father did not like Consuela as a name. He thought it was too lower class. Perhaps he was right, but I hated being called Connie, and they finally stopped."

"Why? I like it. It's . . . I don't know . . . it's kind of Americanish."

"Exactly. It made me feel like a gringa. I didn't like that."

"Well, señora Maria Emilea Consuela Connie Ashworth that should be your new name now. You married a gringo, so now you are a gringa, and you sure seem—"

She was on him like a cat, her kisses smothering his face, her fingers tickling him unmercifully. "You call me what you like, you big gringo. I love you more than words can say."

Like an unwanted flood, the early morning sunlight began spilling through their window and across the floor, driving the night from the room and filling their hearts with a joy that seemed to banish the feelings of impending loss that lay beneath their happy struggles.

It is a sad reality, but true, that only rarely do a man and a woman come together who are so perfectly matched that every attribute of their being—every emotion, every desire, every quirk and characteristic—is perfectly attuned, one in unison with the other, to such a degree that if any adjustment was necessary it was scarcely recognized by either of them.

So it was with Clay and Consuela—Connie—Salinas Ashworth, together for so short a time, but each feeling, no matter what the future might bring, they had shared a lifetime, and never again would life be complete for one without the other.

# CHAPTER 26

★  ★  ★

Porter Rockwell sat sullenly watching Wolf Striker across the fire. Hours before, he had leaned Striker against a large log, his feet toward the fire, the snow blowing into his flushed face.

Striker's eyes fluttered open for the first time since he had passed out, snowflakes sticking to his eyelashes. "Like to kill me, wouldn't you, Rockwell? It's written all over what little can be seen of your ugly face. Well . . . do it, then, you poor, simple fool. I've got nothing to live for, not even to kill you."

"What's this Christian charity you're suddenly feelin' toward me, Striker?"

"Christian charity?" the big man croaked, attempting to sit up straighter against the log, but lacking the strength and slumping back. "That's a joke. Charity's got nothing to do with it, preacher. I've seen too much, done too much. I just don't care anymore, Rockwell. Can you understand that? I just don't care anymore."

Rockwell got up and took a large coffeepot from the fire. Filling a tin cup with a dark, greenish liquid, he walked around the fire and helped Striker into a more comfortable position. "Here, drink this. The stuff's called Mormon tea. It ain't too bad if there's enough sugar in it, but I ran out of sugar weeks ago. Here . . . drink it."

"Ugh . . . you *are* trying to kill me," Striker croaked, gagging on the hot brew. "Just use a bullet and get it over with. Poison isn't a man's way to go."

"Nobody I know ever accused you of bein' a man, Striker."

"The devil, you say."

"No, sir. Just a low-down, back-shooting killer."

"Low-down, no doubt," Striker said, his voice low with resignation. Straightening his back, Striker looked Rockwell in the eyes. "A killer, for sure; but I shot those two friends of yours from the front. Both of them, from the front, right in the chest."

"Don't you provoke me, Striker, you no-account cutthroat. Those two boys were like sons to me. Had you killed any other man in that town, I'd not have spent half the effort to find you. But when you killed them, you signed your death warrant—at my hands."

"What I'm trying to say is, I've never back-shot anyone."

"Front or back, you shot the wrong people this time, Striker. I'm taking you over to Fort Union for a proper hangin'."

"Then why all this loving care, preacher?"

His thick, dark beard white with snow, Rockwell sat down in front of the man whose nemesis he had sworn to become, contemplating both the man and the question. There were reasons enough, maybe a million or more, but why bother with explanations now? Rockwell's face clouded, and he said, "Just drink that stuff and get some strength into yuh. Hangin' a dying man some-how lacks the gratification I've been dreaming of."

Striker took a sip of the hot tea, winced at its bitter taste, and chuckled. "You're a good man, Rockwell. I like a dedicated man. It's too bad we couldn't have been friends."

"Yeah, a sorry thing, alright. But what I got planned for you, one friend don't do to another. You think on that for a while—*friend*."

Striker's eyes had begun to flutter closed, and it was obvious to Rockwell that the man was too weak to go anywhere without a great deal of rest and hot food. "Rockwell," Striker said, his voice hoarse and thick, "you can believe this or not. I've regretted few things I've done in my life, and I've done plenty. For a man blessed with the opportunities I was given, I've led a miserable, rotten existence. I could be hung a dozen times over and never pay all my debts to those I've killed or maimed. But, Rockwell, I'm genuinely sorry about those two boys back at Platte River Station." A sudden chill shook the big man, and he grew visibly weaker. "There was something about them," he said, his voice trailing off. "I don't know what . . . they were stand-up men, both of them. Real soldiers . . . they were real soldiers, Rockwell." Striker slumped over, his voice faint and reedy. "Genuinely sorry."

"Yeah, and bulls wear bloomers," Rockwell grumped. But Striker could not hear him. "Striker, you sorry . . . you're not going to die on me," he said, leaning forward and shaking the unconscious man. "You hear me? You're not going to die. You'll live to pay for what you've done, and pay proper. I don't care what it takes or how long."

Rockwell spent the next day gathering pine boughs, brush, and Aspen poles with which he built a snug, comfortable wickiup for himself and Striker and a shelter for the horses. Careful to keep an eye on Striker, Rockwell went about his work, but the man never moved. He had lost a great deal of blood, and getting some substantial nourishment into him became an urgent necessity.

For each of the next two days, Rockwell left the snug camp before sunup in search of desperately needed food, not returning until well after dark. The snow made hunting difficult, but the exhausted marshal managed to bring down a good-sized doe, two rabbits, and gather some skimpy forage for the horses. Had Striker attempted to escape during one of Rockwell's prolonged absences, he would have had to carry the two saddles to which he had been securely manacled, but Striker never regained consciousness, and if he had, in his weakened condition, he could not have gone far.

Within several days, thanks to the hot, meaty rabbit broth Rockwell managed to get down his half-dead prisoner, the man finally regained sufficient strength to sit up and begin eating small portions of broiled venison. Between the hot broth, red meat, and Rockwell's care of his wounds, Striker's strength slowly began returning.

Late one evening, with the wind howling around their snug, smoky wickiup and snow falling heavily, Rockwell turned from the fire and handed Striker a bowl filled with broth and venison. "Here, get this down yuh," he said, his voice more harsh than he intended.

Persistent exhaustion smothering his voice, Striker said, "I can't. No reflection on your cooking, friend, but the stuff tastes lousy."

"You get that into yuh—and I ain't your *friend*. Such as it is, this stuff's the only thing that's kept you alive when anybody with more scruples woulda had the decency t' die."

Striker chuckled as he watched the bearded marshal putter around with cooking utensils, throwing more sticks on the fire, and otherwise trying to appear busy. It was a surprise to Striker, but he was actually coming to feel some fondness for this large, hairy lawman who was so determined to get him healthy just to hang him. "Why are you bothering, Rockwell? I'm not worth all of this effort. Listen to that storm. You should have at least saved yourself. I'll be surprised if both of us don't freeze to death out here. Where will that have gotten you?"

"That's my worry, and I told yuh why I'm here. You're going to hang for what you did, and I want yuh good and healthy for the party."

"Yeah," Striker sighed, "and I might just get to feeling good enough to kill you instead."

Rockwell leaned back against his saddlebags and contemplated the miserable figure before him. "Well, now, if that don't sound like the old Wolfgang Striker everyone knows and loves so much. My administrations must be working, though if I handed yuh a gun, I doubt you'd yet have the strength to lift it."

Striker leaned back, staring at the smoke hole a few feet above them. "It takes more than strength, my friend. It takes will."

Rockwell watched him for a moment, not really sure how he felt about this broken, defeated man. Striker seemed to lack not just the will to live, but any interest at all. This was not the destroyer of villages, the killer of men, and terrorizer of women, he'd heard so much about. "What happened, Striker? You're like a grizzly that's had all his teeth pulled. Who or what pulled those bloody teeth of yours, Striker?"

Striker's eyes closed, and for a moment Rockwell thought he had fallen asleep. Finally, his voice low, he said, "Have you ever felt like you'd seen everything, done just about everything, and never gave so much as a single thought to who it hurt? Like the world was yours to take and rape and ravage at will?"

"Can't say as I have. Oh, I'm no angel. Truth is, in some circles, I'm called the Avenging Angel, which might tell yuh I've done my share of dubious deeds—for one reason or another. But whatever I've done, I've had sufficient reason."

"Vengeance is one thing, Rockwell, though a person can justify just about anything to placate his conscience. Self-defense is always justified. But few of my crimes can be justified, and I never thought I'd see the day I wished I could. I've always just reached out and taken what I wanted—usually as violently as possible, and if I got paid to do it, all the better. So, you see, my friend, hanging is something for which I'm well suited."

Falling silent, Striker's breathing became heavy and labored, and Rockwell suddenly felt concern. Before he could move though, Striker seemed to jerk back and said, "Remorse—I just wish I could feel remorse. Why can't I feel remorse, Preacher?" he said, his eyes searching the thatched wall of the wickiup, as if there were an answer to be found there. "Well," he said finally, "I guess the truth is, Rockwell, I don't know how remorse feels. I don't think I would know it if I felt it, so I just don't care anymore. Hanging, shooting, whatever, it's all the same."

"But why, man? Why? What happened to make yuh feel this way?" Rockwell said, his cold blue eyes searching Striker's drawn face. "I ain't sure, but for some reason, I think I liked the man I tracked across half the western wilderness better."

"When you crawl with snakes, I guess you should expect to get bitten, and I was crawling among snakes. I've crawled among them for years now.

"We had ridden into this small farming village. It was about two weeks after we left Platte River Station. Maybe you bypassed it in your hurry to catch up with us. It was no more than four or five houses, two of them just muddies, the farm fields scattered out around them. It was a Sunday, and I had given orders to loot the place for whatever we needed, maybe even grab some women, if there were one or two you could stand to look at. But when we got there, four wagons full of small children were parked between the houses—little Indian kids, they were. I don't know what kind, they all look alike to me. These little kids—just children—had been stolen—kidnapped—by this bunch of bucks who were up in the wagon with knives to the throats of some of the littlest ones.

"When we rode up, some women came running toward us begging us to stop what was happening, but the Indians started hollering and cutting the throats of those little kids. Oh . . . the sound! As long as I live, I'll never forget the sound of those little children screaming in terror, and their blood was everywhere. It was a merciless slaughter of the innocent. Those little Indian kids had no idea what it was all about. They were screaming in terror. Screaming for their mothers, I guess. I don't know their lingo, but who else would little kids be screaming for? And the women of the village, I've never seen such panic and terror. Not for themselves, but for those children they were helpless to save.

"Oh, dear God in heaven," a half-stifled sob caught in Striker's throat, "it was awful.

"When the few white men that were there broke and ran for their guns, my men started shooting at them, and the dogs of war broke loose. It was pure havoc. I tried to stop it, get some control, but the blood—all that blood seemed to ignite the rabble I was supposedly leading, and they went crazy . . . blood crazy . . . killing crazy. The Indians were shooting anything that moved, little kids were running in terror, some of them covered in blood. It was absolute hell. I shot one of my men who was shooting in almost every direction, and then it seemed like a half-dozen guns opened up on me. The next thing I remember was coming to, surrounded by bodies, weeping women everywhere trying to find anyone left alive, and I just crawled into a ditch and passed out again.

"I guess what finally brought me out of it was my horse snuffling at my face. Why they didn't take him, I'll never know. Everything else of value was gone, including the wagons—all those guns and that ammunition. Knowing that rabble, it'll wind up in the hands of the highest bidder. Those kind know no allegiance.

"So there it is, Rockwell. I just wasn't ready for what I stumbled into. I thought I'd seen everything, but the horror of those little kids literally shocked me senseless. Believe it or not, I've always had a soft spot for children. Looting those farms would have meant nothing to me, but I would never let harm come to kids. As long as I live, I'll never forget the horrible sound of those little Indian children, and those poor, helpless women wanting to stop the horror but unable to do anything about it."

"Mmm . . . I reckon," Rockwell said, studying Striker's face. A confession such as he had just heard was the last thing on earth Rockwell expected. The whole thing was incredible, coming from Wolfgang Striker. But given all Rockwell knew about him, it had to be true. Besides, given the shape the man was in physically and emotionally, there was just no strength left for much of anything short of the truth. "Where's your gang now?"

"*Gang?* Huh . . . *gang.* The word denotes some sort of organization. That rabble left me for dead, I guess. They thought they'd killed me and they took everything. I suppose they'll find someone to sell it to—Indians, outlaws, somebody."

Watching Striker slump down into the robes that covered

him, Rockwell said, "If you're up to it, we'll leave tomorrow. It's at least a three-day ride from here to Fort Union."

Striker cleared his throat and said, "Makes little difference to me—one way or the other."

# CHAPTER 27

★ ★ ★

R APIDLY SLIPPING BEHIND THE frozen mountains to the west, the sun stained everything it touched a portentous crimson. In contrast to the dark violence of the wind-driven blizzard that had raged throughout most of the day, the broken clouds that lingered after the storm's passing were lined with a silver brilliance. Yet their soft, benign bellies remained darkly purple, somehow mitigating the harsh, sun-bloodied snow that covered the Mora Valley, in the middle of which stood Fort Union. The high-desert valley was situated at the westernmost edge of the Great Plains, where eleven years earlier the military post had been built to protect travel along the Santa Fe Trail. The fort's strategic importance could not be overestimated.

As the heavy double gate swung open to admit Porter Rockwell and Wolf Striker, the clear, clean air was sharpening with the cold of the coming night. A large man with three stripes on each sleeve stepped in front of Rockwell's horse. "State your business!" he demanded.

After three, freezing, miserable days in the saddle, Porter Rockwell was in no mood to put up with the irritating demands of some stuffed-shirt, self-important, blue belly sergeant. "Get your commanding officer out here," Rockwell demanded, his sharp tone allowing for no argument. "You tell him Marshal O. P. Rockwell is here with a prisoner. I need to lock this fella up until I can take him back to Utah Territory for hanging. Either that or hang him here. Now, do it! I'm cold, I'm tired, and enough's been said."

The icy blue eyes of the bearded man on the horse left little room for argument. "Shut the gate!" the sergeant demanded of no one in particular, attempting to shift the focus of his affronted authority. "Corporal Haddock, go inform the commandant this gent's askin' for him."

Striker snickered, knowing the irritation it would cause. "'Marshal'? Look around you, Rockwell," he said, his eyes taking in the busy fort, "you don't have any jurisdiction here. This is a federal installation, not Salt Lake City. Your legal authority ended when you left the Utah Territory, my friend."

"I don't want to tell you again, I ain't your *friend,* and all the 'jurisdiction' I need is right here," Rockwell said, patting the large pistol holstered at his side. "Mister Colt has given me all the *legal authority* I need, and best you don't forget it—*friend.*"

"If you'll get down off'n them horses, I'll have 'em looked to," the big sergeant said, his attitude somewhat mellowed. "Looks like they've been rode kind of hard, a'right."

"Busy place," Striker said to no one in particular.

"We're gettin' ready to move south," the sergeant responded, taking the reins of each horse. "Them Texas rebs have moved into

Albuquerque and Santa Fe, and now it looks like they're headed our way."

A corporal stepped out of the dark. "Marshal? The commanding officer sends his compliments and asks that you come to his office, sir."

"Ah, West Point training," Striker said, throwing his leg over the saddle horn and sliding to the ground. "You can tell a West Point man every time."

"Who you talkin' about?" Rockwell grumped.

"The commandant, sending his *compliments.* That's the Point talking, just as sure as we're standing here."

"You don't even know the man's name," Rockwell snapped. "You've got no idea if he's a West Pointer."

"I'll bet you the key to these cuffs I'm right. What do you say, *Marshal?*" Striker said, half mocking Rockwell's title—anything to needle the Utah lawman.

Entering the headquarters building, the two men followed the corporal into the commandant's office.

"What can I do for you, Marshal?" the fort commander said, rising from behind his cluttered desk, his hand extended. As he spoke, his eyes were drawn to Striker. "Well, will you look here," he exclaimed, before Rockwell could respond. "If it isn't Wolfgang Striker. I'd have thought someone would have hung you a long time ago, Striker."

"That's exactly the nature of my business," Rockwell said, taking the commandant's extended hand before it could be withdrawn. "I'm Marshal O.P. Rockwell, Utah Territory."

"Colonel Paul, Marshal. Take a seat—both of you," Paul said, settling behind his desk. "You'll never know how glad I am to see two more men."

"Gabe. How in blazes are you?" Striker said, the rattle of the shackles belying the relaxed tone of his voice.

"I'm—that is to say, *we*—are about to go into battle. You ready for *Boots and Saddles* again, Striker? Ready to become a soldier again? Maybe the kind you could have been—if you'd have stayed at it and mastered that mean streak of yours?"

Colonel Paul's face grew solemn with momentary reflection. "As I recall, it wasn't what you did so much as how you did it."

"If war is about to overwhelm us, is this any time for nasty recriminations among those who are about to die, Gabe?" Turning to an irritated Porter Rockwell, Striker said, "As you can see, Marshal, the colonel and I go way back, clear back to the war with Mexico, and West Point before that. If you and I can ever sit down and exchange a civil word, I'll explain it all to you. Believe it or not, I was a hero once."

"Hero, my foot," Paul exclaimed, not altogether good-naturedly. "You're good, one of the best, but heroes don't do the kinds of things you and your men did in the Forest of Chapultepec. It not only cost you your command, but your commission."

"That wasn't all my doing, Gabe. I really never got a fair shake in that court-martial."

"Perhaps not," Paul said, turning his attention to Rockwell. "But that is neither here nor there, Marshal. The point is, I can't incarcerate your prisoner right now. I need him—and you. Your prisoner is an ex-soldier, an officer of some experience. A dead shot with anything that shoots, and as I recall, he can ride anything that wears hair, wool, or horns. Isn't that right, Wolf? You still as good as you were in Mexico?"

Porter Rockwell did his best to hide the surprise that must have been partially hidden beneath his beard, not trusting his ample camouflage. Yet the more he learned of Striker, the more his feelings seemed to moderate toward the big desperado. If the truth were known, he was actually coming to like this man of many surprising parts, in spite of himself. What troubled him most was the thought that there might actually be something worth saving in Wolfgang Striker.

But Rockwell was quick to dismiss such soft-headed thinking. The Cartwright brothers had been shot down in cold blood attempting to keep an armed Confederate force out of their town, and what happened at Platte River Station had to be atoned for, regardless. Besides, Brigham Young's counsel aside, there were some people to whom you just didn't give any benefit of a doubt. The man had to die, and that was all there was to it.

"Oh . . . some would argue better, some worse, Gabe. But under the circumstances," Striker chuckled, "I'm willing to do my part—as always."

"Uh-huh," Colonel Paul said, watching Striker closely. "Just as viciously, too, I suspect. Well . . . the point is, we are all going to be one big happy family—for the time being, anyway. In the next day or so, we're going have the opportunity of whipping some rebels and saving this fort in the process—and the Union, perhaps. If our reinforcements get here from Colorado in time, that is. There is a rebel column reported to be marching on us from Santa Fe. They've already taken Albuquerque, and we have the dubious honor of being next. The word is, they're pretty well strung out and desperate to capture our supply depot, so we're making preparations to march out and meet them."

Not liking what he was hearing, Rockwell said, "Well, I don't like to add to your problems, Colonel, but this man's wanted for murder—two, in fact, for certain, and maybe more—the burning of the town of Platte River Station and leading a rebel force to invest that town. I guess you'd have no way of knowing, but Striker here is a so-called rebel himself, so I can't help but wonder just how useful he'd be to yuh. More than likely, he'd find some way to stab yuh in the back.

"Wars, battles, floods, the sky falling in—none of it matters to me. I fully intend to take him back to the Utah Territory for trial and sentencing."

"That true, Wolf?" Paul said, a half-smile of distrust crossing his face. "You have Confederate sympathies? I don't know why I'm bothering to ask you, it does sound mighty like the Wolf Striker I used to know."

"You know me, Gabe," Striker said, softly. "The worst is nearly always true, and I do have to admit to some southern sympathy."

"Sergeant!" the Colonel hollered toward his office door. "Very well, Marshal, I'll have our friend—Mister Striker here—locked up for the time being. But I must tell you that we are making preparations for an all-out engagement, and I can make you no promises until things begin to fall into place around here."

"Sir?" the clerk said, stepping in from the outer office.

"Call the Sergeant of the Guard. We have a prisoner to be escorted to the guardhouse and locked up."

Wolfgang Striker lay curled on his bunk, almost in a fetal position, his arms wrapped tightly about his chest and shoulders. A big man, his back was pressed painfully into the rough log wall, and his knees hung well over the iron frame of the bed. He had no idea what time it was, but the darkness outside his cell window gave no welcome indication of light, though the noisy activities of the fort never seemed to cease. Sleep had come only fitfully, and at this early hour, he lay shivering beneath his single army blanket, staring unseeingly at the opposite wall, his eyes unnaturally large with the horrible visions he could not expel from somewhere deep within his head.

The little Indian children refused to leave him in peace, let him go. In turn, one after the other, they floated up to his face, their naked eyes haunting him with their deadened pleas for mercy from the horrors of the big knives that took each life over and over again. There were no screams, only the awful silence and the large, vacant eyes that grew closer, begging him, until they seemed to envelop him, making way for the next child, and the next.

Is that what they were doing? Begging *him* for mercy? *Him?* How could *he* save them? His existence had been one of unbridled cruelty, seldom giving any thought to those whose lives he shattered or snuffed out. Salvation lay not in *him.* It was not *he* who had imposed this horror on them. Or had he? By just being there, being what he was—had been—was he somehow guilty of their hideous pain? Why did they plead with *him?* What were they demanding of *him?* He had been helpless to stop their terror then; he could do nothing now. Could he?

How could he purge their torture—and his? Was there some way to atone, or was there no relief? If there was none, then did he really want the night visions to stop? Did his life of guilt make this torment somehow deserved and, therefore, good? Was his expiation—and theirs—to be found in his sleepless anguish, in this unrelenting nocturnal holocaust? Or was such a thought just another expression of pride, the hubris that had led him to this miserable end in the first place?

Somewhere nearby a door slammed and a pump handle squeaked. The blessed relief of morning had finally come—one more time. How many nights had it been? One? Two? Ten? How many more must he endure?

Tossing his blanket aside, Striker shuffled stiffly across the small cell to a water basin on a rickety wooden table near the cell door and splashed a handful of cold water across his face. It was almost a rebirth. Taking a deep breath, he dashed his face with the invigorating water once more, and even his aching joints began to seem more pliable and less painful, his mind clearing after the terrors of the night.

There is an odor common to all jail or prison cells. It is the odor of human filth—unwashed bodies, encrusted slop buckets, and straw-filled mattresses that are seldom changed and often found crawling with lice. Such places constitute their own form of punishment.

Refusing to breathe, his nostrils stinging from the stench, Striker stepped to the barred window and filled his lungs with clean, fresh, mountain air. For a cell window, it was rather large and provided an excellent view of the east wall of the fort, only twenty-five or thirty feet away. The window was one of those things that is so much a part of a prisoner's limited world that it is seldom really seen, looked *through* rather than looked *at.* For the first time in the days since he had occupied the small room, Striker looked at the window itself, his eyes roaming its heavy frame. The cool iron bars felt good in his hands, but of even greater importance, one of the bars moved, and with further investigation, so did the one next to it.

Without paying some attention, it would be easy for a jailer to overlook the cracked and crushed mortar around two of the bars, as had obviously been the case. Some previous prisoner had carefully chipped away at the frame until the bars had come loose, but then replaced the chipped material carefully enough that his handiwork had gone unnoticed. With a little more work, the two bars might be pried from their frame. His size notwithstanding, Striker felt certain he could work his way between the remaining bars and out of the guardhouse. He knew from the sloppy fit of his clothes that he had lost weight, a great deal, in fact. Slipping out would be the simple part. Where to go next was the real problem.

Sinking back on his bunk, Striker assessed his situation. Escaping from Fort Union was as difficult a problem as assaulting it. Union was a new star-shaped fort and had been built out in the middle of a broad valley, away from the original stockade. There was not a single wall of the fortress that was not covered by one opposite, the walls forming a circular series of large Vs in relationship one to another. Attempting to seize such a fortress by scaling its walls would be suicidal. Trying to sneak over a wall in an effort to escape without being seen might prove equally foolish. If attempted in the dark, however, it might just be accomplished. Being an experienced mercenary and soldier, Striker was fairly certain it could be done. And if so, he was the man to do it.

A commotion in the main compound stirred Striker from his determined tactical reflections. There was nothing to be seen from his window, since the parade ground and center of the fort's activities were on the other side of the guardhouse, but two guards were just entering the jail with Striker's breakfast.

"What's all the ruckus outside?" Striker asked.

"None of your affair, is what it is," the surly Irish sergeant answered sharply.

"No need for that, Irish," Striker said. "I was just wondering."

"Well . . . since you asked," the sergeant said, unlocking the cell door, allowing a young private to place Striker's plate on the table, "some of our reinforcements have arrived from Denver City," he said, the clang of the closing cell door emphasizing his words. "Three hundred miles they've come, the 'Governor's Pet Lambs,' they've been called, and hisself to boot."

"The governor?"

"Aye, the governor, hisself. Worried sick the rebs'll take his state away for the Confederacy, he is."

"*Boots and Saddles* pretty soon, then?"

"Now, that *is* none of your business, Laddie. But if you must know, war's upon us. Be it here or there, upon us it is, and a bloody one it's goin' t' be."

Porter Rockwell stepped down from the boardwalk and hurried across the parade ground to where Clay Ashworth had just given the command for his Utah troopers to dismount.

"Ashworth!" Rockwell hollered, as the tall Utahan swung down from his horse. "Clay Ashworth!"

Ashworth's face cracked into a wide smile. "I'd know that voice anywhere," he said, turning and thrusting his hand toward his old friend. "And there's no missing that beard. I'll be, Port, you're the last person I expected to find here. What are you up to, Marshal?"

"Truth be known, I'm trying to get Wolfgang Striker hung, or get him back to Utah where I can hang him myself."

"Mmm . . . the latter sounds better to me. One way or the other, though, I'm glad you caught up with him. But, Port," Clay said, turning to loosen his saddle's cinch, "somehow hanging just seems too good for Striker. For all the suffering he's caused, there must be a more fitting way."

"Uh-huh, you'd think so," Rockwell said, scratching his beard, his hand lost to view. "But . . . well . . . the odd thing is, Clay, Striker's not the same man he was at Platte River Station. He's changed, somehow. He just ain't the same."

"Really?" Clay said, skeptically. "Better? Or worse, as if that were possible?"

"Well . . . I don't know exactly. He's like he died, compared to what he was. Striker's softened. The short of it is, he acts . . . different. It's almost like he's a new man, Clay."

"Had some religious experience, has he? An epiphany of some sort, maybe?"

Rockwell's hand found his beard once again. "Don't know about such as that, but he has changed. You ought t' go have a talk with him over to the lockup. But you'd better make it fast. I'm taking him out of here the first chance I get."

"I might just do that. I'm always interested in things miraculous, Port. But first, I've got to report to Colonel Paul, along with Colonel Slough and the other officers. I've got a hunch things are going to heat up pretty fast. I'll be surprised if there isn't a blow-up between Paul and that stuffed shirt, Slough."

"Slough?"

"Oh, some Denver lawyer that got himself appointed colonel of the First Colorado Volunteers. He thinks he's going to replace an experienced soldier as commander. His time in rank exceeds that of Colonel Paul, a career soldier and a West Point graduate. Slough's been in the service all of six months. Hand it to a lawyer—we've got Confederates marching down on us, and this lawyer's worried about his seniority in rank."

"Yeah, well, that's the army for yuh. Anyway, I ain't stickin' around here to find out. I'm taking Striker back to Utah for trial and execution, and the two of us are leaving tomorrow morning, come hell or high water. I don't care what Paul or that Colonel Slough fella or any of the rest of 'em think or do."

"Now, don't go off half-cocked, Port," Ashworth warned. "Wait until things settle down a little. This is the wrong time to cause any trouble. They know Striker's a rebel, don't they?"

"Your friend, Colonel Paul, does," Rockwell said, a tone of irritation in his voice. "That was the only way I got Paul to lock him up—he kept carryin' on about needin' all the men he could get. But once Striker admitted to Confederate sympathies, Paul changed his mind, alright.

"One more thing, Clay," Rockwell said, his eyes hardening. "I ain't never gone off half-cocked, causing trouble or no. That's the main reason I'm alive to be standing here talking to yuh. That's a fact best not to be forgotten by anyone. And you can tell them other Union blue bellies, anything gets between me, my prisoner, and those guards won't be perpendicular long enough to regret it, and that's a natural fact."

The two old friends stood looking at each other. Clay was bone-tired, and each had spoken more sharply than either had intended. The big rancher was the first to break the awkward silence. "Whatever you decide to do, Port, I'll back you to the hilt."

"Yeah, I know, Clay, and thanks." Briefly taking Clay's offered hand, Rockwell turned and made his way across the busy parade ground toward the commandant's office.

He could hear the argument between Paul and Slough from outside the building. It was heated and blunt, and the two men seemed all but reduced to name-calling, if not outright fisticuffs. Entering the empty outer office, Rockwell had only to listen for a moment to know that now was the time to nab Striker and head for the western hills. With the crowded fort's troopers busying themselves with preparations for a forced march through the Sangre de Cristo Mountains toward Santa Fe, and the two senior officers brawling over who was in charge, no one was likely to notice his departure with ex-soldier Striker in irons.

# CHAPTER 28

$\star$　$\star$　$\star$

Air exploded from the young soldier's lungs as Rockwell heaved him against the wall. "What do you mean, he escaped?" Rockwell roared. "How could he escape? Where the devil were you? You're the guard, ain't yuh?"

"I don't know how he done it, Mister," the soldier said, his breath coming in heaving gasps. "I just . . . come on duty . . . walked in just before you, Marshal. It musta been late last night. Look . . . you can see in there," the soldier said, pointing through the door and into the empty cell. "Looks like he musta worked them bars loose, there. See?"

Rockwell strode into the empty cell and examined the window ledge. "Well, I'll be. . . ." he huffed. With even a cursory inspection, it was obvious what had happened. Striker had finished what others before him had started. It could not have taken him long to work the bars free from the frame. And now, there

297

was no telling how long it had been since he escaped or where he might have gone.

Walking back into the outer office, the Utah lawman took the young soldier by the shoulders, twisted him around, and shoved him through the open door. "Go tell the sergeant of the guard his prisoner's escaped. He needs to close the gates and search the fort, and we need to do it fast. Now, git!"

Less than an hour later, after a quick, but fairly thorough search, the sergeant of the guard, the same burly, middle-aged Irishman, stood in the center of the compound with Rockwell and Clay Ashworth. After the final squad of searchers had reported, the sergeant said, "'Tis a sorry thing, but the man's not t' be found."

"*Sorry* ain't exactly the word that comes to my mind, Sergeant," Rockwell grumped.

"I don't think you've got any chance of finding him, Port," Clay offered. "With all of the activity around this fort, troopers coming and going, his trail is long gone. By now, he's well on his way to joining up with the Confederate force somewhere south of us. That's my guess, anyway."

"Uh-huh," Rockwell said, slowly nodding his head in agreement. "He's headed south for Glorieta Pass, alright. I'm tellin' yuh, Clay, that man has changed. He'll join up with those rebels— unless I can head him off."

"Aye, there's little doubt of his sympathies," the sergeant said, in hurried agreement. "And the one thing we did discover was the lad helped himself to one of our finest horses, a dappled gray. Wherever he's gone, he's movin' in style."

"You do what you think best, Port," Clay cautioned. "But maybe you ought to give some thought to what President Young would think. You're not military, and you are close enough to him to involve his name in what you do next."

Lost in thought, the Utah lawman seemed not to hear Ashworth's advice. "With a good horse under him, he's sure enough headed south. I'm just wonderin' . . . if I lit out right now, I—"

"Orrin, President Young won't want you caught up in any of the coming fighting," Clay said, knowing exactly where Rockwell's thinking was taking him. "You're too close to him. We're here as militia; you're not."

"Yeah," Rockwell said, absently, gathering up the reins of his horse. "Well . . . reckon I'd better head out. You watch your backside, Clay."

"You take care, Port."

"Sure," Rockwell said, leading his mount toward the gate. A mile from the fort, Rockwell began cutting back and forth across the trail in wide, circular swings. Within fifteen minutes he had found Striker's trail. A hard-ridden horse headed south, toward the Sangre de Cristo Mountains and Glorieta Pass.

Darkness had fallen by the time Wolfgang Striker dismounted, tying his exhausted horse to the rail in front of the main house at Pigeon's Ranch, the largest hostelry between Fort Union and Santa Fe on the Santa Fe Trail. The ranch, located a mere two miles from Glorieta Pass, was owned by a well-known Frenchman from Missouri, Alexander Pigeon, who for some reason, had recently changed his surname to Valle.

The Frenchman, known to be a man with Union sympathies, had built the ranch eleven years earlier as a way station along the Santa Fe Trail. Aside from the main house, there were a number of outbuildings on both sides of the trail, a well-house, corrals, and ample space for wagons and draft animals. The place provided a welcome stop for any weary traveler.

Having stolen a handsome big gray from the fort's remuda, Striker had pushed his mount hard throughout the day, putting nearly sixty miles behind him by nightfall. Stopping only for brief intervals to spare his horse, he had given Las Vegas, a small Mexican Village some twenty miles south of Fort Union, wide berth because of a rumored smallpox epidemic and had ridden on past Kozlowski's Ranch at the east end of the Glorieta Valley, thinking it still too close to Fort Union. Instead, he had pushed on another five miles to the Frenchman's comfortable way station.

Striker was exhausted both physically and emotionally. The ride had not only been difficult, but the threat of recapture added a dimension of anxiety that doubled the tension. Reaching Pigeon's Ranch was a welcome relief. The night was cold, the fire in the large fireplace gave the pleasant feeling of warmth and safety, and the steaming mug of coffee was hot and strong. The comfortable room, the good food, and the welcome warmth could give a man the relaxed feeling that nothing was wrong in the world, everything was as it should be—a fact Striker knew full well was completely false.

Valle leaned across Striker's table with an air of confidentiality. "As you undoubtedly know, Mister Striker, this is the best hostelry on the Santa Fe Trail. Consequently, we have many travelers each night, as you can readily see. There is a great deal of talk, and it is most alarming. Even now, a large force of Texas rebels has camped at Johnson's Ranch, at the west end of Apache Canyon. I'm told those Texans are making preparations to move through Glorieta Pass and march on Fort Union—perhaps as early as tomorrow."

"Why, that is shocking," Striker said, making an effort to share the Frenchman's sense of alarm. Sipping the hot coffee, he continued, "You must be quite worried, Mister Valle. But, perhaps it's not as serious as some would have you believe. People have a way of exaggerating," he said dismissively.

"Oh, but I believe it is not exaggeration, *mon ami.* Only this morning I saw four men in what looked to me to be Confederate uniforms surveying my ranch and riding back toward the pass. I gave it little thought then, but talking with various travelers from Santa Fe has convinced me the worst is true."

"Have you seen any Union troops?"

"*Non.* I have seen none of them. When they come, I expect there will be many of them—an army. What happens then?" the Frenchman said, with a Gallic shrug. "All I have will be ruined."

"Well, Mister Valle," Striker said, pushing his cup forward to be refilled, his tone reassuring, "I have had some experience in this kind of thing. When they come—either side—give them all they ask and more. Don't betray any sign of loyalty or allegiance. Give only your full cooperation. That way, unless the battle is fought right here," he said, tapping his finger on the table, "it is very likely your ranch will receive only minimal damage, if any."

"But surely I should try to convince any occupiers that I am loyal to their cause. Don't you think it—"

"Trust what I say," Striker interjected, his voice friendly but firm. "Neither side would believe you, anyway. And as most battles go, you're likely to play host to both sides at one time or another—perhaps repeatedly. That kind of duplicity would only serve to arouse suspicion and perhaps get you burned out. Play it straight. You'll be alright."

Morning came early for both man and horse, and the air was so cold, it almost seemed solid. But anxious to reach the

301

Confederate lines, wherever they were, Striker urged the big gray away from Pigeon's Ranch at a ground-consuming trot, recapture being his biggest worry. Given the army's problems, it was unlikely that there would be any military pursuit, but knowing Rockwell, as he had come to know him, it was altogether likely the Utah marshal would be hot on his trail.

As he rode, his worries of recapture aside, Striker carefully observed the peculiarities of the canyon with the practiced skill of an experienced soldier, one more than capable of command. From Kozlowski's Ranch, which he had passed the night before, to Pigeon's Ranch he estimated the distance to be approximately five miles. That ranch, also an excellent bivouac area, lay in the open valley of the Pecos River, but from there, the Santa Fe Trail left the Pecos to follow a small tributary, Glorieta Creek.

The valley of Glorieta Creek became increasingly constricted as it wound northwest into the mountains and neared Pigeon's Ranch. A few hundred yards short of the ranch the narrowing valley became split by a heavily wooded ridge, which ended abruptly across the trail from the ranch buildings. It was more than obvious to Striker that with a couple of artillery pieces—even just one—the entire southeast end of the narrow Glorieta Valley could be controlled with ease. The valley where Pigeon's Ranch was located was very narrow, with only room for the ranch buildings and the trail. The valley, with its steep sides, could be stopped-up like a bottle—a fact Striker would not forget.

For the next two miles, from Pigeon's Ranch to the top of Glorieta Pass, the valley continued to narrow, and at the point where the trail turned southward, the pass became severely constricted. The walls of the canyon were at times very steep, and the surrounding mountains were heavily timbered with pine, with thick stands of piñon and juniper growing on the canyon floor. It was a defense force's dream come true; for an attacking force, it would be a nightmare.

By the time the Confederate pickets stopped him just outside Johnson's Ranch, four miles from the pass, Striker had covered a total of eleven miles from the Kozlowski place. Leaving Glorieta Pass, he had ridden southward along Galisteo Creek into Apache Canyon, which was not a canyon at all, but a fairly small valley of cultivated fields that was split in half by Apache Creek. Further south, Apache Creek joined the wide and deeply eroded Galisteo Creek arroyo, which ran parallel to the trail. At this point, the trail dropped down into the steep-sided bed of Galisteo Creek itself where it passed out of Apache Canyon to Johnson's Ranch, which lay in a wide valley a short distance outside the mouth of the canyon.

As Striker rode out of the canyon, leaving the main trail and heading for Johnson's Ranch, two men stepped out of the trees, their rifles held at their hips, the muzzles pointed directly at his chest. Neither of the two wore what could be identified as a uniform. "You better stop right there, mister," one said, his speech heavily burdened with his Texas background. "Jest step down careful-like an' state yer business."

Striker's glance was cold and calculated. "I'll get down when I choose and not before." It was almost the old, reckless Striker who spoke. Somehow the abrupt challenge had stirred something deep within him, an old way of looking at things, something hateful. "Unless you two boys know how to handle those coon-shooters, you'd better lower them before I really take offense."

The old itch was there, the twisted desire, the need to draw and put a quick and final end to these two backwoods irritants. The murderous sensation felt good and was almost overwhelming—but, no, too much had happened, and too much remained to be undone. He could not go back. Not now, not to what he had been. The purgative trail had been long and hard, and he still had far to go. His voice softened. "Now, suppose you tell me, am I getting close to the headquarters of the Texas Confederates?"

"Maybe so, and maybe no. A question like that'n can be bad fer yer health. Besides, Major Pyron, he don't just see anybody. Mister, you better step down off'n that horse."

Before either man could move, they were suddenly looking into the deadly mouth of a cocked .44 Colt Army revolver. It was level, and it was steady. "Let's not be hasty, and nobody will get hurt," Striker said softly. "After all, it's your health we're concerned about here. Now, lower your weapons, and one of you boys take me to your commanding officer. I've just escaped from Fort Union, and I have information he may find useful. And believe me," he said, his face creasing into a deceptively friendly smile, "I'm in no mood for further argument."

The two guards looked doubtfully at one another, neither willing to make the first move. They had not mistaken the meaning of the intimidating stranger on the big horse. Much more palaver, and somebody was likely to get hurt. Finally, recognizing the danger of Striker's growing impatience, the smallest of the two, a wiry little man with a big Texas drawl, reluctantly stepped forward and said, "Yuh better faller me, Mister. But if yuh ain't what yuh say yuh are, we all'll have t' shoot yuh."

"If I ain't what I say, then y'all can *try* t' shoot me," Striker said, his soft mockery filled with menace and the barely discernable southern drawl in his speech genuine, though not heard even to himself for a very long time. The sound in his voice was almost startling. Something was coming back for Striker, something from deep within, something long lost to insensitivity, lust, and cruelty, something from a genteel upbringing that had been smothered and repressed nearly to extinction, and it felt good—like breathing clean air.

★　★　★

Topping a rise that overlooked Kozlowski's Ranch, Orrin Porter Rockwell reined his lathered horse to a stop and stepped out of the leather for a short breather. The animal needed the rest. Though he had ridden hard after cutting Wolf Striker's trail, Porter's determination had waned with almost every mile. Clay Ashworth had cautioned him not to pursue Striker into rebel territory, and Clay was right.

The trouble was, no one was certain just where the Texas rebels were. Were they on this side of the mountains or on the other? How far was it to the other end of the canyon? Could he take a chance on running into them and getting stopped and questioned? He wasn't a soldier, and with his face lost in a bushy, thick beard and his hair well over his shoulders, he surely didn't look like one. But should he take the risk? There was no doubt in his mind where Striker was headed. In fact, it had become so obvious, he hadn't bothered to look for sign in the last ten miles. But how important was it, at this point, to run him to ground? In the end, what good would it do?

The more Rockwell thought on the matter, the less he liked it. It wasn't just the rebels and the danger of capture, it was Striker himself. When he got right down to the core of the matter, if he had a noose around Striker's neck, with the man standing right in front of him on the trapdoor, and the lever was right here in the palm of his hand, could he pull it? Even more importantly, was it the right thing to do? The man had changed. There was little doubt of that, and truth be told, Rockwell sort of liked the new

Wolfgang Striker. As Brother Brigham would say, there seemed to be something in the man worth saving.

But there was still another knot in this tangled rope. The predominantly Mormon element in the Utah Territory had taken a strong stand against the southern rebellion. Mormons held the Constitution to be a sacred thing, and secession was seen by most Utahans as something almost blasphemous. No state had the right to withdraw from a Union that had been established under divine inspiration. The Constitution aside, Brigham Young had not only promised Lincoln that Utah would stand fast with the Union, he had committed the Utah militia—at least some units of it—to protecting federal property and the telegraph lines.

Now, there it was, clear as could be: Utah was with the Union, Rockwell was a Utah peace officer, and Striker had headed south to join the Texas rebels. On top of that, he was a murderer. He had committed willful acts of war against Platte River Station and its citizens, murdering its law officers and who knows how many other innocent citizens, and all of that supposedly in the name of the Confederacy. Now, escaping from a military guardhouse, he was running to join the rebels. It just couldn't be stated more plainly.

"If I've ever seen a philosopher more lost in thought, I don't know where or when."

"What the . . ." Rockwell said, jumping to his feet. "Clay Ashworth, you liked to have scared the daylights out of me. Where'd you come from, mister?"

Clay grinned at his bearded friend, knowing how Rockwell hated being caught flat-footed. "Well," he said, throwing his leg over the saddle horn, "I've been sitting here for some time. If I'd been a Comanche, I think I could have lifted your hair, and you'd never have known it. What are you doing, anyway?"

"Well, I'm about to mount up and go fetch Striker."

"Mmm," Ashworth said, thoughtfully shaking his head. "Not a good idea, Marshal."

"Look, Clay, I've thought this thing through from every angle, and I'm going after him. He's got to be brought to justice."

"If you'll just stop and look behind you, Port, you'll see an entire Union army strung out almost as far as the eye can see. The van will be here within an hour, and they are going right on up into those mountains. By this time tomorrow, there is every likelihood that a major battle will be raging somewhere between here and Santa Fe—probably right in the middle of Glorieta Pass. Now, as much fun as that is likely to be, do you really think you should be caught in the middle of a shooting war between the states? Think about it, Port. The political fallout could be very bad."

Rockwell gathered his reins and swung into his saddle. "There's nothing in this world I hate more than leaving a job undone," the lawman grumped. "He's beaten me, and it just plain eats at my innards."

"Better that than a lead ball eating at them, Port," Clay chuckled. "And Striker hasn't beaten us, because we're not going to let that happen. I've got a better idea, one that won't get either of us into trouble."

"And just what might that be?"

"Don't forget, I'm part of that army coming up behind us, Marshal—I and a bunch of other Utah Militiamen. We have no choice but to be in the upcoming fight. I'll go into that fracas with the intent of our finding Striker and capturing him—if he isn't killed first. Every one of us will be on the lookout for him. If he's captured, I'll personally see to it that he is delivered into your hands for trial and punishment. If he's killed, our worries, at least where Striker's concerned, are over. Don't forget, I took my licks at Platte River Station, too. I want to see the man caught and hanged every bit as much as you do."

"Yeah, I guess you're right," Rockwell said, swinging his horse around. "I don't like it, but you're right. I'll tell yuh something else, too."

"What's that?"

"I get the sick feeling I ain't ever going to see that villain again, and I don't like it one bit. Not one bit." Before Ashworth could answer, Rockwell had spurred his horse into a gallop heading back toward the Mora Valley and the distant peaks to the north, away from the Glorieta Pass, still uncertain if he was doing the right thing.

Clay watched Rockwell until he had nearly disappeared from sight. The last thing he saw of the Utah lawman was Porter Rockwell standing in his stirrups looking back toward the Kozlowski Ranch. Clay Ashworth smiled and shook his head. At best, dealing with Orrin Porter Rockwell was an uncertain thing, and he knew that was just how Rockwell wanted it.

# CHAPTER 29

★   ★   ★

$\text{I}$N HERE," THE TEXAS REBEL SAID, pushing the tent flap aside, allowing Wolf Striker to step into the cramped tent. Major Charles L. Pyron sat behind a small campaign desk rapidly scribbling on a large piece of paper. Viewing it upside down, across the desk, Striker could see that it was a status report of some kind. The communiqué was addressed to Brigadier General Henry H. Sibley, C.S.A.; that much he could make out.

"I knew General Sibley way back when," Striker offered, nodding toward the report Pyron was hastily preparing.

Sliding his hand over the report, Pyron raised his eyes, a look of irritation on his face. "Sit down," he said, nodding toward a small wooden folding chair, his attitude militarily abrupt. "I'll get to you in a minute."

"Sorry, I didn't mean to pry."

Finishing the report, Pyron slid the papers into a leather folder and set it aside. "So you've just escaped from Fort Union." It was a statement, not a question, and the tone was none too friendly. "If that's true, you're more clever than most, Mister . . . ?"

"Striker. Wolfgang Striker. I'm known by most as Wolf Striker."

"Well, Wolf Striker, where did you know General Sibley *way back when,* as you put it?" Pyron said, leaning back in his chair.

"I served with him during the Mexican War—well, not with him, exactly, but I was at Vera Cruz and Chapultepec."

"Chapultepec?" Pyron said, a thoughtful look crossing his drawn face. "Oh, yes. Now I know where I've heard your name. Whatever became of you after the Chapultepec problem? Let's see . . . what was it? Weren't you and some of your men supposed to have—"

"Every story has many sides," Striker declared, "and every side many facets, Major—not all of them true, let alone accurate."

"Yes . . . I suppose so. Well, be that as it may," Pyron said with a wave of his hand, as if he could brush an unpleasant thought aside, "you're supposed to have escaped from Fort Union?"

"Yes, sir. The night before last."

"And how did you manage to pull that off?"

"The entire garrison is preparing to march on you, Major. I just took advantage of all the confusion. More troops were arriving every day—most from Colorado—and the place was in an uproar. Escaping was not all that difficult."

Straightening in his chair, Pyron said, "When are they likely to march?"

"Yesterday sometime. They're altogether likely to be at Kozlowski's Ranch by now."

"But they're not in the canyon?" Pyron queried doubtfully, his face creased with worry. "At least my scouts have not reported seeing any of them."

"Your biggest advantage, Major, is that they have no idea where you are. Since the battle at Valverde, they know you've taken Albuquerque and Santa Fe, but their information is scanty, mostly based on tales told by travelers passing through and on rumor. You have the opportunity of catching them unawares somewhere in the canyon, or at Glorieta Pass itself. But you'd better act now."

"Mmm . . . yes, I suppose you're right," Pyron muttered, lost momentarily in thought.

"Look, Major, I came here because I want to get into the fight. I want a commission with the Confederacy, and right here is a good place to start. Let me help. I'm experienced. I've been a commissioned officer in the United States Army in the past, as you know. I was field grade before my resignation."

"Yes . . . yes, I know," Pyron said, almost as if he had not heard the man standing in front of him. Finally, apparently having made a decision, he looked up. "And you've already been of help, Mister Striker; however, I'm not in a position to commission you, as experienced as you no doubt are. That will have to wait for General Sibley. Given your military background and experience and our present needs, that should not be a problem. And, I take it, he's familiar with your background?"

"To some extent, yes."

"Very well. Now, tell me, Mister Striker," Pyron said, leaning forward, "what are we up against? What is the strength of the Union forces we are likely to encounter, and what kinds of units?"

"As you can imagine, Major, I left Fort Union in somewhat of a hurry. I did manage, however, to glean some idea of what they had assembled before I escaped. I would estimate their total strength to be in the neighborhood of four hundred men as of the day before yesterday, both mounted and infantry. It's only a guess, and more men and equipment seemed to be arriving almost every hour."

"Mmm . . . I'm relieved to hear that. If that's the case, and their strength remains at that level, we are fairly matched. As of this moment I can field four hundred and forty men, and a good many of them are battle-seasoned. What do you know of their make-up?"

"Their advanced column is being led by some parson, a Major Chivington. I understand he's a man of the cloth, but from what I heard, you should not let that fool you. It's rumored the parson's a real fire-breather, and he's popular with his men. There is infantry, a Colorado bunch, and what looked to be at least two hundred cavalry or mounted infantry. I heard the name 'Pike's Peakers' bandied about. I think it applied to all of the Colorado volunteers, but I'm not sure. They looked to be a ragged bunch—not too well-trained, if at all—but most of them seem eager for the fight."

"Yes, the inexperienced usually are, until they taste blood—their own. Well, we'll give them what they want, all right," Pyron said, a tone of finality to his statement.

"One other thing that will give you some advantage, Major. From what I heard, I don't think they are planning on bringing any artillery with them, at least not initially. I could be wrong, but I overheard a couple of men complaining that they would be bringing no cannons."

"Come with me," Pyron said, rising from his small desk and brushing past Striker. "If your information is anywhere near correct, you've been of enormous help." Turning to the guard near his tent, he said, "Corporal. Find Captain Phillips, and tell him to report to me at once."

Striker stepped from the tent and filled his lungs with the

cold, clean, mountain air. Suddenly life felt good—for the first time in many years. He had a place in what was happening here, and it had meaning—the Confederate rebellion had real meaning. He was born to be a soldier. It was his destiny, and this was the right cause—a fight for liberty and independence.

"What can I do, Major? I want to be a part of this."

"I've sent for Captain John G. Phillips. You'll like Phillips. He is the leader of a group of irregulars we call the Brigands. You'll soon see why. They like to think of themselves as the 'Company of Santa Fe Gamblers'—thirty roughnecks rounded up from the bars and brothels of Santa Fe. That might give you an idea of what they're like. They're a motley group at best, some quite unsavory, but you can help Phillips give them the leadership they need. Some are from Texas, some from Arizona, and some from New Mexico—all of them volunteers, and only a few with any real experience.

"I'm going to suggest that Phillips make you his second in command. Because it's an irregular outfit, I can do that. There are other units of that kind, but this bunch has promise, and they need some real leadership. Phillips is very good, but he can't do it by himself."

"There are those who would say they sound like my kind of unit," Striker chuckled. "I should fit right in."

Striker and Phillips lay hidden in the deep grass at the edge of the bluff, a mile or more down the canyon from Pigeon's Ranch. "How did those bloody fools get themselves captured?" Phillips hissed. "I count . . . great Caesar's ghost! . . . thirty men and horses in all. That's what too little experience gets you."

"They must have stumbled right into those Union troops,"

Striker said, as the two scrambled back from the edge of the bluff. "Listen to those blue belly Pike's Peakers cheer, and they're stripping those men of what little equipment they carry. You can bet your last nickel that Union major is going to move his men down the canyon on the double-quick and do his best to catch us flat-footed. That's got to be Chivington. I don't know much about that preacher, but from the looks of it, he's somebody to watch out for."

"He's almost caught us flat-footed now," Phillips said, the outrage in his voice unmistakable. "Let's hightail it back down the canyon—fast.

"Hell's fire," he said rising to his feet. "Thirty men lost—and all those horses and equipment." Phillips was almost beside himself with anger.

Both men were on their feet and moving rapidly. "This ain't no way to win a war," Striker grumbled to himself. His first involvement had thirty of his men captured and him on the run in the wrong direction. Nothing could be more humiliating to the born soldier; the only direction for any combat-hardened fighting man was forward. Under most circumstances, any retreat was a direct attack on a professional's competence. He could only hope this was just an initial setback, and things could yet be saved— they had to be saved. There was no option.

"Those two six-pounders had better be in place at Galisteo Creek," Phillips said, his breath coming in short gasps. "You find those artillery pieces, Striker. Get them turned on those cussed Yankees," he huffed. "I'm going to the rear to warn Pyron the Feds are in the canyon. He needs to get his men deployed, if he hasn't already—and fast."

Striker was too angry to reply as he leaped over the edge of a cutbank and descended in a cascade of falling rock and dirt down the steep slope to the road below. Regaining his balance as he scrambled onto the road, Striker took off at a dead run, moving faster than he had in years without a horse beneath him. No sooner had he hit the ground than behind him Chivington's men rounded a bend in the road, double-timing it down the canyon, their cries of impending victory loud in his ears.

At that moment, both Striker and the charging Union troops came into sight of the two Texas six-pounders and the main body of Pyron's command. Almost simultaneously, both field pieces belched white smoke from their black mouths, and a pair of balls shrieked over Striker's head, aimed at Chivington and his charging men, not more than one hundred yards behind him.

The cannon balls overshot their mark, landing harmlessly behind the Union troops but bringing their charge to a disorderly halt. For many, it was their first taste of the reality they were about to face. The next blast from the two cannon was obviously grapeshot, and it suddenly dawned on the enthusiastic Pike's Peakers that things were going to get serious. This was not a game among boys; it was not a romp in the woods, a hunt for deer; this was war, and it was going to become ugly. A body could get himself killed—right here and now!

Abruptly, the noisy Union charge to a quick victory turned to confusion, bordering on panic for many. Men began milling about, a number retreating back up the canyon as more cannon shots fell just short of their position. Lacking in military experience, more began moving further to the rear, seeking safety from the Confederate guns and the scattering debris from the pulverizing balls.

The growing panic threatened to bring the entire Union move against the Confederates crashing down in failure, and if that were to happen, Fort Union would lay open to a Confederate siege and eventual capture. Such failure was not acceptable to Major John M. Chivington, soldier and man of God. Moving among his men, oblivious to the rifle fire whistling amid his confused command and the shells exploding around them, the stocky, bearded major urged the men to stand fast and do their duty to God and country. With faith, they were not only superior to the Texas rabble that confronted them, they were invincible.

A popular leader, the Colorado parson, decked out in his finest uniform, gradually restored order, putting a halt to any precipitous move to the rear. His fearless presence was an inspiration to the men he commanded. He moved among his troops as a Moses in the Camp of Israel, rallying them to the fight.

Not wanting to lose any advantage his charge down the canyon might have given him, Chivington quickly ordered two of his infantry companies to deploy up the mountainside to their left, in among the pine trees, in a flanking maneuver above the Confederate force. Another company was dispatched to the broken mountain slopes above the Confederate left, in the hope of catching the rebels in a brutal, flanking crossfire. A company of regular cavalry, under the command of Captain George Howland, and a mounted company of Colorado volunteers, under Captain Samuel Cook, were to be held in reserve. On Chivington's command, they were to charge down the canyon in an effort to overwhelm the Texas artillerymen and capture or nullify their two field pieces. Clay's Utah cavalry contingent was ordered to the rear in reserve.

Chivington seemed a man on fire, a man filled with some divine spirit, as if he were a disciple of the true and living God, sent to lead these men to a sure and righteous victory. In truth, as he moved among them, issuing orders as if by revelation, he almost appeared as a prophet-commander in uniform, bringing order to his flock and leading them toward the victory that was rightfully theirs. In almost immediate response to his words, Chivington's Pike's Peakers became inflamed with his passion, and following his lead, they began moving down the canyon.

Chivington's performance and the tactics of his deployment were brilliant.

Reaching the two cannon and the Texans manning them, Striker hollered, "Get those two pieces limbered up, and let's get out of here." Doubling over, his hands on his knees, Striker fought for breath. "If those blue bellies capture these guns we are going to be in real trouble," he gasped," and they're a lot closer than anyone thought."

For the first time, Striker was struck with the sobering realization that the years were beginning to catch up with him. "I'm getting too old for this kind of stuff," he muttered to himself, his breath beginning to come easier.

No more depressing thought can assail a man's mind than the realization of decline, and had Striker the luxury of time to reflect on what he had just said, depression would surely have followed. But the balls whistling around him, balls shot by an enemy force regaining its determination and threatening to outflank his position, filled his aching body with renewed vigor.

"Let's go!" he hollered. "We'll make a stand down where the canyon narrows—where we can really hurt them. Now, let's get those guns outta here!"

"What in heaven's name are you doing, Striker?" Pyron shouted as he ran up to Striker, Phillips close behind him. "We must stand firm here. Unlimber those pieces!" he hollered to the gun crews.

"Major, if you do, they are going to overwhelm us. This position is untenable. Look back there," Striker shouted, pointing up the canyon. "They're going to flank us on either side. We can't stay here. Let's move down to where the canyon narrows, then we can lay it to them."

As the Confederate troops began moving back down the trail and the artillery pieces rattled out of sight, Chivington's men began laying down a brutal fire from both sides of the canyon on those covering the retreat. Not waiting for further orders, the remaining Confederates turned on their heels, hightailing it down the road, the rallying cries of the Union troops filling the canyon behind them.

★　★　★

The retreating Texans could hear Chivington bellowing commands and encouragement to his troops, and the sound was chilling. "We've got 'em on the run now, boys! Let's send 'em back to Texas with their tails between their legs!" he hollered. Pulling two large Colt revolvers from his belt he tucked one beneath each arm. Drawing two more from their holsters at his waist, he began firing, taking careful aim at a retreating rebel soldier whose torn, lifeless body soon lay bleeding in their path. "Let's go get 'em, men!" he yelled. "Follow me! We've got them on the run!"

With each word, Chivington's Colts barked, punctuating each command with a kind of divine authority and laying waste another rebel soldier. The effect was galvanizing. Every man within the sound of his voice became energized, seemingly beyond physical limitation—both Union and Confederate.

"Charge!"

From where Clay Ashworth sat, it appeared the entire length of Apache Canyon was in utter confusion, the air filled with the shouts of men and the reports of rifles and small arms. The canyon echoed with the violent sounds of war, the voices of men locked in the extremities of life's darkest hour. Without his being aware of it, Clay's head slowly shook in refusal of the bloody violence that seemed to surround him. How could such a thing happen to his young nation, not yet a century old? This was not a fight to settle the West; it was not a fight between the white man and the Indian over territory and rights of way; it was war between the states in the East, and now it had infected the West— a war between Americans.

This was civil war, war among men of common national history, of common language, for the most part Christians all— brothers—men who shared a love of freedom. But in such a dark hour as this, men saw themselves and their brothers in war from perspectives made vague, clouded by bias, bigotry, economic discontinuities, and inconsistent loyalties. In the midst of such violence as that raging in Apache Canyon, the foundations of any unifying brotherhood crumbled beneath the weight of death and carnage.

Was such ruin as he was now witnessing to be his country's true manifest destiny? Is this all there was to look forward to? Was this the future? Where would war and violence spread from here? Would this bloodshed reach *Rancho los Librados*—and Consuela, his Connie? That simply could not be allowed to happen. Could he stop it here? However it ended in the East, would that be the end of it?

The entire Utah cavalry squadron had been ordered to the rear of the Union cavalry, which was only now in a position to enter into the fighting that was moving further down the canyon. From where Clay sat, the Yankee skirmishers were pouring rapid and effective fire down on the flanks of the retreating rebel force. Now was the time for the cavalry to charge and capture their big guns. This war of rebellion had to be brought to an end, and now was the time, regardless of how hideous the furies might appear before the end was seen.

Turning to the man next to him, Clay shouted, "Why is our cavalry waiting? Why doesn't Howland charge those Confederate batteries now, before they unlimber?"

Spurring his horse, Clay cantered up to where Captain George Howland sat his horse watching the action further down the canyon. "George, what are we doing sitting here? Let's go after those cannon before they turn around and get unlimbered."

Not taking his eyes from the action further down the canyon, Howland said, "Just sit your horse and keep your men under control, Mister Ashworth." Howland spoke so low Clay could barely hear him above the din of battle, nor did the man bother to look in Clay's direction. "Before we could get to them," Howland said, his voice rising, "those Texans will have those pieces unlimbered on the far side of that bridge down there, and we'd be charging into a solid wall of canister and grape. Just because that zealot Chivington acts like he has some kind of divine protection doesn't mean I need to lead my men in a needless suicide charge."

Clay wheeled his horse in disgust and rode back to the Utah contingent. Reining up before Lieutenant Jeb Smith, he said, "This day is all but lost, Jeb. For some reason Howland refuses to charge those retreating Texans. He has disobeyed direct orders."

"It's small wonder, Clay," Smith said, as his horse shied and pranced in nervous response to the noise and confusion that filled the canyon. "Look at this mess. This isn't cavalry. This is chaos. There are horses all over the place. Howland's unit is not formed to move yet, and it probably never will be."

"Look down there, Jeb. We could have routed that Texas trash completely and captured their cannon if he'd just done something," Clay shouted above the tumult, fighting to keep his own horse under control. "All the man had to do was yell 'charge,' and those mounted men behind him would have ridden over him to get into the battle.

"This cavalry needs some of Chivington's kind of leadership. Look at him down there, Jeb! Can you see him? The man's obsessed. He's got a pistol in each hand; he's shooting at anything in front of him that moves, and it looks as if he's got two more pistols, one under each arm. Now that's leadership! That is how this madness will be brought to an end, not sitting here fighting our horses!

"Where's Captain Cook?"

"He's over there on the right, and it looks like he's ready to move, Clay. Let's move with him!"

Twisting his prancing horse about, Clay waved his hat in the air. "Who's with me?" he hollered. "Cook's about to charge, and the fight lies before us!" Drawing one of his horse pistols, Clay fired it into the air, his horse rearing beneath him. "It's now or never, boys! It's now or never!

"Charge! Now! Charge!"

# CHAPTER 30

★  ★  ★

Close behind the two cannon, Wolf's horse's hooves drummed a rapid staccato as it crossed the bridge above the dry arroyo of Galisteo Creek. "Unlimber those pieces over there," Wolf hollered, pointing to a shallow talus slope that had formed at the base of the steep hillside and protruded out into the trail forming a natural barrier, one that offered the gunners enough protection to deploy the two artillery pieces in relative safety.

Dismounting, and shouting above the din, Wolf grabbed the nearest man by the arm and pointed up the trail. "Two of you take some powder and blow that bridge. It won't stop them, but the ravine's deep enough to slow 'em down. The rest of you men," he hollered, his hand sweeping their position, "take up defensive positions around the guns. Those blue bellies are going to do their best to capture them—and here they come!"

"Watch yourselves," Pyron yelled, "they're trying to outflank us up there on the slopes. No!" he cried, as the men began shooting wildly. "Up there, on our right. Don't waste your ammunition! Make each shot count!"

"Look at that lunatic!" Wolf roared, almost in unbelief, pointing up the canyon at the oncoming Union phalanx. Grabbing a carbine from the man nearest him and taking careful aim at the Union major leading his men in their wild charge toward the Confederate emplacement, Wolf vowed, half to himself, "That man's got to go. He'll have those blue bellies all over us if he isn't taken down." The carbine jumped, and Wolf could not believe his eyes. He had missed. "I don't believe it! I never miss—not at this range."

"You missed, you idiot!" Phillips hollered, taking careful aim at the Union officer, now no more than fifty or sixty yards away. The rifle jumped in his hands, as he yelled, "How could you miss at that distance?"

"I don't know, Captain," Wolf said, again taking careful aim, "but you just did. If I'm an *idiot,* where does that leave you?" The carbine punched into Wolf's shoulder, and to his utter dismay the man in blue came on, as if invincible, unscathed, his pistols spitting flame. Lowering the weapon Wolf gaped in disbelief. "That man is either a complete fool, or he leads a charmed life."

"All of you take aim on that crazy Union officer," Phillips hollered at the Texans surrounding the two cannon, "and fire on my command!"

Every man facing across that bridge leveled his weapon on Major John M. Chivington, a man possessed, each taking the greatest care he had ever exercised, many of them experienced marksmen. Each was confident his shot would be the one to bring the man down. With careful aim, there was nothing to it. Why, it couldn't be more than thirty yards now. Child's play.

"Fire!"

As the volley cracked the canyon air, mixing with the clamor of the oncoming charge, the bridge between the two forces exploded. Large chunks of timber, shards of wood, and rocks of all sizes formed an acrid, choking cloud of dirt, dust, and smoke. Debris rained down like a biblical plague sent to torment all. The accompanying concussion thundered up the canyon, echoing off the sides of the surrounding mountains, almost a thing alive. The size of the small bridge aside, it was the most impressive event of the day, and men and horses alike, pelted with stinging debris, were stunned by the enormity of the blast.

"How much powder did them boys use?" a sergeant asked no one in particular.

"Can't say, exactly," one of the men answered, "but they sure done the job."

As the smoke began to clear, the stunned rebels could see the Union major, apparently untouched by any human effort to bring him down, standing in the middle of the road, wildly waving the Union cavalry on as it thundered past him and toward the gully and the now-missing bridge.

"I don't believe my eyes," a stunned Phillips said, almost as if to himself, rubbing his smarting eyes. "I don't believe it. The man is still standing. That man is still there!"

"Turn those guns," Wolf shouted, shouldering the awestruck Phillips aside, "and get them down the canyon fast! The rest of you men form up and start firing into that cavalry before they breach the arroyo. If they get our cannon, we're finished!"

Earlier, as the Confederate force had retreated across the now destroyed bridge, Major Pyron had decided to employ some of the flanking tactics used by his ineradicable Union counterpart. Seeking to secure his right flank, he had sent a company of Texas rebels up the mountainside to harass the enemy advance and secure that flank against any Union effort to attack a possible retreat. Some of his dismounted men had also been sent scrambling northward along Apache Creek into the hills and fields there.

Given the tide of battle now faced by the Confederate force, it had been an insightful maneuver. Now, as the Union cavalry thundered down on the dry arroyo, the Texans on both sides of the wide canyon opened fire, and the winding trail once more reverberated with the din of rifle fire and the cries of death.

As the battle heated, Pyron rode up and dismounted. "Captain Phillips, hurry and get those guns back down the canyon.

"Mister Striker, can you hold this position until we are safely withdrawn?"

"Consider it done, Major. Just leave me sufficient men."

"You can have Company A of the Fifth Texas. Now hop to it, if you will, sir!"

As the Confederates began their withdrawal, Wolf led his men along the right flank of the now reformed Union battle line. "Pour it to them, boys! Pour it to them!"

Swords and pistols drawn, leaning across the withers of their charging mounts, and screaming at the top of their lungs, Clay and his cavalry squadron thundered past Major Chivington and his men, racing toward the arroyo that separated them from the rebels' big guns.

Clay felt his horse leave the ground as if in flight and stretch out for the opposite bank. In an instant, he was in the middle of a swarm of angry Texans, each intent on bringing him down. His pistol spitting lead, the faces of those nearest him blossoming in obscene ruin, he plunged on, left and right, back and front, the smell of powder burning his eyes and nose.

Ugly and deadly as it was, this was what war should be: close, personal, and brutal. You knew your enemy. His screaming, distorted face was right before you. These were not innocents, they were warriors, men intent on the kill and winning the day in the most decisive and final way possible. Somehow it was exhilarating. Somehow the face of death gave a meaning to life found nowhere else.

Now, in the midst of this terrible maelstrom, no thoughts of Connie or of the ranch entered into his dark work. This was war, and the quickest way to end it was to press it to the extreme. Later there would be time for thinking, for reflection upon the moral issues involved, the dangers and, possibly, the regrets. But here, surrounded by his enemies, he simply reacted, spurring his horse, directing the animal with his knees, the reins draped over its neck, a pistol in both hands barking out his fatal demands.

Clay felt the tug and sting of something hot biting at his left arm, and then he was surrounded by his own men wheeling their screaming horses in every direction, some forced to leap their mounts back and forth across the wash. It was one of the most daring and unforgettable cavalry charges in Clay's memory, and he had participated in a number and studied many. For its unyielding impetuosity, it was one for the books.

"Major Ashworth!" It was Captain Cook. "You're hit, sir. Fall to the rear!"

No sooner had Cook spoken, than he was hit in the thigh, and his foot was bleeding profusely. "We can't both risk being killed or taken prisoner. Fall to the rear, sir!"

"It's only a scratch, nothing to be concerned about," Clay

responded, swinging his arm about as if to demonstrate his point. "They're falling back. Now's not the time to quit."

The audacious Union cavalry charge quickly proved too much for the Texans. Overwhelmed by the sheer ferocity of the slashing horsemen among them, the Texas rebels began falling back, fighting for their lives and the protection of the two precious six-pounders, now rattling down the canyon and out of sight, several hundred yards from the fighting.

Finally, under the relentless Union onslaught, the Confederate resistance dissolved into a full-blown retreat, men fleeing in every direction, their arms and equipment littering the trail behind them.

Stunned by the obviously impending Union victory, Wolf Striker watched the Confederate defense of the west end of the canyon crumble into an outright rout. It was one of the most disheartening sights he had ever witnessed, and he had witnessed more than a few. But what worried him even more was the fact that he and his men now were nearly surrounded by Union troops, and those troops were so energized by their impending victory, capture would certainly mean death for many and internment for the rest. For Wolf Striker, such an unthinkable thing could not be allowed to happen.

As Wolf frantically began gathering his men for a break through the Union lines, Major John Shropshire suddenly burst through the milling Union troops who had begun withdrawing back up the trail, taking them completely by surprise. "Wolf! You and your boys follow me!" he hollered, bringing his horse to a skidding stop in front of Wolf. Grabbing Shropshire's extended arm, Wolf sprang onto the back of the man's horse.

"Let's get out of here, Major," Wolf hollered. "Come on, boys! We'll get 'em another day!"

★   ★   ★

That night, in his tent at Johnson's ranch, his body aching with fatigue and attempting to unwind from the day's violence, Wolf lay on his cot unable to relax. Something kept nagging at the back of his mind, something he could not quite bring to the surface. The fight had been wild; things had happened so fast when that Union cavalry officer and his men jumped that arroyo, it was almost impossible to review the battle in any detail at all. That Union officer had. . . .

*That Union cavalry officer!* The thought brought Wolf straight up in his bed.

"Clay Ashworth!" Wolf Striker almost shouted. "That Union officer was Clay Ashworth!"

Ashworth's presence lent a new meaning to the battle for Glorieta Pass. For Wolfgang Striker, the fight, when it resumed, would be altogether different. It was now a fight for his personal freedom, if not his life.

Back at Pigeon's Ranch, four miles from where Wolf sat on his cot, Clay Ashworth also bolted upright in his bed. "Wolfgang Striker! That was Wolf Striker!"

Just the thought of Striker's presence sent adrenaline coursing into Clay's veins. "Tomorrow," Clay hissed. "Tomorrow you'll come to justice, Wolf Striker. Before this battle is over, you'll come to justice—and you'll know why."

Morning came early in late March in the high country, and the air was cold and invigorating. Two or three deep breaths gave a man a sense of renewed life and sharpened perspective—except when trying to shave. Clay stropped the razor, only slightly favoring his wounded arm, and turned back to the badly cracked mirror. The wound was not much more than a minor irritant. Besides, the lather on his face had already started to dry. This was an annoying way to start what promised to be a painful day. By agreement between hostiles, this was to be a day of retrenchment, for gathering and burying the dead and providing for the wounded. Given what others had suffered, perhaps a little personal discomfort was only right.

Beyond the fractured face in the almost useless mirror, the canyon seemed broken into pieces by exaggerated fault lines running every which way. Somehow the image was fitting. War shattered everything it touched—men, equipment, the animals, the earth itself. It was as true in yesterday's bitter fighting as it would be tomorrow. The fight in Apache Canyon had been a bloody one, and the engagement was not yet over, merely suspended. If anything, what remained would be even more violent and unforgiving, because the battle for Glorieta Pass was of decisive importance for both sides, and that meant pulling out all the bloody stops. Clay's side knew it, and the Texas rebels knew it.

"Ouch," Clay mumbled half aloud, as a tiny red spot appeared around the self-inflicted sting. It was the second or third nick. Thinking was just plain dangerous, especially while one attempted to shave.

Still, men had died yesterday in the most violent way, others had been wounded and were in agony, many would be crippled for life. Almost as disturbing was the havoc raised with the animals, especially the horses. The big rancher loved horses. Coming from southern stock, he was born to the horse—and to the gun. The big, beautiful animals were the true innocents in man's inhumanity to man—loyal and determined as that wonderful creature could be. Wild at times, yes. Hard to control in the noise and confusion of combat, a horse was still the best friend a man had under such circumstances, and the suffering they were called to bear caused him pain. If he closed his eyes, Clay could still hear the desperate screams of the horses as they were hit by flying lead. The screams of the big animals—they sounded intensely human—as they reacted to the pain brought on them by the men who used them so shamefully were almost as hideous to him as the cries of wounded and dying men.

"Nuts." Another self-inflicted wound.

Any way you measured it, war was the greatest anomaly in human experience, despite the fact that war more than any other human factor seemed to be the driving force in history. If life was so precious, why did human issues—abstractions, really—and their differences become so intense, so hardened, as to lead to such suffering? How could the most virtuous and ideal of human desires result in such horror—men willfully killing and maiming one another with organized determination?

In this war, were men fighting over the ideal of freedom? Not a Texan nor a Coloradan nor a Utahan engaged in killing one another yesterday likely could be found who did not hold the ideal of freedom among his highest and most precious values. Yet there they were, fighting over that which they all held most highly and, in all likelihood, would agree they held in common.

The real issue, of course, was not the question of freedom, but how one institutionalized that freedom. Could the states survive independently, or was a strong, centralized federal government necessary? And how extensive should the powers of that central government be? Was this a union of independent states that could not be dissolved over economic and cultural differences? If the several states had entered into that union voluntarily, could they not dissolve that union in a like manner? Was that what the fight was about—that and slavery?

"March twenty-seventh, eighteen hundred and sixty-two," Clay murmured with a sigh, giving his razor another slap on the strop. Was this really about slavery? As repugnant as slavery was to him, that was not the primary issue. Union was what it was all about—at least so far.

*I wonder what Connie is doing this morning?* Clay reflected as he rinsed the remaining lather from his face and the imponderables of war from his mind. *What's happening on our ranch? I wonder if I'll ever see her again?* Clay took a deep breath. "I'll see her again!" he declared aloud. "After all I went through to win her, I'll be with her again!"

Taking one last look at his disassembled reflection, Clay wiped his face dry and threw the towel on the makeshift shaving stand. Minor cuts aside, nothing made a man feel cleaner and more alive than a fresh shave.

"Major Ashworth!" It was a sergeant from Chivington's staff. "We're pulling back to Kozlowsky's Ranch, sir."

Clay nodded his understanding and strolled over to the fire where his Utah companions were huddled against the early morning chill, two or three of them attempting to cook some sort of breakfast. A small quantity of flour and corn had been found in one of Pigeon's sheds, and as inadequate as it was, mush or fry bread—or something!—was being made from it. The Union force was running short of supplies, and, for hungry men, trite as it sounded, desperate times called for desperate measures.

The announced pullback was no surprise. Chivington had been fearful of Confederate reinforcements and a renewed push toward Fort Union. The order to move back down the canyon to Kozlowsky's Ranch was strictly a precautionary measure. The good news, which Chivington had earlier shared with his commanders, was that a large number of Union reinforcements had arrived from Bernal Springs, both infantry and cavalry.

After Chivington and his troops arrived at the ranch, Colonel John P. Slough was to take command. The change of command was no reflection on the man known to all as the "Fightin' Preacher." He had more than proved his daring and effectiveness as a commander. The big Methodist minister had turned down an appointment as chaplain for a strictly fighting role. It had been a good move. Under Chivington, the Union had carried the day. Union troops had advanced toward Santa Fe and repulsed the rebel force they had encountered. The only worry now was the arrival of Texas reinforcements and what that might do to alter the balance of power.

By agreement, hostilities would begin again sometime around eight o'clock in the morning, March 28, 1862.

# CHAPTER 31

* * *

WOLF STRIKER ROLLED OVER IN HIS blanket and lay listening. The noise outside his tent had reached a level he could no longer ignore, and further sleep was impossible. By agreement, both sides were to spend the next day clearing the canyon of their dead. The day would be physically and emotionally exhausting, and Wolf was not looking forward to it. Once that gruesome task was completed, the war would resume. Under such circumstances it was difficult not to think on the inconsistencies of war, and every war had them. At the end of a busy day of killing one another, men of great animosity would sometimes suspend their murderous rage long enough to treat their wounded, collect the dead, and pay their respects before resuming their bloody work.

Throwing his blanket aside and pulling his boots on, Wolf stepped out into the predawn darkness. A shadow loomed before him, materializing into Major Pyron. "What's all the noise, Major?" Wolf asked.

"What are you up for, *Major?*" Pyron said, a smile creasing his weary features. "You've got another two hours before we roust you out." With each word, Pyron's breath formed small clouds in the cold air.

"Who can sleep with all of this racket?"

"To answer your question, Wolf," Pyron said, turning and pointing into the darkness, "Colonel Scurry and his men have just arrived. They've marched all night over the mountains to get here as quickly as possible. A baggage train with supplies and an additional one hundred men should arrive sometime later today. Things are looking up. We'll whip those blue coats now."

"Oh," Wolf said noncommittally. "Well . . . it's not like we need the help," he yawned, turning to reenter his tent. "Is it, Major?"

"No, *Major*," Pyron said, with a chuckle, "it surely isn't."

The flap dropped behind Wolf as he sat down heavily on his cot and began tugging off a boot. Another two hours of sleep under such exhausting conditions was a treasure not to be lightly taken. Wolf looked up. "*Major?*" he whispered to himself. "What'd he say?" Jumping up he pulled the flap aside to see a grinning Charles Pyron.

"Here, Major Striker," Pyron said, thrusting a paper at him. "It's your commission. I wrote General Sibley about you and included it in a field report. He sent your commission with Colonel Scurry. The general was delighted to hear you are here with us. He'd lost track of you." Tapping the paper, Pyron said, "It's field grade. Scurry just handed it to me, and I was in the process of delivering it when you stepped out of your tent. Congratulations. The Confederacy needs men of your experience and caliber, not to mention the needs of Texas."

Wolf, at the same time, was both stunned and delighted. He

had been caught totally off guard by the good news, not expecting to be commissioned until he had had a chance to talk personally with Sibley. But here it was. He was back where he belonged, back in the military, back in the cavalry.

Reentering his tent, Wolf lighted a candle and tilted the parchment into the dim glow. The document was not a Texas document, it was a document of the Confederate States of America. He was now a major, assigned to Sibley's Army of New Mexico, an officer in the service of the Confederacy—presently assigned to the Fifth Texas Regiment, a mounted battalion.

At this moment and in this place, life could not have been better for Wolfgang Striker. Sleep had become an impossibility, his mind too filled with thoughts and emotions. This was a fresh start, a chance to begin anew, to rise out of the ashes of failure and self-loathing, and to do it in fulfillment of what he had been trained for: a military career. Now, once more, he had a life, in a time and place where he could—to some extent, at least—atone for the past. He would not fail. Not again.

In the dim light, the document seemed to swim before him, and Wolfgang Striker realized his eyes were brimming with tears. Tears! The last time he had cried had been . . . ? He couldn't remember the last time. If somehow he could ever again believe there was a God, now would be the time to fall to his knees in gratitude.

But . . . if Ellen could somehow . . . be here . . . she would help him. She would know his proper response. But Ellen would not—could not—be here. Perhaps not ever again.

How long ago had it been? Another lifetime? Yes, another lifetime—maybe another world—a world of gentility, of music, of books, of art, of civilized living. But in his world—the world in which he had so long existed—he had been left empty, devoid of purpose, an empty hulk subject to any devious wind that blew his direction, always driving him further and further from what he could have been. Much of what he had done was simply retaliation, striking out blindly at a world that had suddenly become beyond his understanding, or at least, his willingness to accept. But now another chance had just been handed him.

"A commission," Wolf murmured, half aloud. "A commission. And Ellen . . ."

"Major? Major, are you alright, sir?"

"What?" Wolf looked up. He had been staring into the candle, struggling to pull himself away from the dark void he had come to know all too well.

"Are you okay, sir?"

"Yes, Sergeant . . . I'm fine. What is it?"

"Colonel Scurry has issued an officer's call—fifteen minutes, sir."

"Thank you, Sergeant. I'll be there."

The meeting was decidedly upbeat. Even in the face of their losses of the previous day, the arrival of Colonel Scurry and his reinforcements had given all of the officers and men at Johnson's Ranch a much-needed boost in morale, and the cheerful demeanor of the other officers quickly added to Wolf's brightening mood. The feeling was now one of impending victory—for him a very personal victory, win or lose.

"Gentlemen," Scurry said, tapping the small field desk with a finger, "we need to get on with this. Let me have your attention.

"Despite our agreement of armistice for the day, I think it would be prudent to anticipate a possible attack sometime after daylight. To that end, I have ordered a thorough reconnaissance of the canyon, and we will post pickets to guard every approach to this encampment. In the event of an attack, I think we are in an excellent defensive position. I do not think we need fear any flanking maneuver against us. The sides of the canyon at its mouth are simply too precipitous. Therefore, I am having four artillery pieces placed on top of the knoll at the mouth of the canyon. Plainly, any attack must come down the trail. In short, gentlemen, our position is formidable, if not impregnable. And judging from reports so far, it would appear that the enemy is not close upon us. Still, we must be on our guard.

"Now, being ever mindful of our situation, let us attend to the duties of the day and lay our dead to rest and continue to see our wounded cared for. There will be an officer's call for eight o'clock this evening.

"Unless there is further business, good day, gentlemen."

It was a beautiful early spring day, filled with the grisly work of gathering the dead, transporting them back down the canyon to Johnson's Ranch, digging graves, and burying each man in a manner that would lend some meaning to his death. Still, burying the dead and caring for the wounded—some seriously so— was a harrowing chore at best. Not a soldier looked into the gray face of a dead comrade or listened to the moans of the wounded that day without wondering why and how he had escaped some fatal blow, and there but for the grace of God . . .

The new commandant, Lieutenant Colonel William R. Scurry, a balding, bearded, and austere man, spent the day pacing throughout the encampment. To his men, he almost appeared to be everywhere at once. One moment he would appear on the hill inspecting the field pieces aligned up the canyon, hoping the federals would violate the truce. Mere moments later he could be seen sitting in his tent scribbling off orders to be delivered to his subordinates. Whenever a grave was being dug, he would be there to offer supposedly needed supervision, then speak words of

Christian and Confederate fervor over the freshly tamped mound—words intended for the living, not the dead. His seeming omnipresence tired everyone—some suggesting to their weary comrades that the dead, if not the living, should be allowed their rest.

Long before the appointed hour of eight o'clock, nervous exhaustion finally overcame Scurry's nervous omnipotence.

"Bugler, sound officer's call!"

Within moments the officers were crowded around their commander, and dozens of enlisted men were hovering nearby hoping to be the first to spread the news of whatever momentous decisions would be made.

"Gentlemen, I am not content with just defensive measures. You have in your hands the order of march for tomorrow morning. Frankly, I had hoped the enemy would violate our truce and give us the opportunity to prosecute this war immediately. We are going to move on the enemy at first light. However, in the heat of combat, let us not forget that taking Fort Union and its supplies is our ultimate objective. We must take Fort Union!

"Majors Pyron, Ragnet, Shropshire, and Striker, I want the Texas Fourth, Fifth, and Seventh regiments ready to pull out before first light. And I want an independent company of volunteer cavalry, under Major Striker, to be ready, also. They will form on our rear in support of our infantry. In addition, we will move a battery of three guns forward with us as well. This will give us a command of approximately eleven hundred men. I think that will be adequate. If we catch the Union force off-guard, we should be able to overwhelm and destroy them.

"Reaching Pigeon's Ranch will be our initial objective. We should anticipate the enemy to form up on the other side of the pass. Therefore, about a mile this side of the ranch we will move into battle formation and proceed forward to destroy the enemy!

"Are there any questions?"

"What of the supply wagons, sir?"

"Yes, thank you, Lieutenant. Given the terrain we'll be fighting in, the supply train would only impede our progress. It will remain here, where it can be moved forward as our needs require, though I expect we may return back here by the close of day. I am detailing Chaplain Jones to remain in command of the supply train. With the wagon masters and teamsters, as well as the sick and wounded men—some two hundred in all—the supplies should be safe. Sergeant Nettles and his gun crew will remain behind with their six-pounder, covering the trail from where the gun is now located. Given the highly defensible nature of this encampment, that should suffice.

"Major Striker's cavalry detachment can be sent back to insure the train's safety, should that become necessary.

"Gentlemen, we move out at first light."

★　★　★

"Gentlemen!" Colonel John Slough said, tapping his small field desk, behind which sat his senior command staff. As Slough addressed his assembled officers, the scene was, in a way, a mirror image of the tactical meeting being held on the other side of the pass. "Gentlemen, I know your feelings are running high, as are mine, but if we are to win this battle, we must get down to the work of it. I have called you together to outline our tactics for the upcoming engagement.

"Our spies have reported that the Texans have been strongly reinforced by both men and supplies, all of which are currently encamped at Johnson's Ranch at the west end of the canyon. My best guess is that they will launch an attack up the canyon tomorrow morning, hoping to engage us somewhere around Pigeon's Ranch. It will be our determination to offer them as much disappointment as possible.

"Our goal remains the same as in the past. We will obstruct at all costs the movements of the Confederate force and prevent it from overrunning Fort Union or impeding in any way traffic or the flow of supplies along the Santa Fe Trail.

"As many of you know, gentlemen, since being commissioned I have become an ardent student of Napoleonic tactics—as are the Confederates, I might add—and such tactics will be the basis of our coming engagement.

"I have asked Major Chivington to present our proposed plan of attack. I believe if we execute that plan as he outlines it, we can defeat the Texans tomorrow, once and for all. Major Chivington?"

Chivington, the Fighting Parson of Colorado, his face drawn with fatigue, rose to an unexpected round of applause. His leadership in the Apache Canyon fight had earned him the respect of every Union soldier who had fought with him in that chaotic engagement. He was, without doubt, the most popular man present. Acknowledging the affection of his fellow officers with a wave of his hand, Chivington began, as all knew he would, with an enthusiasm that belied his exhaustion.

"As you may all remember, our Texas friends have shown their susceptibility to flanking movements; and knowing the density of most Texans, I doubt that they have learned their lessons at all well."

Laughter greeted his assessment of the enemy and gave momentary relief to the tensions of the moment and the anticipation of the coming fight. Chivington was clearly not only admired, but loved.

He continued. "Colonel Slough and I propose a two-pronged attack, as follows. Colonel Slough will lead six companies of Colorado and New Mexico Volunteers, two small detachments of regular cavalry, and two batteries of regular artillery up the Santa Fe Trail to Pigeon's Ranch. He will be leading a total of some seven hundred men in a frontal attack on the enemy. We anticipate engaging the main Confederate force just the other side of the pass."

"In Napoleonic terms, gentlemen," Slough broke in, "we will encounter them with *masse de decision.*" It was in no way a pompous statement, as it might have sounded coming from anyone else. Coming from Slough, the scholarly lawyer, it somehow added a note of unfeigned formality to what was being said.

"I, with nearly five hundred men," Chivington continued, "will take the road, in a circuitous route, toward Galisteo, but for only a short distance. We will then climb to the top of Glorieta Mesa and cut across the plateau south of Glorieta Pass to reconnoiter the Confederates and attack their rear."

Unable to restrain his unflagging enthusiasm for Napoleonic warfare, Slough again broke in. "*Maneouvre sur les derrieres,*" he said, with appropriate Gallic solemnity.

"Does that mean we'll kick 'em in their derrieres?" a young lieutenant offered.

"Indeed, it does," Slough laughed. "Right in their Texas behinds!"

"With luck," Chivington chuckled, "we will be able to cut off their supplies, destroy them and, if conditions permit, attack the main Confederate body from the rear, while Colonel Slough and our main force attacks directly through the pass.

"Major Ashworth, you and your Utah contingent will accompany me and my men, as we have already agreed."

"We'll be ready, sir," Ashworth said, happy the assignment had at last been announced. He had spoken earlier with Chivington, somehow knowing that if he was to confront Striker, it would be in the heat of combat. But it would have to be at a time and place that would allow for what had to be done—up close and personal. If anyone could get him to that point, it would be the audacious Chivington. The Preacher's plan for striking the Confederates from their rear was a brilliant tactic and would more than likely open the needed opportunity.

"Sergeant Peavey is handing out the unit assignments and order of march," Chivington said. "Study them well, gentlemen. This next engagement will be the decisive one. We simply must not fail."

As Chivington took his seat, Slough stepped forward and said, "So, gentlemen, that is how we propose to proceed. Given the terrain and the disposition of the enemy, these tactics should bring us success by end of day tomorrow. We will form up at first light. All unit commanders adjust your schedules accordingly.

"Are there any questions?" he asked. None were forthcoming. "No? If not, then my friends, best of luck to you and your men, and God bless."

# CHAPTER 32

★　★　★

T HE CLIMB TO THE TOP OF Glorieta Mesa through San
Cristobal Canyon seemed impossibly difficult to the four hundred
eighty-eight men under Chivington's command, as they struggled
to keep up with their energetic leader. As with armies everywhere,
there were endless complaints and frequent curses, but not a man
among them would have turned back.

The narrow canyon with steep walls through which they
climbed was strewn with boulders and overgrown with brush. At
times the rocky defile seemed to be almost vertical, men frequently balancing themselves by simply reaching forward and
touching the trail a couple of feet in front of their faces. Thick
clouds of dust kicked up by their scrambling ascent filled the nar-
rower parts of the canyon, making the climb all the more miserable. Bandannas or other pieces of cloth quickly appeared over
many sweat-streaked faces as men fought to keep from breathing

and swallowing the swirling grit, repeatedly stirred by so many slipping, shuffling feet.

Long before finally emerging from the brutal canyon and reaching the top of the mesa it was obvious to all why the so-called shortcut trail to the village of Galisteo was seldom used. Whatever time a traveler might think he was saving would be more than paid for by the pain. Though the morning air was cold, and in most places the sunlight did not reach the canyon's floor, the difficult climb quickly caused the sweating men, straining and grinding up the steep trail, to chill from their perspiration-soaked clothes. All except the officers, of course, who managed to stay mounted even in the most difficult spots, as had Clay and his squadron of cavalry.

The mounted Utah troops had taken to the trail ahead of Chivington's main command and now sat waiting at the top of the trail, resting their horses and listening to the clanking of equipment and curses of the struggling soldiers below.

"Why in the world would a body want to be a infantry sojur," one of his men asked aloud, "when there's horses t' be had? I mean, jest listen to those boys, all loaded down with their noisy plunder and climbin' almost straight up. Did those boys think they was goin' on a picnic when they joined up for this shebang?"

Before anyone could share his wisdom on the subject, some of the mounted officers began pouring over the top of the trail, among them Lieutenant Colonel Manuel Chaves. Chaves was with the Second New Mexico Volunteers, but because of his intimate familiarity with the surrounding mountains, he was temporarily acting as Chivington's scout, at least for the present flanking expedition. It was his responsibility to get Chivington and his men to a spot directly above the Confederate encampment at Johnson's Ranch, ideally at the same time Colonel Slough's men reached the ranch by coming down the Santa Fe Trail.

"Ah, Major Ashworth," Chaves said, reining his winded horse in next to Clay, "things look much better from up here, no?"

"After that trail," Clay said, nodding at the declivity out of which the tired, sweating men now struggled, heaving from the exertion, many on the edge of collapse, "anything would look good."

"*Si,*" Chaves said, with a chuckle. "Indeed, it is so, but from here, as you can see, Major, it will be not so bad. No? Much sage, much juniper, and pine, but only little problems, I think."

The relatively flat top of the mesa south of the Santa Fe Trail was a welcome sight to every man in Chivington's command. After a brief rest, the march was resumed. For another mile and a half, the Galisteo trail wound southwest around timbered hills and knolls that gave definition to the top of Glorieta Mesa. Then, at a point where the trail turned south toward Galisteo, Chaves led Chivington and his command off the trail. They were now only two and a half miles directly east of Johnson's Ranch. Here, with no trail to follow, the going got tougher.

In places the trackless mesa was forested, dotted with thick stands of piñon and juniper, in other places it was thick with sagebrush. Occasionally the men were forced to climb through gullies and dry washes. Rocky ledges frequently had to be scaled, more of a problem for the horses than the men. For most, however, the going did not prove too difficult.

By early afternoon Chivington gave the order that the entire command was to maintain absolute silence. They had reached the rim of the mesa and were now directly above the Confederate encampment at Johnson's Ranch.

Giving the signal to dismount, Chivington said, "Colonel

Chaves and Major Ashworth, come with me." Turning to two of his captains, he said, "Have the men strip their gear and prepare for the attack, but have them do it as quietly as possible. We are no more than two hundred yards from the edge.

"We're going to reconnoiter the situation below us."

Wolf Striker threw his arm in the air. "Dismount! Horse handlers to the rear!" Waving his big Colt in the air, he hollered, "Up in those trees, men, and hold this end of the line!" As his men climbed among the pines and began pouring fire on the advancing enemy, the Confederate battle line now extended the full width across the narrow canyon, and with Colonel Scurry's infantry occupying the center and left flank, the line held.

From where Wolf stood, emptying his two big Colts, firing across the heads of the men kneeling in front of him, the canyon looked and sounded as if the mouth of hell had opened and was disgorging all of the malevolence it held. The tumult was deafening, every shattering sound amplified by the surrounding canyon walls. Everything from cannon to short arms was being used by both sides. The noise was horrendous, and Wolf's heart sang. "*Confusion worse confounded!*" he shouted into the din. "Milton said that, y' know! A great man, Milton! Pour it to 'em, boys!"

Wolfgang Striker was in the middle of one of the most violent battles he had ever witnessed, in the middle of all he had ever trained for. His entire life seemed to have sharpened him for this very moment. Here, in the face of death, was meaning; here was purpose. For the first time in his turbulent, incoherent life, he felt invincible, beyond harm, as if for the first time the world was almost within his arms. "Keep pouring it to them, men!" he hollered, attempting to be heard above the din and the ringing in his own ears. "We'll break 'em right here and now!"

Quickly reloading the empty chambers of the cylinders of his two heavy revolvers, Wolf studied the Union force crowding the canyon before him. For some reason, the blue coats did not seem as formidable as they had in the Apache Canyon battle. Maybe it wasn't them; maybe it was him. Somehow their numbers seemed less overwhelming, less something . . .

Behind him, the Confederate cannon opened up with terrible effect, grapeshot brutally ripping through the Union ranks. As men crumpled and fell in agony, the Union line broke and men began falling back toward Pigeon's Ranch, slowly at first, then more quickly, finally a seeming rout.

"Now's the time, lads!" Wolf hollered, as he scrambled down between the trees and through the brush, toward the trail below, rocks and dirt cascading around his feet. "Let's go get 'em before they can re-form!" It was as if his feet had wings, and the blood coursing through his veins drummed loudly in his ears, beating to the cadence of war.

"Charge!"

The words had hardly left his breathless mouth when, rounding a slight dogleg in the trail, he saw the Union cannon no more than fifty yards away, their mouths belching unexpected smoke, and the balls whistling their eerie death songs above his head. From behind the cannon, the retreating infantry swarming around them, the Union cavalry broke forward, their officers waving their swords above their heads, their mouths wide with command, and the cannons roared again.

"Back to our guns!" Wolf hollered, turning his charging men back to the wavering Confederate line. "Save the guns!"

Scrambling desperately, they fled before the thundering Union cavalry in a furious effort to save the Confederate field pieces. Before Wolf could reach the three-gun battery now being limbered up, one of the caissons suddenly exploded in magnificent color and light, and an iron-rimmed wheel flew gracefully over his head, landing with splintering impact directly in front of the leading horses in the Union charge. One of the racing animals abruptly tumbled over its front legs, a large splinter of a spoke buried deep in its chest. Its rider, thrown violently to the ground, was immediately crushed as the big animal landed on top of him, struggling in its death throes. At least four more horses went down, sprawling over and around the thrashing horse and its now dead rider.

The Union charge was broken as men and horses piled across the trail in a confusion of legs, hooves, and clattering equipment.

"Unlimber those guns and train them on that mess up the trail. We've almost got them now!" Wolf yelled at the lieutenant who had given the orders to withdraw the guns. "Quickly, they're falling back! Scurry and Pyron have cleared our flanks. We've got 'em, now! We must outnumber 'em two to one!"

Scurry and Pyron had been successful in clearing the Confederate flanks. The fighting had been furious, in some instances opposing forces were firing at each other from the opposite sides of the same juniper trees. Every bloody inch of hard-fought ground was fiercely contested, but the outnumbered federals retreated toward Pigeon's Ranch, reluctantly giving ground before the hard-driving Confederate advance.

Watching the fighting from the vantage point of the two remaining Confederate guns, Wolf Striker could not shake his misgivings about the inferior numbers they were confronting. They had almost been overwhelmed by Union numbers in the Apache Canyon fight. Where could those men have gone? Several answers were possible: the Union casualties were heavier than thought; a large force was being held in reserve to attack when the Texans were too strung out; or they had found a way to attack the Confederate rear and supply wagons.

Lost in thought, Wolf did not hear Scurry ride up and dismount next to him. "Striker! We've got them almost in full retreat now. Have your men follow up on our rear."

"Colonel, they're going to attack *our* rear, if they haven't already done so."

"What? What are you talking about?"

"Their numbers, sir. We outnumber them two-to-one. This canyon was full of blue coats the day before yesterday. Where are all the rest of them today? Their casualties were not that high."

Scurry stood stunned for a moment. "Oh, no," he moaned. "You could be right. Why didn't I see that? If you are right, we've lost it all.

"Take some of your men and get back to the supply camp as fast as you can! Don't waste a minute!"

Before Scurry could finish issuing orders, Wolf was mounted and headed back down the canyon, three of his men close behind him. The remainder, it had quickly been determined, would stay to act as a rear echelon guard in case their rear was attacked.

# CHAPTER 33

★ ★ ★

C LAY SLOWLY ROSE UP BEHIND the Confederate picket standing at the cliff's edge, looking down into the canyon. Silently, Clay stepped from behind the sagebrush that had concealed him, grabbed the unsuspecting man by his chin, and at the same time thrust his knee up into the man's back and yanked him backward. The guard was short and had been wounded in his left shoulder, and he gave little resistance. Clay gave the man's head a hard twist and struck him sharply. By the time the Texan hit the ground, he was unconscious. "Sorry, fella," Clay muttered, as he rolled the unconscious guard onto his stomach and tied his hands firmly behind his back. Pulling the man's head up by the hair, Clay stuffed a wadded bandana into the gaping mouth and secured it with another, tied around the man's head. "That's one Texan who won't be going anywhere," he said, letting the guard's head drop unceremoniously into the dirt.

Waving Chivington forward, Clay crawled to the edge of the

cliff and lay on his stomach to study the Confederate encampment below.

Quietly Chivington crawled up beside him and peered down into the canyon. "What do you think, Major?" he asked.

"I think it's almost too good to be true," Clay said, studying the scene below. "I count something like eighty wagons parked among the ranch buildings. There could be one or two more somewhere behind the buildings. Those guards, if that's what they are, look like they're on vacation."

"Mmm . . . looks like they've left the wounded and some teamsters to protect their supplies," Chivington said, pulling himself closer to the edge for a better look. "One gun emplacement above the trail."

"I don't see much of a problem, do you?" Clay asked with a chuckle.

"No, I don't; so let's get the job done so we can all go home."

"Major, you have no idea what those words do to me. Let's go."

Bringing his Union force forward, Chivington laid out his simple plan. "Men, there's no easy or quiet way to do this. Therefore, on my command, we'll all go over the edge. Use whatever means you can to get down, and don't worry about the noise. In fact, make as much noise as you can. The more dust, dirt, and confusion the better.

"Near as we can tell, there are about two hundred men down there, but most of them appear to be walking-wounded and teamsters. A noisy, confusing charge down the side of the plateau might scare some of them into running off. I've got a hunch the teamsters won't stand and fight, and the wounded may have had enough already.

"Once we are down there, subdue any resistance, and burn the wagons–every one of them. Save nothing. Everything must be destroyed, including the animals if we can find them."

With Chivington's mention of the animals, a low groan spread among the men. These were miners, ranchers, farmers, and cowhands—people who made their living from the earth, and animals were precious to them. The thought of slaughtering the horses sickened every man present.

"I know," he responded. "I don't like killing the stock either, but we can't leave them for the Confederates to use against us. It's dirty work, but it must be done.

"Officers to your posts, and let's get this done!"

After the men formed up, the command was given, and Chivington's army spilled over the edge of the plateau. It was as if a human dam had burst, and nothing could contain the pent-up rage that tumbled forth. The descent down the face of the mountain was headlong, dirty, and loud. Men jumped, crawled, and slid with little thought of their safety. In a few of the more difficult places, some were lowered by ropes, but wherever they were on that mountainside, whatever their rate of descent, they screamed, hollered, and cheered. It was an avalanche of shrieking devils, almost something pouring out of another world.

With so large and reckless a force clamoring down the mountainside, rocks were loosened and rolled to the bottom, crashing onto the valley floor, while dusty earth slides carried many of their screaming attackers precipitously toward the startled Texans below. It almost appeared that the entire mountain had been loosened and was tumbling upon the Confederate encampment, enveloping everything in a dense cloud of dust, dirt, and debris.

One dumbfounded Confederate teamster said to another, "What d' yuh make of that?"

"I dunno," came an almost awe-struck response, "but I'm lightin' a shuck outta here—and right now!"

Less than an hour before the wild Union charge down the mountainside, Wolf and his three subordinates had ridden into the Confederate camp at Johnson's Ranch. The encampment lay peacefully in the early afternoon sun, and a quick survey of the area revealed no apparent threat. It was, in fact, hard to imagine how an unexpected attack could possibly take place. The only danger Wolf could see was the totally relaxed atmosphere of the place. Most of the wounded lay in whatever shade could be found, and the teamsters sat around in small groups talking, some sleeping, as if no battle were in progress.

"You two take another turn around the ranch," Wolf said, his disgust more than apparent. "If I were going to attack this place, I think I could take it by myself. Look for any sign of activity around the perimeter."

"What're we lookin' for?" one asked.

"Anything. If something looks out of place or in anyway suspect, come and get me. I'll be trying to convince this rabble there's a war going on."

Wolf dismounted near a group of teamsters lounging in the shade of one of the wagons. Tying his horse at the rear of the wagon, Wolf looked at a wounded soldier sitting away from the others. "Where's the officer in charge?"

"There ain't none." The soldier was just a boy, not more than fifteen or sixteen, Wolf thought. A bloody bandage covered one eye and the side of his head, and blood had soaked the front of his shirt. "Chaplain Jones, well . . . he took off after them German immigrant sojers. They wanted to get in the fight up the canyon yonder, there."

Turning, Wolf looked at the knot of teamsters reclining near the wagon. "If the enemy were to attack this place," he said, "they would go through you sisters like knife through warm butter. Now get on your feet, and stay on your feet! This supply area is likely to be attacked, and if we lose our supplies, we lose the battle. It's as simple as that. I might be wrong, but we can't afford to take any chances."

A big teamster guffawed as he removed the stub of a fat cigar from his mouth and spat at Wolf's feet. "Wrong? I'll say yer wrong. Mister, you gotta be nuts. You jest come down that canyon. I seen yuh ride in here. Jest where do yuh suppose that attack's gonna come from, huh? Look around yuh, man," he scoffed belligerently.

Picking up on the big man's insolent attitude, several of the others spat in the sand and snickered derisively.

"Yeah," another scoffed, a lazy tone to his voice. "Can you see them blue bellies flyin' over them cliffs like bluebirds, 'r somethin'? Geez, mister."

"Ain't nobody gonna attack us here," the first teamster said, an ugly sneer raising the corner of his lip, revealing a row of rotting, tobacco-stained teeth. "The whole Texas army is up that canyon betwixt them an' us, an' you oughtta be up there with 'em."

Deep inside Wolf the old beast stirred. "Get up," he said.

"What'd you say?"

"I said, get on your feet, and I'll show you just how it's done."

The big teamster slowly got to his feet, not sure of Wolf's meaning.

The back of Wolf's hand caught the side of the startled man's face with a teeth-rattling smack that seemed to echo off the surrounding sheds and hillside. The force of the unexpected blow slammed the big teamster into the wagon behind them. Wolf's hamlike fist, which, to the startled men around them, looked as if it had come up from the ground, as if suddenly appearing out of the dust, sank deep into the man's ample brisket, driving the breath out of his bloody mouth. Knees folding, he fell forward into Wolf's up-coming knee, which crushed the teamster's nose and lifted his big head sharply up with a crack that was heard by all. Stepping to one side, Wolf let him fall into the dirt where he stayed, a dark pool of blood spreading from his broken nose, staining the ground beneath him. In the quiet that followed, no one moved.

Those who had witnessed the fight, if it could be called that, were stunned by the sudden, explosive violence. No one had expected such a reaction from the officer standing before them, and no one could believe the finality with which the encounter had so quickly ended.

"All an attacking force has to do is take their objective by surprise, catch the enemy off their guard, while they're taking it easy in the shade." Wolf look disdainfully down at body slumped in the dirt at his feet. "He's lucky I didn't kill him," he growled. "Three weeks ago, I would have.

"You two," he said, pointing to two of the nearest stunned spectators, "drag this lump of garbage off into the brush. If I see him again, I might really lose my patience. Move!

"Now the rest of you, which of these wagons holds the most ammunition and stores?"

The wagons were quickly point out, and Wolf said, "All of you, get on your feet and harness some teams. Let's see if we can get these four through those trees and on the other side of that knoll—behind the barn, there. Move it! We've got no time to waste."

With the wagons at last out of sight from the encampment,

the men were unharnessing the teams and returning them to their corral when the cliffs opposite the ranch suddenly seemed to crumble from the top, bursting into a noisy, dusty landslide, bringing Wolf's feared attack into the reality he had dreaded. It was sudden, not fully expected, and in the end overwhelming.

At the moment the attack erupted, Wolf was trying to estimate the military value of what was in the wagons. Crouching in the brush near one of the wagons, he quickly saw that there was absolutely nothing he could do to resist the descending force. By the time the first of the Union troops had reached the canyon floor, many of the camp guards and teamsters had mounted whatever horses were at hand, including Wolf's, and were hightailing it for Santa Fe. Others broke away and headed east, up the canyon, looking for the main Confederate force, now fighting near Pigeon's Ranch.

Wolf had simply arrived too late. And, truth be told, he had not expected a wild, almost reckless charge down the more than declivitous side of the Glorieta Plateau—an irresistible force of men plunging and screaming like wild banshees, intent on overwhelming anything in their way.

It was, in fact, as fine a military action as Wolf had ever witnessed, given the terrain and the tactical limitations imposed on both sides. Within mere minutes, the Union force had spiked the cannon at the mouth of the canyon, surrounded the wagons and ranch buildings, and were following the order to burn the wagons. The entire Confederate supply train, with its clothing, ammunition, medical supplies, everything, all went up in flames—all but the four wagons Wolf had pulled away and hidden.

From where Wolf lay, he counted three Confederate soldiers dead, several wounded, and seventeen who had been rounded up and taken prisoner. "Well," he hissed to himself, "this shootin' match is over. There's nothing left to do now but sneak out of here with our tails between our legs."

★   ★   ★

Chivington had every right to feel good about how the operation had been handled. The stragegy was, in a word, *brilliant.*

"Major," Clay said, with an appreciative chuckle, "this could not have gone off better. It was a textbook exercise. Wagonloads of Confederate supplies have been reduced to ashes, and we took no casualties, not one."

The knot of officers in which they stood joined in their congratulations, and Chivington said, "Thank you, gentlemen. You each performed with professional vigor. I'm proud of you all. Now, let's discuss our route out of here."

A sergeant who had been guarding the prisoners appeared around the corner of a shed and pushed his way toward Chivington. "Beg pardon, sir?"

"What is it, Sergeant?"

"I don't mean to butt-in, Major, but I just overheard one of the prisoners tell one of his rebel buddies that a large Texas reinforcement was expected any time from Galisteo."

"Well, now," Clay grumbled, "wouldn't that ruin our day?"

"Suggestions, gentlemen?" Chivington said, with a chuckle. The irony of their possible situation was lost on few.

Before anyone could offer a suggestion, shots were fired across the encampment, and someone yelled, "Shoot! Don't let 'im get away!"

A wounded rebel, hanging off the far side of his horse for protection, pounded past the astonished officers at full gallop, the horse lunging up the slope onto the Santa Fe Trail, and disappearing into the canyon.

"Well, that does it," Clay said, slapping his thigh with a glove. "Our plan to attack their rear just rode up the canyon ahead of us."

"But what can he tell them?" one of the officers said. "The news went earlier with those others. We won't be able to surprise them. They'll know we're here, but we will still have them between two superior forces."

Several nodded in agreement. "We still have them where we want them," another offered.

"That's true enough," Clay countered, "but if the rumor of a force coming from Galisteo is true, we'd be hoisted on our own petard. Who would be caught between whom? I mean, when you think about it, it's kind of funny."

"We've no choice, gentlemen," Chivington said, removing his hat and wiping his ample forehead. "We go back up the way we came, and we need to move with some dispatch." Turning to Clay, he said, "Major Ashworth, would you and your Utah boys go up first? As soon as you get to the top, file out along the ridgeline and cover our climb. Then, when we're on our way, will you bring up our rear?"

Clay turned on his heel. "With pleasure, Major."

"Bugler, sound assembly," Chivington ordered.

Within minutes the Utahans were struggling up the steep, rocky cliffs of the Glorieta Plateau. The infantry followed them, scrambling up the steep canyon wall. It was another brutal climb. Men already tired from a long day of marching, climbing, and fighting were now slowly making their painful way back up the six-hundred foot precipice they had only a few hours earlier descended. The Pike's Peakers on the canyon floor watched the advance party on the cliffs above and wondered—some aloud— how they had ever let themselves get into such a fix.

Among the first to reach the top, Clay gave the order to spread out along the rocky edge of the cliff and watch for any enemy intrusion from the canyon or along the trail from Galisteo. Laying down in the bunch grass, he took out his binoculars and began slowly scanning the smoldering Confederate encampment below. The place appeared completely wasted. Most of the buildings had been spared, but every wagon had been burned to ash, only their metal wheel rims remaining. Thick smoke drifting in the ambient breeze made it difficult to see anything. Shifting his attention to the hills that partially surrounded the ranch, he slowly scanned the small gullies, ditches, and side canyons.

"What the . . ." Refocusing the glasses, he searched the small hill that lay partially hidden behind the barn. "If I didn't know better, I'd swear that was the top cover of a wagon," he said, poking the sergeant next to him and handing him the glasses. "Take a look. See . . . behind the barn, just over that hill there?"

"It is. It surely is. We missed one, for certain, sir. Could be more back there. But that ain't all, Major. There's a reb down there. Look . . . there in the bushes near the wagon's tongue. See 'im?"

Clay rubbed his eyes and peered once again through the binoculars.

"Looks like he's going to make a run for it. What do you think?" the sergeant said. "I think I can pick 'im off from here," he chuckled, pulling his Sharps carbine up and taking a bead on his target. "Any of you fellers a bettin' man?"

Clay lowered his binoculars, almost refusing to believe his eyes. Laying his hand on the sergeant's arm he said. "Hold on. I think I know that man." Refocusing the glasses he studied the rebel officer carefully as the man emerged from the brush and ran toward the barn. "Well, I'll be. So it is you, Mister Striker—and about time. Give me your carbine, Sergeant. I think I need to be the one to do this."

★   ★   ★

Ducking low, Wolf raced across the open ground to the barn and flattened himself against the gray, weather-bleached wood. The day was not too warm, but the sun beating on the silvered wood next to the stall door made it seem so. Peering around the corner of the barn he watched the Union soldiers struggling back up the rocky side of the plateau. Only a handful of men remained at the base of the steep cliff, waiting to begin their ascent.

Something brushed the back of his head, and hot breath blew down his perspiring neck. "Great Caesar!" he yelped too loudly, ducking, expecting a blow from behind. The horse nickered and blew softly, taking comfort in the nearness of the man.

"How did they miss you, fella?" Wolf whispered, reaching up to stroke the animal's nose. The horse shied and backed away from the stall door into the barn. Reaching through the open top of the stall door, Wolf grabbed the horse's halter. "Whoa, boy. Stay with me, and you've got a future. You don't want to wind up like those other poor animals, with your throat cut."

It was one of the cavalry horses. Someone had put the big gelding into one of the stalls at the back of the barn. Somehow, in the confusion and rush of the Union raid, the animal had been missed when the slaughter of the others had taken place, and the barn had not been burned. The top part of the two-piece outside stall door was missing, and Wolf slowly opened the bottom, hoping the thing did not squeak, and led the nervous animal out.

After tightening the cinch, Wolf jabbed his foot into the

stirrup and raised himself off the ground, swinging his leg over the cantle of the small Campbell saddle.

★   ★   ★

Sighting down the barrel of the .50 caliber Sharps carbine, Clay watched Wolf tighten the skittish horse's cinch. As he slowly squeezed the trigger, a montage of images raced before his eyes, and with each, a question.

Connie was there, and he wondered if Wolf had a Connie somewhere, someone he loved almost beyond reason and who loved him. Or was he about to die truly alone?

An image of Brigham Young sitting behind his great writing table flashed through his mind. How would the Mormon leader feel? Would he approve of such an execution? Though he was not a Mormon, Clay Ashworth respected Brigham Young more than any other man he knew. Losing the Mormon prophet's respect and approval was something Clay knowingly would never do.

But in his mind Clay could also see the two Cartwright brothers, Will and Luke, shot dead, their lifeless bodies hanging from the awning of the Birdcage in Platte River Station—ordered there by the man now in his sights.

And behind all was Porter Rockwell, the Marshal of Salt Lake, the so-called Avenging Angel—a man of mystery, a man feared by many but respected by all who knew him, telling him *justice* had to be done.

Yes! There had to be *justice!* Justice, in a western wilderness where there was little to be found. He could hear Rockwell now: *Shoot, man! Shoot before it's too late! Shoot!*

Steadying the rifle, Clay slowly drew the trigger back, taking up the slack until he felt resistance.

Suddenly Wolf Striker stiffened, his body somehow arching

BRAD E. HAINSWORTH AND RICHARD VETTERLI

backward as he stood, one foot in the stirrup, the other cocked crazily across the saddle. Slowly, Wolf fell away from the horse, and the report of a rifle shot echoed across Johnson's Ranch.

Clay looked up, then looked at the carbine. The hammer remained at full cock. Laying the piece aside, he grabbed his glasses and scanned the scene below. Disappearing into the brush beyond the cluster of ranch buildings he saw a dusty shadow disappear from sight. It was a buckskin-colored horse.

"What horse was Rockwell riding when he left for the Utah Territory the other day?" He shouted down the line. "Anybody remember?"

"I ain't sure," someone hollered back through the dust and noise of the men scrambling over the edge of the cliff, "but I think it was a buckskin. Can't say fer sure, though."

There was no agreement among the men sprawled along the crest of the plateau, but the question hung in the air like some kind of accusation.

After sending four men back down to destroy the remaining wagons, it was nearly dark before Major Chivington gave the order to his exhausted troops to move. Chivington had received a message from Colonel Slough that he was in desperate need of reinforcements in the fighting around Pigeon's Ranch.

Later, as the four men struggled up over the cliff edge to rejoin the others, the fire from the four wagons glowing in the darkness below, Clay grabbed one, and said, "That officer down there . . . the one shot mounting his horse . . . is he dead?"

"Didn't look close, Major, but he ain't goin' nowheres."

Wolf Striker's body lay motionless on the blood-soaked ground, crumpled almost in a knot. There had been no movement since his body at last relaxed after stiffening from the shock of the bullet that tore through his side. It was the temperature, barely above freezing, that reached a flickering consciousness that kept threatening to go out, like a candle flame struggling in the wind.

When Wolf's eyes finally opened, he was lying face down in the damp dirt, sticky from his own blood, and there was no recognition of where he was or what had happened. He knew nothing but the cold, and it was penetrating. He was so cold, in fact, that after what might have been hours, awareness began to gather from the darkness, and he could smell the blood.

Somewhere in that dim, shapeless awareness was a thread of will that began to thicken and weave into recognition and then—determination. The will to live had grown into the determination to fight.

Wolf Striker struggled to regain control of his body, finally rolling over on his back, and a tiny pinpoint of light reluctantly came into focus. It was a star, and it was at that moment Wolfgang Striker somehow knew he was going to live.

An exhausted Clay Ashworth reined his tired mount to a stop just where the trail dipped down to the buck-gate, not far distant from the large ranch house snuggled beneath the sheltering stand of Ponderosa pines that surrounded it. He had thought the forty-five mile ride from Salt Lake City would kill him, but now he knew it had been worth every painful mile. The place was just as he remembered it—just as he would always remember it.

Beneath each window of the ground floor, oblong splashes of light gave the wet, heavy snow a soft, golden hue. Only the sound of clumps of snow falling from the overburdened trees could be heard. All was quiet, a place of safety and rest, a place far from the din of battle, far from the ugly, blood-stained canyons of Glorieta Pass.

It had been weeks since that bloody battle, perhaps the most significant battle ever to be fought west of the Mississippi, at least one could hope for as much. There were never adequate words to describe the horror of war, the hideous atrocities men could perpetrate on one another in the name of one ideal or another, but the pain was there nonetheless—an agony only time could heal.

Wet and cold as he was, Clay sat quietly, savoring these first precious moments home. He had dreamed of this for weeks on end, and right now there was no room in his life for Mister Lincoln or Brigham Young or the Utah Battalion or the Union Army or any other demand that might take him away. For now, there was only *Rancho Los Librados*—and Connie. Emily would be there, of course, to squeal and run into his arms, all the while scolding him for being away so long and tracking mud and snow into her house. He loved that old woman with all of his heart. But it was Connie—Maria Emilea Consuela Salinas Ashworth—who would always fill the center of his being.

Without urging, the big gray began to trot down the hill and through the gate, the warmth of the big barn behind the house adding urgency to each step. Clay made no effort to hold him back. They were home.

# EPILOGUE

⋆　⋆　⋆

IT WAS THE SECOND DAY OF THE STORM, and as evening darkened into night, a heavy rain continued to fall, turning what passed for the south lawn of the White House into an even more muddy pasture. The windows streamed with water as the wind continued to gust out of the southeast. It was not a night to be out, and the fire burning in the grate across from the president's desk filled the otherwise dark study with a sense of cheeriness he felt was unwarranted.

The President of the United States—a title, the irony of which was not lost on Mister Lincoln—sat watching the lights of Virginia, across the Potomac, as they seemed to lose their shape and dribble down the glass. His large, gangly frame was slumped loosely in a swivel chair that, somehow, always seemed too small. April was promising to be an unusually wet month in the nation's capital, and so far each day had seemed wetter than the last.

The dreary days caused the president to reflect more and more

369

on whether what he was elected to be president of could still be called a *nation.* The term ostensibly denoted something more than the squabbling clutter of humanity that daily sank deeper into almost constant, and increasingly violent, turmoil. Still, the war was not going all that badly. Union armies at long last seemed to be on the move, advances finally being made that might end in the capture of Richmond, bringing the conflict to a merciful conclusion, thus restoring the Union—maybe, perhaps, if. . . .

McClellan had finally gotten off his trouser bottoms and was moving his vast army to the peninsula. Federal troops were in the Shenandoah Valley and western Virginia. Fort Macon was under siege by federal forces down in North Carolina. Further south, the threat against Savannah was growing. Burnside seemed to be chewing a big hole in Confederate territory. The federal army in Tennessee was threatening the state of Mississippi, and a move was being made on Alabama, maybe even Chattanooga.

If all of this was true, things were not going all that badly, actually, and word had just arrived that the Confederate advance in the far southwest had not only been stopped, but totally defeated.

Even so, Mister Lincoln, as he was known, could not shake the dark feelings of depression that assailed him more and more. Maybe it was the rain, maybe it was McClellan—*never really cared for the man,* the President thought. *Too much strutting, not enough marching.*

Picking up the dispatches that the War Department had delivered only a few minutes earlier, Mister Lincoln reread the dispatch describing the Union defeat of a Texas army at a place called Glorieta Pass, way out on the Santa Fe Trail in New Mexico Territory, sending the rebels (or what was left of them) back to Texas with their tails between their legs. *Why the devil couldn't*

*McClellan do that back here?* Until recently, the man just couldn't seem to get off his military behind and start taking it to the enemy.

*What was that major's name?* Lincoln wondered to himself, scanning the dispatches. *The one from Colorado? Oh, yes. Chivington. Maybe I ought to get him back here. I wonder if he could perform as well if he had a couple of stars on his shoulder? What is it about those stars that made a man so cautious, anyway?*

Scanning the page further, another name jumped out at him. *Clay Ashworth! Yes, now there's a man I need back here,* Lincoln thought, scribbling a note to himself and sliding it to the top of his desktop blotter, where he would be sure to see it. *Ashworth has never been a man to sit around when action was called for. Come morning, I'll just have John see to it that Clay is transferred back here as soon as possible. He can send a telegram to Brigham Young first thing in the morning. Yes, sir, Brigham Young'll know where to find Ashworth, if no one else can. Wonder why that is?*

Almost immediately the president felt better. Good enough, at least, to find his way upstairs to bed. "Yes, sir," Mister Lincoln muttered to himself. "Ashworth will like that."

# BIBLIOGRAPHY

★ ★ ★

Alberts, Don E. *The Battle of Glorieta: Union Victory in the West.*
College Station: Texas A&M University Press, 1998.

Boman, John S., ed. *Who Was Who in the Civil War.* New York:
Crescent Books, 1995.

Colton, Ray C. *The Civil War in the Western Territories: Arizona,
Colorado, New Mexico, and Utah.* Norman: University of
Oklahoma Press, 1959.

*Illustrated Atlas of the Civil War.* Alexandria, Virginia: Time-Life
Books, 1998.

Krauze, Enrique. *Mexico: Biography of Power: A History of Modern
Mexico, 1810–1996.* New York: HarperCollins Publishers,
1997.

Long, E. B., with Barbara Long. *The Civil War Day by Day, an
Almanac 1861–1865.* Garden City, N.Y.: Doubleday, 1971.

Roberts, David. *Once They Moved Like the Wind: Cochise,*

*Geronimo, and the Apache Wars.* New York: Simon & Schuster, 1993.

Sweeney, Edwin R. *Cochise, Chiricahua Apache Chief.* Norman: University of Oklahoma Press, 1991.

Utley, Robert M. *The Indian Frontier of the American West, 1846–1890.* Albuquerque: University of New Mexico Press, 1984.

Vetterli, Richard. *Mormonism, Americanism, and Politics.* Salt Lake City, Utah: Ensign Publishing Company, 1961.